A Dirty Game

A Dirty Game

David Lowe

Eloquent Books
Durham, Connecticut

Eloquent Books
An imprint of Strategic Book Group
P. O. Box 333
Durham, CT 06422
http://www.StrategicBookGroup.com

ISBN: 978-1-60911-853-2

Book Design by Julius Kiskis

Printed in the United States of America
18 17 16 15 14 13 12 11 10   1 2 3 4 5

Dedication

To my wife, Kathleen
With heartfelt love and thanks for all your support

List of Acronyms
Abbreviations and UK Police Jargon

ACC Assistant Chief Constable
BKA The Bundeskriminalamt, Germany's national police force that investigate serous federal crime and counter-terrorism
BTP The British Transport Police who police the rail UK's rail network
CIA The Central Investigation Agency, the USA's agency that investigate external threats to the USA
CPS Crown Prosecution Service (equivalent of the USA's District Attorney)
DC Detective Constable
DCC Deputy Chief Constable
DCI Detective Chief Inspector
DI Detective Inspector
Drum Police slang for a house/flat
DS Detective Sergeant
Europol The European Union's policing agency, staffed by police officers on secondment. Main role - intelligence agency and assistance to member states' policing agencies in transnational crime and counter-terrorism
Eta Basque separatist terror group based in Spain and south-west France
FBI The Federal Bureau of Investigation, the USA's federal policing agency that investigates serious federal crime and internal terrorist threats
FSB Russia's security service that investigates threats to Russia, it is the former KGB
GCHQ Government Communications Headquarters – this agency listens to all communications around the world and intercepts those that they think pose a threat to the UK

GMP Greater Manchester Police

IPCC Independent Police Complains Commission

ISB Integrated Special Branch

ISI Pakistan's national security agency that investigates terrorism

Jack Police slang for a detective

MI5 The UK's security service that investigate internal threats to the UK

MI6 The UK's security service that investigate external threats to the UK

MO Modus Operandi – pattern of behaviour, usually associated with criminal behaviour.

Obs Spot Police slang word for a location used by the police to conduct static surveillance

PIRA The Provisional Irish Republican Army, a faction of the IRA that broke away in the late 1960's from the IRA and was the main group active in acts of terrorism against Britain during the war in the north of Ireland 1969-1998

Reccie Police slang for when the police survey an investigation scene checking out possible observation points, population and any potential danger spots.

S013 Metropolitan Police's counter-terrorism unit, the Met's equivalent of the Special Branch

The Met the Metropolitan Police

Preface

Wednesday 30th August
02.15 hours
Georgian/Chechnya Border

Being captured by the FSB or the Russian military was what Leonid feared the most. He knew if they found him, they would kill him.

The relentless rain hammered into his face. Being cold, wet and tired made it harder for him to remain positive. An optimist by nature, his resolve to remain upbeat was being sorely tested. His only possessions were the wet, muddy clothes he was wearing, a flashlight, a handful of roubles, an AK47 assault rifle and the few rounds left in its magazine. The numbness running through his body, brought on by laying still in the cold muddy riverbank intensified his impatience for Al Qaeda to turn up.

On hearing a rustling further down the riverbank, his instinct to survive took over. Leonid grabbed his rifle. Pointing it in the direction of the sound, he placed his finger on the trigger as a bird flew off the riverbank. 'Something or someone disturbed it,' he thought. Straining his eyes, he looked through the dark for any movement that might indicate someone was closing in on him. Not seeing anything, he reflected on how he ended up having to scrabble down the side of a riverbank waiting for his rescuers.

'Too ill disciplined and they just don't fucking listen,' he muttered, thinking of the Islamic Ingushetian faction he helped to train over the last six months. After leading an attack on a Russian Army general on the outskirts of Nazran in Ingushetia four days earlier, he was the only Chechen fighter to survive.

Although he and his Chechen comrades killed a general and two senior army officers, it was a botched job. 'Why didn't they turn up at the escape route and provide covering fire like they were told to?' He kept running through the attack, trying to work out why the Ingushetian faction failed to support him and his now dead Chechen comrades.

Because of their incompetence he covered nearly a hundred miles, mostly on foot. It was no ordinary journey to the rendezvous point. Escaping from Nazran, he had to move mainly at night to evade the pursuing Russian military. This slowed his progress. He could not take the gamble and seek shelter as he made his way to the Chechen/Georgian border for fear of being captured. Spending five nights in the open, being permanently wet because of the unseasonal heavy rain and having not eaten for two days was starting to take its toll both physically and mentally.

His negative thoughts were disrupted by the sound of an engine in the distance approaching at speed. 'It's doesn't sound like a heavy Russian army personnel carrier,' he thought. Cautiously, he raised his head over the top of the riverbank. As the sound of the engine got closer, Leonid carefully edged his way up and lay on top of the riverbank to have a clearer view.

Leonid took the flashlight out from the inside pocket of his rain sodden coat and switched it on to see what time it was. 'If its Al Qaeda, they're early,' he thought, but reassured himself that in such a dangerous part of the world it was difficult to keep to a strict timetable. The driving rain was falling even harder causing him to squint as he looked in the direction of the approaching vehicle. Seeing only one pair of headlights coming from the direction of the border with Georgia, his spirits lifted. Al Qaeda had made it. He was finally on his way to England. As the vehicle got closer, the numbness and tiredness receded. Now his thoughts turned to his new venture in the fight for Chechen freedom from Russian rule.

He remembered his Chechen brigade commander telling him how important it was the fight is taken to Russians living in other European states. 'It's time those millionaire bastards that made their money from running their oil pipelines through Chechnya know what it's like to feel Chechen pain,' Leonid thought. Being selected to organize the new front in their war with Russia, Leonid felt proud to be the first to lead these operations. It was to start with an attack at a summit meeting in London in a couple of month's time. 'And with help from Al Qaeda as well,' he thought. The two groups assisting each other was also a first. Both Al Qaeda and the Chechens had been trying to get a foothold in Ingushetia to control the uprising in the Russian province. Key to the Chechens getting Al Qaeda assistance in Western Europe was the reciprocal assistance the Chechens gave Al Qaeda in getting into Ingushetia, the intelligence they exchanged and the realization they had some common ground.

When the approaching vehicle was a few hundred meters away, Leonid stopped thinking about what he would be doing in England. The vehicle, which he recognized as an Isuzu four-by four, stopped roughly fifty meters away from him. No longer conscious of the cold, driving rain, Leonid's optimism returned. The front passenger and two rear passenger doors opened, illuminating the vehicle's interior. He saw the driver remain in the vehicle as three men got out of the Isuzu. With a flashlight, one of three men gave three short flashes followed by two longer flashes to signal to the waiting Leonid they were Al Qaeda. 'It's them,' he thought. Lying on the top of the riverbank, Leonid picked up his flashlight and returned the recognition signal of one short flash followed by three longer flashes and one final short flash.

Just able to make out their silhouettes, Leonid saw one of the men go over to the one who gave the signal and say something to him. The three men walked slowly in a line towards him.

Leonid rose up to his feet and slung his AK 47 over his shoulder. On seeing Leonid's shadowy figure rise up on the riverbank, the three men stopped. Even though his eyes were accustomed to the dark, it was still difficult to make out exactly what the man in the middle was doing. 'He can't be,' Leonid thought as he saw the man raise his hands. He was pointing a pistol at him. 'He's being cautious. He needs to be certain who I am'. With his flashlight he gave the recognition signal once more.

'He's over here,' Leonid heard the man shout out in Russian to the other two.

Leonid's heart sank. They were not Al Qaeda. They were FSB. Frantically he reached for his rifle from his shoulder. Shots were fired, but not from Leonid's rifle. Three bullets entered his chest throwing his body backwards. Lying motionless on the top of the riverbank, he became aware once more of the heavy rain as it fell on his face. He felt no pain, just a warm feeling running through his body. As the three men stood over him, no matter how hard he tried, he could not move. He looked up at them.

One of the men standing over him heard a rattling sound come from Leonid mouth. Blood hemorrhaging internally from his wounds was seeping out of his mouth. Mixing with the inhaled air in the short breaths Leonid took as struggled to breathe, it made a haunting sound. 'He's still alive,' he said.

The man who shot Leonid pointed his pistol at Leonid's head and pulled the trigger three times. Venomously kicking the lifeless body, his hatred of Chechens came out. He stopped kicking the body and said, 'The Muslim bastard's dead now.'

The driver of the Isuzu walked over to the three men as they stood over Leonid's body. 'Is the job done?' he asked.

Laughing, the man who shot Leonid spat on his body and said, 'The old Leonid Kashinov is dead, long live the new one.'

'Good, I'll get his papers,' the driver said. He knelt by Leonid's body and rifled through his pockets. He took an envelope out of Leonid's coat pocket and switched on a flashlight to read the papers inside. As he took the papers out of the envelope, a creased photograph fell out on the ground. He picked it up and looked at it. 'It's a picture of his wife and children. That'll help my cover,' he said putting the picture back into the envelope. He read the papers. 'These are from his brigade commander. It's outlined the arrangements how he's to get to England to carry out his operation, but there are no details as to what the operation is. All it says is that once in England, an Al Qaeda operative called Sayfel has to be contacted to get further details.'

'Is there a contact number for this Sayfel?' one of the men asked.

'No, I'm to be taken to an Al Qaeda cell in Turkey where I'll get further details. Let's move the body before they arrive. We can't leave it here or dump in the river. We need the Chechens to believe Kashinov got out of the country as planned.'

The four FSB agents picked up Leonid's body and carried it over to the Isuzu. The FSB agent who was going undercover as Leonid looked at his lifeless face, now distorted with the three bullet holes. Having had to learn everything about Leonid before going undercover, he gained a grudging respect for the experienced Chechen fighter who had evaded them for so long. Unlike many of his colleagues, he did not have a deep rooted hatred for the Chechens. He had never suffered personal tragedy from a Chechen terrorist attack unlike the FSB agent that shot Leonid. 'I don't know how I'd cope if I lost both my parents and my eldest son in a Chechen bomb attack like he did,' he thought as he looked at his colleague who was still sneering at the dead Chechen.

As they got to the Isuzu, one of the agents opened up the boot as the other three dumped Leonid's body into the vehicle. The FSB agent going undercover shook hands with the three men. 'Go to the pre-arranged position and wait for Al Qaeda to turn up. If I think anything's likely to go wrong, I'll give you the

signal. Tell the military to hold off and give them a free passage
back to Georgia. Once they've got me across the border to their
safe house I'll contact you. With luck, while I'm in Turkey I should
find out what the Chechens are planning to do in England. Once
I know, I'll pass it onto Moscow.'

One

Monday, 23rd October
06.50 hours
Integrated Special Branch Office, Manchester

Detective Sergeant David Hurst locked his car in the staff car park outside the modern concrete building with large mirrored glass panels that housed Greater Manchester Police's Integrated Special Branch Office. Walking over to the entrance, he stubbed his cigarette on the floor while looking at the time on his watch. 'Made good time there,' he thought, swiping his warrant card in the security entrance to the department's suite of offices. Signing in, the security guard said, 'I didn't have you down as the early officer for your team this morning David.'

'I'm not. My DI rang me earlier. Apparently we're getting a visit from our new MI5 liaison officer and he wants me in early to meet him,' David said putting his pen back into the inside pocket of his jacket.

'It's not a he, it's a she and she's here already. She arrived ten minutes ago and she's with George now,' the security guard said pointing to her name on the visitors' sheet, 'that's her signature there.'

David looked her name written in block capitals next to her signature, 'Debbie Heron from MI5's regional office in Leeds. What's she like?'

1

'I'd say she's in her early thirties and very well dressed. Unlike you scruffy lot, she looks very professional. I noticed how immaculate her hair was. She's obviously got long hair but it's tied up and there's not a hair out of place. She was very pleasant, but then they all are when they're new to a post,' the security guard replied adding new 'signing in' sheets to the clipboard on his desk to be ready for the morning shift to sign in. 'She's certainly an improvement on that arrogant bugger we had as liaison officer before her.'

'Cheers Frank, I'd better get moving seeing how she's already in George's office. You know how he hates to be kept waiting.' David walked through the large open plan office to his desk. The atmosphere of the room had that first thing in the morning calmness about it, as the only staff in the office was those officers on the early shift that had to be in by six. Among the handful of officers in the room was Steve Adams, the senior detective constable on Hurst's team. Being his team's early man for that week, he was working on his computer on the desk opposite to Hurst's.

'Morning Davey,' Steve said, 'so you've been called in early as well? George was in before me and he whisked this attractive, very smartly dressed lady into his office about ten minutes ago without saying a word. So something's up.'

'It's good see your detective training's finally starting to pay off!' David said smiling. 'I'm not too sure what's going on, but that woman you saw with George is Debbie Heron. She's our new MI5 Liaison officer. All I know is, it's got something to do with an MI5 target coming onto our patch that's going to be meeting up with the two we're watching in Ashton. I'd better go to his office and see what it's about. I just hope this doesn't mean Five are going to start taking over and pushing their noses into our job. You know what it's like when they do.'

'I've got used to fetching and carrying for you, so it makes no difference to me who's in charge, be it you or some MI5 officer,' Steve said grinning. As Hurst was putting together the paper file on his desk relating to the two Al Qaeda targets he and his team had been keeping under surveillance, Steve said, 'As your team lost again, I take it your day off yesterday was a bit of a bummer? You should be supporting United by now. You've been living and working in Manchester long enough now that you don't have to support Everton any more.'

'Just like the other glory hunters do? I don't think so. Once a Blue, always a Blue Stevey,' Hurst said picking up the file that now had some semblance of order. As he walked off to the DI's office, he said, 'Do me a favor, while I'm with George get the rest of the morning crew to come in early so we're ready for whatever it is that MI5 want from us.'

Walking up to Detective Inspector George Byrne's office, Hurst was wondering what Debbie Heron was like. During his many years as a counter-terrorist investigator, Hurst's mistrust of MI5 stemmed from working alongside them. Although they willingly passed on ninety-five per cent of their intelligence to the ISB, the five per cent they held back tended to be the most important. Hurst found that not knowing what that five per cent was, had on occasions nearly proved fatal to Branch officers. 'Give her a chance Hursty, she might be alright,' he said to himself as he approached the DI's office door that was slightly ajar. Hurst was about to knock when the voice that woke him up so abruptly at a quarter past six that morning boomed out, 'Come in David, we've been waiting for you.'

As Hurst entered the office, George walked towards him with a mug of steaming hot coffee, 'There we are David, strong and black with three large sugars, just as you like it. That should help wake you up and once again I apologize for disturbing your beauty sleep this morning.' After introducing Hurst to Debbie Heron, he added, 'Apparently your two targets are going to have a visitor that's of great interest to MI5.' Turning to Debbie he said, 'David's team is in Ashton-under-Lyne looking at the two Al Qaeda operatives you think your man is going to join up with.

His team has been watching them for six weeks now. David, could you take it up from there?'

'Yes sir,' Hurst said applying the CID protocol when addressing a senior officer in the presence of people from outside the department where rank is recognized rather than use first names. 'We've been watching two males, a Moosa Khan and an Ibrar Aatcha. Both are Manchester born. Khan's twenty-seven, and first came to notice when he was at a terrorist training camp in Swat Valley in Pakistan eighteen months ago. Little is known of him before then. However Aatcha's been known to us for a while. He's thirty-five and first came to notice when he was in an Al Qaeda training camp in Afghanistan nine years ago. He met Khan at the training camp in Swat Valley eighteen months ago. Aatcha's also been active in France, assisting another Al Qaeda cell based just outside Marseilles last April. Since his arrival in Ashton eight weeks ago, he's been working in a take-away pizza and kebab shop in Ashton owned by his cousin Mohammed Aatcha.

'Aatcha and Khan are currently staying in a flat above a local convenience store owned by Aatcha's uncle. There's no intelligence to suspect that either Aatcha's uncle or his cousin is involved with Al Qaeda. To date, we've struggled to gain entry into the flat to place any covert recording devices. The best we've been able to do is trace their mobile phone calls, tap into their landline and monitor their Internet traffic. Even that's been difficult to do at times as they've been using pay-as-you-go phones and we think they change the SIM cards on a regular basis. We've been using a hand held tracer to try and listen in to what they're saying in the flat, but there's too much secondary noise to get anything of real value. From the phone calls and emails that we've managed to intercept, they're in constant contact with a male we know only as Sayfel. We've worked out that Sayfel's from an Al Qaeda cell based in London. He seems to be pulling the strings on whatever it is our two are up to.

'There have been a few callers to the flat. I have the full

file here on whose been visiting it.' David passed the paper file over to Debbie. 'We've managed to identify most of the callers. Although at this stage we believe they're only innocent associates of our two targets. We've kept the information on the innocent callers on our intelligence system just in case they crop up in any other investigation. To date, we don't know exactly what it is Aatcha and Khan are planning, but I can take you through all the intelligence we have in greater detail now if you wish,' he said. Pushing to the back of his mind the thought that the MI5 officer had come to interfere with the investigation, and trying to sound as though he was welcoming her presence, he softened his voice and added, 'We'd welcome another pair of eyes to analyze the intelligence and spot something we may have missed.'

Debbie placed her hand on the file and said, 'Perhaps I could go through the intelligence with you later?' From the first impressions she made of the two officers, Debbie assessed that to get the fullest co-operation with Manchester's ISB, it would be best to directly address the older, grey haired, more portly George rather than the tall, fair haired DS who she noticed had a Liverpool accent, yet was working for the police in Manchester. 'We received intelligence late yesterday from one of our officers currently undercover in a London based Al Qaeda cell that a Chechen male, Leonid Kashinov has entered the country and is heading up from London to stay with your targets in Ashton-under-Lyne. We've been referring to him simply as Leonid. He's a leading member of a Chechen rebel group based in Argun, Chechnya. Of late he's been training and assisting Islamic groups in the neighboring Russian province of Ingushetia. With help from Al Qaeda, he escaped the FSB in Chechnya and stayed with one of their cells in Istanbul for a couple of months. Last Friday, the French Surete passed onto us that he arrived in Marseilles. We believe he's travelling using false documents supplied to him by Al Qaeda. We know he travelled onto Paris and caught the Eurostar train to London yesterday evening, but we've lost track of him since he's arrived in the UK. Obviously they're reducing our ability to track his movements by avoiding any air travel.

'Last night both MI5 and GCHQ intercepted emails that your man Aatcha received from the same Sayfel you've been monitoring. The ISP was located at an Internet café in Camden Town. We also intercepted a call made by Sayfel from the London area to Aatcha's mobile phone. He gave brief, cryptic instructions for Aatcha to be prepared to meet Leonid today. Sayfel wasn't on the phone long enough for us to get an exact fix. MI5 officers from Thames House, with assistance from SO13, are checking out the location of the call in the Brent area as well as the Internet café in Camden Town.

'It's important we locate Leonid. According to the FSB, he's wanted for a number of bombings in Moscow and St. Petersburg, as well the assassination of a local Russian politician and military personnel in Grozny. Over the past few months he's been in Ingushetia, training local Muslim militants to attack the Russian military, mainly around its capital, Nazran. Intelligence reveals that only a couple of months ago he was involved in an attack on senior Russian Army officers on the outskirts of Nazran. Because he's such a dangerous man, it's important we find out as soon as we can what he's up to in the UK. We don't think he's here to lay low. He could have gone to any number of safer countries to do that. So based on that premise, we can only assume he's planning something to take place in the UK. For him to run such a risk in coming here, it's believed that it's going to be something big.'

For MI5 to take an active interest and share information openly with the Branch so early in his investigation, David realized they must see Leonid's presence as a serious threat to national security. He also adduced that if such a high profile Chechen terrorist was going to be the area, the FSB would also be sniffing around his investigation. He said to Debbie, 'I'm assuming that you won't be the only MI5 officer involved with Leonid. Also, if he's so dangerous, it sounds like the FSB would love to get their hands on him before we do. Has MI5 been liaising with the FSB over Leonid since he entered the country?'

Debbie paused for a moment, her senior officer's words ringing in her ears that there were aspects to the intelligence related to Leonid that the ISB did not need to know at this stage. Knowing that she was only to pass on intelligence directly related to Aatcha and Khan, she said, 'Well I agree there's a very strong possibility that the FSB could join in the activities, but we've no intelligence to confirm this. Naturally, there'll be a higher profile of MI5 officers in and around your investigation once Kashinov joins your two targets in Ashton. For the moment, the only MI5 officer working on this job with your team is me. Once my colleagues from MI5 join us, I'll make sure they don't step on your toes and vice versa.'

'You still haven't answered my question,' Hurst said. 'I can see the possibility of the FSB also joining in the "activities" as you put it. I want to know if Five have been liaising with the FSB over Leonid. Did your intelligence come from them?' he asked more forcefully.

Unlike most of the detective sergeants she had met in her short time as MI5's police liaison officer, she could see that Hurst was more astute. From her psychological profile training, she sensed Hurst's resentment at her presence. She also got the impression he was incisive and a thinker. Noticing she was in a quandary as how to answer the question, George said, 'Let's not embarrass Debbie and push her on this point David. We understand if you're not in the position to tell us at the moment.'

Debbie said, 'It's alright George. Obviously if other agencies are going to be hovering around your investigation, it's understandable that David would want to know what the bigger picture is. I'd feel the same way if I was in his position. All I can say at the moment, MI6 picked up reports about Leonid after he left Chechnya and was staying with an Al Qaeda cell in Turkey. They monitored his movements while he was there. Once it looked like he was on his way to this country, they contacted us. I've no idea if MI6 had been liaising with the FSB during that time. Just like you feel about MI5, I feel there are times that MI6 don't fill us in on the whole picture. It was only yesterday evening that we got wind that Leonid was coming up to the Manchester area to meet up with your two targets.'

'That's an intuitive observation Debbie, but I'm only concerned for the safety of my team. The way I read it, my team will have to watch out for FSB and MI5 agents, as well as our two targets.' David said, looking at George as he spoke.

Debbie replied, 'I'm telling you straight. Initially, I will be the only MI5 officer anywhere near the Aatcha and Khan investigation. My role is to make an assessment of the situation once Leonid's arrived in Ashton and report back to my senior intelligence officer. Don't worry. I'll keep you in the loop if I request the assistance of other MI5 officers. Even if we get a whiff of the FSB coming anywhere near Leonid, you'll be the first to know.'

'That seems fair enough,' George said looking at Hurst. 'That leads me onto the fact that for the foreseeable future or certainly while this Leonid character is with Aatcha and Khan, Debbie will be heading the investigation with you David. That means that you will share everything with her. That includes what we have already as well as what we find out in the future. Debbie, all the resources we have at this ISB office are at your disposal.'

'Thanks George. I appreciate that,' Debbie said as she stood up out of her chair. 'I need to download some intelligence so I can update your team at the static obs point in Ashton-under-Lyne. Could I use your PC David?'

'It sounds like I don't have much choice do I?'

Two

Ibrar Aatcha answered his mobile phone. 'Meet the Chechen at Huyton railway station by two this afternoon. It's on the outskirts of Liverpool,' Sayfel said curtly.

'Did he give a time when he'll arrive at the station?'

'No, just be there by two this afternoon. Don't worry, it's a small station, so it'll be hard for the security services to follow you without making themselves obvious,' and the phone went dead.

Aatcha looked at his watch. He only had one hour to get there. He cursed Sayfel under his breath at setting such a tight deadline. He turned to Khan, 'Moosa, you'll have to stay here. I've got to go to a rail station just outside Liverpool to meet that Chechen I told you about yesterday. If I'm not back by five this afternoon, ring this number and tell Sayfel,' Aatcha handed over a note with Sayfel's telephone number. He picked up the road atlas and the keys to the car his cousin, Mohammed had lent him. 'I've got a bad feeling about this Moosa.'

Sensing Aatcha's concern Khan said, 'Sayfel wouldn't send you somewhere that would be dangerous.'

'It's not the danger I'm thinking of, it's picking up the Chechen that bothers me. I've got a bad feeling about this. What the fuck's Sayfel thinking of letting him stay with us now? We're so close

9

to finishing up here.'

*   *   *

Waiting on the Manchester bound platform at the small
suburban station consisting of two platforms at Huyton, Aatcha
reflected on the straightforward drive he had getting to the
station. The traffic had been light with no road-works to delay
him. Carrying out the counter-surveillance techniques he had
been taught, he came off a few motorway exits and immediately
rejoined the motorway as well as going around roundabouts a
couple of times to make sure that no one had been following
him. 'I just hope the train arrives soon,' he thought. Aatcha's
concerns did not emanate from having the British security forces
keeping him and Khan under surveillance. He expected that.
Having MI5 and Special Branch as adversaries was something he
was used to. As Sayfel had told him Leonid was an important
Chechen fighter, his concern was that Russian FSB agents would
be on Leonid's tail. During his time with Al Qaeda he had a
good idea how the British operate. They were patient. 'They only
make a move when they're certain,' he thought, 'but the Russians
are different.' Stories he heard of FSB agents' ruthlessness along
with the reports he read from Al Qaeda fighters operating in
Ingushetia ran through his mind as he looked down the platform
for the first glimpse of the train coming up from Liverpool. 'The
FSB were bad enough over there,' he said to himself. 'If they're
here, they'll have no interest in keeping us alive for a show case
criminal trial like the British do.'

With his over-active imagination working overtime, he looked
around the small station. 'Sayfel was right,' he thought, 'it would
be difficult for the security services to carry out covert surveillance
here.' It was a small suburban station having only two platforms,
the one he stood on and opposite the two sets of rail tracks was
the second platform to catch trains bound for Liverpool. The

only form of electronic surveillance at the station was two small static cameras, one on each platform pointed to watch the edges of both platforms. 'I don't know why I question Sayfel at times,' he thought, 'this is an ideal place to meet Leonid.' The only other people at the station were a couple who he estimated to be in their twenties on the opposite platform.

A train pulled up on the opposite platform bound for Liverpool. Aatcha watched the couple as they boarded it and sit in the second of the two carriages. They did not look at him. There was not even a sly glance. That reassured him they were not from the security services. As he looked at the young couple, he became aware of a woman carrying two plastic shopping bags walking onto the Manchester bound platform. Trying not to make it obvious he was looking at her, Aatcha watched the woman walk past him to the end of the platform. She stopped and looked down the line. A few seconds later she turned round and began to walk towards him. As she approached Aatcha, she briefly glanced at him and continued to walk past him. He watched her put her bags on the platform. With her back to him, she reached into her handbag and took out a mobile phone. Watching out of the corner of his eye, Aatcha saw the woman press a couple of buttons on the phone. He tried to hear what she was saying, but could only make out that she was talking to a 'Jenny' about her brother and that she would be catching the next train to Manchester. It was a brief call and she put the phone back into her handbag. 'Obviously she's a woman who's been shopping and making her way home,' Aatcha thought as he looked back down the platform towards Liverpool, eagerly waiting for the arrival of the next train.

*   *   *

'Hello Jenny, our brother's still working in the same place. I can't really talk right now, as my hands are full of shopping and

I'm getting the next Manchester train that's due any minute. Can I ring you later?' Debbie said on her phone from the Manchester bound platform at Huyton rail station to Hurst who was sat in an ISB car with Steve Adams. They had parked up a safe distance away from Aatcha's car after successfully following Aatcha from Ashton to the station in Huyton. Hurst's team had five vehicles following him. They did not fall for Aatcha's counter-surveillance techniques. They were expecting it.

'That's fine. Let us know the moment you see Aatcha meet Leonid. If he does, you get on the train and stay on it until it gets to Manchester and we'll see you back at the office,' David said closing his phone. Turning to Steve he said, 'Aatcha's still on the platform. It's a shame Andy and Tracy had to get on the Liverpool train. They had a good eye-ball with Aatcha on the Liverpool bound platform.'

'Credit where credit's due, Debbie showed good initiative there. At least she checked the train times unlike you. Also, it was a good idea of hers to nip into the supermarket and pick up a few items and pass herself off as a shopper,' Steve said approvingly. 'She seems to know her stuff. To be fair, she didn't interfere with our set-up at the static obs point opposite the flat in Ashton. I know its early days, but I reckon we'll get on fine with her. She's not treading on your toes, telling you how you should run the team unlike that last prick of a liaison officer did at times.'

'So you think I'm wrong to be suspicious of her?' David asked, surprised that his closest friend would challenge his judgment.

'Yes I am,' Steve said. 'Give the girl a break. When she briefed the team at the static obs in Ashton, she passed on quite a lot of intelligence that Five has on both our two targets and this Leonid bloke. It was more than I've seen an MI5 officer pass at this stage of an investigation. You've got to realize that she's got a lot at stake in this too. If we cock-up in keeping tabs on Leonid, it'll be her who'll have to answer to her bosses not us. All I'm saying is lay off her for a bit and let's see what she's like before we make any judgment on her.'

David grinned as he said, 'You've always been a sucker for a pretty face and a smile. She's taken to you and I'll tell you why. She's trying to get to me through you. She's realized that we're more than just workmates.'

'Stop being paranoid, you're just pissed off with the fact that she's having a shout in running the investigation and the team. There are times you can be just like the bosses you criticize.'

'I'm not that egotistical that I can't share in the running of an investigation.'

'It comes across like that at times,' Steve said looking Hurst in the eye.

'I'm just saying it's early days yet and we've got to be careful before we open up to her. You know as well as I do MI5 hold back intelligence from us most of the time, or at least until they think the time is right for us to know. She's got to do more than check rail times and buy some groceries before I trust her.'

'I'll admit there are some MI5 officers that I've come across I wouldn't trust as far as I could spit, but most of them are alright.'

'How can you say that? You were nearly killed because of them not keeping us fully in the picture in that Cleveland Road job.'

'For fuck's sake, that was years ago. You've got to let it go. I have. Before you forget, it was me the three PIRA lads surrounded at gunpoint, not you.'

'It was Five's intelligence that diverted the rest of the team to that address in Prestwich leaving us two on our own. Before you forget, it was me that shot them, not you.'

'You never let me forget it, do you? What annoys me is that every so often it's like this spectre comes back to haunt you, and it normally happens when MI5 send an officer to change our plans. Let it go. Give her a chance and judge her by the end of the week. After all you're far from perfect yourself Davey. Let's not fall out over this.'

'You're right, I suppose,' David said as his close friend pricked his conscience that he was too suspicious of people at times.

'Less of Debbie,' Steve said sensing the mood between the friends was getting a little melancholy, 'it's a good job you know your way round here. I always knew having a Scouser on the team would come in handy. Have you heard anything from Merseyside's ISB yet?'

'Only that they're watching Lime Street station in Liverpool city centre while some of our lot are watching both Piccadilly and Victoria stations in Manchester. If you ask me, I think Leonid's got the London to Liverpool train and is going to come up here from Lime Street on the Manchester bound train. I can't see him going to Manchester first and then travel across towards Liverpool.'

'From what Debbie said, this Chechen sounds like he's one smart, ruthless bastard. Apart from the bombings he's done, the FSB haven't managed to catch him for fifteen years! What I don't understand is why is a Chechen getting mixed up with Al Qaeda? As far as I can remember, they've never worked together before.'

'I can't think of it happening before either. It says something when MI5, with all their resources don't know why they're meeting up.' David's mobile phone was still in his hand when it rang. Registering it was from technical support, he quickly answered the call. 'Hello.'

'The tag's on the target's car,' the voice said at the other end.

'Thanks, I'll call you later and let you know how it goes.' David put his mobile phone on the dashboard of the car. 'The techies have got a tagging device fixed on Aatcha's car. At least if we lose sight of them when they move off after meeting up, we can trace where they go.'

*   *   *

The Manchester bound train trundled to a halt and the automatic doors opened slowly. Watching Debbie get on the train, Aatcha saw a disheveled man walking towards him, whose dark hair was sticking up, suggesting to Aatcha that at some stage during the journey he had fallen asleep in his seat. Unlike the other passengers who were walking purposively, this small, stocky man was looking around the platform, as though he was expecting someone to meet him. 'He must be Leonid,' he thought. Watching the small man walk towards him, Aatcha noticed a taller man wearing a bulky green coat standing away from the rear of the train paying a lot of attention to the man he thought was Leonid. The man in the green coat nodded to someone behind Aatcha. He quickly looked round to see a woman, playing with something in her ear nod back. As the man wearing the green jacket began to walk down the platform, Aatcha quickly walked up to the small stocky man and whispered in his ear, 'Are you Leonid?'

'I am,' he said, 'Are you Ibrar?'

As Leonid answered, Aatcha noticed the man in the green jacket stop walking and for a brief moment look directly at Aatcha. Then glancing quickly at Leonid, the man looked over to where the woman would be standing behind Aatcha, as if to catch her attention. This was enough to confirm to Aatcha that Leonid was being followed. As the train's automatic doors were about to close, Aatcha grabbed hold of Leonid's arm, bundling him back onto the train he said, 'You're being followed. Get back on the train.' As the doors closed behind them, Aatcha pushed Leonid into an empty seat and sat down next to him. 'That man wearing the green jacket with the cropped hair standing by the Perspex waiting area talking to the dark haired woman in the blue coat. It's them. I'm sure they're following you,' Aatcha said quietly in Leonid's ear.

As the train began to move out of the station, Aatcha saw the woman frantically looking at the windows of the train trying to spot Leonid. Just as she was going out of Aatcha's sight, he saw her make a call on her phone while the man stood staring, tight lipped as the train slowly moved away. 'Did you notice them following you?' Aatcha asked Leonid.

Leonid pointed to some seats in front of him and said, 'She was about five rows further down from where I was sitting when we left Liverpool. She got on after me. I looked at her, but she didn't seem to be paying me much attention. I didn't notice the man. He must have been behind me.'

Even though he had a thick Russian accent, Aatcha was impressed at how well the Chechen spoke English. 'When you were walking towards me, I saw him stand for a moment by the train doors. He looked at you and then he looked directly at me and nodded his head to that woman who was standing behind me on the platform. When I turned round, I saw her, fixing what looked like a radio ear-piece into her ear while she nodded back to him. That was enough for me to suspect they're from the security services.'

'How do the British know I'm here already? Sayfel virtually guaranteed me that they would have no idea that I had entered the country,' Leonid said putting his head into his hands. The tiredness he was feeling from his long journey was beginning to wear him down.

'Don't criticize Sayfel. If he hadn't arranged for me to meet you at that small station, I might not have noticed them. Anyway, what makes you say they're British? They could be the FSB. After all, you're a Chechen and they could've found out you're here.'

*   *   *

Sitting in rear facing seat, a few rows down from the automatic doors, Debbie saw Aatcha bundle Leonid back on to the train as the automatic doors closed. 'Shit! They're not using the car to get back to Manchester,' she thought, not being able to take her eyes off the two men. 'Something spooked them at the station.' Knowing the original plan of her remaining on the train to Manchester Victoria Station could change, she sent a text David:

'Aatcha and Leonid made contact. Both back on the train.
I have them in view. Ring me.'

*   *   *

Waiting for Aatcha and Leonid emerge from the station, David and Steve's eyes were trained on the station exit. 'They should have left the station by now,' Steve said. 'We can't have missed them.'

David radioed through to the two members of his team watching the exit on the opposite side of the station to check if they had seen Aatcha and Leonid leave when the text message signal sounded on his phone. 'Hang on, Debbie's sent me a text,' he said to Steve as he opened the message. David quickly scanned the message. In disbelief at what he saw, he read it again. Losing sight of the two targets was not Hurst's immediate concern. His concern was Debbie being in a vulnerable position. Any reservations he had for her were put aside. 'The bastards have got back onto the train. Debbie's got eyeball with them but she's on her own. I'll ring her to see what happened and make sure she's OK.'

'Can you talk?' David asked Debbie as she answered his call.

'Yes,' Debbie said. Talking quietly, she bent slightly in her seat, turning her head towards the train window to minimize the chance of Aatcha making out what she was saying. 'I don't know what happened there. I saw our friend make contact with his visitor. Then for no reason, he bundles him back into train as the doors were closing. Something spooked him, but I don't know what. I tried to see if any of our lot was on the platform, but all I saw were the passengers that got off.'

'Are you alright?'

'Yes, I'm fine but there's not a lot I can do if they get off. Before the train pulled in the station he had a good look at me, so I can only follow them to the exit of any station they get off.'

'What are they doing now?'

'Our visitor looks tired. He's sitting back in his seat looking out of the window. You can tell he's been travelling for a while. Our friend's been clocking everyone in the carriage and he's the one that's looking really on edge.'

'All I can think is it's either an unplanned train journey because as you said, he's seen something that's made him get back on the train or, he could simply be checking to see if he's being followed. Let's hope it's a check, as he'll more than likely get off at the next station or maybe the one after that and double back to the car here at Huyton. If he's been spooked then god knows what he'll do next. There weren't any of your mob around the station that you didn't tell me about were there?'

For a brief moment Debbie was annoyed that once more Hurst was showing a lack of trust in her. She took a deep breath to remain calm and said, 'No. Trust me, there was only us at the station.'

'OK, I'll let George know what's happened. He can contact the rail company and get the train stopped before it pulls into the next station. That'll give us a chance to get some back-up to you. I'll speak to you later,' David said terminating the call. He turned to Steve and told him what Debbie had seen while he called George.

'What's going on? I take it Aatcha's made contact, but has he got on the train with Leonid?' George asked answering the call.

'He has. They're both on the train and Debbie's got eye-ball with them. She's got no back-up and I'm worried about her safety. Do us a favor and contact the rail company to stop the train before it gets into the Whiston station. It's the train to Manchester that left Huyton at 14.25. See if you can get some Merseyside ISB officers to join Debbie to back her up. If Aatcha and Leonid get off at a station before the train gets to Manchester we're fucked. Aatcha's clocked Debbie, so she can't follow them. Either something or someone spooked Aatcha or he's simply checking to see if he's being followed. If he's checking, then it's highly likely he'll double back to Huyton and get back to Ashton in the car he came down in. If Aatcha's been spooked, then we're fucked.'

Sensing the exasperation in David's voice, George said, 'I'll get onto the train company straight away. You're most probably right, Aatcha's just being cautious and he'll return to Huyton station. Regardless of what happens, I'll square it off with the DCI. We can be pretty positive in assuming Aatcha's returning to Ashton. I just checked with the boys at the static obs spot and Khan's not moved. Aatcha wouldn't leave him on his own. So either way we'll catch up with him.'

'It's not Aatcha I'm bothered about, it's the Chechen. If we lose him and something happens to Debbie, not only will MI5 come down heavy on us for being inept, Edge'll chew us up, me in particular.'

'I told you. I'll deal with DCI Edge. In the meantime you and your team stay at Huyton and I'll get some Merseyside ISB officers to Whiston station. The train company can make it look like it's had to stop for a red light. That will give us time for Merseyside to join Debbie on the train.'

As David finished speaking to George, Steve said, 'Showing concern for an MI5 officer? Not long ago it sounded as though you wanted her to fail and you didn't give a shit what happened to her.'

'I might not trust her firm, but I don't want anyone getting hurt. We're still on the same side.'

*　　*　　*

'Ladies and gentleman this is the guard speaking. On behalf of North-West Transport I apologize for the short delay before we get

*into Whiston station. A blockage has been found on the rail tracks.
We are expecting it only to be a short delay of approximately ten to
fifteen minutes'*

Mumblings of discontent from the passengers followed the
train guard's announcement. A passenger sitting close to Debbie
sounded off in a loud stage whisper how frustrating it was, as the
train was so close to Whiston station. As Debbie glanced over at
Aatcha and Leonid, she saw Aatcha getting even more agitated.

'It'll be those two I saw at Huyton station that got the train
to stop,' Aatcha whispered in Leonid's ear. 'That tells me they
could be British not the FSB. They'll have arranged for the train
to stop long enough to have agents covering both platforms. If
we get off, they'll follow us. If we stay on the train they'll get on.
The bastards have got all the bases covered.'

'Why don't we get off now and run down the side of the
track until we find a gap in a fence or a wall high enough for
us get over,' Leonid asked, thinking this was the last thing he
wanted to do after his long journey.

'We can't open the doors while the train's stationary until
the driver or the guard releases the lock. We trapped like fish in
a barrel.'

'Fish in a barrel?' Leonid asked, not understanding the metaphor.

'It's just a saying. It means if we stay here, we're fucked,' Aatcha
replied looking around him to see if there was any possible way
to get off the train before it moved off to the next station.

*   *   *

Calling David on the phone, Debbie said, 'The longer the
train remains stationary the more anxious our friends are getting.
George did well to get the train stopped before it pulled into
Whiston station, but the delay is clearly getting to our friend.
However his visitor looks as thought he's too tired to care at the
moment. Have you any idea how long we're going to be waiting

before the train moves off?'

'Merseyside came over the radio just before to say they were two minutes away from the station. They've got four officers on the way to cover the station. It shouldn't be much longer now.'

'If the tension's getting to me, god knows what it's like for those two, especially our friend. He's getting really fidgety now. I'm worried he'll do something silly to get off the train before it moves off. He's clearly suspicious why the train's stopped. Whatever suspicions that triggered him to get on the train in the first place this delay is just fuelling them.'

'I think you're about to move off as the Merseyside officers have just arrived at the station. You stay on the train all the way to Manchester and leave those two to Merseyside. If you get off and try to follow them, it'll only add to Aatcha's suspicions.'

'You're right,' Debbie said. The train lurched forward slightly as it began to move off. 'Let's hope they don't let us down. I'll ring you back when I see some movement from our two.'

*   *   *

The train stopped at Whiston station. Debbie was watching Aatcha and Leonid as they stood up to get off the train. She tried to keep them in view for as long as she could while remaining in her seat.

'We'll get off here,' Aatcha said picking up Leonid's bag.

As they stepped out of the carriage, Leonid said, 'What if they're waiting for us?'

'It's not a case "if",' Aatcha said, looking around the platform, 'they're here alright.'

Debbie telephoned Hurst to inform him Aatcha and Leonid had left the train. She watched them walk along the platform to the exit. It was difficult for her to tell if anyone began to follow them as over a dozen passengers got off the train with the two targets. Debbie asked Hurst, 'Do the Merseyside officers know what Aatcha looks like?'

'George forwarded some pictures we have of him to their i-phones. Sit back, enjoy the trip to Manchester and leave it to us.'

'Let me know what happens. Just so you know, they've both gone out of the exit and I've lost sight of them. I can't tell if Merseyside's picked them up, as they were followed by most of the passengers that got off the train.'

*   *   *

Aatcha led Leonid out of the station and saw a sign-post indicating the way to Whiston Hospital. 'We'll walk up to the hospital. If anyone's following us on foot, we stand a better chance of losing them there and we're more likely to get a taxi from the hospital,' Aatcha said, checking to see if anyone was following them.

'Do you know where you are?' Leonid asked. Struggling to muster up the energy to walk any further, he was hoping they would not have to walk too far. After travelling for nearly three days, all he wanted to do was sit down and rest.

'No, but it can't be far. There's a large building just ahead. That must be the hospital.' Aatcha could see Leonid was starting to struggle as his gait was turning into a shuffle. 'It's not far now and if we see a taxi on the way to the hospital we'll get that.' Leonid looked up at Aatcha and gave a strained smile.

After walking along a wide sweeping right hand bend, they eventually saw the entrance to the hospital. Aatcha looked behind him to see four people walking directly behind him, while on the opposite side of the road there were another two people walking in the direction of the hospital. It concerned Aatcha that one was walking around twenty yards behind the other, not side-by-side. At the entrance of the hospital Aatcha said, 'Let's wait here and see where these people behind us go. If any of them are security services, they'll have to walk past us and that will piss them off.'

A man and woman in their early twenties entering the hospital grounds, paid no attention to either Aatcha or Leonid as they walked passed the two men. Aatcha noticed the woman was close to crying. The young man put his arm comfortingly around her as Aatcha heard him say, 'Mum's in good hands now. Their doing all they can.' They were closely followed by a man of medium height that looked like he was in his mid-thirties. As it began to rain slightly, the man pulled up the collar of his brown leather coat as he walked passed them. He was immediately followed by a woman in her late twenties. She briefly glanced over at Aatcha and Leonid as she approached them, then continued to look straight ahead of her. He nudged Leonid and said quietly, 'I reckon she's one of them. Let's see where they go. As we go into the hospital grounds keep an eye on the two who were on the other side of the road. I noticed they both walked off down that side road opposite, but it wouldn't surprise me if they reappear once we go in.'

On entering the grounds, Aatcha saw the woman walk into an entrance to a building on his right. The sign above the door said 'Orthopedic Outpatients Entrance'. 'She didn't look injured,' he thought. As they walked past the door, he saw the woman had stopped by the entrance and was watching him and Leonid walk past. Ahead of them, Aatcha saw the entrance to the accident and emergency department. To the right of the entrance was a taxi rank with a number of taxis waiting for a fare. He saw the young couple walk into the main entrance of A and E while the man in the brown leather coat stopped, took out a packet of cigarettes, put one to his mouth and light it as he turned to face Aatcha and Leonid. 'I reckon he's one of them too,' Aatcha said to Leonid. He looked behind him. As he expected, he saw one of the men emerge from the side road and enter the hospital grounds. 'They're onto us alright,' he said to Leonid. 'We'll get one of those taxis and head back to Huyton. We can get the car

there and drive back to Ashton. Before we do, I've just got to
make a quick call.'

*   *   *

'Stick as best as you can with them,' Hurst said, cursing
under his breath. 'Is the name of the taxi companies on the
side of the cabs? If they get one, at least we can contact the
taxi company to find out where they're going?' he asked Laura
Darwin, the Merseyside ISB officer stood inside the entrance to
the Orthopedic Clinic.

'It depends how long he's going to be on the phone, but if he
gets the next cab in line, it's from Alpha Taxi's based in Prescot.
The next two have no company names on them, they must be
owned by the driver. Jim's standing by the entrance to A and E and
he's going to try and get the taxi plate numbers without alerting
Aatcha. It's going to be difficult as I'm sure he's clocked us.'

'Tell him to go into A and E. He can call it quits as you're
most probably right that Aatcha's clocked him. You and the officer
you've got across the road try and get the taxi plate numbers
when they drive out. I'll pass it onto the SIO in our incident
room so he can try and track the satellite navigation, or at least
listen into any radio comms they have.'

'Will do David. I'm sorry but there was nothing we could do.
There were only the four of us and no cover for us to use,' Laura
said with a note of frustration in her voice.

'Don't worry about it, there was fuck all you could have
done. It's not your fault. Aatcha's experienced and is no fool. We
saw that when we he got onto the train at Huyton. I'd love to
know what happened when he met Leonid. From the way he's
behaving, I'm more convinced than I was before that he saw
something or someone to make him this ultra-cautious.'

'It could be that Aatcha's just paranoid about being followed,'
Laura said trying to sound upbeat, even though she suspected

that Aatcha had realized they were following him.

*　　*　　*

Aatcha put his mobile phone back in the inside pocket of his jacket. 'When we're driving back to Manchester, Sayfel's going to help us get back to the flat in Ashton,' he said picking up Leonid's bag. 'Let's get a cab to the car at Huyton station and we'll drive back.'

'What's he going to do?' Leonid asked hoping that whatever it was, it brought to a swift end what had seemed like a never ending journey.

'You'll see when we get to Manchester,' Aatcha said slapping Leonid on his shoulder. 'Come on let's get a cab before this rain gets any heavier and you get really wet. The last thing we want is you getting a cold.'

Three

'To confirm, it's a black hackney Austin FX4, registered number Mike Alpha zero eight Yankee Tango November. Taxi Plate number is Five Six One and is issued by Knowsley Council and the company is Alpha Taxi's in Prescot,' Hurst informed George at the incident room in Manchester.

'I'll make a subtle enquiry with the company and get back to you. In the meantime I still want you and your team to stay in Huyton. If they're heading down the A57 towards Prescot, it looks like they're coming back to your location,' George said.

'Thanks George,' David said. He placed his phone back onto the dashboard of the car and said to Steve, 'George'll get back to us once he's been in touch with the taxi company, so we should know for definite where Aatcha's going.'

'We could do with something going our way. Since the Chechen's arrived everything's gone to rat-shit. You'd better let Debbie know what's happening.'

'She's been in touch with George, but I'll give her a courteousy call anyway.'

'And so you should. After all, she's still joint leader of the investigation,' Steve said laughing.

'Before you shit stir it any more, I suggest we get out of the

26

cars and try to blend in before our friends come back to the Ford Mondeo. Having three cars with two people sat in the front seats will certainly look suspicious to Aatcha.'

'You're right. Why don't you go and wait by the entrance to the supermarket, while I get one of the shopping trolleys. I'll pretend I'm putting shopping in the boot. One could go to the garage over there and pretend to put air in the tires. Alex and Tony can get out of their car and pretend to be having a chat.'

'Good idea Steve, I'll sort that out now,' David said as his phone rang. He picked it up off the dashboard to see it was George calling him. 'Alright boss.'

'At last, we have some good news. I spun the radio controller of the taxi company some yarn about the driver being a possible witness to a traffic accident. The controller said that she'll get the driver to ring me back in a few minutes after he's dropped off his fare at Huyton station. So expect them to turn up any time now.'

*   *   *

The black hackney cab drove up to the entrance to the supermarket by Huyton rail station, ten yards from where Hurst was standing. Recognising the cab's registration number, Hurst lit a cigarette and walked to the ATM cash machines. 'The last thing I need now is for them to clock me,' he thought. He joined the queue for the ATM's. Standing slightly to one side, he tried to catch a glimpse of Aatcha and Leonid as they emerged from the cab when he heard Steve's voice in the radio earpiece he was wearing.

'To all units, our two are out of the taxi and are walking up to the blue Mondeo. Aatcha's carrying a brown hold-all. I'm going to close the boot and take the trolley back. Anyone who can take up eye-ball?'

Hurst knew he could not continue with a commentary as the others in the ATM queue would overhear. Turning round, he

saw Steve pushing the empty trolley to the trolley park as Alex
Bullard, from his team took up the commentary. 'He's unlocked
the Mondeo's doors and the Chechen is getting in the front
passenger seat. Obviously he's not used to right hand drive cars
as he went to open the driver's door until Aatcha told him to go
into the other door. Aatcha's gone to the back of the car and is
opening the boot.'

A young woman at the head of the queue was taking her
time at the ATM, placing a third card into the machine. To
Hurst it made no difference how long he had to wait. The longer
the better, but he sensed others in the queue were becoming
frustrated at the woman taking so long to get cash out of the
machine. Now the two targets were getting into their car, he
used this mood to leave the queue suddenly without bringing
too much attention to himself. As he walked off, he put his cash
card back into his trouser pocket and muttered, 'For fuck's sake.'
As he began to walk off he heard the man waiting behind him
say, 'I don't blame you mate.'

As he walked up to the ISB car, Steve had already got into
the driver's seat as Alex continued with the commentary. Hurst
got into the front passenger seat and looking at Aatcha, said to
Steve, 'He's taking no chances.' They both watched Aatcha as
he moved around the car with a small mirror. He held it under
the wheel arches and underneath the car looking for any small
tracking devices.

Steve said, 'When I saw him open the boot to put the holdall in, I was worried he would have found the tag.'

'Thank goodness he didn't check properly inside the
boot,' David said as Aatcha finished his check and got into the
driver's seat. David looked at Steve, 'It looks like our man's on
the move. Let's hope it's a straight forward trip back to Ashton,
if that's where they're going.'

*   *   *

Detective Chief Inspector Paul Edge was the acting detective superintendent of GMP's ISB. It was a temporary promotion following the previous detective superintendent's promotion to chief superintendent two weeks earlier. Over six feet tall, he still had a muscular, stocky build even though his rugby playing days were now behind him. Apart from his height and build, his shaven head and permanent unnerving stare made many officers fear him. Knowing the importance of having such an important MI5 target on his patch, Edge joined George in the incident room to monitor David and his team as they followed Aatcha back to Manchester. He knew if Leonid was successfully housed in the Manchester area, not only would it reflect well on his officers, but it would reflect well on his management of the department and help ensure that his acting rank became permanent. To the annoyance of Hurst, Edge thought nothing of stealing the glory from other's work that would reflect well on him. The two already had a number of run-ins in the past, as Hurst enjoyed using every opportunity to show him up regardless of who was present.

'Looks like the teams have done a good job so far,' George said trying to gauge Edge's mood.

Edge kept his eyes focused on the pictures relayed from the CCTV cameras as Hurst and his team having left the M602 was heading through Salford along Regent Road towards Manchester city centre. 'It isn't over yet George. They'd better not lose them this time or I'll have Hurst's bollocks on a roasting spit. They nearly fucked up when Aatcha went back onto the train with that Chechen. If he'd lost him then, it would have been very embarrassing for me in a particular. It wouldn't be just the chief on my back. I'd have had the Home Office asking me hard questions as well.'

'It wasn't totally their fault, no one expected Aatcha to get back on the train with Leonid,' George said calmly, suppressing his desire to tell Edge he was being unreasonable. 'At least they didn't panic. David kept me briefed throughout and we were on top of Aatcha and Leonid all the time.'

Edge took his eyes off the screen and looked straight at George, 'We should always expect the unexpected. For fuck's sake, we ended up having an MI5 officer on her own with no immediate back-up and then the fucking Scousers cocked up by getting themselves compromised at the hospital. As usual, it was you who was on top of things George, not Hurst and his team. It was you that got the train stopped and it was you that contacted the taxi firm to see where they were heading after we lost sight of them.'

'I couldn't have done that without David's quick thinking at the scene. Strangely enough, he had a feeling Aatcha and Leonid would return to Huyton.'

'That shows me he's not just a cocky bastard, he's a lucky cocky bastard. I'm watching him closely this afternoon especially with MI5 breathing down our necks. One more fuck up by him today and I'll do what it takes to get him out of the Branch.'

*   *   *

'Targets are through the traffic lights and approaching the Mancunian Way. They're still in the offside lane passing two white vans,' Tony King, from Hurst's team relayed over the radio. He and Alex Bullard was the lead ISB vehicle in the mobile surveillance as they followed the targets along the dual carriageway and entered the flyover that went over Manchester's busy city center streets. Alex accelerated to pass the vans to get closer to Aatcha and Leonid as Tony kept up the commentary. 'We're about to pass the vans now... Fuck!'

Alex slammed on the brakes and swerved to the left as one of the vans pulled out without warning into the path of the ISB car. 'We've lost sight of the targets, this bloody van's just pulled out on us and is doing around thirty miles an hour to get past the other van that's doing around twenty,' Tony relayed to the incident room and the other officers.

'We're still on the Salford side of the Irwell. Can you tell from the tag where they've gone?' David radioed through to the incident room. They were still travelling along Regent Road as he and Steve had dropped back from being the lead car at Huyton at the start of the surveillance and was now the rear ISB vehicle.

On hearing David's transmission, one of the technical officers in the incident room logged onto the tagging device placed on Aatcha's car, 'DS Hurst, the car is still mobile. It's come off at the Mancunian Way at the junction with Medlock Street and is travelling towards London Road.'

Steve switched on the siren and the blue lights hidden behind the car's grille as he raced along Water Street through the city centre as David said, 'We're in Water Street now. We'll try and catch them up.' He looked at Steve, who was concentrating as he drove through the heavy traffic, 'Fuck, all the other's are caught on the Mancunian Way. Come on Stevey let's catch up with the bastards.'

As Steve was about to reply, they heard Tony King's voice come over the radio, 'I don't believe it! The van that fucking pulled out on us has now hit the other van it was overtaking. They've stopped on the Mancunian Way blocking the traffic. We're stuck, we can't get past them.'

'Are there any other units to back up DS Hurst's car?' George asked over the radio.

Following a short silence, Hurst said over the radio, 'I think we're the only ones that didn't go onto the Mancunian Way. The others are stuck there. Any update on the tag?'

The technical officer in the incident room replied, 'Aatcha's car has just turned from London Road by Piccadilly station into Fairfield Street.'

'We're in Whitworth Street just passing Minshull Street now. We'll be there in thirty seconds,' Hurst replied.

As they were close to the location, Steve switched off the

siren and the blue lights. He did not want Aatcha to be aware
of their approach. 'The target vehicle's stopped in Fairfield Street
and it looks like it's under the railway bridge,' the technical
officer relayed to David and Steve.

'Just as well,' Hurst passed on over the radio, 'we've got caught
in traffic and we're stuck at a red light. Let us know if they move
off.' When the traffic lights changed to green Steve drove into
Fairfield Street to look for the now stationary target car. As they
passed Piccadilly Station, Steve slowed the car to a near crawl as
both officers searched for sight of the blue Mondeo.

'There it is, it's parked up about fifty yards ahead,' Hurst
said to Steve, and relayed the information over the radio to the
incident room.

Steve stopped the ISB car thirty yards behind the Mondeo.
'Oh fuck,' he said, 'it looks like there's no one in it.'

'You're right,' David said banging his fist in frustration on
the dashboard. 'The bastards have done a switch. The van that
pulled out on Alex must be Al Qaeda.' He got back on the radio,
'Alex, are the vans still there?'

'Yes,' she replied, 'it looks like the drivers have exchanged
details.'

'Get the details of the vans and any pictures you can of the
drivers and follow them. I think they're Al Qaeda. George, can you
get uniform to get a patrol car in the area and stop the vans?'

'I'll see if there's one nearby,' George replied, 'what makes you
think they're involved with our targets?'

'Aatcha and Leonid have abandoned the Mondeo and done a
switch,' David said, 'I think the vans were used to slow the traffic
behind them to let them get away.'

In a fit of temper Edge grabbed the transmitter from the desk
George was sitting at. 'Hurst, get in straight away and report to
me in my office.'

'Yes sir, but first we need one of our units at the scene to
keep an eye on the Mondeo, just in case someone returns to pick

it up. We'll stay here until another unit arrives and then we'll come in.'

'You'll come in now! Leave the Mondeo,' an enraged Edge said. Turning to George, he said, 'who the fuck does he think he is telling me to wait? He's fucked up again. George, direct another unit to park up near that Mondeo.'

'He's right sir. We need someone to relieve David and Steve before he comes in, just in case we miss someone picking up the car,' George said. 'A few more minutes won't hurt.'

'A few minutes won't hurt what?' Debbie asked, standing at the door of the incident room.

Edge turned and saw the MI5 officer walking over to one of the monitors displaying the CCTV pictures of David Hurst and Steve Adams walking away from the Mondeo. 'I'm sorry but due to the incompetence of a couple of my officers, mainly DS Hurst we've lost your target.'

'I've been stood here long enough not to see it that way. As far as I can see, the incident on the Mancunian Way was what caused you to lose Aatcha and Leonid, not your officers' actions. So what happened?' she asked.

'There was an accident on the Mancunian Way that blocked our mobile units. As a result they couldn't follow Aatcha. He drove off to Piccadilly Station and parked up underneath the railway bridge and did a switch. At the moment we've no idea where he or your Chechen is. Hurst's coming in and don't worry he'll be taken off the investigation,' Edge explained to Debbie, feeling highly embarrassed.

'Why are you going to take him off the investigation? Was it is his fault?' Debbie asked.

'He was in charge of the surveillance operation, so he has to take the rap. I'm sorry we let you down. I'll personally take responsibility in investigating what went wrong and ensure that if any officer was found to be negligent they will be severely dealt with,' Edge said.

'If you're suggesting David Hurst or any of his officers were at fault, I can tell you that having been with them today, you would be barking up the wrong tree. What happened at Huyton station was out of David Hurst's control. Everything that was in his control he had covered. When I was on the train with Aatcha and Leonid, it was his suggestion to get the train stopped so other officers could back me up and keep on the Aatcha's tail. From watching Aatcha, I think he's a wily old fox. I'm telling you Mr. Edge, Aatcha's no inexperienced jihadist. Apart from being very surveillance conscious, he's also smart. It could have been any one of us that lost him,' Debbie said, in a polite, but firm manner. 'Also, the incident with the vans is quite clearly a diversion set up by Al Qaeda. It wasn't you I heard requesting that other units follow the vans, it was David Hurst. From my one day of working with him, I can see that he's the one that's the most switched on in this operation Acting Detective Superintendent Edge.'

Taken aback, Edge perceived these comments from this five foot two female MI5 officer as an affront, an attempt to show him up in front if his own staff. He said, 'For your information, I run a tight ship here Ms Heron. If that's how you and your department want to play it, that's fine by me. I'll order Hurst to stay at the scene, but it's under your orders. If anything else goes wrong then I'm assuming no blame will be placed at my door and that you're prepared to shoulder the responsibility?'

'Don't worry Acting Detective Superintendent Edge, I'll take full responsibility. As you know Mr. Edge, all ISB SIO's have to liaise with MI5 before they make a major decision. As MI5 police liaison officer, I'm the one you take instructions from. George, I'm assuming you're still the SIO on this operation?'

George said nothing. He looked at Paul Edge. 'Yes he is,' Edge snarled back at Debbie.

'Good. George, request DS Hurst and DC Adams to remain at the scene. Get some other ISB mobiles in the area to support them. They're to keep obs on the vehicle and wait to see who comes to pick it up. As DS Hurst correctly pointed out, see if we can get some uniform officers to stop those vans and get them checked out,' Debbie said as Edge stormed out of the incident room, slamming the door behind him.

Four

'Aatcha and the Chechen are walking up to the entrance of the flat. We have them in sight,' John Davies, a DC on David's team radioed through the incident room from the static observation point opposite the flat Aatcha and Khan were using.

'Thanks John, you and Andy keep an eye on them. Let us know straight away if any of them make the slightest move out of that flat,' George said tuning to Debbie who was sat next to him. Mainly out of relief that they had returned to the flat, he winked at her, and said, 'We've got them back on our radar. Just like you said they would, they've come back to the flat.'

'It's no surprise to me. Our intelligence source is very reliable. He's an informant controlled by my senior intelligence officer and the source was adamant they would end up back in Ashton,' Debbie said.

'I'll go and tell Edge that our targets have returned. That should cheer him up a little.'

'If you don't mind, I'll do that George. The way he belittled David Hurst earlier only confirmed the original impression I had of him that he was an insufferable bully. It will give me great satisfaction to go and personally let him know. Any experienced

36

detective worth their salt could see that some of the events that happened earlier were out of our control. Aatcha's a worthy adversary and it's how you respond to the unexpected that marks out those who can from who those can't do the job. From what I saw earlier, I think I know out of those two who can do the job.'

'I'm glad you two are getting along. I know David can seem to be a stand offish when you first meet him and that he comes across as a little difficult to get along with. But I've known him since he was a young DC. Once you prove yourself to him, you'll find no greater ally. He'll fight your corner regardless of the consequences. That's why his team is so loyal to him.'

'I appreciate loyalty has its place, but my main concern at the moment is who in this office can do the job. We can't afford to lose Leonid. From what I've seen in David Hurst, he's meticulous in his planning and responds well to the unexpected, unlike that buffoon of a boss of yours.'

'As the roadside recovery fixed whatever Aatcha did to his cousin's car when he abandoned it, Mohammed Aatcha's on his way back to Ashton. David and Steve should be joining up with the rest of his team at the static obs point shortly. I'll let you know straight away once we've more intelligence on the two van drivers.'

'At least we've housed those two,' Debbie said. 'I've passed on the details we got on them onto my firm.'

'And I've assigned some of Ray Baskin's team to keep an eye on them for the moment. Go and enjoy your moment with Paul Edge.'

*   *   *

'Has there been anything of note while we were out and about John?' David asked John Davies as he entered the static observation point.

'No. It's been as quiet as a mouse this end. The only excitement we had was seeing Aatcha and Leonid arrive back at the flat. While Aatcha went out to pick him up, Khan's stayed in the flat all of the time. However we've news that the flat next-door to Aatcha and Khan's going to be empty and we could be in by the weekend. Perhaps we could use that chance to have the techies place some listening devices so we can hear everything they're up to?'

'It'd be great if we could. The problem is getting into the flat unseen. I take it we've got the details of the occupier of the flat?' David asked.

'We've got the details of the landlord. The current tenant's leaving on Wednesday. So it's going to be vacant as from Thursday morning. Andy Lewis has been making some enquires. We didn't want to bother you while you were on the mobile surveillance, so we told George and he gave us the green light to make some enquiries.'

David patted John on the back and said, 'Good work John. It's time we got more of an in and heard what our two are up to. I'll go back to the hut and sort out the relevant authorities we'll need to get into the flat next-door, as well as get in touch with the techies so they're ready to install the equipment on Thursday.'

'When you say "our two" I take we're not involved with the Chechen then?' John asked.

'No. Our role is to simply monitor Leonid. We've had a "hands off" warning as he remains Five's man,' David answered.

*   *   *

As he sat at his desk in the ISB office preparing the written authorities, David was reflecting on the day's developments. He could not stop wondering why Leonid would be coming up to Manchester as well as wondering what he might be planning to do in the area. As he clicked on the print icon to print off the authorization requests, a voice right behind said, 'Getting the paperwork ready?'

At the surprise that someone was right behind him, he bolted upright in his seat and turned round to see Debbie standing there. 'Jesus! You gave me a start there. I thought you were the rubber heel squad,' he said, taken aback at how stealthily Debbie crept up on him without him noticing.

'There's another piece of police jargon I'll have to familiarize myself with. Who are the rubber heel squad?' Debbie asked.

'They're the complaints and discipline department, or as they're known officially, Professional Standards. They investigate the poor bastards on the frontline as they try to do their job. These days the bosses just can't wait to catch you when you make a mistake.' Hurst's face turned into a scowl. He hated most police managers. 'I can't stand this new breed of boss in the police. To help them get their next promotion they'll stab anyone in the back. I don't trust any of the buggers. I take it you've got something for me then?'

'I have. Can we go to one of the briefing rooms and I'll go through the latest intelligence I've received in relation to Leonid.'

'Sure, we can use one of the side rooms,' David said getting out of his seat.

They both went into one of the side briefing rooms where Debbie produced a number of paper files along with a memory stick. She passed it over to David who loaded up the data so it could be shown on the screen in the room. As he was doing so, she said, 'My management instructed me to emphasize that Leonid remains an MI5 target. The ISB can look, but under no circumstances are you to touch him. They were very clear on this. I know it's frustrating, but I also have to carry out orders just like you. Any information you find on Leonid you have pass onto me and vice versa.

'MI5 have been analyzing possible targets of a Chechens attack. There are the obvious targets such as the Russian embassy in London, but from the intelligence we've received so far, it's unlikely.' Debbie clicked on the electronic folder MI5 had on Leonid. As the details appeared on the screen, she said, 'Leonid's an interesting character. Both of his parents are Muslim. His father was born in Uzbekistan and his mother was born in Chechnya, and of course our Russian FSB friends don't have any good words to say regarding Chechen Muslims. Although Leonid was born and raised in Moscow, he began to take more of an interest in the Islamic faith after he had visited his grandparents and extended family in Chechnya. His faith took a more fanatical angle after his mother, maternal grandparents and members of his family were killed in Grozny by the Russian military.'

'Does MI5 have any notion what he's up to in the UK?'

'We're only surmising here, but there are some wealthy Russian businessmen in the north of England who may be targets of a Chechen attack, but it's only a tenuous connection. We've nothing concrete to say that he's going to attack them. That said we're still checking Russians in the area. We're looking at their background to see if they have had any connection or dealings in Chechnya. Of course the fact they're Russian could be enough of a reason for Leonid to attack them. That would go against the MO of Chechen terrorists. Unlike the Al Qaeda, they tend to be more discriminatory in who they target.'

David sighed. 'What you are saying is we know fuck all about Leonid's plans? We need to get into the flat as soon as we can to find out what's going on. We're still in the dark as to the target Aatcha and Khan are planning to attack.'

'I know. It's so frustrating.' Trying to remain upbeat, Debbie said, 'MI5 got a snippet of intelligence regarding Aatcha and Khan. Apparently they're planning an attack in the Manchester area that's going to involve a large number of civilian casualties and it's going to be soon.'

'Well that's a fucking big help! Stop the press, MI5 have earth shattering news, Al Qaeda are targeting Manchester. I know you're not from round here, but you do know Manchester is a big city don't you?'

'Less of the sarcasm! I know it's not what you wanted to hear, but at least we know they're going to be staying in the area. It means we'll have to watch all three of them very closely. If you were Aatcha and Khan and you had to make an impact, where you target?'

David looked up to the ceiling and thought for a moment. 'Well ... it is late October so it could be they're planning to attack a shopping precinct in the area in the build up to Christmas. It could be the Arndale that's actually in the city center, or if I were them I'd target the Trafford Center. If they're planning something big, with it coming up to Christmas, it could be Manchester Airport. That or the Trafford Center would maximize casualties and hurt local businesses, as well as maximize the fear affect.'

'You could be right, they would make good target. It's important we watch what they do when they're out and about. I'm sure they'll want to check out wherever it is they're planning to attack. It's been a good day. Leonid arrived and is with your two targets and we've housed two more from Al Qaeda that didn't know about.'

'Yeah, those two lads who were driving the vans, that turned out alright in the end.'

'George told me that some of DS Baskin's team has been assigned to watch them.'

'That's right. Ray's got a good team. I'm confident they'll do a good job on them. I'm gasping for a ciggie. Would you mind if we carry on this conversation outside while I have a smoke?' David asked, reaching for his packet of cigarettes and lighter from his jacket pocket.

'No, not at all, I could do with some air. Is it only you and Steve that smokes on your team?' Debbie asked following David out of the main ISB office.

'Yes, we're the old dinosaurs. The rest of the team is quite young and a cross between fitness fanatics and health Nazis.

They try to give us two a bit of grief over the fact we still smoke, but we still give them a run for their money at the annual fitness test,' David said holding open the door to the ISB department for Debbie.

'Thanks.' As Debbie stepped outside, she said, 'Doesn't anyone complain about the smell of smoke in the cars you two use. I noticed you ignore the rule about no smoking in the cars.'

'We tend to use the same car. We've been in the Branch that long, Steve and I are like part of the furniture here, the others leave us alone and put up with it,' David said as he lit his cigarette. 'So, as we were saying, we've got another two from Oldham to add to our Al Qaeda collection. It'll be worth keeping an eye on them to see if they've got anything to do with the attack Aatcha and Khan are planning.'

'Like you said before, that's why it's important we get the covert equipment into the flat next door to Aatcha and Khan as soon as possible. I know you've been running off the authorizations, but George has only just told me what you were doing. He told me about the flat next to Aatcha and Khan's becoming empty on Wednesday night and I've already made arrangements for MI5 techies to install equipment. I said it was to get what we can on Leonid, but we may as well kill the two birds with one stone. I'm sorry if you think that you've just wasted your time, but I only got this intelligence about fifteen minutes ago. Get your authorities signed anyway, just in case there's a delay.'

'That means you are with us for the duration then?'

'It looks like it, certainly while Leonid stays with Aatcha and Khan. Have you any complaints?'

'None at all. You can't beat inter-agency co-operation. All I ask is that you keep me in the loop regarding anything that Five get. All I want is to get those two before they do any damage. I don't care who gets the glory, except if it's Edge of course. I forgot to say, thanks for sticking up for me earlier with Edge. George told me what happened in the incident room. George said that not only did you stick up for me but you put Edge firmly in his place. Thanks for that.'

'All I saw was the man losing it at a vital point. He seemed to be more upset at what repercussions might come his way if we lost Leonid than doing what he could to find him again. He went on a rant about you and I told him that neither you nor any of your team was to blame. Obviously there's a history between you two?'

'You could say that.'

'I'm not into point scoring and I'll do what it takes to get the job done. From what I saw of you today, you seem to have the same approach as me.'

'I do, but as you'll find, the more contact you have with the police working as our liaison officer the more you you'll come across incompetent pricks like Edge.'

'I'm finishing for the day. I'm only staying at a hotel round the corner and I noticed a nice pub close by. Do you fancy a night cap before going home? I know I could do with a drink.'

'Thanks, I'd like that,' David said, surprised at the offer, 'but maybe another time. Unfortunately I've had to rearrange the duty rosters and I'm going to take over from Steve as the early man in the morning. I've to get back to the static obs point and have a final check with the team. Thanks anyway. If things quiet down this week, maybe we could go for a drink then, I'd like that.'

*   *   *

David called at the small terrace house opposite the flat Aatcha and Khan his team were using in Ashton as the static obs point. He was about to knock on the back door, when it was opened by Steve Adams.

'Davey, I thought I heard your size elevens coming up the yard. Coffee?'

'Please Steve. It's only a quick visit before I go home. I'm only calling in to see what's been going on and give the new duty roster out. You've been on long enough today so I'll take over as the early man tomorrow morning. It'll give you an extra hour or so to see Lena and the baby. I was going to ring you at home and tell you. I'm surprised that you're still here.'

Steve poured the recently boiled water onto David's coffee. 'I was getting ready to go home when Nick was suddenly feeling a bit under the weather. He was chucking his guts up earlier so I sent him home. I thought I'd cover for him until the night shift come on. Don't worry, I'm not going to claim any overtime, these are more hours I'm giving to the Queen. Now get that down you.' Steve placed a mug of hot coffee on the kitchen table and said, 'It's nice and strong with three heaps of sugar, just as you like it.'

David sat down by the table and reached out for the mug Steve placed on the table, 'Thanks Steve.' He looked at the mug that Steve handed to him. Seeing it was a Manchester Untied mug, he said, 'Oh very funny.'

'You're the only Everton mug out here! Anyway gossip time, is our rather attractive Five officer still with us?'

'She is. We got talking earlier and she seems genuine. In fact, she's quite nice really. George told me that when we lost Aatcha and Leonid by Piccadilly station she firmly put Edge in his place and countermanded his order for us two to come in. He said she was pretty impressive, putting Edge in his place as well as putting in a good word for me. According to George she was singing my praises to Edge. Having a woman put him in his place wouldn't have gone down well with his ego. There again, George is prone to exaggerate at times. That's not all, after she finished work she asked me if I wanted to for a night cap with her.'

'What?' Steve started to nudge David's arm winking as he did so. 'Don't tell me there's romance in the air? I'm impressed. You didn't waste any time in that direction.'

'No, it's nothing like that. She was only asking me to go for a drink.'

'And we all know where that leads to don't we?'

'Pack it in. She's still trying to find out about us.'

'You should have gone and seen what you could have found out about her and relayed it back to the team. You know, find out what makes her tick, what her inner thoughts and fears are. You have to admit, being free and single, or should I say divorced you're best placed on the team to get the pillow talk,' Steve said grinning widely.

'I've told you leave it. It was nothing. Anyway you know what I think of women off duty. They're nothing but trouble.'

'The problem with you is that you've never met anyone like our Lena. I still love her to bits, four kids and twenty years of marriage later.'

'You're right there. I wish I could meet someone like her. She's a gem alright. You certainly put your hand in the lucky bag and came out with the top prize in Lena. While I finish my coffee, do us a favor and call the others down so we can have an update. Just leave one upstairs to monitor events.'

David and Steve were joined by John Davies, Tony King and Alex Bullard who had been working with Steve during the evening watch and Andy Lewis and Chris Gibbons who had arrived fifteen minutes earlier for the night shift. 'What's the latest?' David asked.

Alex spoke out first. 'Since Aatcha and Leonid returned this afternoon we've not had any sightings of Leonid or Khan. The blinds are still closed or semi-closed. It's still hard to see into the flat. We're still struggling to pick up any conversations.'

David interrupted her briefing, 'With luck we should be in the flat next-door to theirs by Thursday morning. So that'll be a big help to us. I'm sorry, go on Alex.'

'While we haven't seen Khan or Leonid, we saw Aatcha leave the flat earlier this evening to work in his cousin's kebab shop. He's still there now. Nick called in earlier to buy some food and Aatcha served him. Apart from that there's no other movement to report.'

David's face tightened with anger as he said 'You know I don't like it when you have a face-to-face contact with a target so soon into the operation. For fuck's sake we're not dealing with normal criminals or smackheads here. These are two experienced, highly dangerous Al Qaeda operatives. They'll kill without any mercy. No more initiative from any of you unless you've squared it off with me or George Byrne first. If you do I'll have you out of the Branch before you know it wearing a big hat directing traffic. Have I made myself clear on this? Especially you Steve, you're the senior man.'

John stepped into the briefing saying, 'It had nothing to do with Steve, Sarge. He wasn't here at the time it happened.'

David stared angrily at the officers standing before him as he raised his voice. 'Don't tell me Nick's fucking well got food poisoning! Jesus. For the last time, until you have further orders you're to stay here. Have I got that through to you? I can't be any clearer on this. After today's events, you all know Aatcha's very surveillance conscious. He won't switch off simply because he's working in his cousin's shop. This is not a game we're playing.'

Apart from Steve, they all reacted like naughty schoolchildren hanging their heads and dropping their arms in front of them with hands clasped as they realized that they had let David down. Although he was strict, his team had a high respect for their DS. They knew that underneath his harsh exterior, he supported them to the hilt if they were doing their best. After he finished speaking, in a quiet but humbling tone John said, 'Sorry Sarge, it won't happen again.'

'Too fucking right it won't!'

Steve interjected and in a more jocular tone said, 'Now that's been sorted, our leader's blood pressure is high enough with having to deal with the bosses and a very attractive MI5 liaison officers for you lot to add to it. Pray silence for our glorious leader as he has something else to tell us about our investigation that he found from our new MI5 liaison officer.' Steve bowed giving a wave of his hand.

'Thanks Steve, you piss taking bastard.' David passed on the small amount of intelligence he received from Debbie in relation to Leonid and potential targets for attack. After he finished updating them he said, 'That's all for today. I'm the early man tomorrow. If anything happens from now until I'm on duty in the morning, phone me straight away. I'll see you all tomorrow here at the obs spot.'

David got out of his chair and started to leave. 'Wait for me Davey boy', Steve said. Both the officers left the rear of the house and began to walk down the rear alley. 'Don't worry. I'll keep them in check. The incident with Nick was just an unfortunate one-off. It could've happened to any of us. In saying this I'm not trying to cop off with you like Debbie was, but do you fancy a drink before we go home?'

'No thanks Steve, I fancy an early night. I've a feeling we're going to be busy from tomorrow. Having this high-profile Chechen arriving on the scene is going to make things a bit more interesting. For starters apart from having even more Five officers joining us in the area, the FSB are likely to be crawling all over this one as well. I've a feeling we're going to face some problems we haven't come across before. The team will have to be completely switched on. It's going to be a sharp learning curve for some of the younger members of the team. We'll all have to play it straight down the line and that means no going off doing your own thing. That's why I was so mad with Nick just before.'

'I get the same feeling. But let's end the day on a positive, we've got our two linking up and housed with the Chechen and we never lost them.'

'You're right. It wasn't a bad day's work. It'll do you good to get back home to Lena, get some rest and help her with the baby.'

Five

Monday 23rd October
22.25 hours
Ashton-under-Lyne

ngrily pacing up and down the living room of the flat, Aatcha kept looking at Leonid. 'I'm telling you, British Intelligence are onto us. We've had no problems until today when you fucking turned up,' Aatcha said, pointing at Leonid. 'We've been here for weeks and there's been no sight of the bastards. Then from the moment this Chechen prick gets off the train outside Liverpool, MI5 and Special Branch have been crawling all over us. For eight weeks we've been planning our job and you being here is likely to fuck it up. They must know we're staying in the flat, as one of them came into Mohammed's shop tonight.' Aatcha walked up to Leonid putting his face right into his and said, 'I knew you were trouble the moment Sayfel said you would have to stay with us. I should kick your arse out of here right now.'

Khan moved in between them, placed his arm around Aatcha, and shepherded him away from Leonid to the furthest end of the room. 'For fuck's sake Ibrar just calm down. Let's think this through. OK, so they were following Leonid, but you said yourself that you were sure you'd lost them. Then when the vans blocked off the Mancunian Way, you said that you would have definitely lost anyone who might've been following you.

48

Then you see this man come into the shop tonight and you immediately think he's MI5 or Special Branch. You're working yourself up over something that may just be a coincidence. Think about it. You're senses are heightened at the moment after what happened at the train station. Don't blame Leonid.'

Leonid calmly added, 'Moosa's right, let's work though what happened. Go through what happened in the shop again in detail.' Aatcha walked across the room and stood by the window pulling the Venetian blinds slightly open to one side to see if he could see any MI5 or Special Branch officers. Leonid went over to Aatcha, 'Come away from the window and tell us what happened.'

Aatcha stopped shouting and glared at Leonid as he sat down in one of the dilapidated armchairs. 'I was working in my cousin's shop when this bloke I've not seen before comes in. After I took his order he kept staring at me. He was watching everything I was doing. Normally the customers look around the shop or out of the front window when they're waiting for their food. Not him, he just kept watching me. He never took his eyes off me. So I went into the rear kitchen where he couldn't see me and I got his kebab and put all sorts of shit in it. I thought if he's local then he'll be like a lot of the bastards that live around here and come in shouting racial insults. Mohammed's had trouble like that before. I'm telling you, with what I put in that bastard's kebab, he'll be really ill, but he never came back. That bastard was either MI5 or Special Branch. I know it. I just fucking well know it,' he said starting to work himself up into another rage.

Khan looked at both men and said, 'If that's the case we shouldn't take any chances. I suggest we move out of here to another safe-house and we move as soon as we can.'

'Because of you,' Aatcha said pointing at Leonid, 'we've got to fucking move from here. No one knew we were here. Not even my uncle knows why we're here. We were out of the way and now we've got to move. Do you know how risky that is?'

Before Leonid could respond, Khan said, 'Ibrar, shit happens. Rather than waste time having a go at each other, let's start organizing a move. It's not Leonid's fault.'

'I'll ring Sayfel and organize it,' Aatcha said reaching for his phone from the coffee table. 'I'll tell him what's happened and that we need to move. I'll see if he can find us a place in the city centre. There's more cover for us there,' Aatcha said.

*   *   *

Hurst was sitting at his desk sipping his first coffee of the morning. It was just before seven o'clock and he decided to contact the night watch at the static obs spot.

'Andy?' Hurst asked as the phone was answered.

'Morning David.'

'Anything of note happen last night?'

'No. All three were very quiet. All we picked up were some strange calls between Aatcha and that Sayfel character. That was around eleven o'clock last night.'

'What did they say?'

'Aatcha made the first call. He asked Sayfel if there was enough money in the kitty as he needed to go and see his mother. Sayfel seemed to know what he was on about as about fifteen minutes later he rang Aatcha back and told him to go to see a mutual friend who would have all the necessary arrangements in place for him. Even stranger than that, he added that Aatcha could, "see his mother first thing in the morning just after eight". We tried to make sense of it but we didn't have a clue what they were on about.'

'I've a good idea what it could be, especially after yesterday's events at the train station and then Nick's trip to the kebab shop last night. Why didn't you tell me about this as soon as you heard the calls?'

'It wasn't long after you left when we heard it.' Realizing he should have rung David, Andy added, 'I mean we didn't want to wake you if it was nothing. I was aware that you had a long day yesterday and ...'

David interrupted Andy. 'You should have rung me and let me decide if it's nothing. My guess is Aatcha's realized that Nick was one of us. Add that to what happened with Leonid at the train station and the hospital yesterday, I reckon they're planning to move out of the flat and they're going to move soon. Tell the others who were on last night to stay on until further notice. I'll get the others to come in straight away and meet up with you at the static obs spot. I'll brief George and get up to Ashton to join you with Steve as soon as I can.'

'What shall we do if they move before you get here?' Andy asked nervously.

'For fuck's sake, do what you're supposed to do, follow them. Listen I know you're all tired, so go and have a strong coffee and just stay awake. If we lose them we'll be in shit-street not just with the likes of Edge but with MI5 as well. So for fuck's sake don't let me down.'

'We won't.'

'Remember, if you hear anything or see the slightest movement from any one of those three, you let me know straight away. It doesn't matter how trivial it is. Even if they fart, I want to know about it. It doesn't matter if it leads to nothing. I'll see you later.' As soon as David finished the call he rang George. After informing him of what Andy and the rest of the night watch had heard, George agreed with David that they could be on the move. As a result he rang the other members of the team ordering them to join the night crew at the static obs spot straight away. There was only one officer, DC John Davies he could not get through to. Still holding the phone in his hand he started to dial Steve Adams' home number but stopped half way through, deciding he should wait for Steve to arrive at the ISB office so the two of them could go up to the obs point together. Replacing the handset, he opened up his emails to see one from Debbie:

> 'Dear David,
> I'm meeting with Thames House colleagues and my
> senior intelligence officer this morning. Whatever I learn
> from this morning's meeting I will pass onto you when I
> see you. That should be around 11 am. Do you want to
> meet at the ISB office?
> regards
> Debbie'

David paused for a moment. He was thinking whether he should inform her of the phone calls between Aatcha and Sayfel. His first reaction was to keep this information within the ISB office. The fact he continuously accused Debbie and MI5 of holding back intelligence from him and his team persuaded him that he should practice what he preached.

'Good morning David,' Debbie said answering his call. 'Seeing how it's just gone seven in the morning I've a feeling this is not a personal call and that's a shame as you could've taken me out for breakfast.'

Ignoring her flirting, David answered, 'You're right it's about work. I've just read your email. I thought I would try and catch you before you attend your meeting this morning. There have been a few developments last night that I think you and MI5 should be aware of.'

'Go on.'

'Firstly, one of my team fucked up last night when he decided to buy a kebab from shop where Aatcha works. It looks like Aatcha got suspicious of him and added some ingredients you don't normally get with a donner meat kebab. It looks like he got food poisoning and he had to go home.'

'Is he OK?'

'Even though he's continuously throwing up, he'll live, but

he's not OK with me. After that incident, the night crew at the static obs spot overheard phone calls between Aatcha and Sayfel last night and it looks like they're moving out of the flat this morning to another location.'

'What was said?'

'Aatcha made the first call around eleven last night, asking if there was "money in the kitty" as he "needed to see his mother". Sayfel returned the call about a quarter of an hour later saying that everything was in place and that he could see, "his mother in the morning" just after eight. As they're suspicious that we're keeping them under surveillance, I think this was a code for moving location.'

'Thanks for passing this on so early David. I appreciate this. I'll contact my boss straight away and I'll get back to you as to what they think it could mean. Thanks for showing faith in me by passing on the latest intelligence so soon. I'll reciprocate this.'

'I hope you do Debbie. I've got to go. If anything happens I'll let you know straight away. Don't switch your phone off at your meeting as I'll ring you as soon as anything happens.'

'I won't and thanks again David. I look forward to meeting up with you later.'

'Me too.'

As David put the phone down he heard George's voice behind him say, 'It's nice to see you liaising with our lovely MI5 officer. So what's the latest?'

'Do you want to go into your room boss and I'll brief you there?'

'Always been the suspicious one. Come on.'

As soon as David walked into George's spacious office he began to update him. 'It looks like we've been compromised in Ashton. Nick Evans had to go home sick last night because he was vomiting quite badly after eating a kebab he bought from the shop where Aatcha's working. As a result of the face-to-face Nick had with Aatcha, it looks like Aatcha got suspicious of Nick and put some unexpected ingredients into Nick's kebab sandwich. I gave the team a bollocking last night, reinforcing the point that there's to be no unauthorized face-to-face contacts with any of the targets. That's not all, after I left the night crew intercepted two calls between Aatcha and Sayfel late last night. Both calls were cryptic and suggest they're suspicious that we're listening to them. I've got the details of what was said here.' David placed a piece of paper file containing the transcript on George's desk. 'Reading between the lines, I suspect they're going to move to a new address and soon, possibly first thing this morning. To make sure we don't lose them I've ordered the night crew to stay on and I've called the rest of my team to come in early. They're going straight to the static obs spot.'

George rubbed his jaw as he took in what David was saying. 'Firstly, don't worry about Nick. He's a good lad. He's keen and his heart's in the right place. If we've been compromised, this is going to be a real pain in the arse in more ways than one. How certain are you that if they move this morning they're simply changing address?'

'You can never be one hundred per cent sure, but if you look at what was said between Aatcha and Sayfel,' David said pointing to the relevant passages on the transcript, 'they talk about moving to see people and that they need more money. Also this part says they can see "mother" at eight this morning. Going by what we've had in the past this looks too much like a move they're planning, not an attack. When we've intercepted similar communications in the past, it's been a move of location. If they do, going by the information we have, I think they're going to start moving address around eight this morning'

'I agree with you. Al Qaeda wouldn't have allowed a Chechen to stay with them if they were making an attack today. Edge will have to know of this. If you're right and they move at eight, I'll call Edge now as the management meeting is at ten this morning and it might be too late by then. He'll put the blame for Nick's antics firmly in your court so make sure you keep a tight rein on your team, especially with Five hovering over Edge's shoulder. One more mistake will be just the ammunition he needs.' Trying to be upbeat, George said, 'I'll make a couple of calls to MI5 to see what they make of what was said. I know Debbie's boss quite well. I've worked with him on a few operations in the old days when he was an intelligence officer. He's full of his own importance and a pompous git, but he's more than manageable from my point of view. He owes me a couple of favors anyway.'

'Thanks George. I've passed the transcript onto Debbie already and don't worry, I'll keep the team's heads down for a while.'

'What time are you going up to Ashton?'

'Shortly, I've a couple of emails to sort out and when Steve gets in we'll get up there straight away."

'Make sure you do. I'll contact Ray Baskin and the rest of his team to get them up to Ashton and help you out. It's a good job they finished that investigation last week or I'd be struggling to find bodies to help you out. Also I want you out of here when I tell Edge what's happened.'

*   *   *

After arriving at the static obs point, DC John Davies was preparing to take over from the night watch. 'Morning Andy, anything happen after we left?' he asked, looking out of the front bedroom window onto the terraced street.

'Enough for Hursty to ask us to stay on this morning.'

'You poor bastards. Why is making you stay on? Something heavy must have happened last night.'

'There were a couple of calls between Aatcha and a contact in London. I told Hursty about them and emailed him a transcript of the calls. He thinks because of Nick's kebab last night, we may have been compromised and that Aatcha and Khan along with the Chechen may try to move location today, so he wants all of us here this morning.'

'Do you think he's just trying to teach us a lesson after what happened last night? That was some bollocking he gave us. I haven't seen him in such a bad temper for a while.'

'I know he can be a bit of a nark at times, but it was serious what Nick did last night. One of us should have stopped him. He's the probey and he's trying hard to create a good impression.'

'We don't wear the stripes. It's not our role to make the decisions.'

Irritated by John's selfish attitude, Andy said, 'I know we don't wear the stripes, but we're all responsible for how the investigation goes, not just Hursty. I've known him long enough, when he asks us to stay on then there must be something in it and it's usually something serious.'

As they were talking, Alex Bullard arrived at the static obs point and walked into the front upstairs bedroom. She brushed past the two officers and looking out of the window said, 'Are you two griping about Hursty asking us all to come in early and you lot on nights having to stay on?'

'He didn't contact me?' John replied.

'He contacted everyone, I know you were due in anyway, but I thought he'd have given you a ring,' Alex said, surprised her DS had not been as thorough as he normally was.

John took his mobile phone out of his pocket and noticed he had a missed call, 'Oh shit, I had it switched off. He'll fucking kill me for this.'

'And that's why he gets pissed off with us at times,' Alex said. 'You know he can't stand anyone being sloppy, and that's what we were last night, sloppy.'

'It's just a mistake. I'll tell him I was at the hospital last night as my niece was badly hurt in an accident and I forgot to switch my phone back on. He'll be alright,' John said looking at his phone as he switched it on.

'Oh I'm sorry to hear that John. Is she OK?' Alex asked, feeling guilty at the way she had just spoken to him.

'You stupid mare, it's a lie. He won't know any different,' John replied.

'You're a stupid prick at times John,' Alex replied.

'You would say that, as you want to be a DS yourself. I've seen how he treats you just because you've passed the sergeants' exam. We all know why you'll soon get promoted don't we?'

At first Alex could not believe what she had heard. 'What do you mean by that?'

'You know exactly what I mean. You're a woman and you're black. You know as well as I do that the job likes to keep up its quota.' A stunned silence descended on the officers as Alex and Andy looked in total disbelief at John. John just shrugged his shoulders and said 'You know what I'm saying's right, you both do.'

Struggling to restrain her anger at John's comments, Alex said, 'So you don't think I can do the job then? I hate prejudiced pricks like you. Don't you know how hard it is for a woman to prove herself in the jacks, especially a black woman?'

The normally thick skinned John Davies was taken aback at her response. 'Hey, I wasn't saying that you can't do the job Alex. Fuck me you're as good as anyone on the team. What I was trying to say was how lucky you are that not only can you do the job, but you've got assets that you can play to their full advantage to help you get promoted.'

Alex was about to explode when Andy said, 'You're an insensitive prick at times. Drop it now before I drop you, because what you're saying I find offensive.'

'OK, OK, I'm sorry Alex. I didn't mean it in a racist or a sexist way. I'll drop it, but you have to admit that you do suck up to Hursty.'

'Not only are you an insensitive, racist and sexist pig, you're also very childish. Of course he treats me differently. When I'm the acting DS, he has to brief me. You know...' Alex stopped

mid-sentence. On seeing one of the targets leave the flat she said,
'Khan's coming out of the front door of the flat. Andy, ring Hursty
and tell him that we've got movement. John, you go out and
follow him. I'll organize the others to carry out foot surveillance.'
Alex looked John, 'Do you ever stop to think that Hursty could
just be right?'

*   *   *

As Steve Adams was walking over to his desk, David shot
up out of his chair and began to put on his jacket, 'Keep your
coat on Steve, there's movement in Ashton. Andy's just rung me
from the static obs point, Khan's left the flat. Go and get the car
started while I go and tell George.'
'You mean I can't even have a brew?'
'No you can't.'
Steve picked up the set of keys to the ISB car they usually use
muttering in a stage whisper, 'And there's me thinking he was a
vampire as we only see him come out at night.'
David ran into George's room without knocking. 'Sorry boss,
job on. Khan's on the move, by foot at the moment. I've got one
mobile up there and three that can follow him on foot. Steve
and I are heading up there now. Can you get Ray and his team
up there to back us up as soon as they can?'
'No problem, I'll tell Ray. You get up there now. It's a shame
Khan couldn't have waited until you got there but we'll just have
to work with what we've got. I'll go to the ops room right away
and get things in place. For fuck's sake don't lose them.'

*   *   *

'Khan's approaching the shops in Market Street. You should
all catch sight of him now. He's crossing the road and careful ...
it looks like he's going to double back,' John passed to the rest of

the team in Ashton as he followed Khan on foot.

'Tony do you still have eye-ball with Khan?' David asked as Steve was driving as fast as he could to join the rest of the team.

'Yes, yes.'

'He's walking back towards the direction of the flat', John whispered into his mobile phone walking towards the shops as Khan walked past him. Being the only two in the immediate vicinity, Khan looked over at John. 'I think he's clocked me,' John reported back as Khan crossed the road walking away from him.

'Pull off John. Tony do you still have eye-ball?' asked David.

'Yes, yes.'

'Tony, you take over following Khan and keep your distance.'

'Will do. Fuck me, he's double backed again. He's heading towards John.'

On hearing this, John walked into a newsagent's shop to deflect any suspicion Khan may have had towards him. He picked up a newspaper and was paying for it as Khan walked past the shop, looking over at John. Knowing that he could not look directly at Khan, John tried to look out of the corner of his eye to see if he had passed the shop.

'Khan gave you good eyes left there John. He's clearly surveillance conscious. He's walking to the taxi office on the corner of Ryton and Market Street. I know I might be stating the obvious here, but he might be getting a taxi, not just checking if he's being followed,' Tony reported back.

'John head back to your car. You're no use on foot now. He's clocked you good and proper,' David instructed him as they drove over the M60 on their approach to Ashton-under-Lyne.

'Will do.'

Tony was a short distance behind Khan, following him on the opposite side of the road. He was the only foot surveillance unit left. 'Why now? Why not wait until we had a full team on? If I fuck this up, never mind Hursty, Edge'll have me for toast,' he thought. 'Khan's gone into the taxi office,' Tony reported back,

'I'll walk past the office, there's a good static point ahead where I can keep an eye on the front door, but I won't have a view of the rear of the office.'

'No problem, I'm dropping Alex off at the back now. Chris has taken over at the static obs point,' Andy said updating the team.

'John, leave your car. Seeing how he's clocked you, get back to the static obs point and join Chris. He'll become suspicious if he sees you still hanging around the area.' instructed David.

Will do.'

'Park up around the corner from the bus stop Steve, it's a good vantage point to see who is best placed to follow Khan if he gets a taxi,' David said. 'Bronze, have you anything for me?' he radioed back to George.

'Three mobiles will be with you shortly to assist. MI5 have been informed. They agree this looks like a change of safe-house. I'll keep you posted if anything else comes from their end.'

'Thanks boss. Just to let you know Khan is in the office of Ace Taxis. Could you monitor their radio traffic?'

'I'm on it,' replied George. As he was organizing a member of the control staff to monitor the radio of Ace Taxis, he was aware of someone next to him. Without raising his head from the screens in front of him George said, 'Mr. Edge sir you've joined us at a very interesting time. It looks like the Al Qaeda targets in Ashton are on the move. Khan has left the flat and DS Hurst's team is watching him now. We have two mobiles at the scene and two on foot. They'll be joined by three further mobiles from DS Baskin's team very shortly and MI5 have been made aware of the developments sir.'

'Let's hope they stay on Khan and don't lose him. I don't want any repeat of what happened yesterday. With MI5 watching us, if we lose Khan it'll be another embarrassing situation especially when we're supposed to keep an eye on their man at the flat in Ashton. How did this come about?'

'They intercepted cryptic messages between Aatcha and

Sayfel, their man in London last night. The best we could make of it is that looks like they're moving house.'

'Whose opinion is this? Hurst's?'

'Well partly...'

'George I've told you before not to trust him. If we haven't seen Khan out and about much it only tells me one thing and that is this could be the start of their attack. I don't want us caught with our pants down. Tell all of the officers involved that this is a possible attack. At least Baskin will be there to pick up any mess Hurst leaves. I'll drop this file off at my office and then I'll come and join you,' Paul Edge instructed George.

'But sir, there's been no pattern of behavior to suggest that this is an attack. I ran the messages past MI5 this morning and they agree with mine and DS Hurst's assessment of the current situation that this is a move to another safe-house.'

Edge glared at George. 'DI Byrne, do I have to remind you who the senior officer is here? I think it's going to be an attack and you will make sure that we do everything possible to stop them, even if that includes lifting the bastards now.'

'I understand your concerns sir, but you've literally walked in on this without being fully briefed on the intelligence that came in overnight. Trust me it would be a grave mistake to arrest them now.'

'Don't you understand English DI Byrne? If you don't do as I say I'll get another DI to step in as bronze commander. I'm the fucking SIO here. You'll do as I say.' The volume of Edge's voice rose to just short of shouting, causing the staff in the incident room to stop momentarily and gaze at the exchange between the DCI and the DI.

'I know you're the SIO sir, but it's my job to make you aware of all the relevant facts. If we lift Aatcha and Khan now it will seriously affect MI5's investigation into Leonid and the Chechens. If you order the arrest they won't be too happy with you and you know with the contacts they have it could cause you a problem or two in the future.'

Edge reflected for a moment and said 'I still think this is an attack. If Aatcha moves out as well, lift the two of them. That will leave the Chechen in the flat and we can hand over the whole thing over to MI5. Unless I hear to the contrary from MI5 that's what you and the officers will do. That's an order.'

'What's that about MI5?' Debbie said entering the incident room.

'Ms Heron,' Edge said glaring at the MI5 officer, 'you have a nasty habit of creeping up on people.'

As Debbie walked up to George, she said, 'Mr. Edge, you have a nasty habit of coming to the wrong conclusion. As we heard Khan has made a move out of the flat, I got a call from my manager to come straight here to assist you. He's read the transcript of the calls made between Aatcha and Sayfel last night. Have you?'

'Not yet, but then that's what junior officers are for. They're here to save me time reading copious amounts of reports and put me in the picture as to what's going on.'

'Then I suggest that you listen to your junior officers as they put you in the picture, seeing how they've read the transcript. If you order the arrest of Khan and Aatcha now, I'll countermand it and request that another senior officer be placed as SIO. I take you are the SIO Mr. Edge?'

'I am.'

'I'm telling you that I agree with DS Hurst and DI Byrne's view that they're simply moving to another safe-house. I suggest that we leave George and David's team to it for a few minutes. I'd like to speak to you alone. Shall we go to your office?'

*   *   *

'A taxi to Piccadilly Gardens via an address in Droylsden please,' Khan asked the receptionist at the taxi office.

'Take a seat and I'll call one for you,' the receptionist said picking up the radio handset. 'Is there anyone free to call in at the office for a pick-up to Piccadilly Gardens, Manchester?' After receiving a reply, the receptionist turned to Khan and he said, 'A taxi will be with you in about five minutes.'

'Thank you,' Khan said as he took a seat in the customer waiting area.

*   *   *

'David, radio transmissions from the taxi company reveal our friend is going to Piccadilly Gardens. I'll arrange for support to be in the area when they arrive at the Gardens,' George radioed to David, who was waiting impatiently in the car with Steve.

'Roger. Thanks for that. Ray, are you position yet?' David radioed to Ray Baskin whose team was static at various strategic points in Ashton.

'What position do you want me in? The one I was in last night with this blonde I met?' Ray laughed over the radio.

Having just re-entered the incident room with Debbie, Edge grabbed the microphone from the desk George was sat at and said, 'Maintain radio discipline. Hurst, you're in charge so set an example. Although DI Byrne as bronze command is the SIO, I'm watching how you perform this morning. Although this may be a move to another safe-house by our targets, I want you to be prepared for this to be an attack. If anything goes wrong you'll have me to answer to. Have I made myself clear Hurst?' Edge replied over the radio.

'You've made your point crystal clear sir. I don't think it's an attack. After what happened yesterday and last night I think our targets are simply changing address.'

'You're not paid to think, you're paid to do as you're told. I'm the one paid to think,' Edge instructed David. As he did not reply, Edge asked David, 'Hurst did you receive my last? I'm in charge and you'll do as you're told.'

'I heard you sir but unless you are now the SIO and you've officially taken over bronze, I will follow standing orders and only take instructions from bronze command.'

'Detective sergeant! You'll do as your fucking well told'

'I think I should remind you that you should also maintain radio discipline ... sir.'

·   George took the microphone from Edge and said, 'I'm not being funny sir but I suggest we get on with the job at hand. If you wish to deal with DS Hurst, do so when he gets back to the office. Do I have to remind you that MI5 are monitoring our transmissions?'

'No you don't DI Byrne. No junior rank speaks to me like that.'

'Gentlemen,' Debbie said, 'I suggest that we stop arguing about what rank can say what to each other and we concentrate on Mr. Khan. Mr. Edge, I suggest if you want to speak to David Hurst you do so when this surveillance operation is over. What you want to say to him is beyond me.'

*   *   *

David turned to Steve, 'Fucking wanker. Why does he always blame me?'

'I think he's jealous of your great wit and repartee as well as that great command of the English language you have,' Steve said as David's phone rang. 'It'll be Edgy giving you another bollocking.'

David answered his mobile phone, 'You alright Ray?'

'Sorry about that, I didn't know Edgey was listening,' Ray Baskin said, 'Mind you that took balls to speak to Edge the way you did. I could hear the cheers from the others from where I was. I just want to let you know that we're in place should our friend take the "new road".'

'No problem, once Khan's on the move I'll let you know.

Regarding Edgey, I'm not taking that shit off him or anyone unless I've done something that warrants it.'

*　　　*　　　*

'Your taxi's here,' the receptionist informed Khan. As he walked out of the taxi office he raised his collar as the early morning drizzle had turned into heavy rain. Walking over to the waiting taxi, Khan looked around to see if there was anyone or a car that looked like they might be MI5 or the Branch. Not seeing anyone, he got into the taxi and instructed the driver to take him to Piccadilly Gardens in Manchester, '...Could you go via Dunkirk Street in Droylsden? I'm picking up a friend on the way. Please.' As the taxi moved off Khan looked behind him to see if any cars started to follow the taxi.

*　　　*　　　*

'Khan's got into a blue Ford Mondeo registration number Delta Alpha five Yankee Oscar Lima. It's on a Thameside taxi plate number three two seven. They're on Park Parade. We'll have to wait to see if they go down the "new road" or the "old road" when we get down onto Manchester Road. Let's go,' David relayed over the radio to the other surveillance units. 'Alex and Tony go back and join John and Chris at the static obs point and keep your eyes peeled for the other two. Bronze control, is there any chance of getting "sat nav" traces on the vehicle,' he radioed to George.

'We're on it and we are locked into the CCTV to follow your progress,' George replied.

It was twenty minutes past eight in the morning and the rain was getting heavier. That did not help the surveillance. The traffic going into Manchester was slow moving being virtually bumper-to-bumper. This had its advantages, as it was easier to remain a few cars back and reduce the chances of being noticed by Khan. It also had a disadvantage if the taxi suddenly turned off the main road it would make it more difficult for the mobile surveillance units to follow it. All of the units were aware of this. 'We've locked onto the taxi's "sat nav",' George informed David and the rest of the units over the radio.

'We can't lose him now,' Steve said to David as the taxi carrying Khan turned into Droylsden Road.

While concentrating on the job in hand, David was thinking of potential locations where Khan could turn off. Although the incident control room had locked onto the taxi's satellite navigation system, he knew it was best to keep the target in sight. The last thing he wanted was for Khan to get out of the taxi and back-track or get into another taxi. If Khan did and the surveillance officers did not see it, David knew they would end up following nothing more than a decoy vehicle.

*   *   *

As the taxi entered Droylsden Khan reminded the taxi driver to turn off into Market Street. 'I just want to see if my mate's in, if you go down Market Street, and turn into Dunkirk Street. It's the sixth turning on the right.' This was a pre-arranged meeting with another Al Qaeda operative, Zulfqar Ahmed who was to assist him and Aatcha in their operation. Sayfel had arranged for Khan to meet him in Dunkirk Street for the pick-up to give them the opportunity to see if they were being followed. With Dunkirk Street being a small residential road, it would be easier for both Khan and Ahmed to see if the taxi was being followed.

*   *   *

'We have a detour. Khan's taxi is turning right into Market Street. This could be a surveillance check. Caution everyone.

Stay on your toes,' David radioed to the other surveillance units. He turned to Steve, 'The bastard's checking us out.'

'Do you want me to follow?' Steve asked.

'No, pull in on the left just past the junction,' David replied as he spoke to the other surveillance units over the radio. 'Ray you're behind him, follow but be careful if he turns into one of the roads off Market Street. You'll easily be compromised. Carol you follow Ray, but hold back. If Khan turns off, position yourself to follow him in case he doubles-back down Market Street back towards Manchester, we'll park up off Manchester Road, all other units find a spot off Manchester Road and wait for our man to reappear.'

As Khan's taxi drove up Market Street, Ray radioed to the other units, 'It's turning right, right into, wait...Dunkirk Street, we're going past staying on Market Street towards Moorside.'

David got back onto the radio, 'Carol, see if you can get into a road on the right, like Baguley Street, he's likely to double-back if he wants to go to Piccadilly Gardens. Ray go on up to the end of Market Street to Moorside and turn round. You'll have to go behind Carol when our target returns.' David's calm demeanor hid the thrill of the chase that still got to even the most experienced of officers. As adrenaline pumped through his body, he could also feel the pressure he was under from Edge who had been on his case for the past few weeks now. Although he had little time for David, it was only a few weeks earlier that Edge directed his full attention in his direction after asking David to send some of his officers into a situation without a health and safety check being carried out. Constantly rebuffing all of the protestations and insults that Edge sent his way David refused to send them until the check had been carried out. The confrontation ended with David saying he would make an entry in his pocket notebook that Edge was ordering him to place his officers in a position of potential danger without any consideration for health and safety. He asked Edge to sign the entry adding that he would use this as evidence at any future hearing. As David stood there offering his notebook to him to sign, Edge's face went crimson with rage as he shouted, 'You think you're a fucking smart arse don't you Hurst? I'll sign fuck all. Have it your own way and get your fucking health and safety check done first.' Doing this in front of his team did not help the situation as they clearly enjoyed watching Edge being humiliated by their DS. Edge saw this.

Trying hard not to let his anxieties show to the rest of his team, David fought to remain calm and maintain a placid tone to his voice as he gave out instructions. He did not want the other officers to sense any anxiety in his voice as he thought that anxiety would spread throughout the rest of the officers on the surveillance. He wanted them to maintain total confidence in him. To lose a major target would not only be frustrating as far as the investigation was concerned but it also meant there would be recriminations back in the office.

He was relying on his intimate knowledge of the area. Although he was born and raised in Liverpool, he was familiar with this part of Droylsden. His grandparents lived here and his father was brought up in the area. Along with his brother and sister, David had spent nearly half of their childhood in this part of Manchester staying with his grandparents. This was not the time for him to wallow in nostalgia. He felt the pressure of the chase was starting to show no matter how hard he fought it not to. With butterflies in his stomach and beads of sweat on his brow, Steve took his packet of cigarettes out of his pocket, opened the top and offered one to David. After working with him for many years, Steve could read David's body language. He knew his DS was under pressure. 'Come on let's break the law and smoke in the workplace,' he said offering David a cigarette. Taking a cigarette, he lit it and as he inhaled the smoke a familiar voice came over the radio.

'Bronze Commander to unit one, David come in,' George said.
'Go ahead.'

'Our target stopped in Dunkirk Street and is starting to move off again, it looks like he's turned around and is coming back onto Market Street. I think our fox is rejoining the hunt.'

'I can see him. He's just passing us now,' Carol radioed in, 'indicating to turn right onto Manchester Road.'

'I also have eyeball, we're two cars behind you Carol,' Ray called in.

'OK everyone, let's stay on our toes, with luck that should be it now all the way to Piccadilly Gardens,' David radioed to all the units.

'There are two males in the back now. There's been a pick-up,' Carol reported.

'To all units we now have the target back in view, when we can we will use the cameras to get a decent view of the male that's joined Khan,' George radioed back as Debbie and Paul Edge re-joined the incident room staff. George updated them on the developments that occurred during his brief absence, '.... We're working on finding out who the male is that joined Khan.'

'This just confirms to me that I'm right and they're going to make their attack,' Edge replied sneeringly. 'If they do, we'll be caught with our pants well and truly down. Why hasn't Hurst and his team obtained more intelligence to find out what was going on? They've spent long enough on this investigation to get a proper handle on what's going on. If you ask me they've been idling their time and feeding you and me with bullshit. Six fucking weeks and all Hurst and his team have come up with is fuck all. It's just not good enough.'

'Be fair boss. You know it's still early stages into the investigation. You know as well as I do how difficult it is to penetrate a terrorist cell. We're still in the initial intelligence gathering stage. Added to that very little was actually passed onto us in the original intelligence report from MI5,' George said.

'George is right. There was little to go on and thanks to David and his team, we got them pinned down to the flat in Ashton and the connection with this Sayfel from the London based cell. In addition to that, there is all the intelligence on the callers to the flat during the six week static obs phase. Now we've come across another target and it looks like we'll find a new Al Qaeda safe-house. I'd say that is much more that fuck all Mr. Edge,' Debbie said watching the screens relaying the CCTV pictures.

Six

Tuesday 24th October
08.40 hours
Manchester City Centre

Khan and Ahmed got out of the taxi in Portland Street, by Piccadilly Gardens in Manchester city centre. Crossing over the Gardens, they dodged a couple of trams pulling up at the terminal as they made their way to the top of Market Street where they entered a coffee shop. After being served they carried their coffees to a quiet corner and sat down. 'It looks like our security service friends were not about on our way here,' Ahmed said to Khan.

'Yes, I think we avoided them. If Ibrar's right they will have been watching the house, but with luck we caught them out this morning although I thought at one point I was being followed but it was just a bloke going for his morning paper. Now do you know anything about this Chechen that joined us yesterday?'

'Sayfel contacted me last night. Apparently he's been fighting in Chechnya and in Ingushetia against the Russian military and he's one of the FSB's most wanted terrorists. That's one reason why we got him out of Chechnya. The other reason is because he's planning an attack against some Russians here in England, but Sayfel didn't give me any more details. He only said there are four other Chechen fighters in England who Leonid will be joining up with later. Apparently Sayfel made the arrangements

71

to get the Chechens into England and they've been using our safe houses in different parts of the country. So far they've been keeping their heads down as Sayfel's wary the FSB might be suspicious of their presence here. One problem with Leonid is that if we're being watched by the British security services once they see Leonid it won't take them long to work out who he is.'

'How did he get here?'

Ahmed took a sip of his coffee and said 'One of our cells in Turkey was informed that Leonid needed to escape from Chechnya into Turkey via Georgia. With Sayfel's help they made the arrangements to get him out. Some of our lads crossed over the Georgian border with Chechnya to a pre-arranged point that was just across the border and he was waiting for them.'

'That's risky. From what I've heard the place is crawling with FSB in Chechnya and Ingushetia. Also close by is South Ossetia that's full of Russian military and no doubt more FSB agents.'

'I agree. It took balls to do that pick-up in Chechnya. I wouldn't have been happy doing it, but Sayfel said it went like a dream. When our boys from Istanbul got to the Chechen border it was quiet. Even though they only had to go a short distance into Chechnya, they were lucky not come across any Russians.'

As Khan held his cup to his lips he paused for a moment, 'Was it luck or was it arranged?'

'What do you mean?'

'I find it hard to believe that the FSB or Russian military would leave a border crossing unguarded. It just seems too easy. Think about it. As we said, the whole area's crawling with Russian military and the FSB. If I was on that run it would nag me that it went off so easy.'

'Are you saying Leonid isn't who he claims to be?'

'I'm not saying that, but perhaps the FSB got wind of Leonid's escape and let it happen so they could follow him here hoping he'll lead them to any other Chechens operating in the UK. It's just a thought.'

Ahmed smiled and said, 'Ever since I've known you, you've always been the suspicious one, the one that asks the questions that makes me doubt even my own actions. I'm sure it's fine.'

'It might be that Sayfel's too close to this operation with the Chechens and too eager for a positive result that he's overlooked the obvious. You could be right but I still think that we need to be cautious regarding Leonid. He's only been with us for less than a day and Aatcha had to dodge the security services at the station he met Leonid. On top of that we've had to move from Ashton.'

'If it makes you happy while he's with us we'll keep an eye on him. Now come on let's drink up and go to the flat.' Ahmed handed an envelope over to Khan, 'This contains a key to the flat along with a slip of paper with the address of the flat on it. I suggest we split up, just in case anyone's watching us, especially after the events of last night in Ashton. I'll go down Mosley Street and you go off towards the Arndale then double back where I'll meet you at the flat.' The two got up, walked out of the coffee shop and went their separate ways.

*   *   *

'David we'll have four more officers to join the foot surveillance units shortly, keep us appraised as to developments at your end,' George informed David from the control room.

'Will do. We've parked up in Minshull Street and we're walking up now. We should be with the others in a couple of minutes,' David replied walking past Manchester University's Victorian red brick building towards Piccadilly Gardens.

'I hope Edge isn't right and that we don't have to stop an attack now. Town's full of commuters and early shoppers. If we shoot an innocent bystander they're be hell to pay,' Steve said quickening up the pace as they walked up to Piccadilly Gardens.

'If it turns to rat shit we can blame it on Edge. If he's so sure it's an attack he should countermand George and become silver command. He won't because he hasn't got the bottle to do it, just in case something goes wrong. He'll still be hiding in the shadows of the incident room letting George make all of the decisions. And you know what that means. If George makes one wrong decision then Edge can blame George with impunity for his own actions or should I say lack of action. I can see him now, sat in the control room looking over poor George's shoulder praying that nothing goes wrong but ready to blame me and George if it does.'

'The two targets are sitting down in the coffee shop by Piccadilly Gardens. Both are having a coffee and talking.' Ray Baskin's thick Manchester accent broadcast over the radio.

Due to the cold chill in the air David pulled up the collar of his coat at the back of his neck, grateful that it had stopped raining as they started to cross over Portland Street. 'At least they're still there. Going back to Edge, I'd be surprised if this is an attack that's going down. I think it's a meeting and I'm sticking with the fact they're moving address,' he said to Steve who lit another cigarette.

'I'm with you on that one. When you think of it we haven't seen them do a dry run or even do a reccie of their target. Cigarette?'

David took the cigarette, lit it and as he exhaled the spent smoke he looked around him, 'That said, if they do strike now it will be a coup as they'll have caught both MI5 and the Branch out.'

Both the officers heard Carol's voice come over the radio, 'All units, we have movement.'

David radioed through, 'Boss could you ask the units in Ashton to report the first sign of any movement they see in Ashton.'

'Will do. By the way I have all of you on camera,' George replied.

'He'd love to be here with us,' Steve said.

'Yeah, and that's one reason why I don't want to get promoted. I'd rather get cold and wet rather than be trapped in a dry and stuffy office with the brass looking on. Also I can smoke your cigarettes out here.'

'I have noticed you're smoking your favorite brand, Other People's,' Steve nudged David and pointed to his left, 'Here's a good spot to have eyeball with these two. I can see them both very clearly.' Both of the officers stopped in Piccadilly Gardens standing by one of the bus stops across the road from the coffee shop.

As the two officers focused their gaze on Ahmed and Khan leaving the coffee shop, Edge's voice came over the radio, 'I don't want any complacency from any of you. If any of you mess up you'll have me to answer to. All of you treat this as the real thing.'

David looked at Steve and said, 'Prick. What does he know about being on the street? He couldn't detect his way out of a paper bag.' Ahmed and Khan stepped out of the coffee shop and began to walk off in separate directions. 'Ray and Carol, you follow the unknown target, we'll follow Khan,' David ordered over the radio.

'From control, we have visuals on both targets. We're requesting uniform to call into the coffee shop and get the shop's own CCTV recording that hopefully will have picked up our two targets. We're continuing to run traces on the unknown and our liaison officer is here assisting. Once we have a result we'll let you know,' George informed the rest of the surveillance units.

'That confirms it for me Steve. Unless he has a slim-line explosive body pack I don't think Khan's going for martyrdom today,' David said to Steve forcing their way through the many shoppers entering and leaving the stores in Market Street as they followed Khan.

'Looks that way, I'll break off and cross over to keep eyeball with you and our friend. Do you want to bum some more ciggies off me before we part? There's a tobacconist off Corporation Street if you fancy buying some...'

David smiled and said, 'Cheeky fucker.'

The officers followed Khan up to the junction with

Corporation Street when he suddenly doubled back along Market Street. As Khan was retracing his own steps he kept looking around him. Both David and Steve knew he was carrying out counter-surveillance tactics.

After leaving the music shop, Khan walked up Market Street and turned left into the Arndale shopping centre where the final touches to the Christmas decorations were being put up by the centre's staff. The Arndale was becoming increasingly busy as the early Christmas shoppers arrived. Convinced this was not an attack David still could not take anything for granted. He kept checking he had quick access to his pistol. The two officers followed Khan through the Arndale Centre as he walked in and out of shops. David was bemused as how Khan appeared to be overly surveillance conscious. 'It's as though he's being too careful,' he thought, 'if he keeps this up the security guards will become suspicious of him and think he's a shoplifter. It's as though he's trying to bring attention to himself.' To David, Khan was behaving like more like a drug addict that had not had a fix for a while out on a shoplifting spree than an Al Qaeda operative. After ten minutes of walking in and out of shops, Khan finally walked out of the Arndale Centre by the Corporation Street exit. As did so, he had to push his way past a number of shoppers entering the Centre including Steve. As the two were opposite each other, Steve could not avoid him and bumped into Khan as he walked out of the doors. Steve kept his eyes down and walked on, but Khan looked directly at Steve as though he was waiting for an apology from him.

Realizing that Khan got a good look at him, Steve walked away from the entrance along Corporation Street. Cursing his luck he radioed to David, 'Sorry mate, you're on your own. He got a good look at me as we bumped into each other. It was bad judgment on my part there.'

'Don't worry mate. I was watching you, there's no way you could have avoided him. Just stay back and tail me while I stay with him.'

'Our unknown target has gone into a flat in Granby Row at the corner with Ogden Street, keeping eyeball with the premises,' Ray's voice boomed out over the radio.

'Rest of the units, this could be Khan's destination. Is there anyone in the vicinity to help me out?' David asked. There was no reply.

'I'll cut back up New Market Street onto Mosley Street and try and see if I can pick you up from there,' Steve replied breathlessly, running back to try and see Khan and David. As Steve made his way up to Mosley Street, David followed Khan down Market Street back towards Piccadilly Gardens. Khan was about to cross Portland Street when Steve shouted on the radio, 'I've got eyeball with you now.'

Khan made his way to the block of flats in Granby Row. It was an old Victorian warehouse renovated into luxury apartments. As Khan entered the building David met up with Ray and Steve on the opposite side of the road to the flats, ensuring they could not be seen. 'You two OK?' Ray asked. 'It looks like you were right and the boss was wrong. I don't envy you David when we get back to the hut and bump into Edge. You know how much he hates smart arsed junior ranks showing him up. I'll make some enquiries and set up a static obs point while you go back to the hut and get the ball rolling on where we go from here, especially as George has new intelligence.'

'Cheers Ray,' David said, 'getting a static obs point boxed off that would be a big help. Never mind Edge wanting a word with me, I want a fucking word or two with him.'

*   *   *

Khan entered the flat. Waiting for him in the living room Ahmed had been discreetly looking out of the window and said, 'It looks like the security services don't know we're here. I kept checking to see if I was being followed but it looked like I wasn't. While I was waiting for you I was watching out of the window and it looks like they don't know we're here.'

'I did the usual, kept back tracking, looking in the shop windows and I didn't see anyone following me.'

'While I was waiting for you I made arrangements for Ibrar and Leonid to get the train from Ashton into Manchester Victoria. We'll meet them there and take the long way round back to the flat. We've got our own bugging devices in the flat so we can monitor Leonid or anyone else who may want to snoop around while we're out. That'll confirm your suspicions about Leonid being an undercover FSB agent. If you want, I'll go and meet them and bring them here while you wait in the flat. I'll pick up some food and any stuff that we need.'

'Thanks Zulfqar. I've got to be honest I won't settle until that Chechen's out of here.'

*   *   *

It was gone ten in the morning as David and Steve parked the car in the rear yard of the Branch Office. 'One advantage of them moving into town is that it's only a short walk away from the hut to Khan's new drum. Al Qaeda must have a few bob. That flat won't have come cheap, especially if they're renting it,' Steve said getting out of the car. Walking up to the entrance to the ISB offices he saw George smoking his pipe. 'Hello, it looks like Uncle George is waiting for us, no doubt to brief us before we report to Edge.'

As David and Steve walked up to George he took his pipe out of his mouth and gently blew the pipe smoke up into the air. 'I'm making the most of the lull in proceedings to enjoy the damp morning air to have a few puffs of my favorite pipe tobacco.'

'Very Sherlock Holmes boss,' Steve said.

'After what happened earlier between me and Edge, are

you the warning reception boss?' David asked thinking of the anticipated fireworks that would ignite the moment he and DCI Edge were in the same room.

'No not quite, but I can say that he's really pissed off with you Davey. He was convinced it was going to be an attack this morning. I tried to reassure him that it wasn't but he'd have none of it. Fortunately Debbie Heron turned up this morning at the incident room because of what was happening. She's staying in a hotel only a short distance from here and her boss, Craig MacDonald told her to join us rather than go back to Leeds. It was just as well, as she prevented there being a row between me and Edge. Mind you, she soon put him in his place again. I got to hand it to her, she's no mug. She's clearly sussed what's going on,' George said. 'Steve, it was a nice touch the way you placed the tag on Khan when you bumped into him in the Arndale.'

'What tag?' Steve replied looking puzzled.

George took his pipe out of his mouth, slightly bemused by Steve's question. 'I thought you put a tag on him when the two of you bumped into each other in the Arndale. It was hard to tell from the CCTV cameras how you did it, as there were quite a few people entering and leaving the Arndale at the time. I clearly saw Khan coming out of the Arndale when you bumped into him. When he had to push past a number of people I thought you used that moment to put a tag on him. Since then we've been able to listen to what Khan's been saying to Ahmed since they've been in the flat in Granby Row. You're pulling my leg again aren't you?'

'No boss, it wasn't me. There was only us two following Khan and I had no gear with me.'

David shook his head and said 'Five must have had some of their officers in the field with us and conveniently forgotten to tell us again. I said that Debbie was holding back on us. I wouldn't mind but I phoned her this morning and shared our latest intelligence with her to pass on to the rest of MI5. I'm telling you she knows more that she's letting on.'

Genuinely surprised George said, 'That's taken me by surprise too. Debbie arrived at the incident room not long after you left for Ashton. She even had a quick chat in private with Paul Edge. I thought it was to put him in his place out of earshot of me and the other staff. She was sat next to me and Edge for most of this morning's mobile surveillance and she never said a word. Even when it looked like you put a tag on Khan, she agreed that it was a stroke of genius. That was her chance to say if it was one of her own but she didn't. MI5 were silent throughout our activities this morning except for the fact that they acknowledged that they were picking up and monitoring our transmissions from you lot on the ground. They never said a word about putting officers in the field where you were.'

'I'd put money on it they've definitely got people out there on the ground with us and not told us. Its most probably related to this Chechen and they've most probably got something else up their sleeves that they're not telling us about in case we spoil anything they've got planned. I'll rip into that Debbie when I see her, we are on the same side aren't we boss?' David asked an exasperated George.

George knew David's mistrust of MI5 came from a PIRA investigation they were involved in 1996 where MI5's actions nearly resulted in Steve's death. 'I don't want you to "rip into" Debbie as she's most probably in the dark on this. I suspect her senior intelligence officer, Craig MacDonald was behind this. It has his MO written all over it. Let's play this carefully and wait until we have the evidence that MI5 held back on us before we go on in all guns blazing. Edge is entertaining her at the moment and after what happened in the incident room yesterday and this morning, he's desperately trying to impress her. He'll brown nose anyone he thinks will further his career.'

*   *   *

After David concluded his briefing to the management team on the morning's events, they retired to consider what action to take next on the investigation. Before he left George said to him, 'Wait in the main office and I'll let you know where we go from here. By the way Edge decided that it should be me that bollocks you for your display of disrespect to senior officers this morning. Between us I think that what Debbie said to him has sunk in and he's realized that he was wrong and is skulking with his tail between his legs. So you've got away with this one, but from now on, and I'm serious here, you'll leave him to me. Just bite your lip when dealing with him.'

'OK George.' As the management left the briefing room David turned to Debbie, 'I'd like to run a couple of things past you over what happened this morning.'

'Of course,' she replied walking with David through the main office, 'That was a good show this morning. Not only have we found another Al Qaeda safe house we've flushed out another Al Qaeda operative. I did a check on Ahmed and he's been a very busy boy with Al Qaeda. As we'd lost tabs on him over the past year, my department's very complimentary about your team's actions this morning.'

'It's all coming together, bit by bit,' David said. 'I thought you weren't coming over until eleven this morning?'

'I was, but once Khan emerged from the flat and it was passed onto our office, my boss rang me and told me to join George in the incident room. It was just as well. Edge was also there and close to making a major cock-up. He wanted Khan and Aatcha arrested. He was frightened that we had got it wrong and it was the beginnings of an attack. A move on those two now would have not only have resulted in you and your team struggling to pin anything on Khan and Aatcha, but we could have lost Leonid. I asked to go to his office for a quiet word in his ear. I put him straight that it was likely to be a move to another safe-house. I told him that we had a few officers arriving on the scene this morning in Manchester and how this is a joint operation. I told him that he can't go making decisions without consultation with MI5.'

'So you did have MI5 officers on the ground in the city center this morning?'

'Yes,' Debbie said sensing David's anger. 'I told Edge that four of our officers were arriving in Manchester and would be there to assist you when you arrived in the city centre. I take by the face you're pulling and the slight reddening of your face that he didn't tell you?'

'Did he fuck,' David said. 'To be honest I was ready to have a go at you as I thought you were holding back on us.'

'I told you yesterday that I will let you know of any developments from our end, including when we bring in extra officers. He should have passed that onto you. I wasn't with him and George in the incident room. Once you met up with Ahmed I used your PC and started to make some checks on him.'

Shaking his head, David said, 'I'm sorry I doubted you. What does he think he's achieving by holding back on us?'

'I don't know but no harm's done. Obviously it was one of ours that put a tag on Khan. To be honest, I thought it was Steve.'

'Didn't you recognize your own staff?'

'No, I don't know everyone that works for MI5! Do you know everyone that works for GMP?'

'Fair point.'

'Let's not fall out over this. I have some intelligence to share with you so you can tell the rest of your team,' Debbie said. She looked at Steve who was sat with his feet up on his desk talking to one of the admin staff, and said, 'Steve, will you join David an me in one of the briefing rooms?'

'Do you really need a chaperone?' he replied getting out of his chair to join them.

David ignored Steve's comment as the three of them went into a briefing room that was free. 'I did my best not to overhear the row you two were having, as it's not my place. Have you two kissed and made up now after what happened this morning?'

David looked away and sighed at Steve's ill timed attempt at humor while Debbie laughed, 'If we do it won't in view of others. After all we can't have David Hurst to be seen fraternizing with the enemy? I've some information to help progress this investigation. Regarding Leonid, there are a number of Russian businessmen, the multi-billionaire type who could be his potential targets. One of them recently purchased business interests in this area, including the Aston Towers estate in Lancashire. His name is Viktor Grenko. His brother is General Grenko. He was in charge of the Chechen purge when Leonid's family was killed. Viktor Grenko has to be a top target for Leonid and the revenge angle can't be ignored. However we can't get near Grenko as he has his own private security protecting him. We have intelligence, albeit sketchy at the moment that suggests some FSB officers are working under the pretext of being Grenko's security guards. That hasn't gone down too well with MI5, MI6 or the UK Government especially as Anglo-Russian relations are not very cordial at the moment. As I said it's sketchy and it has not been confirmed. I can tell you that another MI5 team is trying to check this out.

'We also have another potential problem. From what we picked up from Ahmed's conversation with Khan in the flat it appears Khan's suspicious of Leonid. He thinks Al Qaeda got a virtual free hand in getting Leonid across the border adding that it's unlikely the Russians would leave a border crossing unguarded. I have to be honest, I agree with Khan. In that part of the world not only has the Russian military been active in both Chechnya and Georgia but there's currently high tension in the neighboring Russian state of Ingushetia. Over the past few years the FSB have taken a hard line on terrorist groups in the area as some two hundred Russian and Ingush police and soldiers have been killed by Islamist groups with links to international jihadist movements. There have been many suicide bomb attacks in the area, even one left the Ingushetian president critically injured. If Khan's suspicions are right and Leonid is an FSB agent working undercover this puts him in danger with Ahmed, Aatcha and Khan. MI5 have no idea whether or not he is who he claims to be and intelligence on his movements in the last two months is minimal to say the least.'

David said, 'So summarizing, and to make sure I understand this correctly, we have a Chechen terrorist who could be an FSB agent infiltrating an Al Qaeda cell, but who could be kosher and is planning an attack on Viktor Grenko?'

Debbie replied, 'That's right. My boss is trying to see if MI6 have any more intelligence on him and to see if they've had word that the FSB might have an undercover agent pretending to be Leonid Kashinov. My boss has also got one of the directors at Thames House to contact the FSB to see if Leonid is an undercover agent. As usual the Russians are denying it.'

'We'll have to let George know about this Debbie. We can trust him, and he can hold off the police brass while we try and ascertain if any of the intelligence you have has any truth behind it. For Christ's sake don't mention this to Edge and tell your colleagues, including your boss to contact with George only, not Edge. Do you agree Steve?' David asked.

'Too right, George is the only boss from our side on this investigation that we can trust.'

'I agree with both of you, George is the only DI and above I've met in this office that I can trust. I've more intelligence to feed into the systems. Can I use your team's analyst?' Debbie asked.

'Of course you can,' David said getting out of his seat. 'I'll introduce you to Lucy. She looks a bit unconventional but she's a real team player.'

'Good. I'll input this intelligence, do some analysis and then when I 'm done, we can meet up on the ground.'

'Steve and I will be going out once I've drawn up a plan for ensuring we follow Leonid and Aatcha to the Granby flat. You can meet us there.'

*   *   *

As they entered the analyst's office David introduced Debbie to Lucy. On seeing her Debbie realized why David saw her as unconventional. She struggled to contain her astonishment at Lucy's appearance as she shook hands with her. Debbie was trying her utmost not to stare at the varying shades of purple and yellow hair dye on her short spiky hair. Once Debbie got past Lucy's unconventional coiffure she noticed Lucy's spectacles with thin blue and red colored neon wires running through the thick transparent frames and Lucy's body piercing adornments. She quickly glanced at Lucy's bright colored clothes, none of which matched. David saw that Debbie was taken aback by Lucy's appearance and he whispered in her ear, 'Don't worry everyone who sees her for the first time pulls a face like you've just done.' Turning to Lucy he said, 'Lucy my love, I'd like to introduce you to Debbie Heron from MI5. She's our liaison officer and she's been helping me and the team on the Aatcha job. There are a few things she needs to check out and I couldn't think of anyone better than you to help her. Could you do the business for me?'

'Of course no problem, I'll do anything for you.' Looking at Debbie she said, 'Those Scouse vowels of his just so turn me on, don't they you?' Debbie was stuck for words for a moment as Lucy said, 'The things I could do to our Hursty here, if only he was ten years younger, he's all man if you see what I mean.'

'I'll leave you two lovely ladies to it. I've got to get back and check out the rest of the team,' David said smiling, as for the first time he saw a crack in Debbie's calm and collected exterior.

Lucy raised her right hand, put it in the shape of a claw and drew it down slowly saying, 'See you later tiger, and if you're lonesome later, give me a call, you only have to ring me and I'm there.'

David laughed as this was the reception he was normally met

with when he entered Lucy's office. They had known each other for many years and she liked to tease him. When she first met him, she saw he was shy in the company of women who were not police officers. This banter had gone on for so long it had lost its impact on David. On this occasion he enjoyed watching Debbie's reaction.

Lucy looked again at Debbie and said, 'As I said if only he was ten years younger. What do you think Debbie?'

Still taken aback by Lucy's candid behavior she stuttered, 'Err, erm I like him just the way he is.'

'You fancy him then?'

'Erm, no, well yes he's nice but what I mean is...'

Lucy laughed out loud like a horse neighing. 'Don't worry. I've been teasing him for years. I'm only pulling your leg. Saying that, I think he would be a bit of alright if he wasn't married.'

Debbie looked surprised, 'I thought he was divorced?'

'Oh he is,' Lucy replied, "he's divorced from his wife, but married to his job. God help any girl that gets between him and the job. Now what info do you want Debbie?"

'I'll leave you two to do what you have to,' David said. As he left the office he blew Lucy a kiss.

'I'll see you later lover,' Lucy said as Debbie stood there with her eyes wide open not believing what she had witnessed.

*   *   *

'There you go Debbie, just check the information before I send it off. I'd hate to misinterpret your intelligence, but you know what it's like,' Lucy said to Debbie looking at the screen of her PC as she spoke.

'Of course, could you turn your screen round a bit so I can see?'

At that moment Debbie's phone started ringing and Lucy said, 'Is that your mobile's ringtone? Very retro, I do like the sounds of the seventies. That's The Clash isn't it?'

'Yes it is. I'm sorry but can you excuse me for a minute?' Debbie said seeing it was her MI5 manager. She got up from her chair walked out of the analyst's office to a discreet part of the corridor. 'Hello.'

'Debbie, Craig, can you talk?'

'Yes.'

'We need to meet urgently. I'm in town. Meet me in the Weavers' Arms pub in Portland Street. Don't tell the plod that you're meeting me. Keep it hush-hush. Can you meet me in fifteen?' asked Craig McDonald.

'I can make it in ten.'

Seven

Tuesday 24th October
12.15 hours
Weavers' Arms Public House
Manchester City Centre

The distinctive Craig Macdonald sat at a table in the corner reading a newspaper when Debbie walked into the Weavers' Arms pub. She could recognize him from just the briefest of glances. It was not just his well groomed red hair that made him instantly distinguishable, she considered him to be one of the most immaculately dressed men she had ever met. Being one to wear quality clothing when she could afford it, Debbie could see Craig's suits were made from good quality cloth. On one occasion she made comment regarding the quality of his suit and asked if it was bespoke. 'Of course,' he replied, 'it's the sign of a true gentleman.' She also admired his collection of fine cuff links. Debbie had never seen him wearing a shirt buttoned at the cuff. In Debbie's eyes, Craig looked the typical English gentleman. She would never tell him that with Craig being a fiercely proud Scot. If anyone referred to him as English, his admonishment was swift but polite. When he pointed out he came from Edinburgh he would add, 'and it's the true British capital.' On seeing Debbie he waved his hand beckoning her to join him. As Debbie approached the table he was sat at, he said, 'I've ordered you coffee and a sandwich. You don't have to eat it. I just want to make it look like we're a couple meeting for lunch.

Come and sit down.'

'Thanks Craig. It doesn't matter what you've ordered, I'll eat it. I've had no breakfast so I starving,' Debbie said as she sat down opposite Craig. 'Something urgent must have happened to make you come over to Manchester.'

'It's a bit of news that I want keeping between MI5 staff. We're going to be joined by one of our agents from the Southeast. He's been working undercover in an Al Qaeda cell in Brent for a number of years now. He works under the name of Yousef Sayfel, but is known by everyone simply as Sayfel. He's British born from Islamic Pakistani parents and he's passed good quality information onto us over the last few years. He'll be arriving in Manchester on Thursday to meet our target from Chechnya, as well as meeting up with the three Al Qaeda targets the ISB are watching. The plod are not to know Sayfel works for us. I don't want them to treat him any differently from the other three targets.'

'Is this the Sayfel the ISB are talking about in the Aatcha and Khan investigation?' Debbie asked.

'The very one.'

'OK, not a problem, but it will be difficult to keep it from the ISB.'

'I don't care how difficult it is, you're lips have to be sealed about Sayfel being one of us when you're with the plod.'

'I assume Sayfel knows our position?'

'He does. He's only coming up for the day and once he's left, he's going to send onto me what he's learnt about the Al Qaeda targets as well as the Chechen. Talking of the Chechen, there's a bit of a flap on in at the Russian Embassy. GCHQ picked up Russian communications and it appears we've got a couple of FSB agents roaming around the country looking for our friend Leonid. We've managed to confirm there's at least one FSB agent operating here in Manchester. I emailed all of the intelligence regarding this to you before I left Leeds. We think the FSB agent in Manchester is Petrov. He's a very experienced agent. He joined the KGB in the last couple of years of its existence before it became the FSB. We believe he's going around posing as a Russian businessman under the name of Viktor Grenko. Both we and Six have been tracing the movements of this alleged business man. Enquiries with SOCA have shown there is a real Viktor Grenko, a businessman working in the UK. It looks like the FSB have arranged for the real Viktor Grenko to have an extended holiday in Russia while Petrov uses his identity as he goes around the country trying to find these Chechens. Petrov is a very experienced agent and a ruthless man, so we need to keep an eye out for him.

'It was interesting to hear that Khan's suspicious of Leonid. I heard the recordings this morning and I see he thinks Leonid is an undercover FSB agent. It's interesting because from the communications CGHQ have intercepted, there seems to be a bit of panic going on within the FSB and it started after Aatcha met Leonid at the train station in Liverpool. From what we gather, the FSB had followed Leonid through France into the UK. I got in touch with Six to see if they had any idea what was going on. As far as they know Leonid is a Chechen. They have nothing to the contrary to suggest that he is a undercover FSB agent. Together, we've been making a few enquiries and with the help of the Home Secretary we've approached the Russians.'

'Did they say anything?'

'You know what it's like. They denied any activity, just as we would do in their position, but the Home Secretary's like a dog with a bone. He's not going to let this lie. I told him about the suspicions Khan and Ahmed have regarding Leonid's real identity from the conversation we picked up between them earlier. Khan had a point in that it does seem too good to be true that Al Qaeda would have such an easy drive from Georgia into Chechnya, pick up one of Russia's most wanted and drive back.'

'Do you think Leonid Kashinov is undercover FSB agent?' Debbie asked as the server approached their table with the food Craig had ordered.

Craig broke off his briefing and rubbed his hands. 'Ah good, here's our food.'

After the server placed the two plates of sandwiches on the table, Debbie picked up a sandwich and before she bit into it said, 'If the Leonid we're watching is an FSB agent that explains a lot.'

'In what way?'

'When Aatcha got back on the train at Huyton station with Leonid, I looked around to see if any of the ISB team I'm working with were on the platform, but they weren't. I could tell that something or someone had spooked him. I think it was someone. I wouldn't be surprised if FSB agents got off the train to follow Leonid and Aatcha spotted them.'

'That ties in with the apparent panic Aatcha was in.'

'Be straight with me, were any of our lot at the station when Aatcha met Leonid?'

'No, you were the only MI5 officer there,' Craig said picking up his coffee to take a drink. 'I think it's time we put more pressure on the FSB. We're going to need an in to get anywhere with them. So far they're denying having any agents in the area, but that could explain why Petrov's here. He could be trying to locate Leonid. It's going to be difficult for them to get in touch with him if he's one of theirs undercover. The move this morning won't have helped the FSB.'

'Funnily enough, when I was giving the initial briefing yesterday morning, the DS who runs the team I'm working alongside suspected the FSB would be interested in this job. He said that he could see the FSB "sniffing around" and asked if we had been speaking to the FSB about Leonid.'

'I take your talking about David Hurst,' Craig said with a knowing smile.

'Do you know him?'

'I've never met him but I've heard a lot about him. How do you find him?'

'He's a good officer. He's switched on and quite incisive. He certainly runs rings around that acting superintendent they've got, Paul Edge.'

'I heard their little spat over the radio this morning. Apart from being switched on, is there anything else you found about Hurst?'

'He doesn't trust MI5 and he was a bit stand-offish when I first met him. I think he's an officer that sees what he does as a vocation. It's not just a job to him. He also seems a bit surly. He has little time for some of the senior ranking officers and he lets them know except the DI, George Byrne.'

'I know George well. I've worked on a few operations with him in the past. He's been like a father figure to Hurst. George was his DS when he was a young DC in the Branch in the late 1980's, and then was his DI in the former Regional Crime Squad and again when Hurst returned to the ISB. Watch Hurst. You're right about him being switched on, he's bright. I'd keep an eye on him if I were you.'

'If you've not met him, how do you know all about him?'

'His brother, Peter Hurst is a barrister in the same chambers as my brother. Alistair has met David Hurst a few times and said he's got one chip on his shoulder. Apparently Peter's alright, but David Hurst is still fighting the class war. They come from a poor working class family in Liverpool. Peter's done well for someone with his background but Alistair says he's got as high as he'll get for someone of his pedigree, whereas Hurst is bit of a militant and has no respect for authority.'

'That's not the conclusion I've come to,' Debbie said looking surprised at Craig's assessment of the DS. 'As far as I can tell in the short time I've worked with him, he just doesn't suffer fools gladly.'

'So you like him then,' Craig said with a knowing grin.

'And what do you mean by that?'

'Don't tell me you've started fancying a bit of rough?'

'Craig, you're incorrigible. Yes, I like him. He's one of the few I can trust in that office, him, George and the senior DC on the team, Steve Adams.'

'I agree with you about George. He's a good man. He's well connected too. Did you know he's married to a High Court judge and his father-in-law is a Supreme Court judge?'

'No I didn't,' Debbie said wiping her mouth with her paper napkin.

'Oh yes. It caused a bit of a stir at the time. He was a DC when Chloe, his wife, was a barrister. He went to her chambers for a pre-trial conference and apparently their eyes met and the rest is history. Of course, questions were asked regarding how such a bright and attractive professional woman like Chloe could fall for someone as lowly as George. Some said it wouldn't last, but it has.'

'You're such a snob at times. Does it really make any difference what their backgrounds are so long as they're happy?'

'Yes it does. Do you want another drink?'

'Another Coke please, thanks.'

Craig grabbed the attention of the bar server who was collecting empty glasses from the adjoining table and ordered another round of drinks. Handing him a five pound note, he said, 'Keep the change.' Turning to Debbie he said, 'Of course it matters. Fortunately Chloe trained George, but I'm concerned that if you fall for Hurst you couldn't do the same to him.'

'If I do, it's none of your business.'

'So you are attracted to him?'

'Well he is quite handsome in a rugged sort of way. He might look moody but that adds to his charm.'

'I'm afraid the word charm is not something that I'd associate with David Hurst.'

As the bar server came over and placed their drinks on the table, Debbie said, 'I'm nipping this in the bud right now. I find him a good man at heart and he is certainly a good officer that we can work well with. I'll tell you this if we play it straight with him, we can trust him unlike many in that office.'

'How about Adams, you said could trust him.'

'He's a good foil to David on that team. I think they're more than work colleagues, they seem to be very good friends.'

'They did join the police on the same day and in 1996 Hurst got a Queen's commendation for bravery saving Adam's life. They were on a job when the Paddies were at their height. They were watching four PIRA lads at house in Manchester. George was the DS heading the team then. They got called away to check a report of other PIRA operatives at another location in Manchester. George left Hurst and Adams at the house. Apparently the PIRA lads found Adams hiding in the back garden of the house. Hurst could not contact Adams on the radio and went to see if he was OK. He came across them in the back garden and as three of them were surrounding Adams, two pointing guns at him, Hurst shot two of them, killing one. Hurst blamed MI5 for holding back vital intelligence and according to George, he's never forgiven us. To be honest it is a bit of a mystery what happened that night. We had an internal enquiry where we found the additional intelligence that came in did not emanate from MI5. As far as we could ascertain, it came from another Special Branch source. We never did know who exactly passed on the intelligence, but at the time we suspected it was a senior police officer with Irish republican sympathies that played the system and warned the four PIRA lads that the police were there.'

'Well that explains why David's so wary of us and why those two are so close. It wasn't Edge who the senior officer they suspected was it?'

'No it wasn't and I take it he's rubbed you up the wrong way.'

'He's such an idiot. How he got to that rank, I'll never know. No one in the office likes him and he's nothing more than an incompetent a bully. He's got it in for David Hurst, but he's even rude to George. I've had to put Edge in his place a couple of times and I've only been with them a day and a half! I wouldn't trust him Craig. I told him about four of our officers coming to Manchester this morning and they would be available to assist the surveillance op they had running. He never passed the information onto the ISB officers on the ground. If you have anything to pass onto that ISB office and I'm not there, don't tell him anything and see if you can speak to George.'

'Good, I'm glad you used your authority and stood your ground. I was getting that impression from what I heard this morning over the air between Edge and the officers involved in the surveillance,' Craig said looking at his watch. 'I'm not being rude Debbie, but I'll have to shoot. You know what it's like, places to go and people to see. I'm glad you're in effect running the show. I'll pursue the line that Leonid could be an undercover FSB agent. I'll get our four to liaise with George Byrne this afternoon. You know, make them known to the officers involved in the Aatcha and Khan case and don't forget Sayfel is coming up on Thursday. Now you're not to tell the plod in that ISB office about Sayfel being one of ours and keep the FSB thing under your hat for now.'

'Why shouldn't David Hurst and his team know about the possibility of FSB agents being in the area? As I said, he's got an idea they're going to be around anyway,' Debbie asked, concerned that if the ISB officers found out she had been holding back on them it would destroy the fragile trust she had already built with them.

'First of all, I'm your senior officer and I've asked you to. Secondly the FSB and Leonid is an MI5 matter, that's what our four officers and you are there for, the Branch are to simply stay with Aatcha, Khan and this new one, Ahmed,' Craig said getting out of his seat. As he put his coat on he said, 'I admire your wanting to get full co-operation with the ISB and that you think you've won Hurst over, but trust me on this. If they, especially the senior officers get wind of the FSB being in the area and that Leonid is an undercover agent, they won't hold their water and someone will blab it about. Trust me. Once I have more on Leonid and what comes out of the negotiations with the Russians, I'll let you know.'

Eight

A hmed was showing Leonid and Aatcha the rooms they would be sleeping in when Khan emerged from the kitchen. 'Coffee's ready. I'll leave them in the kitchen for you,' he said walking into the living room carrying his mug of coffee. The other three picked theirs up from the kitchen and joined Khan where they sat down.

'This morning seemed to go well,' Ahmed said. 'It looks like we've lost the security services.'

'I fucking hope so, Waiting for instructions to move from Ashton until mid-afternoon was arse twitching. I was expecting a knock on the door all day after Moosa left.' Aatcha said. 'Now we're all here, I think it's time we know what's going on between us.' He looked at Leonid and said, 'seeing you're the cause of all this, we need to know why you're with us.'

'Before I tell you, how do you know this flat isn't bugged?' Leonid asked.

'Trust me,' Ahmed said, 'we've had the flat for ages and apart from ourselves, no one's had the chance to get in and bug it. Over the last couple of months it was used by one of our lads for him to lay low for a while. He left yesterday. Don't worry the British security services don't know we're using it. So Leonid,

96

why did Sayfel arrange for you to stay with us?'

'I've got to meet up with some other Chechens staying in England. I don't know where they are yet. Sayfel told me that I was to stay with you for a couple of days while he made some arrangements. As soon as he'd made them, he said that he would get me out of here once we were sure no one was onto me. Basically I just stay here until I hear from him.'

'He's coming up on Thursday,' Ahmed said, 'so maybe he'll let you know then. We need to know when you're leaving so we can make our own plans. What we're organizing will take place shortly. No offence Leonid, but we could do without you being here when we make our move.'

'I understand,' Leonid said, 'and I don't want to be here any longer than necessary. I want to get my own plans in place to carry out what I came to England for.'

'Having you with us for a few days won't affect us too much,' Ahmed said getting out of his seat. 'Put your feet up and make yourself at home.'

'I understand and thank you, 'Leonid said, 'I'm sorry about causing you so many problems. If it puts your mind at rest, I think I'll be gone by Thursday.'

'Ibrar, it's time to get our coats on,' Ahmed said walking out of the living room. 'We just have a little bit of business to do. Moosa you look after Leonid. We should be no more than forty minutes. We'll be passing a good takeaway so I'll get us all something to eat. Leonid, do you like curries?' he shouted back to the others as he put his coat on in the hallway.

'Yes I do, so long as they're not too hot,' he replied.

'Good, curry all round it is,' Ahmed said zipping up the front of his coat as he walked back into the living room.

Ahmed and Aatcha left the flat and walked down the communal staircase. 'We need to check Leonid out,' Ahmed said. 'There's something about him I can't put my finger on. Moosa's got his suspicions about him and I know you do. Moosa made a good point earlier about it being too easy getting Leonid across the border from Chechnya into Georgia and I agree with him.'

Aatcha opened the communal front door, checked to see who was outside the entrance to the flats. 'It's clear,' he said. As they began to walk into the city center, he said, 'Do think he's an undercover FSB agent and the FSB have fooled Sayfel?'

'I'm not sure. I know Sayfel's happy that Leonid is who he claims to be. I know he was checked out by our brothers in Turkey during the couple of months he stayed with them. I'm going to make some enquiries just to be sure he is who he claims to be. There must be some pictures of Leonid and reports on him I can get my hands on. Even if it's old press reports, there must be something.'

'Good idea. After yesterday we're all feeling a bit jittery and it won't hurt to make sure. When Sayfel joins us on Thursday we can question him further about what he knows about Leonid. One good thing with Sayfel coming up is that we can get on with our own job, as he's bringing up with him the stuff we need.'

*   *   *

'Ahmed and Aatcha are leaving the flat, units one and three to follow, unit two stay in position,' David instructed his team over the radio. 'Control, can you get Ray Baskin's team to Granby Row to assist the two I'm leaving to keep an eye on Khan and Leonid?'

'We're on our way,' Ray Baskin replied, 'you go with your team and follow the other two targets. We'll be there shortly.'

David turned to Andy Lewis and Tony King and said, 'Take a separate obs point each and stay in contact with each other. Don't make any move until you have back-up. I don't want any heroics. Tony, if Ray Baskin and his team aren't here within ten minutes get their ETA. If you see any movement, let me know ASAP.'

'We'll be fine David,' Tony replied.

'From unit three, Ahmed and Aatcha are still on foot going up to Portland Street,' Alex conveyed over the radio to the rest of the team.

'No going off on your own without anyone knowing. If you see any movement inform control straight away, stay put and monitor. Do I make myself clear?' David said.

'Come on Davey, the boys will be alright,' Steve said to David, grabbing him by the arm. As they walked off Alex relayed that Ahmed and Aatcha were walking into Piccadilly Gardens. 'You go on about George being over protective with us two! You're just the same, especially with the young ones. Give them a break and let them learn from their own experiences.'

'I take it that was a bollocking?' David asked.

'No, it was constructive feedback.'

*   *   *

As Andy and Tony were watching the flat in Granby Row the late afternoon autumn sun sank from the horizon. They had to concentrate to see any movement outside the flat in the darkening twilight. While Andy watched the front, Tony positioned himself at the back of the flats. He pressed himself against wall opposite the flats that gave him a view to the side and rear. As Tony was looking up at the rear windows of the flats he became aware of movement out the corner of his eye. In the long shadows brought on by the distant street lights he could just make out the image of a person standing at the rear yard door to the flats the targets were using. He kept looking in the direction he saw the person. As his eyes became accustomed to the dark, he noticed a tall stocky male take a few steps away from the rear yard door and look up at the rear of the flats. Pressing the transmit button on the radio he said, 'Andy, there's a male lurking at the back of the flats. He doesn't look like any of our targets. Any sign of Baskin's lot yet?'

'No not yet. Perhaps the male is one of the blokes from Canal Street who fancies you!'

'Be serious Andy, something's not right. He's by the third light on the right of the entry. He's being careful not be in its glare. There's something fishy going on. Watch my back while I get closer and check him out.'

'Tony, don't move from your position. You know what Hursty said. Stay put until we get back-up.'

'I'll be alright. Contact the boss and see if he can find out if Five has any officers in the area and get an ETA from Baskin's lot,' Tony radioed to Andy. As the man walked back towards the rear yard door, he said, 'It looks like this bloke's going to go into the rear yard of the flats.'

Hugging the line of the wall he was leaning against, Tony carefully approached the rear yard to get a closer look at the man. He paused in between steps to see if he could hear any unusual noises. Apart from the distant sound of traffic, there was an eerie silence in the immediate vicinity. It was so quiet Tony started to breathe slowly. He did not want this man to have the slightest inclination he was approaching him. He turned into the corner of the rear entry leading to the flats. Seeing the man trying to open the rear yard door, he quickly moved back into the shadows. He made sure that his radio earpiece was in place and whispered over the radio to Andy, 'This male's trying to get into the rear yard of the targets' flat. I need back-up.' A burst of static was the only response he got. He repeated his message to Andy.

In reply, 'Don't ... Tony... minutes,' were the only words Tony could make out between the bursts of static.

As his eyes became fully accustomed to dark, he could see the man was about six foot tall with a stocky build. 'He looks a handful,' he thought. As Tony watched him, it was obvious the rear yard door was locked from the other side as the man took a few paces back and ran up to the wall of the flats. Placing his hands on the top of the wall, Tony watched him use his great strength to haul himself on top of the high wall.

The man sat on the wall and momentarily looked around him. 'Jesus I hope he doesn't see me. The way he got onto the wall he must be one strong bastard,' Tony thought. Adding to his already heightened senses was the knowledge he would stand little chance of overpowering this large man if he got into a fight with him. As the man dropped into the rear yard of the flats Tony relayed over the radio, 'The suspect's climbed the wall and gone into the rear of the targets' flat. I need back-up now.' Once again all he heard were loud bursts of static.

Tony decided to move closer to the rear yard door. 'If Hursty was in my place, he'd follow him to see what he's up to,' he thought, ignoring David's warning. Tony's imagination began to run through all the possibilities of what this male was up to. 'What happens if he enters the flats and kills our targets? Or, is he another Chechen we don't know about?' An overwhelming sense of being damned if he did and damned if he didn't do anything added to his natural curiosity. Cautiously, he made his way to the entry into the rear yard of the flats.

As Andy could not get through to Ray Baskin over the radio, he checked his phone. Seeing that he had a signal, he called Ray Baskin as he lost sight of Tony. As soon as Ray Baskin answered his phone, Andy said, 'Sarge, its Andy Lewis. What's your ETA? Tony's seen some a bloke acting suspiciously at the back of the flats and he's gone to check on him. I've lost sight of him as he's moved from his position to get a better look at what he's up to. Problem is that DS Hurst told us not move until you arrived.'

Ray calmly said, 'Don't panic, we're two minutes away. We'll go to the front of the flats. Go and join Tony. I'll also send a couple over to the rear of the flats to back you up. Don't go into the rear yard until we get there. Just stay in the shadows.'

'Will do Sarge.' Andy closed his mobile phone and crept up

towards the last position he saw Tony. Trying to stay out of sight, he thought, 'Hursty will kill us if we cock up. Why didn't Tony do as Hursty said and stay put?'

*   *   *

Victoria rail station was bustling with passengers as David and his team followed Ahmed and Aatcha onto the concourse of the station. David and Steve positioned themselves to the side of the newsagents in the station as they watched Aatcha using one of the public telephones while Ahmed walked over to one of the platforms opposites the public phone booths. 'Aatcha's making a call at the phone booth instead of his mobile phone,' Steve said.

'He's minimizing the opportunity for us to pick up his mobile phone signal. We haven't got that phone booth tapped,' David replied, frustrated they could not hear what Aatcha was saying. 'I reckon Aatcha's acting as minder. He's over there trying to spot anyone watching or approach Ahmed,' he said reaching for the transmit button of his radio in his left sleeve. Pressing the button David relayed to the others, 'Be careful moving around, Aatcha's stood by the entrance to platform eight watching us watching them. No one is to approach Ahmed. Apart from Steve and I the rest of you walk out of the station and stay by the exits. We'll maintain eyeball with the targets.'

'If only we could get closer to hear what he's saying,' Steve said, watching Ahmed intently as he made his phone call.

'Alex, get over to the public phone boxes and see if you can listen what our man's saying?' David instructed her over the radio.

'I'll try,' she replied. As Alex made her way through the busy concourse to the four public phone booths, David trained his eyes on Aatcha while Steve kept watching Ahmed. As she got to the empty phone booth on Ahmed's right, Ahmed hung up the receiver and began to walk towards the exit leading to the Manchester Evening News Arena, followed by Aatcha. She radioed back, 'I'm sorry. I've got nothing.'

'Don't worry about it Alex,' David replied, 'The rest of you follow them and let's see where they go.'

*   *   *

Hunched by the rear yard door, Tony whispered on his radio for Andy to acknowledge him. There was no reply, just another burst of static. 'Bastard radio black spot,' he thought, 'I can't wait for Andy. I'll have to follow him. I'll be alright. Ray Baskin's lot will be here soon.' Tony heard noises coming from the yard and looked through a crack in the door. He saw the tall, thick set man taking a small bag out from his inside coat pocket and conceal it under some bricks below the rear ground floor window. As he only had a limited view into the yard, Tony lent into the door to get a better view. Unexpectedly, the door burst open. The stranger unbolted it when he entered the yard to give himself a quicker exit. The door clattered against the wall and Tony fell into the yard. As he tried to break his fall, he mumbled, 'Shit!'

As he lay on the ground, Tony's fear was realized. Before he could regain his balance, the man was on top of him. As he pounced on Tony's prostrate body, the air in Tony's lungs gushed out causing him to fight for breath, 'Fucking hell, he's stronger than I thought.' The fight to survive overtook any fear Tony felt. As hard as he tried, Tony could not throw off the man. He tried to shout out, but found he could not open his mouth as a strong right arm had a vice-like grip on his lower jaw. Tony's resistance was hopeless. The man's greater strength forced Tony's head to turn to one side. Eyes wide open, and feeling totally powerless, Tony prayed these were not his final moments. A sharp bladed knife was plunged into Tony's neck and sliced his throat from one side to the other. Tony's eyes closed as the experienced assassin held onto him until the life force ebbed from his body. Once Tony's body went limp, the man got up to check the rear alley. As it was clear, he left the yard. Walking quickly down the rear entry, he faded into the ever darkening night.

It was quiet as Andy crept up to the rear of the flats. 'Tony!' Andy uttered in a loud whisper. For a few seconds his eyes were transfixed at the sight of his colleague and friend lying there motionless. After the immediate shock of seeing Tony's motionless body subsided, he knelt down by the body to check for signs of life. He felt the thick sticky moisture around his throat and realized it was blood. Rubbing the blood between his fingers, Andy looked at Tony's throat and saw a trail of blood in the yard. Cradling his friend's body close, tears welled up in his eyes. Andy's mind raced as the consequences of what had happened began to dawn on him. Covered in his friend's blood, he whispered to the motionless body, 'Why didn't you wait! Hursty warned us not to go off on our own.' Pulling all his emotions together, he called David Hurst on his mobile telephone.

*   *   *

'Stay with Tony's body. I'll get Ray Baskin to you right away. Just stay calm and be as quiet as you can. Don't blame yourself Andy. I'll get back to you as soon as I can,' David instructed the young detective constable. He immediately contacted Ray Baskin to inform him of Tony King's death.

After the initial shock at what David told him subsided, Ray's professionalism took over. In a quiet confident tone he said, 'I'll get over to Andy now. We've just arrived at the flat. Leave the scene to me David. Are you going to tell George or do you want me to?'

'I'll do it. Just keep an eye on Andy for me. I wouldn't mind, but I told them no initiative, no fucking heroics. Now look what's happened.'

'Don't blame Andy. He told me Tony had seen someone at the back of the flats and I told them to keep an eye on the male. As I said, I'll get the scene sorted out and I'll make sure Andy's OK.'

'Cheers Ray.' Hurst looked at Steve and said, 'Ray's going to box off the scene but before I tell George, I've an important phone call to make to ascertain if our mutual friends were in the area. If that was a Five officer who killed Tony, he'll regret ever touching one of my team,' David said calling up Debbie's mobile phone number, thumping the buttons on the small keypad as he did so.

'Hello David, is everything alright?'

'No. Tony King's been killed.'

'Oh my god! What happened?'

'I don't know yet. Have any MI5 officers been sniffing around the back of the flats in the last half hour?'

'No, we've only got the four officers who came up this morning and they're sitting next to me checking out some intelligence. We've not sent them out to the flat as your team's covering it and we thought it might get a bit crowded. Where was Tony killed?'

'It was at the back of the flats in Granby Row. Tony saw a bloke go into the rear yard and followed him. Looks like whoever he followed into the yard killed him.'

'Does George know?'

'Not yet, I'm about to tell him but I wanted to check with you first to see if any of your lot were in the vicinity of the flats,' David said, wanting to believe Debbie.

Knowing that David would be going through a mixture of emotions in losing a colleague, she tried to reassure him saying, 'We need my manager and George to meet up and start getting the ball rolling on our next move. Leave George to me. I'll tell him what's happened to Tony and you do whatever you have to at the scene. I'll get them to pull an emergency meeting together. The last thing we need is the local area police turning up, especially with Leonid being there. It's likely to scare them off again.'

'I agree, it's best to keep the locals out and we deal with it. Ray Baskin's boxing off the scene and Steve and I'll be at our office in about twenty minutes. Once you've got the meet arranged let me know and Steve and I'll be there.'

*   *   *

'David, Steve, come to my office, Debbie and her two MI5 colleagues are already in there,' George said to the officers as they arrived at the main ISB office. On entering the DI's office, George introduced them to the MI5 officers, 'This is Detective Sergeant David Hurst and Detective Constable Steve Adams. Tony King was on David's team. David, can you tell us what happened?'

David relayed the few facts he knew regarding Tony's death, '...One of Ray's team found a bag underneath the rear ground floor window containing a mobile phone and small book with a note inside it written in what looks like Russian. One of Ray's team was sent over to the ISB office to deliver what they found. She should have been here by now and handed it over. It could be either another Chechen making contact with Leonid or it could have been an FSB agent that killed Tony.'

'Thanks David. We got the items a few minutes ago and we've had a quick look at them. You're right, it's Russian alright and MI5 are arranging for a translation as we speak. The question is how are we going to go about investigating Tony's death?' George said.

David answered first. 'We're going to have to act quickly. The problems we've got, as Debbie pointed out to me earlier, if we treat it as a normal crime scene, we'll have the local area police all over that rear yard. If that happens, no doubt our targets will be on the move again thinking they've been compromised. On the other hand, the longer we wait, the more questions will be asked as to why the delay. I suggest that we deal with it and deal with it now.'

One of the MI5 officers, Brian Maguire, spoke up. 'If it's any consolation you're summation that an FSB agent killed your colleague could be right. My colleague and I have been trawling though communications flying around between the FSB agents active in the UK over the last few hours Of course they were coded and on top that coded in Russian. That's not helped in trying to work out what they've been up to. It looks like your colleague disturbed an FSB agent. We can't confirm this at the moment, but with help from Thames House, we'll keep working on it. I can say that up to the last half hour there was no confirmed intelligence of any FSB activity so close to the flat. All we've had from, our man on the inside, is there was only a possibility of FSB activity in the Manchester area. Not only is this a very tragic incident, but if it was the FSB that killed DC King, it's going to be very embarrassing to the Russians if one of their agents is found to have killed a British police officer. I agree with David that we deal with the murder. I'm trying not to be insensitive here, but I suggest that we move the crime scene to location not far from the flats. Then we can arrange for the local police to deal with the investigation as though it happened at the new location. I also agree that time is of the essence and we should move the scene as soon as we can.'

Debbie was tempted to mention the conversation she had with Craig earlier that afternoon regarding Petrov being in the area. Knowing emotions were raw, to avoid any conflict she decided to be vague and said, 'I agree with Brian, we'll have to move the crime scene and fast. In the last fifteen minutes GCHQ passed onto Thames House that an FSB officer is active in the Manchester area but there were no specifics. It's believed they're watching Leonid and it looks like there's more than one Chechen fighter in the UK planning an attack. GCHQ believe it's to take place soon on a major Russian target residing in the UK. It looks like the original plan for the ISB to focus on the Al Qaeda targets suspects while MI5 look after Leonid and the Chechen link has to be changed. I've a feeling that from this moment we're all working together?'

George said, 'I think that's a safe assumption to make Debbie. I'll contact you senior officer, Craig MacDonald and I'll work out with him a strategy over how we deal with Tony's death so we can keep it in-house. When I say in-house, I mean all knowledge as to what happened tonight stays between the ISB teams currently engaged on this investigation and MI5. No one on any of the ISB teams not involved is to know and for the moment, that includes Paul Edge. It's not ethical, but, if we have a circus looking into this at the flats, all four of our targets are, as David said, likely to move and we could possibly lose them. I'll pull a team off an investigation that was going nowhere to investigate the murder with DI Andrews from the Port Unit. He can be the SIO.' Turning to the MI5 officers George asked, 'Can you arrange a new venue for the crime scene?'

Brian Maguire replied first. 'I'll get onto it straight away, have you got a number for Detective Sergeant Baskin?'

Keeping an eye on David, George said, 'Yes, I'll give that to you now.' As he wrote Ray Baskin's mobile telephone number on a piece of paper, he said, 'We must do all that we can in moving the crime scene in a way that minimizes potential awkward questions. You've got one hour to get it sorted, after which I'll have to contact Paul Edge. With a bit of luck he'll not get too suspicious over the time delay. Debbie, David and Steve, join me. I want to come up with an alternative version of facts leading to Tony's death that will be acceptable to the chief and the press. We've a lot to do in the next hour so let's get to it.'

After the two MI5 officers left George's office, George said, 'I know you're hurting and I know that you David will be feeling guilty about leaving the lad. But there was nothing you could do. It was an unforeseen event and Tony was doing his job. It could have happened to any of us. I'll notify Tony's wife and sort out the welfare side. There's too much at stake if we lose either Leonid or the three Al Qaeda lads. I don't want any more of this being suspicious of each other. We're all one team now. Understood?'

'Yes,' David replied.

Debbie put her hand gently on David's arm and said, 'I know you've been suspicious of me from the start, but I've always told you everything I could tell you. Believe me I know exactly what you're going through.'

George added, 'Debbie's right, it's not as if the intelligence was specific on this particular FSB agent.'

Steve got up out of his seat and said, 'Definitely a strong sweet coffee is needed for my leader, anyone else for a brew?'

Nine

In a briefing room at Greater Manchester Police Headquarters, Chief Constable Bernard Gamble began his press conference in company with Detective Inspector Bill Andrews. 'Ladies and gentlemen of the press, it is my sad duty to inform you that early this evening a police officer from Greater Manchester Police's CID was killed in Manchester city center while investigating a crime. It happened in Mosley Street near to Nicholas Street. The officer was Detective Constable Tony King. He was making enquiries into a number of thefts that had taken place over the past couple of weeks in the Mosley Street area. As he turned into Nicolas Street, he came across three men who appeared to have been drinking. We have some CCTV footage to show you.' As the pictures were relayed on a large screen behind him, Chief Constable Gamble took the assembled press through the events. 'I apologize for the grainy quality of the pictures, but here you can see DC King walking into Nicholas Street and bump into one of the men holding what looks like a bottle of spirits. As you can see, an altercation takes place between three men. As you watch Detective Constable King being dragged behind a building in Nicholas Street that is the final sighting we have of the officer and his killer. The CCTV cameras could not pick up any more

110

of what happened during the incident. We've set up a murder squad and an incident room at Greater Manchester Police's headquarters. All I can confirm is that Detective Constable Tony King was needlessly stabbed by one of these three men. If anyone watching or hearing this who witnessed the event could contact the incident room on 0161 777 3939 or call Crimestoppers we would be grateful for any information, no matter how trivial you may think it is.

'Tony was married and his wife has been informed of his death. Her family members are currently comforting her and a Greater Manchester Police family liaison officer is supporting her. Tony King had twelve years service with the Greater Manchester Police, most of his service being in the CID. He was a dedicated and popular officer. He received two commendations, one for bravery and one for his investigative work. He will be sorely missed and our heartfelt thoughts go out to his wife and family at this time. Once again we see through the death Detective Constable Tony King the dangers that my officers and all police officers in the country have to face while serving their communities. I trust that you will report the news of this officer's death with sensitivity and respect for the memory of Detective Constable Tony King. Just to repeat, I urge anyone that witnessed the event please assist us by calling the incident room on 0161 777 3939 or call Crimestoppers if you wish remain anonymous. All calls will be dealt with sensitively. I cannot take any questions at the moment, once I have more information I will organize a further press conference. Thank you.'

As the Chief Constable got out of his seat to leave the room, he was faced with the bright flashes of light from the assembled Medias' cameras and a barrage of questions by the assembled reporters. He refused to answer any further questions repeatedly saying, 'I have no further comment to make at this time.'

*   *   *

'Well the Chief fell for it, how about Edge?' David asked George after watching the press statement given by his chief constable on national television.

'So far it looks like he took it hook, line and sinker. He agreed that we avoid reporting the fact that Tony was a Branch officer. His only question was why Tony King was on his own. I told him Tony was returning to the hut as his duty time was over. MI5 did a good job with doctoring the CCTV footage. In that group I recognize two of the men but who was the third man?' George asked David.

'I can't say, you'll have to watch that film with Orson Wells!'

George smiled. 'I'm glad to see your sense of humor's returned but seriously who was the third man?'

'Ray Baskin.'

'You couldn't tell. You have to hand it to MI5. They did a good job transposing the images of Tony into the video clip. Well it's down to Bill Andrews now. He believes that Tony was murdered in Nicholas Street. Five did a good job clearing up the actual murder scene and moving to the back of Nicholas Street. I just hope our targets didn't notice what happened. It's important that you and the rest of the Office involved in our investigation leave Bill Andrews' team alone. What we have to do now is work closely with Five. I've already spoken to Craig Macdonald. I know him quite well. He's very smart, educated at Oxford, with an incisive mind and a photographic memory. We're meeting up with him and MI5 at the Manchester Marriott where we're setting up a temporary control room. Craig's already made the necessary arrangements in setting up the equipment and relevant staff from his department. Get Steve and the three of us can walk over there together.'

'Edge isn't involved with Craig MacDonald and this part of the operation then?' David asked.

'No, Craig was very specific that Paul Edge is to have no knowledge of this meeting or the events that led to this meeting.

So make the most of it as it. It'll do you good to be out of Edge's hair for a while. I thought we could walk up, and have a quick drink as we're meeting them in the bar of the hotel first. Go and get Steve and I'll meet you outside, and remember, not a word to anyone about what's happening or where we're going.'

*   *   *

'George, it's lovely to see you again, it's been far too long. Are these your two friends?' Craig said shaking hands with George in the hotel bar.

'Nice to see you again Craig, let me introduce you to David Hurst and Steve Adams.'

'It's nice to meet you. I've been hearing very good things about you two from a mutual friend. Drink up. I'd like you to come through to the room I've hired so you can join the party.' Craig said shaking hands with both David and Steve. As he shook hands with Hurst there were no smiles from the DS, no pleasantries just a cold stare he gave Craig and a firm handshake. After their introductions, Craig guided them to a room off the hotel's main ground floor corridor that led off from the reception where there was a sign on the door saying, 'Simpson Corporation: Market Survey Analysts'.

George said, 'Simpson Corporation?'

'Best I could come up with at short notice. It's my brother-in-law's name,' Craig said opening the door. Along with other MI5 staff, Debbie, Brian Maguire and Gordon Bascombe were already in the room. Debbie was sat at a table working on a computer while the others were setting out tables and installing computers and television screens. As each piece of equipment was being placed on a table, empty boxes were being stacked neatly at the corner of the magnolia painted room. As David walked in to the large room it obvious to him that Craig Macdonald had hired one of the rooms the hotel use for conferences and meetings. As he noticed the many sockets and telephone points he could see why Craig had hired the room, it was amply equipped for their purposes.

'Come in to our new office and help yourselves to the refreshments I managed to acquire,' Craig said pointing to a table placed against the wall by the door with plates of sandwiches and catering flasks of tea and coffee. The three officers did not take up the offer as they walked over to a stack of chairs. 'I think you all know each other.' Craig said shutting the door behind him.

The three officers sat down in the corner of the room furthest away from the activity and were joined by Debbie, Brian Maguire and Gordon Bascombe. Craig brought a chair over with him and joined them. 'It's an absolute tragedy what happened to Tony King, he sounded a first rate officer,' Craig said shaking his head at the loss of the officer. 'I can fully understand how you must be feeling. We have an idea who killed Tony King. In the last hour Thames House passed on intelligence confirming there's at least one FSB agent presently working in the area. His name is Petrov. He cut his teeth in this game when he joined the KGB in its last couple of years of existence. He's very experienced agent and we believe he's currently posing as a businessman. One important find was the mobile phone and the message written in Russian that Petrov left at the scene. He obviously had no idea we were that close to him and his chum Leonid. Killing Tony would be a last resort for Petrov. He's bright enough to realize after seeing the news that he's killed a Special Branch officer. As a result he'll know that he has to get out of the area quickly. MI5 are trying to keep tabs on him as he'll have to make contact with the FSB based in the UK to receive further instructions.

'From the analysis of the book and the information we found on telephone, it appears the man we thought was Leonid is not him at all, but is an undercover FSB agent whose real name is Gregor Petrolsky. He's a senior FSB field agent and joined the agency when it was still the KGB. Six have confirmed this. The real Leonid Kashinov is either dead or is in some gulag in a

Siberian wasteland. Petrolsky had some minor plastic surgery makeover to make him look like Leonid. Apparently the process was not too severe as he had similar features to the real Leonid. From what we've ascertained, Petrolsky's had quite a productive time while undercover. Not only has he penetrated the main Chechen sympathizers in Turkey but also the Al Qaeda cells in Turkey and France and now the UK. The information he's gathered on these cells would be very useful to us indeed. That could explain what happened yesterday at Huyton station when Aatcha and Leonid got on the train instead of meeting up and going to the car. I reckon Leonid was being tailed by his FSB colleagues and Aatcha sussed them out.

'Obviously we would like to keep tabs on Petrolsky and bring him in so MI5 can debrief him over what he's learnt. As there are far too many Russian names flying around at the moment we shall still refer to Petrolsky as Leonid, seeing as that's how we've got used to calling him. As far as we're aware, the Russian's main interest is in the Chechens he's come across in the last twelve months. MI6 are trying to ascertain from their agents in Turkey if there have been any reported deaths of Chechens living in Turkey. If there are, then Six are looking to tie these into possible FSB actions. It appears that to date there have been no FSB actions taken against Al Qaeda cells, but of course any intelligence the FSB have on Al Qaeda will be excellent bargaining chips in our dealings with FSB and the Russian government over the killing of Tony King.

'What we found at the scene of Tony's death confirmed the FSB was running an operation in the Manchester area. Apart from the politicians and relevant ministries, to date Leonid's activities involves Six, the CIA, the French Surete and the German Bundeskriminalamt as well as ourselves to name but a few. On top of that, from the few communications we've picked up from the three Al Qaeda targets at the flat, it looks like they're suspicious of Leonid being an undercover FSB agent. With what

happened this evening, it might just be getting a bit too hot for
him to stay with them any longer. I suggest we try to get Leonid
out of his current location.' David raised his hand, 'David you
wish to come in here?'

'I didn't realize this investigation was so involved. How are
we going to square this off with DCI Edge? There's going to be
a lot of fall out over Tony's death. For example, questions are
going to be asked about me being the team leader and having
responsibility for the team. One question Edge will certainly
want to know, as well as the team investigating Tony's murder is
where I was. It's just that I can foresee problems down the road
if we just press on regardless of what's going on right now over
Tony's death.'

Craig answered David's concerns saying, 'Mr. Edge has been
put in the picture in relation to what I want him to know at this
stage. He's been told that your team has been seconded to my
control for now along with George's support. He's not just been
told by me but also by greater powers than I. Don't worry, he'll
do as he's told. Regarding the current operation, one problem we
have is finding Petrov. He'll have a good idea we're onto him as
we've found the mobile phone, the book and the note. So he'll
try to get in touch Leonid who we believe is Petrov's controller.
If Leonid does assist Petrov that could mean Leonid having to
break his cover and part company with the Al Qaeda boys that
the Branch have been watching so far. This in turn will have
Moscow preparing a statement to present to the Foreign Office
as well as time to prepare their next move. As a result, we have
to move quickly to get Leonid out of that flat in Granby Row.
Getting him out is down to MI5, as it is our job to try and
orchestrate events if they do not go our way. So Brian, I want
you to take charge of getting him away from the Al Qaeda boys
and bring him in.

'Of course this leaves us with what to do with Aatcha,
Ahmed and Khan. If need be, one last resort is to raid the flat

in Granby, get Leonid out and arrest the three Al Qaeda boys. If that happens, with the little evidence we have on them all we can do is detain the three of them for the twenty-eight days and release them. If that happened, it wouldn't be a total loss as it will be harder for these particular Al Qaeda boys to operate in the UK for a while. That will be our last resort. In the meantime we've got to see if we can get Leonid when he's on his own.'

George interjected and said, 'We can have the legal authorities in place within the next couple of hours and I can have a rapid entry team, including firearms officers ready by morning.'

'Thanks George, I'm sure we can stand down the rapid entry team and the firearms officers if our plan B works.'

'What's plan B?' asked George

'Debbie's acquired the keys to the flat above our targets'. In the past hour we've been arranging for MI5's tech support to install the equipment we need to hear what's going in the Al Qaeda flat below. It's a bit of rush job, but they can give us the support we need. David and Debbie you will play the role of the couple that lives in the flat above our targets' flat. They've been away on holiday, and they return tonight, arriving at Manchester Airport. Once they arrive at the airport I've arranged for an MI5 officer to meet them and offer them an extended holiday. Your holiday luggage awaits you over there,' Craig said pointing to a couple of suitcases next to the table with the refreshments on, 'but instead of dirty washing, the cases contain the technical equipment we need. Once you are in, two of our techies will act as your friends. They will call at the flat to see how your holiday went. Once you two are in, let me know and I'll send them over to the flat so they can install the equipment. The sooner we're in, the sooner we'll find out when Leonid leaves the Al Qaeda flat so we can take him out. George, you and I will be the senior officers running this show. Steve Adams you will run the rest of your ISB team including Ray Baskin's team and keep static obs in Granby Row while David's in the flat with Debbie.'

'So I'm now an acting DS?' Steve asked.

'I suppose you are,' Craig said, 'and David that means you stay in the flat regardless of what goes on outside. I'm sure you've known Steve long enough to trust him to look after your team?'

'I do, I know I can trust him' he replied.

Craig continued saying, 'Brian and Gordon are going to be supported by another two MI5 officers. I suggest we get everything in place as soon as we can. In case you're wondering, all this has been squared off with the Home and Foreign Offices. Has anyone got any questions?'

Ten

Tuesday 24th October
21.50 hours
Granby Row, Manchester

The sound of a diesel engine could be clearly heard inside the flat as Ahmed went over to the living room window to see a man and a woman getting out of a taxi with two suitcases.

'What is it?' Aatcha asked lying on the sofa watching the television.

'It looks like the couple that live in the flat above have come back from their holiday. Mo, who normally stays in the flat got to know them and some of the other neighbors to learn their patterns of routine. At least the flat will be occupied now. That'll make it more difficult for British Security to break in and snoop on us.'

'Have you been worried about that?'

'A little,' Ahmed said walking away from the window and sitting back down in one of the large leather armchairs in the living room of the flat. 'The commotion earlier at the back of the flat has me a little concerned. It's certainly got Leonid on edge. Mo told me that a man in his thirties lives in the ground floor flat. He thinks he's a bit of a gangster, possibly a drug dealer. I asked him if he knew for certain, but he said he was guessing. According to Mo, the fact he drives a Porsche and has a number of frequent callers throughout the night is enough for him to

119

suspect he's a drug dealer. He told me that one night he was walking back to the flat when he saw this man drag another lad outside and really batter him. He smashed his face in and everything. He's got access to the rear yard and the disturbance we heard was most probably him and a couple of his friends sorting out a local difference. That said, I just hope it's got nothing to do with Leonid as it seems to have shaken him up a bit.'

'He's a stranger to the UK and to be honest if I'd been living the way he has over the past few months I'd be on edge. Remember he's a long way from home and he doesn't exactly know us. Put yourself in his shoes.'

'Leonid obviously thinks he's still dealing with Russian militia!'

'Are you sure the couple you saw get out of the taxi are the ones who live in the flat above? You don't think they could've been Special Branch or MI5?'

'I've not seen the couple that lives in the flat above so I couldn't be a hundred percent positive it was them, but it's too much of a coincidence. Mo told me they would be returning today in the late evening. Well it's late evening and there's only two of them and they've got two suitcases with them.'

*   *   *

'The flat looks really nice,' Debbie said as David put the luggage in the hallway.

'I'll put the television on so we have some noise in the flat.' David said walking across the well-appointed living room to switch on the large flat screen television. 'That's better, we can talk now. We've got to be careful ourselves until the room's checked out by your boys. I'm starving, are you hungry?'

'Yes, I only had a sandwich at lunch and I haven't eaten since.'

'Do you like Chinese?'

'I love it.'

David took out his pen and on a scrap of paper wrote down

the telephone number of a Chinese Takeaway he frequently used and handed it to Debbie. 'Ring this number. It's a local Chinese restaurant that does an excellent takeaway. I use them regularly and the food's really nice. You ring them, as they know me. If they recognize my voice they'll wonder what I'm doing at this address. I'll have a special curry with boiled rice. I haven't got the menu but they serve all the usual Chinese food. It's on me, so have whatever you want.'

'Thanks I'll give them a ring now.'

David watched as Debbie took off her shoes and massage her feet while resting the paper with the phone number on the side table in the hallway. A sense of loneliness came over him as he realized how long it had been since he had been alone in a woman's company outside the office.

While Debbie rang for the takeaway, David contacted George on his mobile phone to inform him that they were in the flat and the MI5 tech officers could arrive whenever they were ready. Looking out of the window to see if he could see Ray or Steve or any of the team, he noticed the sodium street lighting lit up the Manchester evening. All was very quiet around the flat. He went into the kitchen and looked out of the window down to the rear yard where only hours before Tony King had been killed. The rear yard to the flats was only small with a few refuse bins lined up next to each other as if on parade along the far wall of the yard. There were no flowerbeds, nothing that made the place pleasant. As David was thinking what a sordid and undignified place for such a talented detective to die, Debbie walked into the kitchen and said, 'They'll be about half an hour at the most.' She saw David looking out of the kitchen towards the rear year and realized that he must be thinking about Tony King. 'I know it's awful when we lose one of our own. Are you OK?'

'Yes I'll be fine. I was just thinking about Tony's wife and what she must be going through.'

'You can't start to imagine what emotions she must have.

Come on I'll make some coffee, they must have coffee in here,'
Debbie said as she started to open the cupboard doors.

'Good idea, I'll put the kettle on. I hope they don't have any
of that weak stuff. I can't drink that muck.'

Seeing a packet of coffee, Debbie took it out of the cupboard
and looked at the packet. 'You're in luck. They've got some Italian
filter coffee. Let's have a drink and our takeaway without thinking
of what's been happening, or thinking about our colleagues and
the targets. Just for one hour let's forget all of that, enjoy the
break and it'll give us the chance to get to know each other a
bit better. Being your liaison officer as well as the fact we've got
to work closely together, I think it's important you know more
about me and vice versa. That's only if it is OK with you?' Debbie
asked, hoping she could use this period of inactivity to get to
know the real David Hurst.

Thinking that he had been a bit harsh on Debbie earlier,
David thought there would be no harm in getting to know each
other better, in fact he thought it could be more productive
to the investigation if they did. 'Yes that's fine. If I think that
you're getting too personal I'll soon let you know. You said at the
briefing that you knew what I was going through. Have you lost
a colleague during an operation?'

'It was nearly two years ago when it happened. I was posted to
Thames House working with a team headed by senior intelligence
officer Jenny Richmond. She's a different kettle of fish to Craig.
Where Craig gives the impression of being cold and aloof, Jenny
cares about her officers and what they're going through. We were
watching a far-right group suspected of infiltrating the major
political parties either as potential Parliamentary candidates or as
aides to senior MP's, even cabinet ministers. We followed a group
of targets into a pub in the east end of London. As this was a
place the targets met on a frequent basis, we ended up following
them to this pub. The last time we followed our targets to the
pub, James Osman, he was the MI5 officer I was working with,

went to the toilets. Apparently they were suspicious of us two and three men followed James into the gent's toilets. As it was busy in the pub that evening, I didn't notice anything unusual except that he was gone for ages. I went to the toilets and asked a man to go in and see what had happened to James. Long story short, the men that followed him kicked him to death. It really shook me up. Jenny took me off the operation straight away and kept me in the office most of the time dealing with intelligence analysis work. To help me get back on track and start getting me out an about, she helped me get the post of police liaison officer for the north of England. So I do know what you're going through, genuinely I do.'

'I'm sorry Debbie, I didn't know. It's a bad thing for anyone to go through. I'm really sorry that I've been a bit of a shit at times since you arrived at our office yesterday.'

Sensing genuine regret in David, she said, 'That's OK. Don't worry about it. You weren't to know. Listen let's get to know each other better. I know your younger brother is a barrister working in chambers in London.'

'How did you know that?'

'Craig told me this afternoon. Apparently his brother works with your brother and they share the same office. It's a small world isn't it?'

'It's too small for my liking.'

'Your brother's name is Peter isn't it?'

'Yes, he's my baby brother by five minutes, we're twins.'

'So there are two of you running around looking the same.'

'We're not identical twins, but there are similarities in our personality, but differences too. He is much more patient than me and slower to lose his temper. He's cleverer than me too.'

'Why do you say that? Because he's a barrister?'

'No, it's just when we were younger, he was more disposed to studying than me. During our teenage years, I easily got bored with schoolwork. I couldn't see the point behind reading books that I had no interest in whereas Peter did. While I was busy playing sports and doing my own thing, Peter was disciplined enough to study. As a result he did well at school. He got his 'A' levels and studied law at Manchester University where he got a first. He then went to the Bar School in London and he did well there too. It cost Mum and Dad a lot of money as well as me. I helped fund him through his studies at the Bar. It was worth it, as he came in the top half of his year and soon got a pupillage. Credit to Peter though, he's repaid our parents once he started to earn some serious money. I've got no doubts he'll become a QC soon and that'll be a major achievement for a lad from the Dingle in Liverpool.'

'I've been meaning to talk to you about that. I noticed that you're from Liverpool not Manchester. Why did you join GMP?'

'They're the only ones who would have me! No seriously, Dad's from Manchester and when I applied to join the police I applied to both GMP and Merseyside. It's just that GMP replied first.'

'Do you have any other brothers and sisters?'

'I only have a younger sister, Siobhan as well as our Peter. Mum had a bad time giving birth to her and as a result she couldn't have any more children. Siobhan's a deputy head at an inner city state school in Liverpool. She's the only one out of the three of us that remained in Liverpool.'

'When I was talking to Craig this afternoon I thought what a small world it is with your brother working alongside Craig's?'

'I think I know who his brother is, it's Alistair McDonald.'

'That's right, that's him.'

'He shares his office with Peter. Peter's says Alistair's a pompous sod who's desperate to take silk and he'll brown nose anyone to get there. In Peter's opinion he's getting a bit too long in the tooth and he's not good enough, even though Alistair's got an over inflated ego of himself. When I met Alistair McDonald I quickly came to the conclusion that he's a right snobby bastard. He looked down his nose at me when Peter introduced us saying,

"I believe you are a flatfoot plod by trade?" Unfortunately my wit and repartee fails me at times as my reply was "At least it's an honest trade not an overpaid profession that has to dress up in fancy dress and act like pompous twats".'

Debbie started to laugh. 'You're so funny and forthright. I like that in a person. I'd love to have seen his face.'

'Well he wasn't too pleased and since then we've never got on. If I see our Peter in London and he's there, he just nods his head and grunts when I say hello to him.'

'I think Alistair got the term "plod" from Craig as that's what he calls officers from the Branch. I can hear traces of Craig's personality in your description of Alistair. How did your parents meet?'

'Dad comes from Droylsden in Manchester and he was an electrician. He moved over to Liverpool in the 1960's working on renovated tenements when he met Mum. She comes from Ballina in County Mayo, Ireland and came over to Liverpool in the early 1960's looking for work. Being in a big city, it was a bit of a culture shock for her as she was raised in the countryside on my grandfather's farm, just outside Ballina. There was a good Irish Catholic support system for girls like my Mum who came over to Liverpool. She met Dad a few weeks after she arrived when their eyes met over a repair job Dad was doing in the tenements where Mum was living and the rest is history. They fell in love and got married and had us three.'

'Whereabouts in Liverpool do you come from?' Debbie asked as she snuggled into the leather armchair sipping her steaming hot coffee.

'We were all raised in a three bed terraced house in the Dingle in Liverpool. I've noticed that when Peter does come home to Liverpool, it always coincides when Everton are playing at home. Not that he's been over that often in the past few years. He's virtually lost his Liverpool accent since he became immersed into the legal social life in London. He speaks like you.'

'I suppose you mean posh?'

'Yes. It's funny how his posh accent slips when he gets exited or angry and he reverts to his mother tongue.'

'So he supports Everton too?'

'Apart from Mum, who's an agnostic in relation to football, we all do including my three children and Siobhan's two. Even Dad's a convert. He's been in Liverpool that long he comes to the games with us and he's an honorary Blue, although I think he still has Manchester City close to his heart. You see you're born an Evertonian you're not made one.'

'I've heard of Everton but I never knew they came from Liverpool. I thought they were a team from Birmingham. It goes to show how much I really know about football. To be honest I know nothing about the game except for the fact that I thought David Beckham was gorgeous.'

'Birmingham!'

'If you supported Liverpool, I've heard of them.'

'Are you doing this to wind me up? If you are then you're succeeding.'

'Enough of football, I like the story of how your parents met. You never know when you are going to meet someone and fall in love do you? It can be in some of the most unexpected situations or locations,' Debbie said seeing for the first time David starting to relax in her company as he sprawled on the sofa with his long legs hanging over the edge.

'How about you, you did say you were going to tell me about you and your family.'

'I'm single. I was born in Oxford as Mummy's family comes from there, although I was conceived in Kenya as Daddy works for the Foreign Office and he was posted to the embassy in Nairobi at the time.'

Mockingly David said, 'Fucking hell! Mummy and Daddy!' He started to laugh. 'Do you still call them that? That's just so middle class. I couldn't imagine me doing that at home when I take Dad to the pub. I'd have the piss taken out of me something bad if I said to him, "Daddy do you want a pint?"' he said attempting a posh accent.

'Very funny. Yes I call them that and if it's alright with you Mr. Northern working class bigot, I'd like to continue to call them mummy and daddy.'

He raised his hands as if to surrender the point laughing, saying, 'Fine by me. It's my turn to be sorry.'

'That's big of you. Anyway, as I was saying, when Mummy was eight months pregnant, she wanted to make sure that she had me in England. As Daddy was still in Nairobi, it was an obvious choice for Mummy to go to Grandma's. So I was born in Oxford not Nairobi. My parents met in London, as Mummy was working as a clerk in the Foreign Office in Whitehall. Daddy had recently returned from a posting and had to pick up a file from Mummy's office. Again their eyes met and apparently Daddy kept finding excuses to search for files in Mummy's office. Eventually he picked up the courage to ask her out to dinner. She accepted and as you said, the rest is history. I was brought up all around the world, but had a boarding school education, supported by the Foreign Office. I went to Cambridge and studied politics. I got an upper second and started working for the Conservative Party in their administration, mainly working for the policy and election committees. I then got a job as parliamentary secretary to an MP and from there I joined MI5. I live in hotels in the area as I haven't had time to find a place to live yet. It's only just over four months since I moved out of Thames House after getting the liaison officer job. I've no children and only ever had one serious romance and that lasted for six years but that ended two years ago. My hobbies are drinking red wine, horse riding and listening to rock music. What's that look suppose to mean?'

'Nothing, it's just that I like all music, apart from rap and country and western, but rock's my favorite too.'

'I just thought you were thinking that a stuffy middle class bird who went to Cambridge, who worked for the Conservatives and is now an MI5 officer wouldn't like rock music.'

'Not at all,' David replied imitating Debbie's accent. 'I was smiling as the music appears to be the only thing we have in common! You're a Tory and I'm not. You went to boarding school, while I went to the local comprehensive. I have a working class background and you've had a nice middle class one. I graduated as a part time student from one of those new universities, but you're Cambridge educated. So you're a Cambridge spy eh? I'm going to have to keep an eye on you. Burgess, Philby, McLean and Blunt were all Cambridge spies weren't they? But for the other side!'

'You needn't worry about me. I know who I'm working for and I'm a loyal subject of Her Majesty like you.'

'I work for me and me mates and to get the pay check every month. I'm afraid I'm not a great royalist. Well I won't be until Roman Catholics have equal rights under the UK Constitution' David replied flippantly.

'Are you a Catholic? I didn't want to be presumptuous just because your mother's Irish.'

'That's between me and my priest. I still have uncles, aunties and cousins in Ireland mainly in the County Mayo and Sligo area. Of course it was very difficult concealing my work with the Branch from them when PIRA were active. That wasn't just for my own safety but also for the safety of my family. They knew that I was a police officer, but they thought I was simply an ordinary detective. There was a PIRA cell in Sligo, not far from one of my uncle's farm so I had to be careful. There was one operation I was involved in with the RUC and An Garda Siochana where I ended up working not far from where my family members lived. It was tempting to go and see them, but I didn't.'

Debbie's stomach gave an involuntary rumble as she was ravenous, but she was hoping that the door bell would not ring just yet as they were finally getting along together. 'There are those in MI5 who have republican sentiments and a similar background to you, but they're just as loyal as any royalists who work for our firm. George told me about when you shot those PIRA lads. That explains why you and Steve are so close.'

'Is it that obvious?'

'You're like a married couple that's been together for years. He knows you better than you think. I've been watching him. It's amazing how he anticipates not only your moods but also your actions. Just watching your team over the last couple of days, I would say you manage it, but Steve runs it. I mean that in a good way. He has the rest of the team prepared for the way you want things run.'

'My god is it only two days since you've been with us, it seems longer than that.'

'Thanks very much,' Debbie said. She laughed as she pulled herself out of the chair, 'Well it's nearly three days but a lot's happened, and that sounded like the intercom, I think our Chinese is here. Get some plates and I'll go and get it. I know you offered, but it's on me, really. You get the next meal, I'd like that.'

As Debbie left the flat to go and pick up their meals, David was looking for the crockery in the well equipped kitchen. He started to think about what Debbie had said, 'No it can't mean anything can it?' he pondered.

*　　*　　*

'Paul everything's in hand. Relax. I've been around the block too often for everything to turn into rat shit. You focus on the murder enquiry and I'll make sure we act before our targets do,' George said to Paul Edge as he rang the ISB office to update him.

'My neck's on the block on this one George. Between you and me, I'm in for the super's post. If anything goes wrong, I can kiss that and any other promotion goodbye. It's not just my temper you lot will have to suffer. If I find out that any officer has been negligent or has deliberately done anything to jeopardize my chance of promotion, my revenge will be swift and painful. Even you George could find yourself back in uniform on three shifts,' as Edge reverted to the use of threats to get what he wanted.

'Don't say that Paul, it's too tempting. The quiet life of running some uniform bobbies where the most serious thing they deal with is the odd fight or a crime report is a lot less stressful than my current role. I can see it now, gently fading into the background and then collecting my pension after having a relatively stress free few final years.'

'I know you're joking George, but I mean it. For example, I would make life for DS's with over twenty years service totally insufferable. You keep me updated, no matter what the time is. I'm sure MI5 will give you everything you need. Tell that Five bigwig that we have no more resources to deploy on this one. All this for three Al Qaeda suspects, it does seem over the top.'

'I know how it must seem from your end. I understand that you're worried that if a big one does go off that it would be your head on the block. Don't worry, I'll make sure your head stays on your shoulders and that promotion of yours will be safe. I'll speak to you later Paul.'

After George replaced the handset laughing Craig said, 'So I'm an MI5 bigwig? He's not deploying any more resources eh?'

'His terms not mine.'

'Sorry to pry George, but I've heard so much about this buffoon, I had to hear how much a prick he is for myself. He sounds a real oaf. How the hell did he get a posting to the Branch?" Craig sat down on the edge of the desk and gave George his full attention.

'It's a combination of a few things, having the right handshake. It still has some influence in the police certainly amongst the middle to senior ranking officers, and being a good rugby union player. I suppose being a bully also helps. In his recent postings he did turn things round, especially in the uniform postings, but only by bullying and intimidation. He didn't turn things round by being an inspirational leader. Although it can't be proved, he also has the black on a couple of bosses.'

'So apart from favoritism and joining that group, for aspiring middle classes, the freemasons, corruption still works in the police then George?'

'I'm afraid so. I could go on and on about him, but I don't have the time! All you need to know is that three months ago he returned to the CID and came straight into the Branch. He's not a Branch man. He's never served in it before. He's trying to run it like an area CID office. He's really out of his depth, but it looks like he's going to become the number one in the department.'

Craig patted George on the back and said, 'We can't be having that George? It's far too dangerous having an oaf who is also a loose cannon rolling around the areas of counter-terrorism and espionage.'

* * *

As Debbie and David finished their meal the intercom buzzer sounded and Debbie said, 'I'll get that. It's most probably our techies arriving. You wash the dishes. You're not sexist and think that's women's work are you?'

'No problem, with being on my own, I can also use a washing machine and iron clothes. You'd be amazed what I can do. I'm one of those new men!'

Debbie's raised her eyebrows to the ceiling, 'New man,' she thought, 'I've never seen such a real man for a long time.'

As David was in the kitchen, the two MI5 technical support officers arrived in the flat and emptied out the equipment Debbie and David brought in the luggage. They removed the rug in the living room and carefully hand-drilled small holes into the floorboards in order to place the recording devices to pick up events in the flat below. David emerged from the kitchen and all he could see was the two officers lying on the floor face down in their overalls, 'Being a new man and not a sexist pig I'm going to put the kettle on, so would you two gentlemen like a brew?'

Amanda, one of the technical support officers looked up indignantly and said, 'If you haven't noticed I'm a woman. Technical support is not a male preserve in MI5, even though it may be in the police.'

David, temporarily tongue tied with embarrassment said, 'Oh, erm, well, I, I'm sorry, it's just that in the briefing Craig said he had two technical support "men", and as both of you were lying down I couldn't tell that you were a woman. I'm sorry.'

'Don't worry it happens a lot. I know Craig's sexist, still referring to us as "lads" and "men".'

'Before I create an even bigger hole for myself, I apologize and will rephrase it, would any of you two like a brew, that is would you like a tea or a coffee?'

'Tea for me please with little milk and one sugar and coffee for Simon, white with two sugars.'

Laughing, Debbie grabbed David by the arm. 'Come on I'll give you a hand, it's better to stay out of the way while technical support do their bit.'

In the kitchen David said, 'Embarrassing that, but she does look like a fella.'

'Actually it was amusing, but not at your expense. Firstly it's taken your mind off the events earlier this evening. In the past hour I've seen a different person from the grumpy, intense and insular DS to one who is a bit more human.'

'Don't repeat that to the rest of my team, I don't want them to think I'm going soft.'

'Don't worry I won't, it's our little secret. Secrets are what you and I are used to dealing with.'

'That's true. It's been a long day and I'm tired and when I'm tired I'm prone to making mistakes.'

'Once Amanda and Simon have their kit up and running they will be monitoring events so there'll be little for us to do at the moment. Why don't you go and get your head down in the bedroom. I could do with a nap too. Don't worry I won't take the acting as a married couple too far. I'll be in the other room. If anything happens I'll wake you.'

'I had no worries on that score. I can be a gentleman when the occasion demands it.'

'Damn,' thought Debbie, 'that's all I need!'

Eleven

Wednesday 24th October
00.30 hours
Granby Row, Manchester City Centre

'I've got to go out,' Leonid said to the three Al Qaeda operatives in the living room of their flat, buttoning up his coat. 'I've just got a text message from one of my Chechen contacts. He's in the area and I'm going to meet him. I won't be long. When I get back, I'll be as quiet as I can so as not to disturb you?'

'Don't worry about keeping us up,' Ahmed said, 'with all of the activity that's been going on tonight, we're taking it in turn to stay up and keep a watch for anything else unusual that may happen outside.'

'I'll get back as soon as I can. If the meeting goes as I anticipate, I'll be out of here by tomorrow.'

'Staying with us for a couple of days more makes no difference to us. If that's what Sayfel ordered, we're more than happy with that,' Ahmed said. As Leonid walked out of the flat Ahmed looked at Aatcha and said, 'Follow him. We need to know what he's up to. If he gets back to the flat before you do, we'll find an excuse as to why you've gone out.'

'OK Zulfqar. If I see anything, I'll ring you.'

Aatcha got his coat, walked out of the flat and descended the stairs to the communal front door. He opened it slightly to see

134

Leonid walking up towards the city centre. Staying in the shadows Aatcha followed him. The closer he got into Manchester city centre, the more people there were milling about. Aatcha focused more intently on Leonid's movements to ensure he did not lose him. He followed Leonid through the city center until Leonid entered a pub in Peter Street by Manchester's Free Trade Hall.

Aatcha waited across the road from the pub entrance. He knew if he entered the pub if Leonid saw him, he could easily be compromised. As he waited he began to think of an excuse to give Leonid as to why he would be in that pub. The last thing he wanted was to make it obvious he had been following Leonid. Standing at a bus stop, he tried to make it look like he was waiting for a taxi while he thought of a solution to his dilemma. He took his mobile phone out of his jacket and rang Ahmed. When Ahmed answered his phone, Aatcha told him where he was and what he had seen, '... I don't want this Chechen fucking things up for us. I'm going to go to the pub. If it's busy, I'll sneak into a corner and I'll see who he's meeting. If I can, I'll take a picture of him and his contact and forward it onto you to check it out on our systems.'

'Good idea Ibrar. If you sense trouble get out of there straight away.'

*   *   *

'Wake up,' Debbie said, shaking David asleep on the bed.

'What, what time is it? What's happened?' he asked eyes wide open after being in a deep sleep.

'Leonid's left the flat and Aatcha's following him'

David jumped off the bed and as he had done so many times in the past, his experience of shift work and being on surveillance operations had taught him how wake-up in an instant. With Debbie, he walked into the living room of the flat where Simon and Amanda were monitoring both the events in the flat below

as well as the officers following Aatcha and Leonid. He checked
his watch and saw it was just after one o'clock in the morning.
He only had two and half hours sleep, but it was enough to take
away the edge off the tiredness he felt earlier. Debbie told David
the three Al Qaeda targets were suspicious of Leonid and as a
result Aatcha had followed Leonid, who had gone out to a pre-
arranged meeting. As David placed a set of headphones to his
ear, he heard Steve Adam's voice on the radio relaying to other
officers involved in the surveillance that Leonid was walking
towards the Duke of Wellington pub, '...Aatcha's stopped and
he's standing across the road from the pub.' Then he heard Brian
Maguire's voice, 'We're going into the pub. Steve you and your
team keep an eye on Aatcha.'

David threw the headphones down. 'We'd better get out there
and give them a hand,' he said walking out of the room.

Debbie grabbed his arm and said, 'Our brief is to wait here.
As Ahmed told Leonid, they're keeping watch and they would see
us leave. That would raise their suspicions of us two. Remember
we're supposed to have just arrived home from a holiday after a
long flight, so there'd be no reason for us to go out at this time.
Also we have our two friends who have just visited us here. So
if we go out and help Steve and the others, there's a good chance
it would blow our cover.'

David stopped, turned to Debbie and said, 'You're right but I
hate it when I can't be where the action is.'

Amanda said, 'One of their mobiles is going off, I'll try and
trace it. It's Ahmed's.'

Simon informed control they were monitoring the call
tracing it in order to get a tri-angulated location fix of the caller.
As they were talking for some time, within two minutes Simon
ascertained the caller was Aatcha and his position was in Peter
Street. He passed on to the MI5 and the ISB officers on surveillance
details of the conversation between Aatcha and Ahmed.

Listening on her headphones to the conversations taking

place in the living room in the flat below, Amanda said, 'Our Al Qaeda trio is discussing their job. They've just talked about it taking place at the weekend ... Good god, it's the airport. They're going to attack Manchester Airport.'

* * *

Brian Maguire and Gordon Bascombe entered the Duke of Wellington pub and saw Leonid standing at a crowded bar waiting to get served. As Brian waited to be served, Gordon walked past Leonid towards the toilets. As he walked through the crowded bar area, he kept saying, 'Excuse me', gently touching some people on their back. Brushing past Leonid, he used the opportunity to place a small bugging device on Leonid's coat. Seeing Gordon place the device on Leonid and continue towards the toilets, Brian telephoned the control room at the Manchester hotel and informed Craig the device had been planted on Leonid. After a couple of minutes Leonid was served. Brain watched as he took two beers back to a table when Gordon rejoined him. They watched Leonid go to a table at the far corner of the bar, where another man was sitting.

'That's Petrov. He looks nervous,' Brian said, as the man was continuously mopping his brow and rubbing his neck.

'Clearly things are not going according to plan for those two,' Gordon said, 'control should be picking up the conversation they're having by now.'

As Gordon spoke, Brian was looking around the pub when he saw Aatcha enter the pub. He elbowed Gordon and said, 'As Simon told us he would, Aatcha's just walked in. He's over there, stood by the door looking around, obviously he's looking for Leonid.'

'Looks like our Intel was right, the Al Qaeda boys are suspicious of the Russian.'

Brian turned away from where Leonid and Petrov were sitting, holding his drink and faced the bar. 'This puts the cat well and truly among the pigeons. If they have the slightest whiff that Leonid is FSB, they'll kill him.'

'And there's the chance that they'll go into hiding and that won't please our ISB friends especially that DS Hurst.'

'I agree, did you see the way he was looking at us in the briefing earlier? I wouldn't like to be on the wrong side of him.'

Nodding in agreement Gordon said, 'Hurst's the least of our worries at the moment, we've got to make sure that we don't lose Petrov or Leonid.'

'You're right. You keep an eye on Aatcha, I'll watch the Russians.'

Aatcha took out his mobile phone out pretending to make a call, waiting for the best moment to take a picture of Leonid and the man sat with him. The pub was busy and he was struggling to get a clear view of both of them. While he stood at the bar one of the bar staff asked him if he wanted a drink. 'I'll have a Coke please,' Aatcha said giving a nervous smile. As the barman walked down the bar to get him the drink, some people in front of him moved away towards a table that had just become vacant and Aatcha got a clear view of Leonid and Petrov sat at their table. Making the most of the moment, he took a picture of the two of them with his phone. Satisfied the picture was good enough, he hurriedly walked out of the pub before the barman returned with his drink.

Gordon Bascombe leaned across to Brian and said, 'Aatcha's leaving. It looks like he's got a picture of the two of them on his phone. I'll go and see where he goes and get the ISB boys to tail him, then I'll come straight back.'

*   *   *

Petrov grabbed his drink off Leonid and gulped down most of the beer in one go. As he finished drinking he banged the glass on the table and wiped his mouth with the back of his hand. In an agitated state he began to speak quickly. 'Gregor I've fucked up big time. I was disturbed when I was delivering the package. As I put the package under the rear window, a man fell through the rear door into the yard. I had to kill him as it sounded like others were coming. If I stayed, it would've been too hard to talk my way out of it. The problem is I didn't get the package back. To make matters worse, I've a feeling the man I killed was a police officer. I was in another pub earlier and I saw a news bulletin about a police officer being killed, and that was only a short distance from where I killed this man. The news bulletin said that the officer was a detective investigating thefts, but it's too much of a coincidence to be a separate incident. Did you get the package?' a worried Petrov asked Leonid.

'No. It would have looked too suspicious to the three I'm staying with if I went out to the back yard with all the activity going on. It wouldn't surprise me if it's a Special Branch officer you killed. He was most probably keeping the three I'm with under surveillance. My concern is that either Special Branch or MI5 or both have the phone and the code book. If they do, they'll know by now that I'm not the real Leonid Kashinov and that an FSB agent has killed one of their own. There'll be hell to pay as, they won't keep it from our Government for too long.'

'If they do then I'm finished.'

Leonid could see the anxiety in Petrov. Knowing that panicking at this stage could lead to mistakes being made by one or both of them, he said, 'We can work this out Uri. I'll try and contact the embassy and tell them that you had no choice but to kill the police officer.'

'This will finish me off with the FSB. Don't you realize this will deeply embarrass the Russian Government as well as the FSB? They'll have to answer difficult questions because of what I did. It'll be my head that will roll over this. You know as well as I do, the British Government as well as MI5 and MI6 will make a lot out of the incident.'

'OK, so things didn't go the way we planned. You were cornered into a situation that none of us would like to be in. You had to make a quick decision. What's done is done. We can't turn the clock back. One thing in our favor is that they don't have you yet, and maybe they've no idea who killed the officer. With luck the British security services may think it was someone else from Al Qaeda or some other Islamic fanatical group that did it. Pass me your phone. I'll put the new numbers you've got of our agents in the area into my phone so I can make arrangements to get you out of here before the British find you. We may still have time on our side. MI5 may not have decoded the information on the telephone and the codebook yet. I'll make arrangements for you to go to the Russian embassy in London. It's too noisy in here to make the calls. I'll finish my drink and go outside to see if we can get you out of here tonight.'

Felling a little calmer Petrov took a sip of his drink and said, 'Have you learnt any more about what the Chechens are up to in England?'

'Apparently there are four Chechen terrorists in the country planning to attack a meeting that's taking place in London next week between members of our government and the Russian business people living here. My man on the inside tells me the Chechens are in the Leicester area at the moment. I'll go down there tomorrow and try and find out exactly where they're hiding. You stay here. I'll make some calls and then get us another drink while we wait for them.'

*   *   *

'George, we have a problem. We're not picking up what our Russian friends are saying. Either the tag's fallen off or it's simply not working. I am not even getting any static off it,' Craig said to George Byrne at the temporary control in the hotel.

'Are your other two officers at the pub yet to assist

Gordon and Brian?'

'They're close by and can be there within seconds.' Running his fingers across his chin, Craig thought for a moment and said, 'I think this is our chance to lift both Leonid and Petrov. A point will come when they will split up. I can have Gordon and Brian lifting Leonid while my other two lift Petrov. Can you have your crew handy to support them?'

'Of course. Steve and officers are outside the pub now. The rest of Ray's team is following Aatcha. Just give me the word when you want their help.'

'Thanks George,' Craig said as he picked up the phone to call Brian Maguire.

*   *   *

'Have you found anything about the man Leonid was with?' Aatcha asked Ahmed, taking his coat off in the living room of the flat.

'Not yet,' Ahmed replied, 'I forwarded the picture to Sayfel. Although he's adamant that Leonid is who is says he is, just to be sure Sayfel has forwarded it on to our Turkish cell in Istanbul. Sayfel says he'll ask them to try and contact the Chechens to check it out. I think it's best to assume that Leonid is not who he claims to be until we hear to the contrary. We'll have to assume he's an FSB agent. If he stays with us, we've got one hell of a problem.'

Pacing up and down the room, Khan said, 'I say we kill him as soon as he gets back to the flat. We can arrange for others to get him out of the flat after we leave here to attack Manchester Airport. That will give the British security services something else to think about.'

Ahmed replied, 'Until we get confirmation from Sayfel about Leonid, I suggest we let Leonid stay with us. While he's with us we say nothing about our own plans. We can keep a close eye on him so he has no chance of contacting anyone. If we do kill him, we'll do it just before we attack the airport on Monday?'

'That's a good idea and with it being Monday, it will give us time to make the final preparations. It'll make great television. I can see it now. Once our other brothers from Oldham have got on board the two aircraft at Manchester, Ibrar and I will hit the two terminals as planned. Apart from the damage, just think of the panic it'll cause. While the police and MI5 start sifting through the wrecked terminals they'll have no idea there'll be two aircraft taking off due to explode once they're over their targets of Manchester and London. It will be like 9/11 all over again.'

Ahmed added, 'I can see the look of shock on their faces now as the planes explode over London and Manchester as well as having caused mayhem at the airport.'

*   *   *

'I'll make a call now and then I'll get us a couple more drinks,' Leonid said to Petrov. As he stood up, he placed his hand on Petrov's shoulder and said, 'Don't worry, I'll sort it out.'

'Leonid's coming over,' Gordon said to Brian as they stood at the bar.

'It looks like he's making his way of the pub. This is it,' Brian said pressing the redial button of his phone. Craig answered the call immediately and Brian said, 'Leonid's leaving now. We'll take him outside. Get the others to take Petrov. He's still at the table in the far corner on the right as you enter.'

'They've got pictures of Petrov, so they should spot him. Once you've got Leonid bring him over to the hotel and go straight to room 116. I'll be waiting for you.'

As soon as Leonid fought his way through the crowded bar area, he walked over to the door and stepped out onto the pavement followed by the two MI5 officers. Leonid walked away from the pub door with is back to the two MI5 officers. He took out his phone and dialed the number to the head of the FSB in Britain. As it started to ring he stopped walking and began to update the senior FSB officer of the situation. A sixth sense told him someone was behind him. Mid-sentence he turned round towards the entrance to the pub to see Gordon Bascombe and Brian Maguire walking towards him. He looked past them to see a man and a woman purposively enter the pub followed by three others. As Brian and Gordon were walking towards him, Leonid could tell from the look in their eyes his time as Leonid Kashinov was over. To take hold of him, Maguire raised his hand as Leonid said to the senior FSB senior officer, 'The British have got me!'

Twelve

'How long are you going to keep me here?' Leonid asked Craig in the hotel bedroom he secured to debrief the Russian agent.

'Have you got any complaints?' Craig asked.

'No, it's one of the more pleasant detention rooms I've been kept in. The coffee was good too. Obviously MI5 have quite a large entraining budget. What do you plan to do with me? You know who I am, don't you?'

'We're not sure, you might be a senior FSB agent that goes under the name Petrolsky or you might be Leonid Kashinov, a Chechen terrorist that my friends in the FSB would love to get their hands on. That's what I'm going to find out,' Craig said hearing a knock on the door. 'Brian, see who that is.'

Brian Maguire walked over to the door, placed his hand on the butt of his pistol as he slowly opened the door a few inches. He turned to Craig and said, 'It's Gordon.' He looked back at Gordon Bascombe and said,' Come in.'

Gordon walked straight over to Craig, pulled him to one side and whispered in his ear, 'The Russians have been in touch. You're needed downstairs. Jenny Richmond wants to speak to you.'

'Did she say what she wanted?'

'It looks like we've got to the let him go.'

'Did she say why?'

'There's been a parley between our government and the Russians.'

'Problems?' Leonid asked

'Nothing for you to be concerned about. I've got to disappear for a few minutes,' Craig said to Leonid, 'but my two colleagues here will look after you. If you need any more coffee or a bite to eat let them know and they'll order it for you.'

*   *   *

'It's nearly two in the morning and the bastard's not back yet,' Aatcha said cautiously lifting the blind of the living room window looking out on the street below for Leonid.

'He might have moved on,' Ahmed said.

'But his stuff is still in the bedroom. If he was moving out tonight, he would have taken it with him,' Khan said.

'If he is the Chechen fighter we were told he was, perhaps the FSB have got him,' Ahmed said.

'Or the British,' Aatcha said walking over to the coffee table in the middle of the room. He picked up the remote control for the television and turned up the volume. He beckoned the other two to come closer to him. Making sure they could hear him, Aatcha said, 'If they have, that tells me they're watching the flat. How else could they have got him? I mean that incident in the back yard earlier had Leonid very nervous.'

'Are you suggesting we go on the move again?' Khan asked.

'If that's what it takes,' Aatcha replied as Ahmed's phone began to ring.

Ahmed picked up his phone and recognized the number as Sayfel's. He walked out of the living room into the kitchen. 'Sayfel, have you anything for us?'

'I'm confirming that Leonid is who he says he is and the man Ibrar saw him with was another Chechen contact. I had one of our brothers who was in the area keep an eye on him after Ibrar left the pub and it looks like the FSB have got Leonid and his Chechen contact.'

'What happened?'

'As Leonid was leaving the pub our man saw two FSB agents grab him outside while a few others went in the pub and brought the man he met out. They were bundled into two cars that drove off at high speed. From what I can tell, MI5 and Special Branch are not onto you, it was the FSB. Look on the bright side, he's out of our hair now and we can concentrate on our own plans. I'll see you Thursday morning.'

*   *   *

'So we've got to hand him over tonight,' Craig said to Jenny Richmond who had telephoned him at the control room in the hotel from Thames House.

'Yes. We have no choice. The PM and the Home Secretary has agreed to this with the Russian ambassador, but at least they're letting us keep Petrov for now.'

'And I can't interview Leonid at all?'

'No. Politically this is sensitive enough without us interrogating one of their senior FSB agents as well.'

'He's knows so much...'

Interrupting Craig, Jenny said, 'And if the Russians are good as to their word, we'll find out what he's learnt about Al Qaeda operations in Europe. Don't forget he was with them in Turkey, right through to France and into the UK. They want to co-operate with us and in return, we've promised them help in finding the four Chechens planning to attack the summit meeting between senior Russian politicians and wealthy Russian exiles, before it happens next week. I'm in charge of that end of things, so don't spoil things for me by having a go at Leonid.'

'Have we got an ETA when Leonid's colleagues arrive at the hotel?'

'They should be with you around two thirty. It's frustrating I know, but it's out of our hands now. I'll speak to you later in the morning and I'll let you know how we get on with Petrov.'

'OK Jenny, I'll speak to you then.' Craig replaced the handset of the phone. He looked at George and said, 'Did you get the gist of that?'

'I take it you've been instructed to hand over Leonid, to the FSB?'

'I have and they'll be here around two thirty. Bugger, we can't even have a friendly chat about what he's found out about Al Qaeda.'

'But it sounds like we're keeping hold of Petrov?'

'For the time being we are. I think the only reason he's been sacrificed by the Russians is because he knows sweet FA about Al Qaeda. The Russians said they were abhorred that one of their agents killed DC King and wanted to show good will by letting us interview him about the death. The trouble is its Leonid that's got the goods we need not that bastard.'

'I take it when you say we can interview Petrov, you mean MI5 will be interviewing him.'

'No offence George, but it's better that way. We should expect the Russians to be claiming diplomatic immunity in a day or two for the bugger. If they do, that means he won't even get him charged with the murder, let alone go to court for it. I'd better go back upstairs and give our Russian friend the good news.'

*   *   *

'They're waiting for you in the hotel foyer,' George said to Craig over the phone as he stood with the two FSB agents that had come to pick up Leonid.

'Thanks George,' Craig said sitting next to Leonid in the hotel room and he terminated the call. Putting his phone back into his jacket pocket he looked at Leonid and said, 'Your colleagues have arrived and are waiting to take you back. Come with me and I'll go downstairs with you to the hotel foyer.'

'Well Craig,' Leonid said getting out of his chair, 'I thank you for your hospitality and I suppose I should thank your men for getting me out of the Al Qaeda flat. If what you told me is true, I would be dead by sunrise.'

'Seeing how you are FSB, what name shall we call you from now on?'

'Leonid. Stay with Leonid, that's my field name.'

As both men walked out of the room, Craig said, 'I'm being straight with you when I told you they were going to kill you. They had strong suspicions that you were FSB.'

'I'm grateful for that and I'll not forget what you did for me. I take it Uri's staying with you for a little longer?' Leonid said as they walked along the corridor towards the elevator.'

'I'm afraid so,' Craig said pressing the elevator call button, 'he did kill a police officer.'

'Is he staying with your officers or have you handed him over to the police?'

'He's with us for now, but eventually we'll have to hand him over to the police so they can charge him with murder.'

'That's if you get the chance, we'll have claimed diplomatic immunity for him by then. You know that don't you?' Leonid said as the doors opened and the two men walked into the elevator.

'I wouldn't expect anything else. In fact, I'd be disappointed if your embassy failed to make such an approach,' Craig pressing the button for the ground floor.

'I can assure you that once I've been debriefed by my senior officer, I'll be in touch with you over what I've learnt about Al Qaeda operations, including the details of the personnel I met and where I stayed.'

'I should hope you do seeing as how our side is going to help you stop this Chechen attack they're planning to carry out in London next week. Just before you go, I need to know one thing and I'm asking this in the spirit of co-operation, not as an interrogator. The three you were staying with, did you find out details about what it was they were up to and when they plan to do it.'

The elevator arrived at the ground floor and the doors started to open. As the two men began to walk out of the elevator, Leonid said, 'Trust me Craig, all the time I was with them they were tight lipped about what they're up to and they were careful not to leave anything about what they're up to that I could read or look at. What I can tell you is they have no explosives with them in the flat. I think they've got a couple of firearms, but I can't be sure. All I know is that a man called Sayfel is running things. He's from an Al Qaeda cell in London. Find him and you'll find the key to what's going on.'

'Thanks for that. Here's your reception committee.'

As Craig and Leonid joined George with the two FSB agents, Leonid extended his hand to Craig. As Craig shook hands, Leonid said, 'It's been nice to meet a British colleague and thank you for your hospitality. I'll contact you soon and see if I can help you.'

Still gripping Leonid's hand, Craig said, 'See to it that you do.'

Thirteen

Wednesday 25th October
07.00 hours
ISB Office, Manchester

Craig and George called a briefing at seven o'clock that morning at the temporary control for the members of MI5 and ISB teams involved in the Leonid and Al Qaeda investigation. That included a very tired Steve Adams. As David was getting himself a coffee from the table supplying tea and coffee for the officers, he saw Steve constantly yawning and got him a coffee as well. He walked over to where Steve was sitting, handed him the coffee and sat next to him. 'Christ mate, you look like shit. Here you go. I've got you a brew. Get that down your neck and you'll feel better. Now you've either been up all night or you've had about an hour's kip and you've literally got out of bed,' David said quietly in his ear.

'Thanks mate, you look good too! Do you have to be so brutally honest to your friends first thing in the morning? Don't you have any sensitivity to the less fortunate than you? Listen while you and lovely Debbie were playing happy married couples in that luxury flat, I was walking around Manchester's city centre streets until the early hours following FSB agents. I got in at three this morning and I couldn't get any kip as the baby was up all night teething. I think I got about half an hour's sleep,' Steve said yawning once more.

150

'Why don't you go back home and get your head down? I'll square it off with George.'

'Thanks but I'll be fine after a couple more of these,' Steve said raising his cup of coffee, 'and a full English breakfast that I'll grab after the briefing. Anyway Lena's looking after the baby and as she was up all night with him, I'd only disturb them if went home. Anyway, you need me here to look after you. How are you getting on with the lovely Debbie?'

'Fine. We had a good chat last night and we've got to know each other a bit better now.'

'If you ask me, she'd like to get to know you a lot better. Haven't you noticed the way she looks at you?' Steve said raising his eyebrows up and down, and smiling.

'Behave, she wouldn't give me a second glance.'

Elbowing him, Steve said, 'I'm telling you, you're in there mate. Leave it to me and I'll put my match-making skills into practice.'

'Not fucking likely, especially after the last time you and Lena tried to set me up on a blind date with that girl from Lena's workplace. She was a right fucking moose head. I'm happy with my domestic circumstances just as they are thank you very much.'

Craig and George entered the temporary control room and Craig opened the briefing. 'Thanks everyone. Can I have your attention please? We've got a lot to get through this morning as we had a very eventful night last night.'

Steve leant across to David and whispered in his ear, 'So you weren't the only one to have an eventful night.'

Craig spotted Steve whispering in David's ear and said, 'DC Adams. Have you anything you would like to share with the rest us as well as your DS?'

'No sir, sorry sir I was just telling DS Hurst how that hair dye he uses works really well for him. There's not a grey hair to be seen.' While the assembled officers laughed, David scowled at Steve.

'I'm glad to see your sense of humor hasn't left you after such a grueling night last night. To update you on the developments following last night's events, MI5 officers, supported by ISB officers lifted Leonid and his associate Petrov last night. Unfortunately, before we could find out what he had learnt about the three Al Qaeda targets we're watching, we had to hand Leonid back over to the FSB in the early hours of this morning. For those of you who were not on duty last night, he is an FSB agent and was working undercover as Leonid Kashinov. However to keep things simple we're still going to refer to him as Leonid. We've been promised by the Russians that once Leonid's senior officer has debriefed him, they will pass over to us what they have learnt about Al Qaeda operations.'

'We still have the second FSB agent, Petrov in our custody. He's with MI5 officers and so far the Russians have let us keep him while Brian Maguire and Gordon Bascombe interview him over the killing DC King yesterday evening. As much as we'd like to, we can't hand him over to our colleagues in the ISB yet. Diplomatic protocol is preventing us from doing so. Until then, MI5 will continue to interview him. I can report that he is being fully co-operative and has admitted to killing the officer.

'I can't stress enough the importance on lips being sealed on this. This information stays within the assembled company in this room. If the media get the slightest whiff there are Russian agents running around the country at this delicate stage of proceedings it will result in one almighty political scandal that will be damaging to the UK Government in particular. More so if the media find out that these Russian agents are killing British police officers.

'Debbie and the Branch officers are to stay on Ahmed, Khan and Aatcha. From intelligence received last night, Al Qaeda intend to attack Manchester Airport next Monday morning. The attack is bigger than we originally thought. According to what we picked up from the targets' conversation last night, Aatcha and Khan are going to be suicide bombers in terminals one and two of the airport. That is not the whole picture. Two more Al

Qaeda operatives from Oldham will join Aatcha and Khan at
Manchester Airport. These two from Oldham will board two
aircraft at the airport and detonate bombs while their respective
aircraft are in flight over Manchester and London. We have a
reliable MI5 source inside Al Qaeda and I contacted him just
before this briefing. He confirms the airport is their planned
attack but knew nothing of the plan to blow up any aircraft
whilst in flight. Therefore we have to find these other operatives
who will be boarding the aircraft as quickly as we can. George
has deployed ISB officers to investigate the Oldham angle of the
operation. They will be looking at those known to be members
of Al Qaeda from the area that are already in the system as well
as those suspected to be Al Qaeda and who have had associations
with Al Qaeda, no matter how remote their association has been.
It's important we leave no stone unturned as we try to find them.
Time is of the essence here. Fortunately we have an MI5 officer
working undercover with Al Qaeda. He has gone under the name
of Sayfel. He's arriving in Manchester tomorrow morning and
informs me that he's delivering final instructions to the three Al
Qaeda operatives we've been watching. I know this may come
as a surprise to the ISB officers in particular as you have been
intercepting calls between him and our three targets.'

David and Steve looked at each other. David scowled and in a
loud stage whisper said to Steve, 'Here we go again, MI5 holding
out on us. You think they'd have fucking told us last night after
Tony was murdered about this Sayfel being one of them.'

Craig heard what David said and still addressing the assembled
officers said, 'I appreciate that some of you will be frustrated
that we in MI5 didn't tell you that Sayfel was our man working
undercover with Al Qaeda. When we have someone working on
the inside, we need all the investigating officers to treat them
no differently to the main targets. We would not want his five
years work to go down the pan just because of one comment
passed at an inopportune moment to someone not involved in

the investigation. It's important we keep this information in this room. Telling you that Sayfel is one of ours at this stage, I have already broken our protocol. The events of the last twenty-four hours deemed it necessary that you all know about Sayfel being one of ours. I need you to just be as vigilant in monitoring his movements when he's in the company of our three targets. Sayfel is very important to us in MI5. He has become one of Al Qaeda's most trusted and senior operatives. This has given him the opportunity to pass on good quality intelligence that's kept us one step ahead of the buggers and prevent them from carrying out their plans. Al Qaeda has absolutely no idea that he is our man on the inside.

'Sayfel assured me there will be no activity of any significance from the three we've been watching today, so this gives us the chance to check out the airport. David Hurst, Steve Adams and Debbie Heron you will go to the airport immediately after this briefing. George has made the necessary arrangements regarding who to meet and what to do. The rest of David's team will work with Ray Baskin's team and keep Ahmed, Aatcha and Khan under close surveillance. We have a twenty-four hour window to catch our breath after the events of the last couple of days. We need to make the most of this to take stock of what we already know. If no one has any questions I suggest that you go to your posts and we get started straight away.'

As the officers present at the briefing got up to leave, David and Steve joined Debbie and George. David asked, 'What have you got for us then George?'

'I want you three to meet up with DI Tim Johnson from the ISB's Port Unit at the airport. He's expecting you. I want you to go through all of the passenger lists with him and identify any possibles that you think could be the two intending to blow up the aircraft. Once you have addresses and their descriptions let me know and I'll arrange for doors to be knocked on. Tim's already digging out details of flights going to London from Manchester as well as those aircraft where the flight path goes over London.

It's going to be a lot harder regarding the aircraft they propose to explode over Manchester as that will include most of them, but Tim told me that this is not always the case as many flights don't fly over Manchester as after they've taken off, they fly towards the Pennines to go south. That will eliminate a few flights for us as we try to work out the likely flights Al Qaeda intends to blow up over Manchester. I know this is tedious work, but it's necessary. In addition to this, when you get to the airport I want you to go around the terminals looking for likely places where Aatcha and Khan can place a bomb.'

'I thought they were going to be suicide bombers,' Steve asked.

'They might be or it might be a bomb drop. I know we'll keep them in our sight on the day, but this is just a precaution just in case we lose sight of them,' George replied.

'Why don't we simply arrest Aatcha and Khan over the weekend? Craig said their inside man is going to drop off their final instructions tomorrow and to be honest he's also likely to be dropping the equipment off they need. We've got the recorded evidence of what they've said so far and no doubt we will find out a bit more from their conversations we'll record today regarding their plans. If we do a warrant on them, add the evidence we find in the flat then we've got them,' Steve said.

'Arresting those two is a line of action we've considered, but I'm looking to cover every angle on this one just in case they bring their plans forward before we can execute a warrant. I just want to be ready for any eventuality. What if they disappear and we miss them? On top of that, we're keen to find the other two from the Oldham area that Khan talked about last night. We don't want to scare them off by arresting Aatcha and Khan too soon.' George said.

'If we do arrest Aatcha and Khan I think the other two will still go ahead with their side of the operation. I'm still puzzled as to why they plan to attack the airport. They know that security's tight at any airport nowadays. How do they think they'll get away with it?' David asked.

'I thought the same as you when I was talking to Craig earlier. He told me about some of the wonderful and ingenious ways they've been trying to conceal explosives and detonators as well as how the likes of Al Qaeda have developed equipment that could evade the security checks. Added to that, if they intend to be suicide bombers and even though they may not make it to the departure gate or even through the security checks leading to the departure lounges, there is the possibility that they may detonate their bombs at the check-in desk areas. So I need to you to look at spots in the check-in desk area that would have the maximum impact.'

'That's true, I hadn't thought about that. In other words you want us to check everything out, but mainly you want us to try and find some names of passengers we think are likely possibles?'

'That's it David.'

Debbie said, 'I've got my MI5 laptop. I'll take it with me so we can cross-check the names and details on the passenger lists with the MI5 intelligence files as well as being able to access all the ISB and SO13 intelligence systems. In addition to those sources I can also access the European Union's Schengen Information System and the FBI's and CIA's systems. I'll get Craig to arrange for the FBI and the CIA to pass on any relevant intelligence in relation to this investigation they have stored that we can't access.'

George was pleased with the positive attitude the three displayed to such a tedious task saying and said, 'That's a good idea Debbie. I want you three to make a move to the airport, as we're fast approaching peak hour traffic and I don't want you delayed getting there.'

'We're on our way boss,' Steve said, as the three began to leave the room.

As they were walking out of the hotel David looked up to the heavens and said, 'What a pig of a job. I hate airports at the best of times.'

'I know its laborious work, but I can see where George is coming from. You never know what we'll learn. We may uncover some interesting information,' Debbie said trying to keep the other two upbeat.

David laughed and said, 'We've already opened enough cans of worms on this one to last a life time. We don't need to open up anymore.'

'So what would you rather do, sit in an obs point all day bored out of your skull or go to the airport and actually do something constructive?' Debbie asked.

Steve and David looked at each other and in unison replied, 'Be bored in an obs point.' David added, 'Come Stevey, let's be positive, Debbie's right. You never know, by trawling through passenger lists we may get lucky and find the other two.'

'Actually do you know what I'd rather we all do?' Steve said, 'I suggest that we all get breakfast. I'm starved and it could be a long day once we get to the airport.'

*   *   *

At Manchester Airport David parked their car in one of the ISB car parking bays by Terminal Two and the three of them made their way to the Main ISB office at Manchester Airport where DI Tim Johnson was waiting for them. As they entered through the swipe card system, David was booking Debbie in when Tim approached them. 'Long time no see David and you Steve. Why don't you two ever call into this neck of the woods from time to time?' Tim said as he welcomed them to the Airport's ISB office.

'We would boss, but David has a terrible fear of flying. Just the smell of aviation fuel sends him over the edge. We had to blindfold on him on the way here in case he mistook us going over the speed bumps as turbulence,' Steve said.

'I see you still haven't lost that sense of humor of yours Steve?'

Tim said smiling.

'Well you have to have a sense of humor working with this miserable sod,' Steve said pointing at David.

'I am sorry,' Tim said as he caught sight of Debbie. 'You must be our MI5 liaison officer. Debbie Heron isn't it? I'm Tim Johnson,' he said extending his hand to Debbie.

Debbie shook hands with Tim gazing up at his gangly six foot four frame, 'It's, nice to meet you Tim.'

'I feel sorry for you having to put up with these two jokers. Mind you, they are two of the finest bobbies I've worked with. I've badgered George many times to get these two transferred to my team at the airport. Talking of George, he's emailed me over what we need to do. I've already got the ball rolling. A few of my staff are already looking at the passenger lists for flights taking off in the next few days. I know George said that it was likely to be Sunday or Monday when these Al Qaeda bombers are going to attack the airport, but I thought it better to be safe than sorry, so I've been pulling out flight passenger lists that take off from tomorrow.'

'Oh great, that means we can go through even more of these lists, how the hours must fly by here at the Port Unit with all these exiting jobs that you have to do,' Steve said.

'I know you two like the cut and thrust of being out there on the street but this is important stuff. Surely it beats sitting in some pokey obs spot on a damp autumn day like this is?' Tim asked.

Both David and Steve looked at each other and smiled and David replied first saying 'I couldn't think of anything finer to do sir than go through passenger flight lists.'

'Except pick my eyes out with an ice pick!' Steve said. Rubbing his hands he said, 'we're only joking boss, come on let's get started. The sooner we get stuck in, the sooner we'll get the job done.'

'I'm glad you see it that way Steve. With David and Debbie, I'm going to check all the terminals and knowing how much you love paperwork, I've already assigned you a desk. So you may as well make a start straight away. The desk is just over there,' Tim said, pointing at a desk by the window on the right of the room.

As Tim handed them both a tag, David and Debbie laughed as Steve made his way to the desk. 'You'll both have to wear these security passes. They'll give you complete access to all areas of the airport and will prevent you being unnecessarily stopped by airport security as we go around the terminals.'

* * *

As they were walking through Terminal Two's departure lounge, Debbie's eye was caught by the duty free shops. Pointing at the display at a perfume shop, she said, 'I wish these were prices of the perfumes in the high street.'

'If you want to make a purchase, I can do it for you on my staff card,' Tim said.

'I thought we were here to catch terrorists not do some shopping!' David said shaking his head.

'Oh come on David, let the girl have some fun. It could be worse. You could be checking passenger flight lists with your partner in crime back in the office. Waiting here for five minutes won't hurt,' Tim said.

'Phrases like women, shopping and five minutes are not the ones I would put together, try eternity instead of five minutes,' David said scornfully.

Debbie tapped David in the stomach with the flat of her hand and said, 'Sexist.'

'If it's this or checking flight lists, then I suppose letting Debbie have a few minutes to do some shopping won't hurt. When you say she can use your staff card, I assume it's the card you use to get the discount and not your credit card as you may regret that decision.'

While Debbie was looking through the various perfumes

with Tim, David's eye caught sight of a woman working at a leather and electrical goods store opposite the perfume shop. 'I know her,' he said to himself, running through the pictures filed in his brain of previous targets he had dealt with. He leant over to Debbie and Tim and said, 'While you're looking here, I'll go and have a look at the cameras over there.'

'See it didn't take you long to get the shopping bug,' Debbie said.

David took off his access pass to all areas. Unzipping his jacket, he placed the pass in the inside pocket of his jacket pocket and walked over to the store. As he was looking at the digital cameras in a display cabinet, the woman he recognized came over to him. 'Can I help you?'

'I'm just looking at the moment thanks.'

She turned round and with her back to David began rearranging the leather bags on the display stand behind the counter. 'There's a sale on today and if you see anything that want, I'll need to see your boarding card,' she said.

'I don't have a boarding card as I'm not flying today. I'm a guest of one of the staff at the airport who's showing me round,' David said, still looking at the cameras on display in the glass cabinet.

She stopped rearranging the bags and thinking that she might make a sale, smiled at David and said, 'That's not a problem you can use their staff card if you see anything that you fancy.'

'Is this your own store?'

'It is, why do you ask?'

David gave a coy smile and said, 'I'm nosey that's all. These cameras seem a bargain. They're much cheaper than the high street.'

'Because they're duty free, on average they're about twenty per cent cheaper.'

'I assume your business does quite well?'

'I can't complain. It's the cameras that sell the best, especially when passengers forget to bring their camera and they're going on holiday. They tend to have a carefree attitude, especially those going on holiday as they like to treat themselves. So trade can be quite brisk at times.'

'It must be a long day for you if you're in the store on your own or do you have any staff to assist you?'

She was beginning to wonder why that this man in front of her was asking so many questions. She said, 'The shop stays open twenty-four hours so I have five other girls who work for me here in Manchester, so it's not too bad. One of them is working with me this morning but she's gone for her morning break.'

'I take you live local if you have your store here at the airport?'

She smiled at him and said, 'You are nosey aren't you?'

David winked at her and said, 'Not really, I'm just trying to be polite by indulging in that old art form called conversation.'

The woman giggled and said, 'It's either that or you're trying to pick me up?'

With a smile David said, 'If I was truly free and single it would be a totally different matter, I'd not hesitate to ask a good looking woman like you out for a date.'

Trying to be coy, she pretended to move some items off the top of the counter and said, 'You're full of yourself and a cheeky bugger too, trying on the charm like that.'

'I'm just a charming bloke. Anyway you didn't answer my question, do you live local?'

'It depends if you would call living in Knutsford local. I can tell that you're not local with that accent of yours. You're from Liverpool aren't you?'

David placed the elbow of his left arm on the counter and leaned closer to her and said, 'You guessed right.'

'I go to Liverpool quite often as I have another store at John Lennon Airport. I sell exactly the same products there. If you can't make up your mind what you want today then perhaps you'd like to visit me when I'm in Liverpool. I can let you know when I'm going to be there and I'll give you a little extra discount,' she said leaning closer to David.

'There's an offer I can't refuse and to repay you I'll take you for a drink."

She stood upright and laughed. 'I knew you were trying to pick me up! What do you mean by you're not "truly single"?'

'I've being seeing this woman for a few months now, but she's trying to tie me down, you know get a house together and all that kind of stuff. Me, I just want some female company and a bit of fun if you get my meaning.'

'I get your meaning alright. Listen I'll go for a drink with you when you're properly single and there are no other female attachments. I don't like complicated relationships.'

'Who said anything about relationships?'

'I did. That's the way I like it.'

'Fair enough. So business must be doing well if you have a chain of stores?' David said trying to change the subject before the flirtation went too far.

'I wouldn't say that having two shops is a chain. So what are you doing here then if you're not flying? You said you were a guest of one of the staff here.'

'You'll have to work that out.'

'It's one of two things. You're either a company rep trying to make me buy something that I don't really want or you're a copper.'

'So, which one are you going to go for?'

Pausing for a moment, she eyed David up and down and said, 'I'd say you're a copper.'

'What makes you say that?'

'Two things, your eyes are never still, even while you're talking to me you're constantly looking round and when you lent over the display cabinet,' she pointed towards his jacket and said, 'I saw the holster and the handle of the gun that you're carrying under your jacket. It's a bit of a giveaway when you've got your jacket unzipped. That's not very undercover is it?'

'Oh shit,' David said pretending he had mistakenly left his jacket unzipped. He stood up and zipped up his jacket to just below his base of his neck.

'I knew the security status went up this morning. When I arrived at the airport we were asked to be more vigilant and report anyone acting suspicious. When you were looking at the display cabinet I saw your gun. As you were not wearing a security pass, I was about to press the alarm button under the counter.'

David took his warrant card out of his wallet and showed it to her and said, 'Don't worry, I am a police officer.'

'So have you received a tip off about something going on?'

'No, if you ask me I think it's just a case of being over cautious. We were asked to come in today to assist the regulars.'

'You wouldn't tell me if there was something expected to happen today anyway. I take it that you don't want to buy anything then?'

'Not at the moment.'

'You weren't using me as cover while you were watching someone were you? That would be quite exiting if you were.'

'No I wasn't. I am actually interested in the cameras as my brother's looking for a replacement. So if I get a chance later, when I'm on a break I'll call in and see you about getting a camera. It was nice to meet you Helen,' David said looking at her name badge on her non-existent cleavage.

'I can see you're a good detective spotting my name badge,' she said laughing, 'If you leave me your name and you come back later to buy a camera, I'll leave your details with one of the girls that work with me so they give you the discount. And perhaps we could meet up later?'

'My name's Duncan Ferguson.'

'That's a Scottish name. Are your parents Scottish?'

David laughed and said, 'Now who's being nosey? My father's the Scot in the family. So what time you do you finish? I'll meet you so we can go for that drink and get to know each other a bit better?'

'I finish up around six this evening. Will you still be here?'

'Yes. Provided nothing happens I'll meet you here at six then?'

'I'll look forward to it.'

'I'd better go before my boss catches me and bollocks me for shopping while I should be working. If it's alright with you, I'll take one of your business cards from the display here and I'll ring you to let you know if I get delayed.'

'By all means take one and ring me anyway to let me know one way or the other. Use the mobile number, it's my business phone but I'm the only one who uses it.'

'Thanks,' David said putting the business card into his wallet, 'I'll see you later.' David walked off to the rows of seats behind the store where passengers were waiting for their flight to be called. David found a seat away from the other passengers and telephoned Debbie who was still at the fragrance store with Tim.

'Where the hell have you got to? Don't just disappear on us like that. The last we saw of you, you were talking or should I say chatting up that woman who works at the leather and electrical goods store,' Debbie said angrily.

'There's no need to be jealous, in fact I never took you for the jealous type. I want you to keep an eye on that woman I was talking to. The name on her name badge is Helen Leyland and I reckon it's the name she's registered with airport security. That's her maiden name. Her real name is Helen Ikram. She's married to a Mohammed Ikram. He's the cousin of a target we were watching two months ago, just before we were assigned to watch Aatcha and his mates. I've no time to go into all of the details over the phone, but we had inputted her as an innocent associate of our target. I was never happy with that. I was suspicious of her and her husband. I think she's an Al Qaeda source working here. I need to know who she meets up with and what she gets up to. Do me a favor and keep an eye on her. If she makes a move in the next few minutes, follow her and try and catch what she says to anyone she meets up with.'

A feeling of foreboding swept through Debbie's body as a

self-imposed pressure to get this right came across her. Trying to suppress these feelings, Debbie said, 'Not a problem, I'll do that. Where will you be?'

'I'll be right behind you, watching your back. Ask Tim to come over and meet me by the seats behind Ikram's store. Don't tell him what's going on. I'll do that when I see him. He can get a bit exited and he's likely to go from blending into the background to sticking out like a sore thumb with neon signs flashing above his head saying "look at me I'm a Branch officer working undercover".'

'OK. Just make sure you cover my back.'

'Don't worry about that. I'm good at looking after my friends.'

'I'll take that as a compliment.'

'A compliment?'

'I'll tell you later. I'll send Tim over to you now,' and Debbie terminated the call. After telling Tim to meet David, she continued to browse at the items in the fragrance store as cover while she kept a watch on Ikram.

Keeping a watch on Ikram's store, David took out his mobile phone and called George. Answering the call, George said, 'David, have you something for me?'

'I have but it's not what you're expecting. Tim Johnson's been giving us a tour of the airport and you'll never guess who I've been talking to ... Helen Ikram.'

'That name rings a bell. Refresh my memory, how do we know her?'

'She cropped up in the last job we were on before this one with her husband Mohammed Ikram.'

George was silent for a moment as he tried to remember. He said, 'I'm sorry David, I've got my mind on other things at the moment, you'll have to tell me more.'

Knowing that George would most probably be under pressure trying to sort out other incoming information that he knew would be coming in thick and fast into the control room, he said, 'She's a white woman, in her early thirties that converted to Islam when she married Mohammed Ikram. Mohammed was a wealthy business man from Knutsford and he was the cousin of one of the targets we were watching who they made regular calls to.'

'That's right. I remember them now. They were recorded as innocent associates on the system, but you were never happy about that. I remember it because you used that old phrase that they "looked a bit shifty". What's she doing at the airport?'

'She owns and runs a leather and electrical store in Terminal Two and she's got another store at John Lennon Airport in Liverpool. While we were talking, I managed to get her mobile phone number. Can you do me a favour and get a fix on her mobile. I'm sure she'll have it switched on and see if you can pick up her calls. The number is zero seven zero six five six eight three nine one eight. I think she's Al Qaeda. It wouldn't surprise me if she's keeping an eye on security developments here at the airport for them. If you like, she's part of an Al Qaeda observer corps they've deployed at the airport. I've got Debbie tailing her, so I'll give you the full run down later.

'I am impressed. If you've got her number, I'm sure you've got more to tell me. I can sense some urgency in your voice, so I'll get onto that straight away. I'll call you back once I've got a fix.'

'Thanks George.'

As David terminated the call, Tim joined David and sat down in the seat next to him. 'What's going on, Debbie asked me to come and meet you here. Have you seen something suspicious?'

'That leather and electrical store is owned by a Helen Ikram. She was the woman I was talking to. You'll most probably know her as Helen Leyland. That's the name on her badge so I'm assuming she's registered with airport security as Leyland not Ikram. She and her husband had associations with a target we were looking at on our last job and I think she's part of an Al Qaeda's observer corps.'

A look of astonishment came over his face that right under his nose Al Qaeda may have been operating in the terminals and he and his officers had no knowledge of it. 'What do you mean by an observer corps?'

'I think she keeps an eye on the security arrangements as well as the security levels operating at the airport. It wouldn't surprise if she's not on her own. I think Al Qaeda have a number of sympathizers working here.'

'All under my nose and I've not seen it. Jesus, if you're right, it's something I could do without at the moment as it'll be another reason for Paul Edge to rip into me.'

'I wouldn't worry about Edge. You wouldn't have known. It was just a bit of luck that you made me stop while Debbie looked around the perfume shop. If you hadn't then I wouldn't have noticed her. I had to think hard to remember where I'd seen her before and to be honest it wasn't so much her that I remembered but her husband. I thought he was up to his neck with Al Qaeda, but at the time no one else believed me.'

'I remember that. You had one almighty row with Edge over it. You don't think she's part of the attack planned for the airport?'

'I'm not sure, but it's too much of a coincidence that she's here and the three lads we've been watching are supposed to be targeting the airport. I've just spoken to George Byrne back at our control room and he's locating a fix and tapping into her mobile. Don't worry, for the moment I asked Debbie to keep tabs on her.'

'How did you get her mobile number? I saw you talking to her, and both Debbie and I simply thought you were chatting her up.'

'I wasn't, I was being a detective and it was detective work that got me the number.'

'I knew you're good, but that's bloody marvelous. How did you get the number out of her?'

David produced the business card and said, 'I'm sorry to

disappoint you, but it was simple. I took her business card with the phone number from the display counter.'

'That was obvious I suppose.'

'My concern is who else among the staff at the airport are working with her. I'm not just talking about those working in the shops, bars and cafes. There could be ones working in security. How well do you know all the airport security staff?'

'I know them quite well, but you could be right. I'll tell the rest of the Branch officers at the airport not to trust anyone outside the office at the moment until we've identified who's working with this Ikram woman.'

'Do me a favor and go back to the office and monitor her movements on the CCTV cameras? That way it'll be easier for us to identify those she makes contact with. It would also be useful to link into our control room at the hotel we're using for this job.'

'I'll give George a ring and sort that out.'

'I don't want to step on your toes Tim, but is there any chance of Steve being relieved from his passenger flight list checking duties and sending him up to me here, and if possible a few more hands you can spare from your unit to carry out surveillance work?'

A surge of excitement came over Tim as the normal routine work at the airport took on a more serious edge to it. He said, 'I'll get Steve and a few others up here straight away. I'll make sure they bring you and Debbie covert radios. It's best if we communicate over the air rather than use the mobile phones. I'll act as SIO here working alongside George in Manchester.'

'That makes sense. I'll wait here until Steve arrives. If I see anything I'll ring you.'

'And I'll get back straight back to the office. If you have to move, be careful and I'll get back up to you as soon as.'

'Cheers Tim.'

Tim got up out of the seat and said, 'I'll give you a call once I've got back to the office.'

*   *   *

Helen Ikram was still at the counter of her store dealing with a few customers as Debbie continued to browse through the shops in the departure lounge keeping her under surveillance. Assisted by the many passengers passing the time before their flight left that provided Debbie with extra cover, from Ikram's body language, Debbie sensed Ikram was getting tense. She continuously kept looking over to a door at the far end of the departure lounge that Debbie noticed was for the use of staff only. 'She's either waiting for someone to come out of the door,' she thought, 'or she's suspicious that David was onto her and she's looking for an exit to get out quickly.' Debbie could still see David sitting behind the store out of sight of Ikram. The fact he was still there while Tim Johnson was setting up an incident room at the airport's main ISB office reassured her. The incident in London where her colleague was killed made Debbie feel fear a lot quicker than she used to. She knew she had to get over this barrier or she would be no good to anyone in the field.

Leaving the fragrance store, Debbie moved to the adjacent clothing store imitating a passenger doing some pre-flight shopping and stood by a display in the clothing store that afforded her a good view of Ikram. While watching Ikram, memories of that night in east London kept coming to the forefront of her mind. Telling herself this was an irrational fear, she continuously reassured herself that David could look after himself. The time for mulling over her fears ceased when a young woman walked to Ikram's store and walked behind the counter next to Ikram. Debbie watched as Ikram had a brief conversation with the young woman, who obviously was a shop assistant working at the store. Once they finished talking, Ikram walked out from behind the counter of her store towards the 'staff only' door. Debbie looked over to David and nodded at him. David discreetly nodded back to her. She knew that was his signal for her to follow.

Ikram was just over ten yards away when Debbie followed her towards the 'staff only' door. Having no idea what to expect when she got behind door, a chill went down her spine. Dreading that it could only lead to a small room, she was trying to think of a plausible excuse to give if Ikram challenged her. Once more the images of her dead MI5 colleague flickered in her mind. Again, she kept telling herself to stop being irrational. She was safe as was David. Ikram got to the door. Placing her hand on the door handle, she started to open it then stopped. Ikram looked behind her. Fearing she had been compromised, Debbie froze for a moment. Then much to her relief, Ikram closed the door and hurriedly walked back through the departure lounge towards one of the cafeterias at the far end of the terminal. As Debbie followed her, she glanced over to look at David. She could not see him. Trying to keep one eye on Ikram, Debbie kept looking around the terminal for him, but there was no sign of the DS. Wave after wave of panic went through her as she feared for David's safety. 'It's happened again! I've let my partner down!' she thought. Feeling her face drain of color and her heart beginning to race, she tried to quell her fears as Ikram approached a member of the serving staff at the cafeteria.

Debbie stopped walking and began to look for an empty seat from which she could see Ikram without drawing attention to herself when she felt someone lightly touch her upper arm. Nervously she jumped and turned round to see Steve standing beside her. 'You look as white as sheet. Are you alright Debs?' he asked.

'It's happened again, David's in danger. We must find him,' Debbie said so quickly, Steve hardly understood a word she said.

Seeing her shaking like a leaf, Steve said, 'What are you on about Debbie? Slow down, what is it?'

She took a deep breath to try and control the panic attack she was having and said, 'Its David, he's in danger. I've cocked up again. He's in danger I tell you.'

Looking perplexed, he said, 'Calm down. Everything's fine and

David's safe. He's behind me over to the right. I just came over to bring you a radio.' He put his arm around her and escorted her to a table at the cafeteria. 'Sit down and I'll get us a coffee while Ikram's chatting with her mate. While I get the coffees calm down and get your breath back and I'll try and listen to what she's saying.'

Shaking and blushing slightly, she said, 'Thanks Steve. I'm sorry, you must think me a right idiot?' and Debbie bit her lips as she tried to fight back her tears.

Seeing tears begin to slowly meander down her cheeks, he put a reassuring hand on her shoulder, 'Hey you big softie, it happens to us all at times. We'll talk about it later but first I'll go and see if I can hear what that Ikram woman's saying.'

'Go on, I'm fine,' she said feeling highly embarrassed about her outburst. Steve gave her a reassuring wink and smiled at her as he walked over to the counter.

As he was waiting to be served, Steve stood as close as he could to Ikram and the woman she was talking to. He could just about hear Ikram's conversation. '...I'm telling you the security's increased and the terminals are flooded with plain clothes coppers. One of them came to my shop before. He was a right cocky bastard, a typical Scouser. You know the type, giving it the charm but full of bullshit. He began chatting me up saying that he was looking for a camera for his brother. I knew he didn't want a camera as he was looking at my tits more than he was the cameras. As he bent down to look at the cameras I saw the gun he was carrying. I asked him if he was a copper and he admitted he was. These won't be any normal coppers They'll be those Special Branch ones. I haven't seen him since, but I just thought I'd let you know. I'm going to go over to Terminal One and pass the word on over there. Tell Cheryl that you need the toilet and pass the word on with the others here at Terminal Two. I'll also get over to our friends in Terminal Three and tell them.'

'Yes love?' the server asked Steve.

'Two cappuccinos please, make them large will you. Thanks love.'

The server passed the coffees to Steve. As he paid for them he just caught the end of the conversation between Ikram and the woman where Ikram said, '...I'll check with our man to see if he knows anything,' and Ikram walked off back towards her store.

Steve looked over at David, who nodded to two other ISB officers from the Port Unit to follow her. As they did so David followed the ISB officers while Steve walked over to Debbie and put the coffees on the table. 'Now get that down your neck,' Steve said passing her some sugar. Steve then radioed through to Tim, 'Ikram's going to Terminal One to tell her contacts about our presence here and then she's going to go over to Terminal Three. The woman she's just been talking to is going to go around Terminal Two to pass on the message that we're around. Debbie and I will stay and watch the woman from the cafeteria as she warns the rest of her mates about us.'

'Roger that,' Tim replied over the radio, 'Anyone to follow Ikram?'

'We're on it,' David replied.

'Just to let you know, we're monitoring all of the cameras in the three terminals,' Tim informed the rest of the officers.

Debbie went to get out of her seat and said, 'Ikram's on the move, I've got to follow her. David said I've got to stick with her.'

Steve placed his hand on hers to stop her from getting up and said 'No you don't, you'll stay right here with me. Strap on your radio and switch it on. David and some of the others are following her. Your role right now is to watch Ikram's mate over there.' Steve raised his eyes upwards as if to point with them behind him towards where the woman was standing behind the counter.

Debbie was struggling to discreetly strap on the radio as her hands were still shaking. The more she struggled, the more she cursed and became frustrated. 'I'm just bloody useless! I'm no good to anyone,' she said as tears started to flow down her cheeks.

Surprised by her behavior, Steve handed her a paper napkin and in a quiet, reassuring tone he said, 'Debs, calm down. Dry those tears, everything's fine. Actually it looks quite authentic, as people will just think that you're frightened of flying. Our job now is to keep an eye on her. As you've got the best view of her, I'm relying on you to tell me if she makes a move away from the counter. Until she does, I want you tell me what happened just before. No offence but you looked like shit, but a pretty shit if you see what I mean.'

Debbie gave a little laugh and said, 'I think that was an insult disguised as a compliment. Thanks for the coffee.'

'Stop trying to change the subject. What happened to you before?'

Steve's comforting demeanor caused Debbie to stop shaking and she began to calm down. 'I just don't think that I'm cut out for field work anymore. I just lost it like I did before,' she said

'You've got plenty of fieldwork experience. What are you on about?'

'You're partly right. It's just that I've not done any real fieldwork for about two years now.'

'That's alright. We all get rusty from time to time.'

'No, this is different. It's not about being rusty. I take it David hasn't told you what happened to me a few years ago on another job I was doing with our lot?'

Looking a bit put out that for once his closest friend had not shared information with him, he said, 'He's told me nothing about a job you were involved in a few years ago.'

'We had a chance to have a chat last night and get to know each other a little more...'

Steve smiled and interrupted Debbie saying, 'I knew it, I just knew it, you do fancy him don't you?'

Debbie remained somber and said 'I'm being serious. It's nothing to do with that! Last night we were talking about Tony King and I told him about the last time I was out in the field with

MI5. We were looking at a far right group suspected of infiltrating the main political parties. During that investigation, my partner and I followed our main targets to a pub in London. They must have guessed who we were and on the last night we followed them into the pub, they lured my partner into the gents' toilets and killed him while I sat in the bar drinking. It really shook me up. After that incident, my old boss had me inside doing intelligence analysis for just less than two years. That's what I did before I took this police liaison job. In getting the job, I never realized that I would be going back out into the field as much as I have done in the last few weeks. I've no problem passing all my annual tests and check-ups. When I know it's not for real my nerves are fine. I did well to keep my nerve on Monday when Aatcha and Leonid got back on to the train. To be honest I was shitting myself as my nerves were getting the better of me. I'm no good to the team. Just before, I really thought it was happening again and they'd got David.'

'I'm sorry Debbie. I didn't know. If I did, I wouldn't have been so flippant. Come on, chin up. You did a brilliant job on Monday. We were all impressed and you even impressed David as to how calm and professional you were. To do that takes something special. You did well just before. Ikram had no idea you were tailing her. It was only when I came up to you that I could tell something was wrong. You smiled when I said that you impressed David. You do like him don't you?'

As hard as she tried, she could not stop herself from blushing as Steve brought up the subject. She asked him, 'How do you know?'

'When you're a sex god that's a pure gift to woman kind like I am, you easily recognize the signs. Regardless of that professional exterior of yours, I've seen one or two looks you've been giving him over the last couple of days. You forget I look out for him, so while you think I'm not paying attention, I'm watching carefully how others react to him. But I've got to ask, what the hell do you see in him?'

As her cheeks returned to their normal color, she said, 'I'm not saying a word to you about what it is I like about him or why I do, as you're his best friend you'll only tell him everything. Please don't say a word as I don't think my wanting to get to know him better is being reciprocated.'

'I wouldn't be so hasty in coming to that conclusion. He's as thick as shit when it comes knowing he's turned a lady's head and secondly he's a bit preoccupied on this job at the moment. Just keep plugging away and he'll come round. I've already told him at this morning's briefing that you like him and he went all bashful. Don't give up on him just yet. Going back to what happened to you before, you stick with our team and we'll have you back in that saddle better than before.'

'You won't tell David what happened will you?'

'I won't tell him that you fancy him something rotten, but I'll have to tell him what happened to you today. If he knows, he'll make sure he doesn't put you in that situation again until you're ready. Don't worry, he'll make sure that you'll be alright and that we all help you get through this.'

Fourteen

Wednesday 25th October
17.40 hours
ISB Office, Manchester Airport

Back at the ISB's Port Unit office at Manchester Airport, David was talking to George on the phone, 'That's brilliant news George. It was great watching them hopping all over the place. We've certainly got them on the run.'

'It looks like we've uncovered a right little nest of vipers at the airport. I make that a total of eleven possible Al Qaeda operatives or sympathizers working at the three airport terminals. Of course that's just from those we know of on the day shift. There's the night shift to come on yet. We just about got a fix on the call Ikram made to her contact. He came from a location in Brent, in London. The call helped confirm it's the airport they're targeting. I'm recommending we don't make a move on the Al Qaeda observer corps as you call them, not yet anyway. We need Aatcha and Khan to believe we've stepped up security. While we've had good news on that front, it's been frustrating trying to find out who the two from Oldham are that are supposed to be going on the aircraft on Monday. We've knocked on a few doors, or I should say we've had uniform in Oldham knocking on doors under the pretext of some neighborhood policing initiative, but they found nothing really to write home about.'

'Have there been any developments at the flat in Granby Row?'

'Not really. Sayfel rang them this afternoon and spoke to Ahmed about his travel arrangements for tomorrow. Aatcha and Ahmed went into town and did some food shopping. Most of the day all they've done is watch TV.'

'So all the fun was at this end then?'

'It certainly was. Do you still have reservations about the target being the airport?'

David hesitated slightly before giving his answer. Knowing his colleagues were celebrating what had been uncovered at the airport, he plucked up the courage to go against the grain and said, 'I'm still not so sure it's the airport. When we call in later, I'll run past you my reasons why.'

'There's no need, we can discuss it in the morning. Why don't the three of you go straight home after you've finished?'

'We've got to call into the hut anyway as we've got the firm's car.'

'Fine, I'll look forward to seeing the three of you before you go off. I'll be here for a good few hours yet as there's that much intelligence to sort out. Put me onto Tim Johnson and I'll brief him as to what he should do at his end.'

After passing the phone to Tim, he sat down by Steve and Debbie and said, 'Not a bad day at the office. That was a bit of an unexpected twist finding all those Al Qaeda workers scurrying around the three terminals.'

'Well it got me out of checking passenger lists, so that was bonus. Mind you I would have much preferred to have been chancing my arm and chatting up the shop staff at the terminals like you were,' Steve said to David grinning broadly.

'What do you mean?'

'This is straight from the horse's mouth. I overheard Ikram say to the girl working at the cafeteria in Terminal Two that you were chatting her up. According to her apparently there were more than simply the cameras that were on display. She said that you were more interested at looking at her chest area! Mind you though she was spot on when she said that you were a typical Scouser, as not only were you full of yourself but that you were also full of bullshit. That was the comment where I recognized immediately who she was talking about.' Both Steve and Debbie started to laugh.

David said, 'The cheeky mare. She's a fucking liar. I wouldn't touch her with a barge pole. What she said was bullshit. I recognized her as Ikram and thought I'd test the water. So I unzipped my jacket so she'd see the Berretta in my holster and put on the charm and talk to her. I thought she might be guarded, so I tried to soften her up by chatting to her about anything under the sun. It worked, as I got a lot of information from her. Tell you what, using her business mobile to call Al Qaeda in Brent shows us that she's not really that savvy.'

'Ah, but Davey boy, Debbie and I know as well as you do that to get some information there must a trade off. What did you trade? Did she get your name and phone number?'

'No, although she asked what my name was.'

'What did you tell her?'

'I gave her the first name that came into my head. I told her that my name was Duncan Ferguson.'

Steve started laughing and said, 'You told her that you were drunken Duncan?'

Not understanding why Steve was laughing, she said, 'Who's Duncan Ferguson? Is he a police officer you both know?'

'Oh no,' Steve said, trying to stifle his laughter, 'Duncan Ferguson was Everton's centre forward until he finished playing a couple of years ago. But what makes it funny is that he was a thug on the pitch and a real piss-head. This lot loved the bones of him and I don't know why.'

David said, 'Because he played with passion and he normally scored against your lot. Anyway Ikram now thinks that I'm a Scouser with a Scottish father. All joking apart, it was a stroke of luck that I saw her. I said in the last job that her and her husband were involved with Al Qaeda didn't I Steve?'

Steve nodded remembering how David was the only one advocating to the rest of the investigative team that further enquiries should have been made on the Ikram's. 'He did. He even persuaded me to come round to his line of thinking. Most of the others, especially the bosses would have none of it. I remember David having a heated discussion in the briefings over the issue as he wanted to investigate the Ikrams further. George was not as convinced as us, but he would have given us a couple more days to follow them up. Edge put his foot down and said that his word was final. Edge then went on a rant about how too much time and money was wasted on ISB investigations. A certain DS, not a million miles away from us told Edge that he didn't know what he was talking about. What followed would put an expensive firework display to shame. If I knew beforehand how these two were going to have a go at each other, I would have sold tickets, it was that entertaining.'

'Let me guess,' Debbie said, 'In their exchange there was lots of swearing as an excess of testosterone was displayed.'

'We didn't quite get to the fight in the playground bit but let me put it this way, the rest of GMP's ISB knew exactly what they thought of each other!'

Tim had finished speaking to George and overheard the discussion the three were having and said, 'I can corroborate Steve on that one. It took less than two minutes after they had their head-to-head before we had a phone call here at the Port Unit to tell us what happened. I would love to have seen it.'

David said, 'In the past he's bullied you enough times Tim. Edge has always taken advantage of your good nature. It should be you that's the DCI not him.'

'That's a ringing endorsement when it comes from you,' Tim said.

'I'm only giving credit where credit's due Tim. It pissed many of us off how he treated you. He's jealous of your style of management because you get the best out of people. That made you a popular DI and he didn't like that, so he shafted you by shunting you over here to the airport.' David turned to Debbie and said, 'Tim was Ray Baskin's team's DI but, and correct me if I'm wrong here Tim, you didn't see eye to eye with Edge in some of his decision making and there were occasions when you politely told him so. And I mean politely.'

'Yes that's true I suppose, but I can't change. It's not in my personality to shout and bark orders out like him. I'd rather encourage others to work with me, as well as encouraging junior ranking officers to feel comfortable in expressing their ideas. You know, let others have their say without there being any recriminations. After all, we're all supposed to be a team and a manger is a conduit to running an effective team. It was clear to me that Edge lacked certain detective and managerial skills. The problem with him is that he always wants quick results that reflect well on him.'

Steve said, 'That's the trouble, you're not only clever but you're also a gentleman and to Edgey he sees being a gentleman as a sign of weakness that he can exploit.'

Basking in this moment of praise, Tim turned to Debbie and said, 'I do miss working with these two. They may come across as a pair of hardnosed uncaring bobbies but they're good for your confidence. I've enjoyed myself today. It's been like the old days. Are you three going back into Manchester now?'

David answered first and said, 'Yes. Is there anything you need us to do before we go?'

'No thanks. George briefed me as to what we have to do at this end. We've got to check the afternoon and evening shifts to see if we can uncover any more Al Qaeda sympathizers. We'll handle everything else from this end.' As David, Steve and Debbie stood up Tim shook hands with all three of them and said, 'Thanks again and when you're passing call in and see us. You're always welcome here.'

While David was shaking hands with Tim, he placed his left hand over the grip, smiled at Tim and said, 'If you need anything, especially on what we found today you know where we are and I agree with you, it was good to work together again.' The three of them left the Port Unit office and returned to their car. Although the cold late October wind hit their faces, it felt good to be out of the stuffy atmosphere of the airport.

'Do you want me to drive back?' Steve asked.

'If you want to, but I don't mind driving,' David said.

'I'll drive. I'll take us straight back to the hut. Are we going to see George before we clock off?'

David nodded and said, 'Yes. I think we could do with a bit of a check on what's been going on so we're fully up to date.'

As Steve was driving out of the car park, Debbie was reflecting on what had happened that day. She didn't know how to approach her personal anxieties with David. To break the silence in the car she said, 'You two surprise me. You really do. I got the impression that you had no time for Tim as a boss?'

'We have little time for him as a bobby as he's a flapper when he's at the sharp end, but as a boss he's like George. The difference between the two is that Tim doesn't have that ruthless streak George has,' David said.

Debbie shook her head and said, 'I felt sorry for Tim. It seems like his heart was in his job and Edge gets rid of him, not because he's incompetent but because he's a threat. It's just so silly. It doesn't make sense.'

David turned to her and said, 'That's the way the police has always been only its worse now. There are no longer any ties of the cloth that bind us to the senior ranks anymore.'

*   *   *

'Hello you three come in and take a seat. I'll order us some tea and coffee,' George said as he welcomed David, Steve and

Debbie back to the temporary control room in Manchester. George rang through to the hotel staff to send in some tea and coffee. 'Well done all three of you. I've had Tim Johnson on the phone singing your praises. Today's events certainly seem to have put that spark of enthusiasm for the job back into him. I haven't seen that in him for a while. Anyway, we've housed all eleven of the possible targets unearthed today, as well as having quite a decent personal profile on them already. It was handy having their airport work records, as we got their tax and national insurance numbers really quickly that helped us gain access to a lot of information from their personal records even down to most of their health records. Craig and I have called for reinforcements from MI5 and the ISB, and we've quite a large team of analysts going through the intelligence on these eleven matching it up to the intelligence on other ongoing investigations. I was going to ask Steve to help with that side of things, but I thought that a morning of going through flight passenger lists would be enough paperwork for him for a while.'

'Thanks boss, I appreciate that,' said a relieved Steve.

George continued and said, 'Paul Edge is like a dog with two dicks at the moment. I think he ran over to headquarters to tell Bernard Gamble personally what a good boy he's been and what he found. It was a nice touch by you David talking to Ikram and getting the ball rolling.'

'You mean Duncan don't you boss?' Steve said grinning.

'Duncan?'

'He only told her that his name was Duncan Ferguson. Claiming that it was the first name that came into his head! It fits as both can be drunken thugs.'

David was glaring at Steve as George said, 'If I remember correctly Ferguson did score a lot of goals against United. David, perhaps in future if you're going to use Everton's forward's names instead of your own you should say you're Alex Young. He was a more cultured player as I remember. Did you have a good look at possible locations where Aatcha and Khan could place their bombs or carry out a suicide attack?'

David answered first and said, 'If it's going to be a suicide attack, the check-in desks would be their best location as they don't have to go through much security. An explosion in any of the three terminals' check-in desk area would cause maximum damage, as well as maximum casualties. It would be harder for them to plant a bomb in the check-in desk area but if they got past the security it would be easier for them to plant bombs in the departure lounge area, but saying that it wouldn't be much easier. I have an issue over this point and looking round the airport only confirmed this for me. The main problem any potential bomber has to overcome is getting past the numerous security checks and points undetected. To be honest, I struggle to see how they would get through the security, especially as it's even higher after what we found today. I still go for us arresting the three of them in the morning.'

'We can't,' George said, 'MI5's undercover agent, Sayfel, arrives tomorrow and Craig wants to get him into the flat to find out exactly when and how they're going to make their attack at the airport.'

'Why not wait until he's gone and lift them then? I mean this Sayfel may bring up some equipment they need for the attack and we'll catch them bang to rights with the gear,' Steve said

'That's a possibility...' George said.

David interrupted and said, 'If we do lift them, this will give us give us more time to find out who the two from Oldham are that are supposed to be detonating bombs in the aircraft.'

'I agree. We've really come up a blind alley on that side of the investigation. It's been really frustrating. We've gone through thousands of names and we couldn't link any of them to this investigation. Hopefully, being at the highest security alert at the airport may be enough to stop them. There again, if we do as you two suggest and lift Aatcha, Ahmed and Khan as soon as we can, maybe we can get something out of them in interview,'

George said.

'Your body language doesn't match what you're saying. You know as well as I do, we're more likely to get the forecast of the winners at the next race meeting at Chester than we are of getting anything out of those three,' David said.

'True, I think any experienced interviewers would struggle to get anything out of those three. Let's not end the day downbeat. I've got time to work on finding anyone else who works in the evening and night shifts at the airport that could also have an Al Qaeda connection and that could help find the two from Oldham.'

'Would you like me to stay with you and help analyze the intelligence?' Debbie said.

'Thanks Debbie, but I'll be fine. I know where you'll be if I need you.'

Debbie looked quizzically at George, and said 'Won't it be awkward if I have to leave the flat and get back here to help you?'

'Ah,' George replied, 'obviously word didn't get through to you and Davey here. You don't have to spend any further nights at the flat pretending to be a happily married couple in Granby Row any longer. MI5 thought it best for the two techies monitoring our three targets to pretend to be the couple that lives there.'

Steve looked at David and said, 'That's a shame boss, these two were really getting into role. You should have seen them today. They looked such a lovely couple.'

Both David and Debbie felt a twinge of embarrassment at Steve's comment and both looked away from George and Steve. Sensing how the two were feeling, George said to Debbie, 'So I'm afraid it's back to your hotel room for now.'

'Ignoring Steve's poor attempt at getting a cheap laugh at my expense, I've got to say I'm a bit disappointed as it's quite a nice flat. George if you need me, just call me and I'll come down and help you. To be honest, it'll be better than looking at the four walls of a hotel bedroom,' Debbie said.

'I might just do that. However, I've a better suggestion. Why don't you go and have a well earned drink and get some rest before tomorrow?'

Debbie said, 'I'm starving. I could do with these two taking me out to a decent restaurant and join me for something to eat.'

'That's a good idea,' George said, 'Go and take this lovely lady for something to eat and a night cap. It'll do Debbie good and that's an order.'

'That's one of the best orders you ever given us. Can we put it on expenses?' Steve said. After they said their farewells to George, the three of them walked out of the hotel and Steve said, 'I'll have to take a rain check on going out with you two. Lena's been with the baby all day and as the baby's teething, I feel I should carry out some family responsibility and do a bit of fathering duties. You two go on without me.'

'Well I...' David said, remembering what Steve told him earlier about Debbie being attracted to him.

Before he could finish his sentence Steve interrupted him and said, 'Davey don't let GMP's ISB down. This young lady has a choice of going around a city that's strange to her and eating on her own or she can eat with someone that has the table manners of a pig and boring topics of conversation. So I think eating with you will be the less of the two evils.'

'Steve's right, I hate eating on my own,' Debbie said.

'OK, I'd only be eating on my own if I went home. Do you like Greek food?' David asked.

*　　　*　　　*

Sitting at a table at the rear, David and Debbie were halfway through their meal at a small Greek restaurant in Manchester city centre that David and a few of his ISB colleagues used frequently. Adorned with pictures of Cyprus, there were only half a dozen customers in the restaurant, as was usual when it was quiet, the staff tried to keep this particular table free for ISB officers when they called in to give them as much privacy as possible. To enhance the mood, traditional Greek music was playing in the background as the two were eating their meal. 'Your glass is getting empty. Shall I order some more beer for you?' Debbie asked David.

'I could do with a top up, thanks,' he said as he drank the small amount of beer remaining in his glass.

Debbie asked one of the waiters for another beer and as David appeared relaxed, she plucked up the courage to tell him what happened to her at the airport. 'I've a confession to make to you about today about my performance at the airport. It was when you asked me to keep Ikram under surveillance.'

'What about it?'

'Do you remember me telling you about that time when my MI5 colleague was killed in that pub in London?'

'Yes.'

'I panicked today and completely lost it when Ikram went to speak to the woman in the cafeteria. When she didn't go through the staff only door and turned around, at first I thought she had spotted me and I'd compromised the investigation. Then as I followed her over to the cafeteria, I couldn't see you. That was when I really lost it. I thought she'd realized I was following her and she went to the cafeteria as a ruse to get me away from you. I know this may sound silly, but I thought that others she may be working with had got you and taken you away. I was really worried about your safety and I thought once more I'd let a colleague down and that you were in danger.' Debbie's eyes started to well up with tears as she spoke. 'I just don't think I'm cut out for fieldwork anymore and that makes me useless to you or any team I work with.'

David took his clean napkin from the table and handed it over to her and said, 'Come on Debbie don't be so silly. Dry your eyes. You were good today and you were really good on Monday when we were at Huyton rail station. Going to the supermarket buying a couple of items and going on your own onto the same platform as Aatcha was a stroke of genius. Not only that, you remained very calm when Aatcha got onto the train with Leonid. We weren't expecting that and you were very professional. If it wasn't for you, we'd have lost Aatcha and Leonid. Today, you were a natural following Ikram at the airport. She never clocked you once. If anyone was at fault it was me. I should have let you know that I was still there watching your back. You're tired. You've been working long hours over the last couple of days and I've been a shit to you at times. It can't have been easy...' As David spoke, she dabbed the tears from her eyes and smiled at him. She put the napkin down on the table, leant across the table and kissed him gently on the cheek while placing her hand on his. 'What's that for?' David asked.

'Just my way of saying thank you for being so understanding. That's two compliments you've given me.'

'Two compliments?

She beamed at him and said, 'Yes, one when I went to keep an eye on Ikram. You said that you were watching my back as you do to all of "your friends". I knew then that you were starting to accept me as part of the team. That's important, especially after what I've been through. It meant a lot to me that you had faith in me. That's something I haven't had in myself for a while now. The second compliment is in you just saying how good I was on both Monday and today. I know that you don't give many compliments. You're a good man David Hurst. I saw that in you when you were with Tim Johnson. You made him a happy man today. I recognized in Tim what I've been suffering from lately and that's a lack of confidence in my own abilities. You restored some pride back in him today, just as you have done with me now.'

Feeling a little embarrassed he said, 'I can understand things like what happened to you today. You can't blame yourself for the death of your colleague. Listen shit happens and on the day it was shitty what happened to your colleague. What would have happened to Tony King if we could turn the clock back? I've asked myself that question a few times today. I most probably would have stayed at the obs point in Granby Row and let Steve and someone else go and follow Ahmed, but I can't turn the clock back. It would be wonderful if we were all blessed with the gift of knowing what happens in the future but we don't. We aren't dealing with normal criminals. We're dealing with people whose main activity involves killing people.' He looked at Debbie's remorseful smile and realized that she not only needed her confidence boosting but also to take her mind off things. 'Debbie Heron, if I need you to go on surveillance tomorrow, I'll have total confidence in you because you're good at it. You're right, we're a team and a team like ours is like a family, we look after each other. The next round of the Mezes is coming over so come on let's forget the job and enjoy the night off. After the meal, we'll go and have some fun. Are you up for that?'

'I certainly am,' Debbie said, placing her hand on David's noticing that again he never retracted it, 'and thanks.'

*　　　*　　　*

After leaving the city centre pub they went to after the restaurant, David escorted Debbie back to the hotel. As they got to the hotel entrance Debbie said, 'Do you want to come up for a night cap?'

'Thanks anyway, but I need to get my head down. I'm feeling a bit pissed and I think we're in for another heavy day at work tomorrow.'

'That's true,' Debbie said. She leant back with her arms outstretched and shouted, 'I'm not just a bit pissed. I'm very pissed.'

David put her arms down and said, 'Be quiet, we don't want anyone to get the wrong impression.'

She put her arms around his body and hugged him saying, 'So you're bothered about my reputation, I like that.'

David released her grip around his body and said, 'Come on Debs, we both need some sleep, it'll be a busy day tomorrow.'

'And I hope George doesn't ask me for any help in analyzing the intelligence tonight as I think I'm starting to see double. Thanks again for a great night and thanks for being so understanding. You made me laugh tonight. I haven't had such a good laugh for a long time. You're a lovely and special man David Hurst, don't change. I love you just the way you are.' Debbie raised herself on her toes and kissed him. 'Thanks for a great night. I'll see you in the morning.'

'You're welcome Debs. I had a great night myself. When this job's over do you fancy doing it again?'

'I'd love that,' she said. 'I'd really love that, but I'd really love you to come back to my room,' she thought. She watched David walk away as he went to look for a taxi to take him home. Just before he turned the corner, he looked back and waved to her. Debbie smiled at him and blew him a kiss. She turned and walked into the hotel foyer. Part of her was pleased that he declined to come back to her room as she thought that this was a gentlemanly thing to do, it showed her that he had respect for her. The other, more dominant side of her was disappointed that he did not.

Fifteen

Thursday 26th October
07.10 hours
ISB Office, Manchester

Nursing a hangover, David walked into the temporary control room and got himself a coffee provided for the officers attending the briefing and sat next to Steve. Grinning he looked at David. 'It's your turn to be looking a bit rough this morning. Was it a late one last night?' Steve said, winking at David and elbowing him in the ribs.

'It's not what you think. We had a good meal followed by quite a few drinks. And before you ask, yes I did escort Debbie back to the hotel but I left her at the entrance and she went to her hotel room on her own.'

Steve shook his head and said, 'You're useless at times when it comes to understanding women and recognizing the signals they give off. You're telling me she didn't come onto you?'

'No she didn't, she's a lady. We just had a good laugh and she needed it, especially after what she told me last night about nearly losing her nerve at the airport.'

'She told you then. That's good. I told her you'd understand. I thought she did a great job yesterday as well as Monday and I told her that.'

'Good, I'm glad you told her the same as me. Quiet, she's coming over to join us. Good morning Debbie,' David said as she sat down, tentatively holding a black coffee.

'Good morning boys, I'm nursing the mother of all hangovers this morning. I just hope this black coffee helps me regain my senses quickly. Steve, it's a shame you couldn't join us last night, we had a really good night,' Debbie said reflecting on what happened at the entrance to the hotel last night.

'I wish I could have, but with the baby teething I had to go home. David said that you told him what happened yesterday. So now you know that both of us rate you and I hope you'll forget it and put it behind you. I'm sure last night helped.'

'It did and this man sat next to you can be quite funny when he wants to be. Don't worry, he didn't say anything derogatory about you, in fact when your name cropped up in the conversation he was very complimentary.'

'So he should,' Steve said still winking at David

Before any more was revealed about what happened the previous night Craig, accompanied by George entered into the room and opened the briefing. 'Good morning everyone, we've a lot to cover so I'll get started. Uncovering the Al Qaeda sympathizers and operatives at Manchester Airport yesterday was quite a coup. We're still collating the intelligence we gathered on them, but I have to say it appears that a few more names have been thrown into the ring from the late and night shifts of the staff working at the airport. I must stress that not all of those whose names came into the mix have been confirmed yet as definite associates of Al Qaeda. At this stage we're not going to make any move on these individuals until we've arrested Ahmed, Khan and Aatcha. That's not going to happen until our man on the inside, Sayfel has left Manchester later today. Sayfel's arriving this morning by train from London Euston to Manchester Piccadilly. He is bringing up the final details of the attack that we believe Khan and Aatcha will be carrying out on Manchester Airport. MI5 have briefed Sayfel to meet Ahmed at Manchester Piccadilly station. The two will then go to the Granby Row flat where Sayfel will instruct

Ahmed to leave the operation telling him that his duty is done. Sayfel will arrange for a taxi to return Ahmed to his safe house, only it will be a Branch officer who will be the taxi driver. Once away from the flat and when the taxi is stationary at a red traffic light, Branch officers will arrest Ahmed. However, once Sayfel leaves Manchester this evening he is instructed to contact me and pass on the details of the attack. Any questions so far?'

George said, 'Just to add about arresting Ahmed. Ray, you and your team will conduct the surveillance and the arrest of Ahmed. DS Luke Walmsley's going to act as the taxi driver. It will be down to you to pick a good spot for the arrest. You can talk to Luke, but bear in mind that as he will only have an earpiece he won't have the ability to transmit. David Hurst and Steve Adams you can go home to rest and freshen up as you'll be interviewing Ahmed following his arrest. We anticipate you being tied up with Ahmed for at most of the afternoon into the late evening as you try to empty him out. By then we'll have plenty of evidence for you two to put to him. We must also prepare ourselves that it'll be around day three of interviewing before we get anything out of Ahmed. When he does, that will be close to when we expect Khan and Aatcha to carry out their attack on the airport. So time is important as we don't have much of it to spare.'

Craig thanked George for his input and continued his briefing. 'Debbie, you're to return to the flat above the targets' in Granby Row and assist Simon and Amanda in analyzing the intelligence we get in when Sayfel arrives. Once he leaves, you're to come straight back here. Just so that you all know, the PM and the Home Secretary have been informed of today's operation and they will be constantly updated on developments. Our aim is to prevent the buggers from carrying out their attack. Has anyone got any questions?'

David put his hand up, 'Which custody suite are we using?'

George responded first and said, 'Platt Lane. Everything will be ready for you and Steve by the time you arrive there. I've contacted the area commander at Platt Lane and she's freeing up the custody suite as we speak.'

After George finished speaking, Craig ended the briefing. 'If there is nothing else, shall we get ready for the next phase, and good luck to you all.'

Debbie lent over to David and whispered, 'I need to get some clothes and freshen up myself before I go to the flat in Granby Row, but need to get a few bits from town first. Once I've finished in town can I come back to your flat to freshen up? It's just that being at the hotel puts me too close to Craig and he'll want me at his beck and call if he knows I'm here.'

'Of course you can,' David said trying not to show his obvious pleasure at the request.

'I'll get some clothes and smellies and meet you at your flat about ten o'clock. Is that OK?'

'Fine, here's the address,' and David scribbled down his address.

'Thanks I appreciate it,' she said taking the slip of paper.

*   *   *

'Come on up Debbie,' David said answering the interconnecting phone from his flat to the communal entrance. As Debbie entered the flat, she was struck by the minimalism and tidiness. The living area was dominated by a large plasma screen television with a surround-sound system and two large black leather couches with a coffee table placed in the middle of the room. 'I've a fresh pot of coffee on the go. Do you want one before you freshen up?' David asked.

'I'd love one,' she said looking up at the original brick vaulted ceiling. 'I like these flats? Was this an old cotton mill?'

'Yes, there were hundreds of cotton mills in the Ancoats area of Manchester in the 19th and 20th century, right up to the 1970's. When I researched my family history I found that some of my ancestors worked in this actual building when it was a mill and they lived around the corner in Henry Street.'

She continued to look around the open-plan room that had a fitted kitchen against the far wall with a breakfast bar. She noticed David had added a small dining table by the breakfast bar, but she was thinking how the room was screaming out for some life and color to make it more homely. To Debbie, it simply looked like somewhere to put your head down. She could tell a single man lived here. Apart from a couple of photographs up in the hallway that obviously were his children, the flat was void of any personal touches. Keeping her thoughts to herself she said, 'You've done it up really nice.'

'Thanks.'

As she continued to look around the flat temptation got the better of Debbie. 'You can tell it's a man's flat,' she said staring at the barren wall above the fireplace.

'Is that because there's no chintz, fluffy cushions or flowery curtains and other stuff like that?'

'No it's the large plasma television, fancy leather couches and lots of stainless steel in the kitchen area. They're very much the tell tale signs that a single man lives here.'

'I like it and that's all that's important,' he said indignantly.

Annoyed that she could not keep her thoughts to herself, she said, 'Don't get me wrong, I'm not being critical, I'm just saying it looks like a typical man's place. I'm impressed how you keep it so clean and tidy. Although I prefer the eclectic look, I'm afraid I can be a bit of a scruff at times.'

Shrugging off Debbie's comments and desperate to show that he was a good host, David said, 'I'll show you to the bathroom. It's the first door on the right off the hall way. Don't worry about me, as there's an en suite in my bedroom. As both the showers are electric, it doesn't matter if they are both running at the same time. I've left you a clean towel and a toweling bathrobe out for you. It's not that I'm trying to be posh. I robbed it from a swanky hotel I stayed in during a job we were on in London a few months ago. You know what it's like. You've got to get your money's worth.' He opened a door next to the bathroom leading to the second bedroom, 'You can put your change of clothes in here and change later as this is the spare bedroom. So make yourself at home. I don't stand on any ceremony here, so if you need anything help yourself. I'm going to make myself a full cooked breakfast. Do you want one or would you like me to make you something else?'

Seeing how different David's demeanor to her was compared to three days ago, she smiled at him and said, 'Don't worry about me. I'll have whatever's going. I haven't had a proper cooked breakfast for ages. I have to keep an eye on my weight but one cooked breakfast won't hurt me.'

David looked at her. She was only five foot three, but in David's eyes she had a great figure. She was not one of those stick insect type of women that he found unattractive and in all innocence said, 'You look great just the way you are. You're not fat. You've got a great figure.' Embarrassed that he had said what he was thinking, he said, 'I'm sorry, that didn't come out right. What I meant to say was that you look lovely, great, you know there's nothing wrong...'

As David's cheeks increasingly reddened, Debbie sensed David's acute embarrassment. Knowing he was only trying to pass a compliment, she placed her right index finger on his mouth to stop him saying anything else. Debbie found it an attractive quality in David that operationally he was a hard edged confident man, but in the company of women he could be like a shy small boy. To save him further embarrassment, she leant over and kissed him on the cheek. 'That's lovely. You've boosted my ego thinking that I look great and I know that came from the heart. That's what I like about you David Hurst, you don't bullshit anyone.'

'Just so long as you don't think that I was being too forward or anything. Listen I'll get breakfast on,' David said, looking over to the kitchen as he tried to avoid any eye contact with her.

As Debbie was getting showered, David heated up the hotplate on the hob of his cooker and set the table for breakfast. This time it was breakfast for two. He did not have many visitors at the flat, and when he did they were usually when his three children stayed over. To set the table for two was a rare occurrence. The only other times he had done it was when Steve occasionally stayed over after a night out.

As he started to cook breakfast the nagging feeling he had regarding the investigation returned. He was thinking how this stage of the investigation seemed to be going all too easily when the smell of bacon cooking whetted his appetite further. David thought how unusual it was for such surveillance conscious targets to talk so openly about their plans in the place they were staying, especially so far away from the day they intended to carry out their attack. The previous day's events kept running through his mind. He came to the conclusion the Al Qaeda targets were setting a trap for them by saying their target was Manchester Airport and two aircraft in flight. 'It'd be nigh on impossible,' he thought remembering how tight the airport security was. 'They wouldn't even get into the terminal with explosives without triggering off alarms,' he thought. Running through his mind what he had seen at the airport, he convinced himself it would be impossible for two Al Qaeda operatives to board aircraft with explosives especially with the X-Ray cameras and the numerous security devices in place. It all seemed too convenient. It was all too easy. When the breakfast was cooked, David placed the food carefully on the plates.

As he put the food on the dining table, Debbie emerged from the bathroom wearing the bath robe with a towel wrapped around her wet hair. Looks like I timed that just right. It smells lovely. You can't beat the smell of bacon cooking,' she said sitting down and sniffing the aroma emanating for the cooked bacon, sausage and black pudding.

'Thanks. Now tuck in and enjoy it. You should never feel guilty about eating good food,' David said as poured some fruity sauce on his breakfast and then offered it to Debbie, 'I've put a bit of everything on, and if you don't like anything just leave it.'

'That photograph up in the hallway, are they your children?' Debbie asked as she began to eat her breakfast.

'Yes, that was taken two years ago. It's one of those professional studio jobs. They've changed a lot since then. All three of them have shot up lately.'

'It's a lovely picture. Do you see them often?'

'Mainly whenever I'm off at weekends and I try to take leave during the school holidays so they stay with me for a week at a time.'

She looked at him. His eyes showed he did not want to discuss his children. 'It looks like you've got something else on your mind,' she said.

Resting his fork on his plate, he paused for a moment and then said, 'It's the attack we're expecting Aatcha and Khan to carry out. Don't you think it's all too easy? I've never known terrorists, especially such surveillance conscious ones like those three to openly discuss their missions, even in their own accommodation. They gave details not only of what the three of them are going to do, but they also threw another two targets into the mix. From dealing with the Provo's to Al Qaeda, I've never known any experienced operatives to be so open about their plans when they think we could be listening. If they were young and inexperienced operatives, I could accept it to a degree. But our three are well-trained Al Qaeda operatives. It's not their style at all. Attacking Manchester Airport and two aircraft just doesn't seem right. Think about it. You saw the high level of security and the measures in place for yourself yesterday. I'm not dismissing it totally, but it doesn't go with how they operate. I think they're testing us to see if we're onto them. If it is a test and we lift Ahmed, it's going to be harder to find out what they're really up to as the other two will go to ground.'

Looking surprised at his analysis of the situation, she asked, 'What's made you think of this now?'

A look of consternation came over David's face. 'When you're in the middle of events, especially events like we've had in the last twenty-four hours, you can as they used to say on the old detective training courses, lose sight of the squirrel,' he said.

'What does that mean?'

'It was a saying on the detective training course. It's from a paper exercise where you're supposed to be in the woods looking for the squirrel but so much else is going on in the woods that you take your eyes off the squirrel. When you go to look at it again it's gone. The point is you lose sight of the squirrel because of other distractions in the wood. The analogy is used in relation to complex investigations where you can lose sight of what your targets are doing because you're distracted by other events that occur. In other words, we've taken our eye off the ball. Since I came home, I've been thinking how this seems all too easy. There's been that much going on from Tony's death, Petrov's arrest and Leonid being handed over to the FSB as well as yesterday's events at the airport that we've lost sight of what Ahmed, Khan and Aatcha are up to. How well do you know Craig?'

'Fairly well, we worked together for a while when I was posted to Thames House. Why do you ask?'

He swallowed a mouthful of his breakfast and said, 'I need to know if he's a lateral thinker. Does he take that step back and review what intelligence he's got and listen to others on the team?'

'From watching him work in the past I've got no reason to think otherwise, he always seems thorough. Perhaps you're being over cautious?' Debbie said helping herself to another round of toast, making the most of the fact that she could eat normally in front of him.

'Maybe, but in the last couple of days Al Qaeda have been forced to go through their own change of plans. I mean they've had to baby-sit what they originally thought was a Chechen rebel who they suspected and were right in thinking was an FSB undercover agent. Then they've had to move safe houses and when the techies came into the flat and were drilling the holes, how do we know they didn't spot any shavings that dropped onto the floor into their flat below? If they did, they'd have guessed that we could be listening to them. These three aren't impressionable youngsters recruited from the local mosque. It just doesn't fit with me that Manchester Airport and two aircraft is the target of their attack.'

She paused for a moment to comprehend David's rationale. 'I see now where you're coming from. You could be right and we could have lost sight of the squirrel. I'll give Craig a ring.'

David looked at his watch. It was a quarter past ten in the morning. 'Ahmed will be on his way to Piccadilly station by now to meet your man, Sayfel. I'll speak to George first. He'll understand where I'm coming from on this one and then he can sell it to Craig. Do you want some more coffee?' he asked picking up the coffee pot, holding it over Debbie's cup.

'Yes please. By the way breakfast was lovely. I was ready for that,' she said placing her knife and fork neatly on her plate.

David rang George and told him what he was thinking. 'If you're right we'll have fucked up big time. Get over here right away while I pass this onto Craig. Tell Debbie to come with you,' George said.

David closed his mobile phone, turned to Debbie and said, 'I suggest that you change into your clothes as soon as you can. George wants us to go and meet him and Craig straight away. I've just one quick phone call to make before we go.' David picked up the landline phone in his flat.

'Good morning, Craigmore Chambers. How can I help you?' said the voice at the other end of the phone.

'My name's David Hurst, and my brother Peter Hurst is a barrister working from your chambers. If he's there could you put me through please, its important family business.'

The operator put David through to his brother. 'David, what is it, it's not Dad is it?'

'Hi Peter. No, Dad's OK, in fact we're all aright. Is it OK to talk?'

'This all sounds very clandestine. Yes, I'm on my own. Why?'

'I don't have time to explain. I'm working on an investigation with Alistair's brother, Craig. Do me a favor and find out as much as you can about him. It doesn't matter what it is. It can be how they were as children, what they got up to at university, anything really. Trust me it's important. If he asks why you're interested, just tell him it's curiosity on your part. Don't tell him I'm working with his brother at the moment.'

'I understand. Obviously you're digging up what dirt you can find on him. From that I take it he's getting on your nerves. I'll see what I can get out of Alistair for you.'

'Thanks for that Peter. I'll ring you later when I've got more time and we can have a proper chat then. I've got to go back to work.'

As David put the receiver back, Debbie shouted out from the bedroom, 'I heard that! You've got a cheek to say that we in Five are paranoid and secretive! What was that all that about?'

David shouted back at her, 'Two can play at this game. I need to know as much about the man who is pulling the main strings of this operation. Not a word to Craig that I'm digging up what dirt I can on him. Come on, hurry up and get changed. We've to go.'

Sixteen

Thursday 26th October
10.45 hours
Temporary Control, Marriott Hotel, Manchester

'Come in and sit down both of you,' Craig said to David and Debbie as they arrived at the temporary control room. 'David, George passed on your message and I have to say it's a very interesting line of thought you've got. However we can't ignore what we have on the three Al Qaeda boys.'

David turned and faced Craig directly and said, 'I understand that Craig. What I'm suggesting is that we hold off on the arrest of Ahmed, just for today. We can continue to keep him under surveillance. Your man Sayfel's going to the flat this morning and meeting the three of them. That gives us an even stronger hand in finding out what's going on. If they are planning to strike on Sunday or Monday, it will give us a few days grace to allow us to see what they're really up to. If this is a trap, then we'll have fallen head long into it if we arrest Ahmed and they'll have the upper hand. If we do arrest Ahmed now, we'll have no real evidence to put to him and certainly nothing to charge him with. We could possibly charge him for preparing acts of terrorism, but the CPS won't go with it and you know as well as I do, it won't get past a jury, it's too thin a case.

'You also know if we arrest them now it will attract national, possibly international media interest, especially if it's released the target was the airport along with two aircraft in flight. You know we will have to release them without charge in the end, and that will result in news stories of how three innocent men were arrested and interrogated by the police and the security services. After what happened with that Ethiopian bloke the other year who was claiming asylum in Britain, we should learn our lesson. If your remember, he claimed that he was interviewed and tortured by the ISI in Pakistan with assistance from MI5 because he was suspected of being involved in an Al Qaeda terrorist plot. You know as well as I do the media and do-gooders will latch onto this. That will only mean more hard questions for the Director of MI5 and the Home Secretary and possibly the Prime Minister to answer. You also know as well as I do that if these three walk free, they and their lawyers will make more of this than what really happened. It'll be their moment in the spotlight and they will maximize the potential propaganda in discrediting us, but mainly you lot in Five. I'm sure you wouldn't really want that would you? And with you being the SIO, it'll be your neck on the block. I'm not saying that Al Qaeda targeting the airport and two aircraft is an old hat tactic that couldn't happen. My main point is this, it's so unlike experienced targets to reveal their hand like they did,' David said.

George responded first and said, 'I think David's got a point there Craig. We could hold off lifting Ahmed for a day or two. So long as we continue to have the birds in our hand we can wait a little longer before bringing them in. I'm inclined to agree with David over the evidence issue.'

'I understand your concerns David, but we cannot take any risks. I stand by my decision. There's too much to lose on this one if you're wrong and it goes off.'

'If I'm right the situation will be worse. We'll have to let Ahmed go after twenty-eight days at the most, that's if the courts let us keep him that long of course. The other two could go to ground and it'll make it more difficult to find out where they've gone. I'm not doing this to spoil anyone's personal plans. I just think they're checking us out to see if we make a move. Think how tight security is at airports. I saw it for myself yesterday. I'm sure we've scaled up the threat at the airport and right now they'll be on a very high security alert. Am I right?'

'Yes and your point is?'

Having thought he had made it perfectly clear, David took a deep breath to try and keep his annoyance at bay. 'If you listen and not instantly dismiss what I'm saying, my point is this, they're testing us. For all we know when the techies installed the equipment, shavings from the drill holes could have fallen onto the floor below and they saw it. Also they're jumpy themselves at the moment. Think about it. With the Leonid situation, along with the activity following Tony's death at the back of the flats, you'd be suspicious that the likes of the Branch and MI5 could be onto you. Put yourself in their position. Too many events have happened in such a short space of time for them to feel completely safe. It could be that Ahmed's willing to sacrifice himself. Look Craig, you're going to have Sayfel with them in a few minutes. You can get him to find out more details of what they're up to. Why not wait a little longer? What will we lose?'

Craig's class prejudices were taking over as David's Liverpool accent with a Manchester lilt started grating on him. His face reddened with anger at a lowly detective sergeant questioning the decision of a senior MI5 officer. He said, 'I'll tell you what we'll lose detective sergeant, two civilian aircraft, two airport terminals and thousands of lives when those aircraft explode over London and Manchester. If that's not enough, we'll lose credibility in the eyes of the British public and across the world, as it'll look like we can't protect our own citizens. Don't forget that's our primary role. We'll also lose politically, as the door of opportunity opens even further for direct political interference in MI5 and the Branch. Is that enough or do you want more?'

'So that's how you play it? You've made a decision and you

will stick to it regardless of whether you're right or wrong. You pompous bastard! Its detective sergeant now is it? Well I'd like you sign my notebook that you dismissed my suggestion out of hand. If it comes to a hearing, if I'm right I'll make sure you'll roast for it.'

'I will do nothing of the sort...'

'Gentlemen, some order please,' George said, 'David, go and wait for me outside? I'll join you shortly as I want to have a smoke of my pipe.'

David glared at George. 'This is not getting brushed under the carpet. All this bullshit he's spouted since yesterday that we work as a team? My arse we do,' David said as he stormed out of the room.

Debbie got up to follow him, and Craig shouted out to her, 'Stay here Debbie, let George deal with him.'

'Craig, let's calm down and look to reason,' George said to Craig in a soft reassuring tone.

'Reason! Reason you say! The jumped up little shit! My brother's right about him. David Hurst's just an arrogant bugger and an inverted snob.'

George placed his hand on Craig's arm to physically reinforce the point that he should listen. 'David Hurst is one of the finest sergeant's on my team. He might be an inverted snob, arrogant, impervious to higher-ranking officers and bad tempered, but he's intelligent and very experienced and I think he has a point. And, before you say anything, I don't say this out of loyalty to David. What difference is a day going to make? You've hardly slept, you're tired and you need a few hours rest. A period of quiet reflection is what we all need to think a little clearer. Think about it. We're still able to keep our eye on the potential airport and aircraft attack, but we could also learn more of any other potential activity that Al Qaeda could be plotting. We've worked together before and never let each other down. Why should we do so this time? There's no loss of face. In fact it would give us even greater credibility with the PM and the Home Sec. Think about it.'

*   *   *

Ahmed paid the taxi driver as Sayfel got out of the taxi and walked to the flat in Granby Row. As he entered, Sayfel was warmly greeted by Aatcha and Khan. They all sat down in the living room of the flat. For the first time there was a cordial atmosphere in the flat as Sayfel reminisced about the times they had together. Although recounting those days caused them to laugh lifting the downbeat mood Sayfel sensed when he walked into the flat. 'Enough of the old days, let's go and get something to eat. I'm hungry after that train journey,' he said.

'Good idea, we could all do with some air to clear our heads. Leave your bags here Sayfel and we'll show you around the city. How was your journey?' Aatcha asked.

'The train was busy. It was full of business people talking loudly on their mobile phones as they tried to make themselves sound more important than they really are. Then there were some children running wild around the carriage ignoring their mother's constant requests to behave. It wasn't exactly a relaxing journey.'

'Come on let's go out and you can forget about your journey as you tell us what's been going on,' Ahmed said.

*   *   *

'Control confirm. Is that abort the arrest of Ahmed?' Ray Baskin asked George Byrne over his radio.

'Affirmative, abort, abort. Stay where you are and watch for developments.' George then turned to Craig and said, 'I'm glad you reconsidered David Hurst's proposal.'

'It was the Home Secretary that swung it. He thought we

should look at the wider picture and not rush in if we don't need to. I just hope Hurst's right. Our man's there now and they're all going for a walk, so alert your troops.'

*   *   *

Walking up to Piccadilly Gardens Ahmed said, 'Moosa and Ibrar, you go off down to the right towards Market Street. Sayfel and I will go down Mosely Street. Meet up at the coffee shop in St. Anne's Square.' As Ahmed and Sayfel walked along Mosely Street, Aatcha and Khan walked across Mosely Street and off towards Market Street.

Sayfel said, 'I like Ibrar and Moosa. Neither of them are hot heads and they're reliable.'

'It was Ibrar's alertness that caused us to move from Ashton to the safe house in Granby Row. Mind you, just when we thought we were safe there was that disturbance in the back yard on Tuesday night. I still think it has something to do with Leonid. Do you still think it was the FSB at the back of the flats after Leonid?'

'I had confirmation yesterday it was the FSB. Apparently they followed Leonid to the pub on Tuesday night where they got him and the other Chechen.'

'I'm glad he's gone as we can concentrate on our own job now. I believe they've stepped up security at the airport?'

'It looks like the diversion we've set up is well in hand. We should have the security services looking the wrong way when you make your attack.'

Ahmed sighed, and said, 'I hope it works. It's stressful not knowing if we are still under surveillance.'

Feeling Ahmed's frustration, he put his arm around his shoulder to physically reinforce his point. 'I know how stressful it can be. You're getting nervous about what we've got to do as we're so close now. I need you to be strong, not just for yourself but also for Ibrar and Moosa. Just look at all of these people walking around Manchester city centre. They're all under constant surveillance and they've done nothing wrong. We're always under extra surveillance and so we play the game accordingly. We never show our hand, we never discuss operations even in our safe houses and we always keep incriminating evidence on the move. The problem for you Zulfqar is that being on the front line you don't have an overview of the operation. We've many people working for us in the background the security services aren't aware of to help you. It was a lesson I learnt when studying how the Provisional IRA conducted their campaign on the British mainland. They only had a small number carrying out the attacks and they were known on both sides of the Irish Sea, yet they were very successful. What helped them were the unsung heroes working in the background. I've a similar set up, only on a grander scale. The number of sympathizers I've recruited to our cause is greater than you realize. Although they carry out simple tasks, these tasks are vital to our success.'

'I know you're right, but another reason to be careful is Leonid. He may have talked to the FSB about us and they may have passed on what they found to the likes of MI5'

'Did he know what you were doing?'

'No, we were very careful. We didn't even give him the slightest inclination of what we've been planning.'

'There you go. I can tell you now the FSB are more likely to speak to us than they are the likes of MI5 or MI6.'

'That's true. By the way, we were happy about the script you sent us to use as a decoy just in case the British have got covert devices near the flat. I'm just hoping they've fallen for it and they expect us to attack Manchester Airport. I was worried when Moosa deviated from the script saying there would be two others from Oldham joining us who would go on two aircraft and detonate bombs over Manchester and London. I joined in to give what he said some credibility. My fear is that what we said would be too far-fetched and they may not fall for it.'

Sayfel laughed and said, 'I had no idea either when I was asked about having planes exploding over Manchester and London. Obviously Moosa got carried away, but my sources have confirmed that they believed you, so you can relax.'

'When do you have to get back?'

'Later on this afternoon. I'm using the national coach service and I'm getting off at Stoke-on-Trent where a car is waiting for me to take me back to London. Have you got everything ready at your end for your operation?'

'Yes. You did well to get that pathogen into the UK for the bombs. It's virtually impossible to get even the slightest deadly virus from establishments in the UK, in fact in all of Europe. Where did you get it from?'

'From one of the scientists working in an establishment just outside Tehran in Iran. He's a member of one of our cells there. Once he got it, it was easy to use our own network to get it over to the UK. Mind you, I wouldn't have liked to have the job of bringing it over here. It was bad enough having it in our house last night and coming up with it on the train this morning. You'll have to take great care with it.'

'We will. Trust me. Moosa's good at dealing with this type of stuff, or so he says,' Ahmed said.

Nodding in agreement Sayfel said, 'Well we both know that he's good with explosives and handling pathogens. This attack will have a great impact once the bombs go off. The north of England down to the north midlands will come to an immediate standstill. I can see it now, none of the hospitals will be able to cope as they fill up with people that have the virus' symptoms. As they struggle to find an antidote, the whole country may have to crawl on their knees to states like Iran that they've looked down on for years and beg for the antidote. Industry will grind to a halt and people will be told to stay in their homes as the Britain tries to prevent the virus from spreading. In effect the whole country will be placed under quarantine from the rest of the world.'

'It's incredible to think that all this can come from the few bombs we set off.'

'Just think of the panic running through the population as they fear contracting the virus. What you, Ibrar and Moosa will be doing will be bigger that July 2005 attack in London, even 9/11. You will be forever remembered,' Sayfel said as they moved in and out of the late morning shoppers that were oblivious to this deadly conversation.

'I know how big this is going to be and how important to our cause it is. That's what is making us so paranoid that we're constantly being watched. It's been hard to sleep lately. We're constantly expecting the door to be kicked in at any time and have a police officer shoving the end of his rifle up our noses. You're right, what we're going through is last minute nerves.'

'And that's why there are people like me here to help and support you. Don't worry, in a few days time, the three of you will be safely out of the UK.'

'You're right. Now we've got the equipment in the flat, we want to bring the attack forward. The longer we wait, the greater the chances of receiving that early morning call from MI5 or the Special Branch.' Pointing to a shop on the corner, Ahmed said, 'Here we are. This is St. Anne's Square. Here's the coffee shop, and the coffees are on me. We can have lunch as the Halal food's good here. It looks like Ibrar and Moosa are already here.'

Seventeen

Thursday 26th October
15.45 hours
Temporary Control, Marriott Hotel, Manchester

'So it's confirmed that Al Qaeda intend to attack the airport. Thanks for this George. If we stop them and get the buggers convicted it will do me no harm,' Paul Edge said with a satisfied smile on his face to George who had rung him with an abridged update on the investigation. As George updated him, he was thinking how the post of detective superintendent would be his for sure. 'George, I want you to make sure there are no fuck ups on this one and make sure the ISB get all the credit they deserve. We can make a lot of hay out of this.'

Sensing Edge's ego inflating by the second, George said, 'I'll make sure the Branch plays a successful role and that you, sorry I mean we get the credit as well as MI5. Have there been any developments on the Tony King murder investigation?'

'No. Poor old Bill Andrews is coming across nothing but brick walls at the moment. The post-mortem results are in and the cause of death was the wound to his neck, he literally had his throat cut. There must have been a scuffle though as the post mortem revealed bruising to his hands and head before he died. We'll get them George, I'm sure of that.'

'I'm sure we will boss.'

210

'Have you anything further on that Russian?'

'You mean the Chechen? He's moved out and MI5 are watching him. We're playing no further part on that side of the investigation for the moment, but MI5 are keeping us posted as to developments on that front.'

'Make sure they do George, make sure they do. If all goes well and we stop the attack on the airport and bag a couple of Chechens too, we'll come out of this smelling of roses. It'll do all of our careers no harm at all.'

'I'm glad you think that I still have a career sir,' George said sarcastically.

George's comment went over Edge's head. 'George you know as well as I do that you could have gone up a couple of ranks if you wanted to. But you've always wanted to stay at the coalface. Anyway look on the bright side. You could always get a few years extension if you wanted. You know the rules, you look after me and I'll look after you.'

George knew only too well that Paul Edge would only look after himself and make sure that he alone got the credit. 'It is nice to know that sir.'

*   *   *

Later that afternoon Hurst rubbed his hands trying to warm them up outside the static observation point opposite the flats in Granby Row. He told Steve about his conversation with Craig McDonald. 'You really do know how not to create a good impression Davey. For what it's worth I agree with you. I think they're trying to get us to look the other way by saying it's the airport they're targeting and they're planning something else,' Steve said.

'Jesus you can tell winter's on its way. It's getting really cold,' David said rubbing his hands and stamping his feet to keep his blood circulation going. 'I just hope this Sayfel comes across with the goods and finds out what they're really up to.'

'It'd save us a lot of time and heartache if he does.'

George's voice came over the radio, 'All four targets are about to leave the flat. They should be in sight shortly.'

David responded first and said, 'Khan and Aatcha have just come out, my team to follow them. Ray's team, you follow Ahmed and Sayfel.'

'Will do,' Ray replied.

As Aatcha and Khan walked out of the flats a light drizzle started to fall making the cold afternoon air even damper. As they spoke, the condensation from their breath was getting thicker. They walked up towards the city centre, passing the old Victorian warehouses that had been converted into flats or housed new businesses. David was wondering how the staff in the photography or in the design business they were passing would feel if they knew that two members of Al Qaeda were walking past their premises and looking into the windows dressed with their loud modern designs and logos. David pulled up the collar of his coat, lit a cigarette whilst offering one to Steve.

'Cheers mate. This could be interesting. It looks like Khan's got something in that plastic bag he's carrying,' Steve said to David.

'What odds that they're doing a dry run?'

'They're walking over to Market Street, you don't think they're doing some shopping do you?'

'Why have they got the bag? That's what makes me think this could be a dry run.'

David and his team followed Aatcha and Khan down Market Street where they turned right into Corporation Street. They walked past The Triangle and the Cathedral towards Victoria rail station. 'Do you think the target's Victoria station?' Steve asked.

'It could or it could be the M.E.N. Arena. Are any big names coming on at the weekend?'

'I'll check when we get back to the hut. I tell you what. A bomb going off at a sell-out concert would be a coup for them.'

David and his team followed the two targets into Victoria rail station. 'On your toes everyone. There are lots of people about on the station concourse. I don't want to lose them,' David said to the rest of his team on the radio. Looking around the station concourse he said to Steve. 'This could be where they're planning to hit. It would make a good target, especially during the morning or evening rush hour.'

As they entered the station, David and Steve split up but kept each other in sight. David stayed close to Aatcha and Khan. The two stopped and started looking around the station. So as not to draw attention to himself, David walked over to the newsagents in the station. As David informed the rest of his team of what Aatcha and Khan were doing, Khan started looking up at the train departure screen. Warning the rest of the team to keep vigilant, he said '...expect them to get a train any minute.'

David picked up a newspaper from the newsagent's stand. As he turned to pay for the paper he lost sight of the targets. Steve's voice coming through his small covert earpiece reassured him that the targets were still being monitored. 'They're moving over to the Costa Coffee shop. Khan's sitting down and Aatcha's gone to order some drinks by the look of it.'

'I'll get a coffee and get as close as I can to them,' David said over the radio to the rest of the team, 'once I've got my coffee I'll sit down and read my paper. Alex, I want you to join me. Give about five minutes after I've sat down before you do and make it look like I've been waiting for you.' David went into the coffee shop and joined the small queue while keeping a discreet eye on Aatcha. When Aatcha received his change, he joined Khan at the table outside the shop. There were around ten tables that David could see, Aatcha and Kahn were at one, and two others were occupied.

After a few minutes David was served. As he was paying for his coffee he heard Steve saying over the radio, 'It's black coffee, but the big question is whether they have enough sugar?' David gave a wry smile and after paying he sat two tables away from Aatcha and Khan. As he was putting the sugar into his coffee, Steve was on the radio again, 'I don't believe it there must be five sashes of sugar used there! I lost, I said four.' After stirring his coffee, David turned to the sports pages of his newspaper, still keeping a discreet glance at Aatcha and Khan. He read in the sports pages a small headline, 'Everton to buy new forward in January transfer window.' It had seemed like months since he went to the last game, yet it was only the previous Sunday and it was now Thursday. This had been one of the most intensive weeks of his career.

He was thinking how surreal it all had been when Alex approached him. 'I hope I haven't kept you waiting long?' she said standing in front of him.

David got out of his seat, leant over and kissed Alex on the cheek and said, 'I always have time for my favorite sister-in-law. Let me get you a coffee.' After buying her a coffee, he joined Alex and they engaged in meaningless conversation whilst keeping an eye on Aatcha and Khan.

*   *   *

'Do you think any of these people here are watching us?' Khan asked scouring the station concourse.

With a hint of caution in his voice Aatcha said, 'That old couple there are far too old to be security services. The three students over there are more interested in showing each other pictures on their I-phones and giggling.'

'How about that man and the black woman sat over there?' Khan asked, nodding towards David and Alex.

'I just heard him call her his sister-in-law. He has his back to us and she's looking at him while they're talking, so we should be OK. It seems none of the station's CCTV cameras seem to be particularly interested in us either.'

'There are two waste bins close to the platform entrances. They're the best places to drop our packages. We should get maximum impact there.'

'I agree. We can be here just after eight in the morning, come into the station use those bins as a drop and board the trains. If we set the timing devices for twenty minutes, we will be well away from here and it will difficult for them to trace it to us. Ahmed's arranging for one of our Oldham boys to buy the tickets today and he'll pick them up from him later. Tomorrow we'll come straight into the station, drop our parcels and get straight onto our trains. Drink up and I'll post this parcel in one of the bins in The Triangle. Zulfqar should be there by now to see if anyone takes an interest in it after I've dumped it. If anyone picks it up straight away, we'll know for sure we're being watched.'

*   *   *

'Have a safe journey. I'm coming down to your area soon so maybe we can catch up then?' Ahmed said to Sayfel as he was about to board the London bound bus.

'That sounds a good idea. Best of luck and God willing I'll see you soon.'

'I hope so Sayfel, I hope so. Don't be offended, but I've got lots to do if we're going to be ready for tomorrow.' The two embraced and Sayfel got onto the bus while Ahmed walked off towards Manchester Cathedral. As he was walking away, Ahmed telephoned an associate in Oldham instructing him to buy two return rail tickets, '... get one for Liverpool and one for Leeds. Make sure they're open tickets so they can be used within the next month. I'll meet you by Victoria station.' As he ended the call he walked up Exchange Square and picked a secluded seat at The Triangle. As he looked out for his Aatcha and Khan he began to eat a sandwich he had bought earlier. The drizzle had stopped but it was still cold. Being late afternoon, the whole area was busy with shoppers and the smell of the nearby cafeterias and bistros made Ahmed wish that he had something more substantial to eat than his sandwich. 'Now let's see if they're onto us. Come on Ibrar. Drop your parcel and let's see if they pick it up,' he muttered to himself.

*   *   *

'Ahmed's sitting down at The Triangle eating a sandwich. He could be waiting for your two Steve,' Ray radioed to Steve Adams and the rest of the Branch officers on the foot surveillance.

'Our two are walking past Cheetham's School of Music now, crossing Fennel Street towards The Triangle. It could be a meet. It's busy enough to hide in these crowds,' Steve relayed back to the other officers.

Steve was following Aatcha and Khan with Chris Gibbons as David and Alex made their way to the ISB office. David and Alex knew it would be too risky for them to be involved in any more foot surveillance that day just in case Aatcha and Khan recognized them. Chris was on the opposite side of the road to Steve, about ten paces behind as they followed their targets into The Triangle. Khan walked up to one of the waste bins, dropped his bag into it and carried on walking towards the Cathedral. Steve walked towards the bin when Ray barked over the radio, 'Ahmed's watching you. Leave the bin alone. I repeat do not pick up the bag, leave the bag alone.'

On hearing Ray's command, Steve carried on walking up to Exchange Square into Corporation Street towards the shops, while Chris carried on following Aatcha and Khan. As Ahmed kept his eyes fixed on the bin, Ray kept Ahmed under surveillance. After waiting for a quarter of an hour, he was satisfied no one was going to pick up the bag. He walked back to the flat believing that no one was following either Aatcha or Khan.

*   *   *

'It looks like that was a close one Steve,' David said as he, Steve, Ray Baskin, George and Debbie were debriefing that afternoon's events in George's office at the ISB department's building where George had been catching up on some paperwork.

Steve said, 'Thankfully, Ray was switched onto what was happening.'

'If we'd gone straight to the bin, we would have been well and truly blown and our three would have moved on,' Ray said.

George added, 'I agree, it was nice work Ray. What do you think they were up to?'

David responded first saying, 'I think their target is Victoria rail station.'

'Why the station?' George asked.

'They were sat at the station's coffee shop for a good fifteen minutes, looking around and nodding their heads to different locations on the concourse. To be honest, the station makes a good target. If they strike either in the morning between eight and nine o'clock or in the evening from four to about half six, the concourse is heaving with commuters. A hit at those times would maximize the number of casualties,' David said.

Debbie joined the discussion and said, 'Added to that I think it's going to be a bomb plant rather than a suicide attack.'

'What makes you think that Debbie?' George asked.

'I've not seen suicide bombers carrying out a reccie of where they intend to attack at a station concourse for fifteen minutes before. If it's going to be a suicide attack, all they need to familiarize themselves with are the entrances to the venue of the attack and in this case where the platforms are. That would only take a few minutes to do at, most.'

'A good point Debbie any other thoughts?' George asked the others.

'As these three are highly trained and experienced, I can't see

Al Qaeda sacrificing these three that easily,' Ray said.

'True,' David said, 'that makes a lot of sense. They might be more confident in making their attack if they think we're not onto them. I go with Ray, it looks like the target is Victoria station and it's as both he and Debbie think, it's going to be a bomb plant. I have this nagging question running through my mind and it may sound strange...'

'Nothing sounds strange, go on,' George said encouraging David.

'I don't think they're planning a single strike. I know there's a potential for a high loss of life by just having the one attack at Victoria, but it's...'

Steve broke his silence and interrupted David saying, 'It could be a triple or quadruple strike. It depends on how many of the three are involved, but personally I think Ahmed's the controller, so I would go with a triple strike. They could be planting the bombs with a timer at Victoria. Then they get on separate trains. You can access Liverpool to the west of Victoria and then Leeds or York, or even Newcastle to the east. While there's panic going on in Manchester, an hour later one goes off in Liverpool. Then while everyone's attention is focused on Liverpool as well as Manchester, another one goes off in Newcastle. The potential can be even greater if they start travelling around the rail network.'

George nodded his head in agreement. 'I suggest you get back into the field and at seven this evening you all return to have a briefing. That includes you Steve. We need the rest of the team to keep an eye on Ahmed, Aatcha and Khan at the flat,' he said.

Steve nodded his confirmation and they all got up and began to leave George's office. David was the last to leave. His hand was still holding the door handle when he looked towards Steve and Debbie. 'Give me a few minutes. I just want to check something with the governor,' he said. David closed the door and turned to George, 'What does Edge know of our operation so far?'

'Only what is nice to know. He's still not on the need to

know list yet. Five made that very clear. So far I've only fed him snippets and lies. It goes against the grain to keep one of our own in the dark, even if it is Edge, but needs must,' George said.

Relieved that Edge would be out of the way for the rest of the investigation David said, 'I take it they're Craig MacDonald's orders?'

'They are.'

'What does Edge know about Tony's murder?'

'He still thinks it was an unfortunate accident. He's no idea what really happened. Also he thinks Al Qaeda is targeting the airport. That suits us, as he keeps pestering the likes of Tim Johnson at the Port Unit telling them to make sure that the security at the airport is at maximum alert.'

'I take it Five want to keep it that way?'

'That's right and it stays that way until Craig says otherwise or some unexpected events militate that Edge be told what's really going on. If anything unexpected does go down, he'll go ballistic. Craig's totally aware of that, but it's the fallout and what he'll do to some of us when this operation's over that bothers me.'

'I know what you mean. But look on the bright side George. If we're successful he'll be able to milk it for all it's worth. It might even get him promoted!'

George shook his head at the thought and said, 'God forbid that happens but you're right. I'm not bothered who gets the glory so long as the job gets done, but there are times it really pisses me off when the likes of Edge go on to others, especially senior ranking officers about how they personally deterred attacks and they don't give the likes of you and me any credit at all.'

'I don't give a shit who gets the credit, all I'm bothered about is that I get paid at the end of the month. When that stops, then I'll start to complain.'

'I wish I could adopt your outlook on life. You're lucky. You don't have to deal with the Edges of this world as often as I do. I envy you at times, I really do' George said, wearily getting out of his seat. Working long hours over last few days was starting to take its toll out of him.

As George struggled to get out of his seat, David could see the job was catching up on him. His former DS was no longer the lithe and athletic figure that nurtured David when he was a junior detective. David said, 'It could be an advantage having Edge thinking the airport's the target. You know what he's like. He'll make sure security at the airport is tighter than ever and that'll get back to Al Qaeda. On top of that, we know Sayfel brought the equipment our three targets need with him from London today. They don't do that simply to have the stuff lying there dormant for too long. They know the longer it's with them, the more likely it is they'll get an early morning call from us and we find the explosives. I think the end of this investigation is going to be sooner than we anticipated, it could even be tomorrow.'

George smiled at David and said 'I agree. Fortunately we're prepared should they strike tomorrow. After you've finished today, I want you to get your head down this evening ready for an early start.'

'Will do George but what about you? You look shattered. I know you've been putting in more hours than the rest of us and you're not as young as you used to be.'

George looked at David for a moment and with a forced laugh said, 'You cheeky bugger. I can still give you a run for your money any day.'

'Don't take it the wrong way George, I can see that you're knackered and I worry about you.'

George was taken aback at this show of concern and said 'I've told you, there's no need to worry about me.'

'I do though. I mean just think what the bosses would do to me if anything happened to you.'

George laughed and said, 'That's more like it, for a moment there I thought you were genuinely concerned.'

'But I am George. I don't want you worrying unnecessarily. I just want you to know that if anything happens to you, I'll be right behind you. You know you have mine and the team's support.'

Still smiling George replied, 'I know and I'm grateful. Now get out and earn that money the public pay their taxes for.'

Eighteen

When the coach left Manchester city centre and was heading towards the motorway, Sayfel took out his mobile phone to text his MI5 controller:

'Looks like Manchester Airport next Monday pm, S'

'That should keep him off my back for a couple of days,' he thought. He then took out a second mobile phone and sent the following text to Leonid:

'L, is all ok for CH'n job? S'

'That's everyone happy for the moment,' he said to himself sitting back in his seat and closing his eyes to have a nap before the coach reached Stoke-on-Trent.

*   *   *

'George, I'm glad you're here,' Craig said to George as he walked into the control room.

'That tells me something's happened?' George asked.

'It certainly has,' Craig said excitedly. 'The FSB have in touch with Thames House. As we expected, they want to do a deal with us over Petrov. They've passed on intelligence the Chechens' attack is going to be at a meeting taking place between three

222

prominent Russian businessmen domiciled in the UK along with a couple of others from France and a Russian Government delegation next week. Apparently the Chechens intend to blow the buggers to kingdom come. Of course that will also mean British casualties if they succeed. In order to maintain good diplomatic relations and they claim for humanitarian reasons, the FSB felt obliged to inform us of everything they know and that includes what our friend Leonid learnt of Al Qaeda operations during his time undercover with them. In return, they want Petrov released straight away so they can return him to Russia. Our response was that more negotiations need to take place before that happens. We suggested that Petrov face trial for manslaughter where he pleads guilty and after a few years of Her Majesty's hospitality, he goes back to Russia to serve out the rest of his sentence so his family could visit him and so on. Of course we're not bothered what they do once he's returned to Russia.'

'Have we had a response?'

'They said that it would be unfortunate if the British press found out that a Special Branch officer was murdered and the British security services and senior British Government politicians lied about the incident not only to the British public but to chief police officers. You can imagine the furor that would follow such a revelation. The repercussions of that coming out are just not worth thinking about.'

'So what have Thames House suggested we do?'

'We need more details of the Chechen operation before we can make any positive moves and the Russians know this. It looks like Tony King's murder is going to have to remain unsolved and lie on file. If in the meantime we foil the Chechen attack, that's the only win-win situation we have at the moment. The only problem we have at the moment is they have no idea of the current location of the four Chechens they believe are going to make the attack.'

George became perplexed as he realized he would have

to keep this information from the ISB officers involved in the investigation and said, 'I take it I can't tell my lot of these developments.'

'Too damn right you can't George, not when you have hot heads like Hurst in your team. This would be the sort of thing that would tip them over the edge, especially over the death of their colleague. It's a dirty game we play. We knew that we joined up.'

Trying to temper Craig's excitement, George said, 'The only trouble is that when one of your own is killed, the game gets that bit dirtier. It'll be hard to keep this from David's team. They're such a close knit unit. That unit includes me, as more often than not they turn to me to deal with the politics and look after them.'

'You have to stay tight lipped on this one George.'

'Have you told Debbie?'

'Not yet.'

'I suggest you don't. I know she's one of yours, but she's getting on well with David's team.'

Craig raised an eyebrow realizing that George's suggestion had a hint of gossip about it. 'Are you saying that she's getting on well with David in particular? I thought as much,' Craig said tapping his nose, 'this old nose can sense trouble and it's never let me down yet.'

'Not particularly, unless you know something I don't. I just know she's built up a good bond with the team over the last couple of days. She's an excellent liaison officer. She's a credit to you Craig.'

'While your compliments towards my staff are always welcome, my concern is any off duty liaisons they have. It happens sometimes, a girl from her background falls for a bit of rough. I believe they went out for a meal and a few drinks last night. I wonder if it led to more, such as action in the bedroom department.'

George frowned at Craig. 'If you're intimating those two have something going on between them of an intimate nature, I can assure you, I've no evidence of that. In fact David's done nothing but constantly battle with her. Anyway Steve Adams was with them last night.'

Craig started laughing and said, 'I think your sources have let you down. When my techies arrived at the flat on Tuesday night, Debbie and Hurst had just finished a meal they had together in the flat. To the techies it looked like they were playing more than happy families. Added to that, Debbie told me that she had a good chat with Hurst that night and that she had got to know him a little better. Then last night Adams actually went home while those two went out for a meal together and both got on very well according to Debbie. In fact, I saw them return to the hotel last night. I have to say it all looked very cozy, very cozy indeed.'

'I'm sure you've got the wrong end of the stick. It was me that ordered them to go out and let their hair down for a few hours after they had worked so hard yesterday at the airport. So what if they're getting on well in their private lives?'

'It causes problems during an investigation. I'm not saying there's anything going on between them yet, but she wants there to be. I can sense this sort of thing. We can't trust Debbie. If I tell her what's happening, she'll try to get round Hurst and feel obliged to tell him. Good thinking there George, I'll also hide it from her.'

'Funny, I thought you had a soft spot for her. Actually what I mean is, I got the feeling you fancied her?'

'Who wouldn't? I mean she is a well bred piece of skirt that brightens up the place. Like many others who may have wishful thinking in that direction, my concern is that she doesn't lose her effectiveness as an MI5 officer by falling for Hurst. You understand don't you?'

Annoyed that he could not get through to Craig, he said, 'Only too well!' George changed the subject. 'Have you heard anything from Sayfel yet?'

'I got a text message from him in the last hour.' Looking smug, he said, 'It looks like your boy Hurst got it wrong. According to

Sayfel, our Al Qaeda friends' target is the airport and the attack is planned for Monday. I think we should concentrate our efforts towards the airport. I knew Hurst's thinking was fanciful. I'm thinking that we should be planning hitting these buggers on Sunday morning at the flat. We should catch them carrying out their final preparations and that includes catching them with the explosives. I'd like you to have most of your officers concentrating on trying to find the two Al Qaeda operatives from Oldham that plan to detonate explosives on the flights over London and Manchester over the next couple of days.'

'I can allocate a few more resources, but you shouldn't dismiss David Hurst's suggestion out of hand just because of what your man on the inside has told you. How reliable is he?'

'Don't you start to question me as well! Who would you rather believe a hot headed philistine of a DS or a highly trained MI5 officer?'

'Don't press me on that one Craig. I think you know the answer to that.'

'Sayfel's been working on the inside of Al Qaeda for about five years now. Admittedly, what he's passed on lately has been a bit patchy. I have confidence in the intelligence he's passing on and I still think the airport is the real target.'

'I'm not saying it isn't, but this afternoon's events also suggest they could be intending attack the rail stations. For all we know, Al Qaeda could be getting suspicious of Sayfel being one of your boys and they've been feeding him the same information as they have us. May I suggest we consider both options equally? David Hurst thinks if they do attack the rail station, it will take place in the next day or two. You can't disregard that suggestion. Your man brought the explosives today. They'll know if they kept them over the weekend until Monday they're running the risk of a knock on the door from us. Even to me that suggests they've brought forward the date of their attack.'

Craig rubbed his forehead as he thought about what George

had said. 'Fair comment, and looking at all of the intelligence I agree that nothing will be lost if we consider the attack as being either the rail station or the airport in the next day or two. You do have a point over them having the explosives in the flat. They wouldn't want them to be there for too long.'

*   *   *

As the seven o'clock briefing came to an end, Craig summed up what had been discussed, 'I think we're getting on top of this one. It's been excellent work by all of you so far. Once I have any more information from Sayfel that's relevant, I will get it out to all of you as soon as I can.'

They got up to leave and George called David and Ray over to him. 'I just need the surveillance rosters from you. I'm bringing in half of D team to assist us, as I think we're close to the end on this one. I want us to be ready for the roles the team will be carrying out after the arrests. David, you will be senior interviewing officer and I need you and Steve as one interviewing team, so I want you to come up with three more interviewing teams. Ray, I need you and your team to be conducting the searches of all of the premises they've been using. Don't worry about the authorizations, I'm going to apply for them this evening and they'll be ready for you when you come in tomorrow morning. I suggest that you two and the officers involved in the interviewing don't put yourselves down for night duties so you'll be fresh in the morning.'

*   *   *

David entered his flat, switched the lights on, took off his coat and kicked his shoes off. It was just after nine that evening. Feeling tired, he walked over to the large couch and flopped down. 'I'm buggered,' he thought. For the next few seconds he closed his eyes and enjoyed the silence. He decided to relax that evening, call for a take away, put his feet up and try to switch off for a few hours watching some meaningless television when his mobile phone started ringing. 'Bastards, can't they leave me alone for just on fucking minute,' he said picking it up to see it was Debbie calling him. 'Hello, Debbie? Are you alright?'

'I was just wondering if there was any room at the inn. I can't stand hotel rooms at the best of times, they're so impersonal. On top of that, Craig's getting on my nerves at the moment. Knowing I'm staying at the hotel, he's constantly pestering me to do little jobs for him. I've got the begging bowl out. Please can I stay over at yours tonight?'

'Yes that'll be great, but I must warn you that I'm not in a sociable mood this evening. What time will you be here?'

'I'm outside now. By the way I've ordered Chinese for us, I hope you don't mind?'

'Bribery will get you everywhere.'

                    *   *   *

David placed his fork on the empty plate, 'I'll do the washing up, now how much do I owe you?' he asked Debbie.

'Just think of it as rent for the night. I'm grateful that you've put me up.'

'If it means you avoiding Craig, feel free to stay as long as you want while we're working on this investigation. I have a spare key if you want one?' Before David could get a reply his telephone rang, he excused himself and he answered it. 'Hello'

'Hi big brother, I've tried you a few times today but you must've been busy.'

'Peter, it's good to hear from you. Have you anything for me?'

'Well a bit, but I don't know if any use to you. I take it Craig McDonald's been getting under your skin?' Peter said with a slight snigger.

'A little, he's a right pompous bastard, just like his brother. We had proper run in earlier today.'

'Now there's a surprise. That's not like you to have a run in with management!'

'Enough of the sarcasm, what've you got for me?'

'Craig McDonald graduated with a first in politics, philosophy and economics at Oxford. Just like his brother, he went to a prep school and then to Gordonston school in Scotland. His hobbies include rugby, union of course where he got an Oxford Blue. Apparently he was a potential Scotland international but a severely damaged medial ligament injury he sustained at the end of his university days put paid to that happening. All Alistair added after that was that he went into the civil service. He then gave me a potted history of Craig's career. He worked for the Foreign Office in his younger days. After a few postings abroad he transferred over to the Home Office. He wouldn't elaborate on what he does, only that he currently works from Leeds. It must be something in your line if you're working with him?'

'It is. You could say he works alongside, rather than for the Home Office. Did you get any dirt on him?'

'All that I could get is that he's divorced with no children. His first wife, Catherine, was well connected and apparently came from a wealthy family. Evidently that helped his early career. He's still got a woman in his life. Her name is Charlotte and she is works for the Home Office here in London. He's down quite often and he stays with her and he's been seeing her for nearly ten years now. That's it I'm afraid. I'll keep digging for you if you want.'

'Peter, that's great, at least I've got some information I can throw back at him if he starts on me again. Thanks for that, you've done a great job there. When are you coming home again?'

'I'm coming up for the home game against Blackburn in two weeks. I've already got my ticket. I thought I could stay with you and we could go to the game together and then go and see Mum and Dad afterwards.'

'Not a problem. Thanks again and I'll ring you soon.' David replaced the telephone receiver and walked to the kitchen area. He looked at Debbie who had washed the dishes and was making a pot of coffee. 'Debbie, I said I was going to do that.'

'Don't worry. You had to take your phone call. I take it that it was your twin brother? Did he have anything interesting to report on Craig?'

'He gave me enough wind up the bastard up. Apparently Craig was a good rugby union player until he got injured. He's divorced from a Catherine, who is a well connected and wealthy woman and he's currently seeing a Charlotte who works for the Home Office.'

'I knew about the divorce. His first wife is Catherine Richmond. She was the youngest daughter of Lord Richmond. Rumor has it the Richmond's helped Craig in the early part of his career. Since he left Catherine they've done all they can to thwart Craig's career. I learnt something new there. I didn't know that he's currently seeing a woman.'

'Add your information to Peter's and now I've got something up my sleeve to throw back at Craig when we have our next outburst.'

Nineteen

Friday 27th October
05.45 hours
Temporary Control, Marriott Hotel, Manchester

George relieved the ISB night officer at the control room in the hotel at a quarter to five that morning. He could not sleep as too many aspects of the investigation were constantly running through his mind. Coming in early, he sat in the quiet solitude of the control room to think clearly. Once more he went through the evidence and the intelligence his teams had gathered on Aatcha, Khan and Ahmed. 'It's got to be here, but I just can't see it,' he thought. For George, this was just as frustrating as tackling the cryptic crosswords where he only one final clue to complete it. No matter how hard he looked, he could not work it out. He gave himself a break, made himself a cup of tea and scanned the newspapers that the ISB officer had acquired from the hotel reception. 'Nice to see the troops are still resourceful,' he thought thumbing through the pages of the paper. After he finished drinking his tea, he logged back onto the ISB web page and once more he trawled through the intelligence.

He was convinced the teams were correct the Al Qaeda attack would be the rail stations. What he could not work out was exactly how and when they would carry out their attack. He placed himself inside the minds of the three Al Qaeda targets

231

trying to work out how he would carry out their mission to maximize the greatest chance of success. Combined with David's observations before he went home the previous evening was the fact Sayfel had brought up from London the equipment the three needed to carry out the attack. He knew it was only at the last minute did terrorists have all the materials they needed in the one place to carry out an attack.

As he felt he was getting nowhere, he decided to contact his reliable DS to employ his lateral pattern of thinking. He needed someone he could rely on, someone who could be objective. 'David Hurst is no "yes" man, he'll tell me straight,' George thought. At this moment that was just what he wanted.

As George called David's mobile. David was in such a deep sleep he thought the 'Z Cars' ringtone was his alarm clock and he fumbled to switch it off. The familiar tune that his beloved football team came out onto the pitch continued and became a clarion call for him to stir into action. Waking up in an instant he picked up his mobile phone and answered it.

'I apologize for disturbing your beauty sleep again, but I need you to get down to the control room. I've been going through the intelligence and thinking what our Al Qaeda targets could be up to and I needed to run some ideas past someone I could trust. So get yourself dressed and when you get down here I'll have coffee and breakfast ready for you,' George said.

'OK George, I'm on my way. I can be with you in around half an hour to forty minutes. Do you want me to contact Steve?'

'No, let him be for the moment. His baby's been teething and I think he and Lena could do with some sleep. It's you that I want to speak to. I'll also give Debbie a shout and get her up as I could do with tapping into her incisive analytical skills as well. I'll give her room a call.'

'There's no need, she stayed for the night at the flat. I'll get her up and we'll come down together.'

'Not a problem. I'll see you in fifteen minutes.'

'I said half an hour to forty minutes.'

'Try and make it sooner Davey.'

He put on his dressing gown and tentatively went to Debbie's bedroom to wake her. As he placed his hand on the door handle he paused. 'Should I shout her from here to wake her up?' he thought. A short debate went through his head as to whether he should enter the room. He plucked up the courage and entered to see Debbie lying serenely. As he looked at her sleeping, he noticed her natural beauty. There was no make-up and her shoulder length hair was spread all over her pillow. He had no time to linger and think of how beautiful she was, duty called and reluctantly, he woke her by gently shaking her shoulder. As she stirred he said, 'I'm sorry to wake you Debs, but George has been on the phone and we've got to go to the control room and meet him there.'

Debbie squinted as she sat up, yawned, ran her hands through her hair and scratched her head. She suddenly realized that David was seeing her without any make up on and her hair in a mess and thought, 'Oh my god, he'll freak seeing me like this!' As she yawned she mumbled, 'No it's alright I'll come with you. What time is it?'

'It's twenty-five to six in the morning.'

'Twenty-five to six! Bloody hell. Doesn't he know what time it is?'

'That's George for you. It's not the first time he's done this to me and he knows that you've stayed the night at the flat. Of course he's put two and two together and got five. I said we'd be there in about half an hour to forty minutes, but he wants us both in as soon as possible.'

'I must look a right mess.'

'You look lovely,' David said as he kissed her on the cheek.

'And you don't look half bad yourself first thing in the morning in that bathrobe,' she said, recognizing it took a lot of courage for him to do and say what he did.

'Don't worry about grabbing a bite to eat, George is arranging for us to have breakfast with him at the hotel.'

'I'd better make a start then,' she said getting out of the bed.

As she did so, David turned around to preserve her modesty saying, 'When you're ready, I'll meet you in the kitchen.'

*   *   *

David and Debbie arrived at the control room at ten past six that morning to see George pondering over the intelligence reports on the desk. As they entered he looked up at them and said, 'I didn't expect to see you so early as I thought there would be a fight for the bathroom.'

'George it's not what you think,' Debbie said.

Sensing the potential for an embarrassing pause in that morning's greeting, David said, 'Before imaginations start running riot and the rumors start, Debbie stayed at mine last night and will be staying at my flat for the duration of this investigation. I've two bedrooms in my flat and I was in my room while Debbie slept in the spare room. The reason she's staying at mine is because her hotel room's dull and Craig keeps pestering her to do little jobs all the time. If it was Steve staying over at mine you wouldn't think anything of it.'

George said, 'But he's a man. Anyway I'm teasing you. Sit down both of you, I've ordered coffee and bacon sandwiches to get our day started off. Now before I start, get yourself a coffee and tuck into those bacon butties while I run some thoughts I have past you both.'

David and Debbie drew their chairs next to George. As Debbie poured out three cups of coffee, George noticed how she automatically put three heaped spoons of sugar into David's cup. The two of them began eating the sandwiches as George started to share his thoughts with them. 'I've been going over the intelligence with a fine tooth comb. I agree it looks like

something's going to happen at Victoria station, or, as is more
likely, an incident at Victoria station is likely to be the start
a series of events. It could be a bomb plant at Victoria and
as Steve pointed out yesterday, possible bomb plants at other
stations. Although they may be bomb plants at the stations, we
can't dismiss the possibility of them carrying out suicide bomb
attacks, especially if they get on any trains. If they do, and the
trains are packed, the devastation doesn't bear thinking about.
On top of that I was thinking that another source of attack could
be the rail infrastructure itself. It's imperative we keep a close eye
on them this morning and for the rest of the day. We have to
stop them before they carry out any form of attack. I've also been
going over when they're likely to make their move and I think
we should expect an attack at any time, including first thing
this morning. We've been thinking it's either Sunday or Monday
because of the misinformation we received. Another factor that
makes me think they'll make their attack earlier that Monday is
the fact Sayfel brought materials with him to the flat yesterday.
What do you think?'

David answered first and said, 'It makes sense to me. I can get
most of the team in as well as all of Ray's team and we can have
a full en masse briefing within the hour. We can ensure we're
tooled up and ready to make a move should the occasion arise.
In fact, I could send a couple of my team over to Victoria station
straight away to keep an eye out for our three targets.'

Debbie said, 'And I can contact Craig right now and get him
here. He's only in one of the rooms above us. Sayfel should have
sent more information onto us this morning. I can check our
intelligence now if you want George and see if anything's been
added since last night.'

'That would be great and Debbie. I'd be grateful if you make
contact with Craig so I can have a quick word with him. I've
already been preparing for the arrest of Aatcha, Khan and Ahmed.
I've booked Platt Lane custody suite again and warned the firearms

section to have officers ready for an immediate briefing. I stressed to them they must be ready to move first thing from this morning onwards, including the weekend. I'm just trying to pre-empt such a move, but I just wanted a second opinion.'

*   *   *

Having just got out of bed, Craig shuffled into the control room yawning. Craig's normal appearance of being dressed in a well-tailored suit with a handkerchief in the top pocket accompanied with a silk tie was replaced by a crew neck jumper and a pair of jeans. He looked at the three who were eating their bacon sandwiches and said, 'It can't be too much of a flap if you've got time to eat.'

'This setting may look deceptive, but I think we should expect a strike by our three targets at any time, possibly this morning. I've arranged for more ISB staff to come in here for a briefing at seven fifteen this morning. Have you heard from Sayfel yet?' George said.

'I have, but first what brought this on?'

'Going through the intelligence it just makes sense,' George said, 'If your man brought equipment up for our targets, they won't want that equipment in the flat for too long. I think their attack is going to be sooner rather than later, and it could be this morning.'

'That doesn't fit with the information Sayfel passed on to me. He sent a report to Thames House late last night saying the attack will be at Manchester Airport on Sunday, Monday at the latest. His email stated the materials he brought up to Manchester were simply change of identity documents along with a confirmation that the target is the airport.'

'I have to hold my hands up at this stage and admit that we don't know for certain whether they have all the equipment they need to carry out an attack. For all we know, Ahmed could have been bringing it in bit by bit and your man did only bring identity documents. To come up to Manchester from London carrying identity documents in two holdalls does seem a bit peculiar to me, especially as he had no hand luggage with him when he went to the bus station to get the coach back to London. Our three targets have the skills to prepare identity documents themselves as well as the fact that there is any number of Al Qaeda associates in the Greater Manchester area that could produce false ID. It makes no sense to risk an Al Qaeda operative to travel all the way up from London to simply deliver identity documents.'

'I suppose it's better to be safe than sorry. Have you put anything in place yet?'

'As well as contacting SO13 and alerting the commander of the Northwest Special Branch region, I've contacted my opposite numbers in Merseyside, West Yorks, North Yorks and Northumbria. This is just in case our three targets catch a train and go to Liverpool, Leeds, York or Newcastle. You have to admit that it would be worth targeting the largest cities in the north. The other forces have arranged to have officers at the major train stations to support us. I've not informed the British Transport Police. I think we're able to cope at the moment and I want things to look as normal as possible. If I informed the BTP, they're likely put extra officers around the stations or do something that may affect the appearance of a normal Friday at the station.'

'That makes sense,' Craig said as he looked at David. 'I hope you're not the main influence behind George's thinking. I've always been wary of the likes of you from the lower ranks that are disrespectful to management. It makes me laugh when you in particular bang on about working as a team, then undermine senior managers. I can't fathom your logic. Is it because you think that only officers working the streets can gather intelligence of any real value? Now is there some coffee and sandwiches left or have you three gannets had the lot?'

David poured a coffee for Craig and handed him the cup. As

he did so he caught Craig's eye and said quietly out of earshot of the other two, 'How's Charlotte?'

'What?' a startled Craig asked David.

'You heard me, how's Charlotte? I suppose if this investigation finishes today you'll have the chance to slip back down to the Smoke and see her and perhaps slip her one.'

Craig snapped back saying, 'What are you up to Hurst?'

David gave Craig a steely eyed glare that gave out the message that he was not to be messed around as he said, 'Just like you, I have fucking sources elsewhere. I know all about you. I know about your divorce, how the aggrieved first wife's family have done their utmost to fuck up your career since you went shagging behind her back. So if you want to start bad mouthing me, you will regret it. It's such a shame that your crocked leg resulted in fucking up your rugby union career. I believe that you were once considered for Scotland? Mind you anyone can play for them as there are less to choose from compared to England! Listen Craig with my background, I'm used to fighting in the gutter unlike you who simply visits it now and again.'

A mixture of shock and fear spread throughout his body as Hurst leant over him causing him to stammer, 'Are, are you th...threatening me Hurst? Have y...you been sp...speaking to your brother?'

David continued to look threateningly into Craig's eyes as he leant closer into his face and said, 'They're not threats Craig old boy.' He emphasized the words 'old boy' while mocking Craig's accent. 'I just want you to know that two can play at your game. When you want to start fighting dirty, you're playing into my hands as I was brought up in harder streets than you. Unlike your public schools with your fagging system and having your little arses roasted over an open fire, you fucking ponce.'

Craig pulled himself together and tried to stare back at Hurst. But he struggled as David was a good five inches taller than him. Trying not to sound frightened he said, 'Congratulations, so you can read. But things have moved on from Tom Brown's

Schooldays. My class has been playing this game a lot longer than yours and we have always played dirty, so don't threaten me.'

David smiled at him. He could see the fear emanating from Craig's face and said, 'I'm not threatening you. Where I come from that's not a threat, that's called a fucking promise you Scottish prick. I don't play mind games like you. I suggest we start to get on, respect each other and watch each other's backs. Here's your coffee, but you'll have to order some more sandwiches, as the oiks didn't know their place and scoffed the lot sir.' He passed Craig the coffee raising his left hand to his eyebrow and mockingly made the gesture of tugging his forelock. David turned to George and said, 'I'm going to make my way to the station now. Could you get Steve Adams to meet me at Victoria station by the newsagent's stand? Alex Bullard can run the team after the briefing until we RV at the station. Don't worry I'm armed.' He took his Berretta Cougar pistol out of its holster to check it. As he did, he pointed the barrel of the pistol straight at Craig who turned even whiter as the gesture was not lost on him.

George said, 'Good idea, I'll get a couple more to get down there to join you ASAP. It sounds like this morning is going to be more of a series of mini-briefings rather than one big one. Give me a radio check when you get out.'

'Will do George,' David said. As he was leaving the conference room he looked straight at Craig and said, 'Take care, I'm watching you.'

As he began to walk out of the control room, Debbie came over to him and said, 'I'll see you out.'

'There's no need for that, I'm old enough to look after myself.'

'I want to.' As they walked out of the entrance to the hotel Debbie hugged David and gave him a kiss on the cheek. David looked surprised and Debbie said, 'Just take care. All I want to say is that I like you and you've become a friend. Promise me you'll take care?'

David looked deep into her eyes and trying to avoid any

sentimentality, he tried to make light of the situation. 'Don't worry, I will. I think it's more dangerous where you are.'

'What do you mean?'

'You're going to have to spend most of the day with Craig!'

'I saw you talking to him before. He didn't seem to like what you were saying. You obviously said something sarcastic as I saw you tugging your forelock.'

'I just gave him a few home truths. I asked him how Charlotte was and I let him know that I've got information on him too. Now come here.' David took hold of Debbie, embraced her and kissed her on her lips. 'I'll take care and you never know after this job's over, but only if you want to, we could become more than just friends.'

Realizing that David had the same feelings for her that she had for him, she hugged him tightly and closed her eyes as just for a second she did not want this moment to end. 'I'd like that very much. I want you to come back to me tonight. If you're late home, I'll wait up for you.'

*   *   *

As George was looking out of the window of the control room, he saw David and Debbie at the hotel entrance. Craig walked over and said, 'You seem captivated by events outside. What's going on George?'

'I think your worst fears for Debbie have happened.'

Craig leant past George's shoulder to get a better view of Debbie and David, just in time to see them kiss. His face reddened and his lips tightened with rage, fuelled by the earlier angry exchange of words he had with Hurst. 'I knew it. I just fucking well knew it. You know what it's like with work romances George. Things are fine when they're going well but once it doesn't, performance suffers,' he said angrily.

'Is that really what you're concerned about Craig or the fact that she fancies David and not you?'

Realizing his mask of indifference had slipped momentarily, he said indignantly, 'Don't be preposterous George. My concern is purely professional.'

Twenty

The morning rush hour saw a greater frequency of trains arriving at the large Victorian built Victoria rail station. The more trains that arrived at the station, the greater number of people there were on the station concourse, making it harder for David to spot the three targets. He was standing by the newsagents stand when he checked his watch. It was just after eight as Steve entered Victoria rail station and strolled up to David, scanning the station for their three targets. 'Morning leader. Any sign of our three targets?'

'No, I can't see anyone but it's hard with all these crowds in the station.'

'I know, its heaving. Shall we go for coffee and keep an eye on the concourse from there?'

'Good idea, I could do with a brew.'

The two walked through the station as commuters were arriving from all over the northwest of England to work in Manchester. Everyone David saw seemed to be in their own little worlds, strenuously avoiding any form of eye contact. He saw very few happy faces as most people's body language displayed this was the last place they wanted to be on a Friday morning. He thought how the picture would have been the same a hundred

242

years before when the workers were making their way in their thousands to the Manchester cotton mills. 'Nothing changes only the clothes,' he thought.

He did see some happy faces on the passengers that looked as though they were travelling away for the weekend. A group of young people with heavy haversacks were laughing and joking as they checked the departure screen. He saw mothers becoming increasingly fractious with their children as they juggled baggage with having to attend to their demanding children. As he continued to scan the concourse, he focused on an elderly man looking anxiously around him while glancing at his watch. 'Whoever he's waiting for must be late to himself,' he thought. It was a normal frantic Friday morning at the station. There were long queues by the ticket office and people coming out of the station shops armed with takeaway drinks, sandwiches and newspapers. Just one small bomb going off would not only cause death and destruction, it would change forever the lives of the survivors and the families of those killed. A shiver went down his spine as the enormity of the responsibility placed on his and his team's shoulders to stop the attack dawned on him. 'We've got to stop them. There's no place for complacency, there's no place for mistakes,' he thought.

As he scanned the concourse this feeling disappeared momentarily when he saw a man greeting a woman on the concourse with a warm, loving embrace followed by a passionate kiss. His mind turned to Debbie who did the same to him earlier. A sense of excitement ran through every nerve of his body. He knew this was no passing fancy he had for Debbie. He had not felt this way about a woman for years

'A penny for them Davey,' Steve asked interrupting David's thoughts.

There was no way that he would share his latter thoughts with his close friend, not now, not this morning. 'Sorry Steve I was just concentrating. It looks just like a normal weekday morning. There are all sorts of people here, commuters, day-trippers and people going away for a weekend. It's getting busier by the minute. I was just thinking of the carnage there'd be if a bomb went off now.'

Steve knew he was still hiding something as he said, 'I was just thinking the same. I caught sight of those young ones over there laughing and joking as they appeared to be showing each other pictures on their mobile phones. Don't worry we're here now, what can go wrong?' They walked up to the coffee shop where Steve asked, 'I take it you want, a double espresso? These are on me.'

'You're a star, thanks Steve.'

'Go and get a table where we can get a good view of what's going on and I'll bring them over.'

The tables outside the coffee shop were busy, but he found a table giving a good view of the station concourse. He sat down and telephoned George to let him know that he and Steve had met up and taken up a position outside the coffee shop, a position similar to the dry run the day before. George informed David the BTP agreed to allow an ISB officer to monitor the station's CCTV. George did not tell the BTP they were the ISB for fear of them changing their security alert status. He told them the officer was from GMP's major crime unit looking for a drug trafficker. As a result the BTP patched up their CCTV to the ISB's control room at the hotel.

'Were you calling George?' Steve asked placing the drinks on the table. He took out ten sachets of brown sugar from his coat pocket and said, 'Two of these are for me, the rest are for your sweet tooth. Quite a few of the team have already arrived at the station. I saw Alex and Chris at the main entrance and I heard Nick and Andy say that they're making their way to a position by the ticket office. With George monitoring the station's CCTV and Ray's team at the targets' flat, we should have everything covered.'

'Having one of Ray's team monitoring the station's CCTV

in the BTP control room will be useful,' David said pouring the content of six sachets of sugar into his espresso.

'A strange thing happened this morning at control. As I was leaving, Debbie asked me to make sure that you stay out of trouble. I said, "That's charming, how about me staying out of trouble?" She added that she meant all of the team, but I didn't believe her. Have you something to tell me?'

'If it'll shut you up, if we get through this I'm taking her out for a meal and see how things go. It'll be a proper date not like Wednesday night. Are you satisfied now? Will you let the subject drop?'

Steve patted David on the back and said, 'Good man, it's about time you asked her out. Now that's out in the open, or should I say between us two for now, let's enjoy our coffee and see if our Al Qaeda friends decide to come out to play.'

*   *   *

'All three targets are leaving the flat in Granby Row and they're carrying bags with them,' Ray Baskin radioed to the other officers and control.

In the control room George noted the time was a ten minutes past eight. He informed all of the officers, 'OK everyone, this could be it. Keep your eyes peeled.' He then turned to Craig and asked him what he thought.

'My apologies for doubting you George, but I think it's show time.'

*   *   *

Ray and his team followed all three targets. The targets split up and mingled with the commuters and early morning shoppers thronging Manchester's city centre streets. Ray relayed that Aatcha and Khan had two bags each and Ahmed was carrying three. George had one of the MI5 technical staff patching the control room into all of the CCTV cameras located in Manchester city centre allowing them to follow events. On entering Market Street, all three targets met up and walked in a single line. Aatcha took the lead with Ahmed about thirty yards behind him and Khan about another thirty yards further behind Ahmed. Ray noticed that out of the three, Khan appeared to be the most nervous. He constantly kept looking behind him more than Ahmed and Aatcha, '...and he's dropping back from the other two,' he thought. The calm tone of the officers' commentary as they relayed the events belayed the tension gradually increasing among the officers on the street and back in the control room.

As Ahmed passed the Market Street entrance to the Arndale Shopping Centre, he nonchalantly placed one of the bags he was carrying into a litter bin, walked a few paces and stopped outside one of the shops.

'Looks like they've delivered one of their packages,' Craig said to George, keeping his eyes constantly trained on the screens.

'Why has Ahmed stopped by the bin and let the other two walk off? I think he's watching to see if any of us pick it up,' George said and relayed this to the officers on the street. 'Do not make a move to the bin. It looks like Ahmed's waiting to see if we make a move. Wait until instructed before anyone makes a move to pick it up.'

Craig said to George, 'Tell your officers to keep with the three targets and not to worry about the bag in the bin. I have officers out there as well. They'll deal with it. Just keep them on the tails of Aatcha, Khan and Ahmed, once he makes a move. He has another two bags with him, so he'll move soon.'

George went back to the radio and said, 'All Branch officers stay with Aatcha and Khan and keep on them. Ray's team, you stay with Ahmed. He may make a move soon.' Both George and Craig watched Ahmed as he lit a cigarette and for what seemed like an eternity, remained outside the shop doorway. As he stood there, Ahmed calmly looked at the bin to see if anyone made a move to take the bag out.

'The bastard's playing with us George. He's waiting to see if we make a move. My worry is the timer on the detonator. I just hope that we have enough time to get to the package and disarm it after he's moved off.'

'Do you want to lift him now and get to the package?' George asked.

Trying to hide the tension he was feeling, Craig said, 'No, we'll take our chances and wait until he moves. If we move too soon it could affect how the other two behave. No, we'll wait. So far we're still in control of events.'

Once Ahmed finished smoking his cigarette, he dropped it onto the pavement, stubbed it out with his shoe and walked off, turning right into Corporation Street in the direction of Victoria station carrying the other two bags he had with him. Once Ahmed was out of sight of the bin, Craig instructed MI5 officers to move in, remove the bag and check it out. While this was going on Debbie was in touch with MI5 headquarters at Thames House when she got a message that made the color drain from her face. 'Craig, George, I think you two need to see this,' she said turning her laptop so they could see the message on the screen.

As Craig read the email his jaw dropped in disbelief.

'Moosa Khan is an MI5 undercover officer. There have been doubts over Sayfel for a while and his brief was to check him out. Khan reported that Sayfel has gone native and cannot be trusted. Al Qaeda will make their attack this morning. Khan has not set the detonator on his bombs, but these are dirty bombs carrying a highly infectious pathogen. We are still waiting for confirmation of what exactly the pathogen is. It is believed that it is a virus similar to the bubonic plague. We are making arrangements for all local NHS A&E units likely to be affected to be on standby for a potential major incident. Khan relayed that Al Qaeda's plan is to close down the north of England and threaten to use similar devices in London if

their demands are not met. Extra caution must be taken. Our officers
in the field are now aware. ISB to arrest Khan at the first opportunity
and he will fully brief all staff involved. Their targets are Liverpool
and Leeds as well as Manchester.

Jenny Richmond, senior intelligence officer'

'Fucking hell, this could get messy,' said a stunned Craig.

'That's an understatement. I'll get this out to all those in the
field now,' George said.

George relayed the information to the officers involved in the
surveillance. The possible effects of these bombs going off began
to dawn on Craig. Repeatedly banging his fist the top of his desk,
he shouted, 'Bastards!'

'What's wrong Craig?' George asked.

'Why didn't they tell me they had doubts about Sayfel? Why
didn't they tell me we had another man on the inside? On top of
that, if these things go off imagine the chaos it will cause. Apart
from hospitals in the north of England not being able to cope,
it will affect the whole infrastructure of the area. Quarantine
will be imposed with people having to stay in their homes. The
whole of the cities in the north of England will simply grind to
a halt. There'll be a national panic. Once this is released, people
all over the country will be going to their local GP with the
slightest sniffle and they won't be able to cope. In fact, none
of the health services will be able to cope. On top of that, the
financial markets will collapse in the UK and that might impact
globally as panic spreads in the knowledge that Al Qaeda could
detonate similar devices throughout the western world.'

The enormity of the situation also dawned on George, who
said, 'I'm going to give the order to lift them before they can
detonate the bombs.'

'You're right. It's too risky to let those three carry on, as we
might lose them and, importantly, we may fail to spot where
they plant the bombs. Why didn't Thames House tell me about

this earlier?'

Debbie looked at him indignantly and said, 'So the tables have turned. Now you know why David Hurst is so suspicious of us.'

Craig's face filled with rage at having Hurst's wisdom passed onto him and he said to Debbie, 'Don't quote Hurst to me. You're loyalty's questionable too. For Christ's sake, this is MI5 holding back on their own.'

*   *   *

'Aatcha's boarding the train to Liverpool. Khan's approaching the bin by platform eight. No sign of Ahmed yet,' David radioed to the other officers as he and Steve got up and followed Aatcha towards the Liverpool bound train. As it due to depart within the next few minutes, the two quickened their walking pace. Walking through the barrier, they discreetly showed their warrant cards to the rail staff at the platform entrance. As Aatcha boarded the first carriage of the four-carriage train, David got on the second carriage. He grimaced as it was full of passengers as he momentarily lost sight of Aatcha. Steve waited by the door of the fourth carriage to see if Aatcha would do a switch and get off the train. The platform staff started closing the doors and the train guard asked Steve to board the train as the driver released the brake. He walked through the packed carriages to get to David, brushing past people with bulky bags, squeezing past rotund passengers, bumping into standing passengers who had acquired the skill of holding onto a handrail whilst reading a newspaper. Constantly saying 'Excuse me' and 'Thanks', he slowly made his way down the train.

Squeezing his way past a fat man with a bulky haversack on his back, Steve caused him to slightly spill down the front of his coat some of the coffee the man brought with him onto the train. The man looked at Steve and said, 'Hey, who are you pushing?'

Although Steve had said sorry, he had enough of struggling to get down the crowded carriages to join David. Steve moved into the man's face and said, 'You, you ugly bastard. What are you going to do about fat man?' Sensing Steve was in no mood to argue and fearing he was about to hit him, fear came across his fat, sweaty face as he turned away to look out of the window. The train was moving slowly out of the station when Steve joined David in the second carriage. They were both standing cheek to jowl with other passengers.

David whispered to Steve, 'I heard you coming. Did the big lad over there fancy his chances?'

'The ignorant fucker. I said I was sorry, but he's stood there with his fucking big bag on his back and he's the about the width of three people. What does he expect? The train's packed and he's stood there drinking coffee taking up the spaces of at least four people.'

'Forget him. He's the least of our problems. Our man is four rows into the first carriage from here. He's facing the way the train's going with his back to us and he's put his bags under the seat he's sitting on.'

'Trouble is we can't relay this back at the moment, we're in a radio black-spot. By the time we get through Salford we should be OK,' Steve whispered back.

'I'll try and get through to them on my mobile,' and as David tried to ring George, it constantly stated on the small phone screen 'no signal available'.

*   *   *

After placing his bag with the undetonated dirty bomb into a litterbin on the station concourse, Khan walked through the barrier to platform eight and boarded the train to Leeds. The train was due to depart in five minutes. He sat there looking out of the window on to the platform. Knowing that Ahmed was watching him, he could not get off the train and contact MI5. He knew if he left the train now Ahmed would become suspicious and relay this to Aatcha, who would then detonate his bombs on the Liverpool bound train. He was looking for people who would be either MI5 or ISB officers, constantly hoping that they would get to him before the train moved off. He had no time to talk to any of the MI5 handlers at Thames House that morning, but he was sure his handler at Thames House received his text message he sent earlier.

*   *   *

'I've got through to all of them except David and Steve. They must be in a radio black-spot. I've even tried to contact them on their mobiles but they mustn't be able to receive a signal,' George informed the other officers at the control room. Debbie turned and looked at George. Picking up on her concern, he said, 'Debbie, keep trying David and Steve for me. We need to let them know that they must make their arrest now.'

*   *   *

After sitting in the carriage for what appeared to be an eternity, Khan was approached by Alex Bullard and Chris Gibbons. The officers entered the carriage laughing and behaving like two women regaling each other of their adventures from the previous night. As they walked towards Khan, they gave him no eye contact. Chris pushed Alex saying, 'You're such a slut at times.'

Alex fell into the vacant seat next to Khan. He looked at her and saw that she was not laughing anymore. He felt something prod against his body. He looked down and saw the pistol she was pointing at him. As Chris stood over Alex and showed him her warrant card, Alex whispered in his ear, 'Mr. Khan you're under arrest for acts of terrorism. Now get up slowly. Don't think for one moment we wouldn't kill you, because it would give me the greatest pleasure to prove you wrong.'

Khan said, 'We work for the same side. Radio your control and verify it. I have the codes to disarm the bombs.'

Alex looked puzzled and said, 'What do you mean?'

'I'm an MI5 officer. I'm undercover,' Khan said quietly.

Disbelieving him Alex and Chris handcuffed Khan and escorted him off the train. As they stood on the platform Khan pleaded with the officers saying, 'I'm not lying to you, I'm an MI5 officer. Check me out with your control. It's important that you do this quickly. I have to call Ahmed and Aatcha, tell them that all has gone to plan and that I'm on my way to Leeds. If I don't, Aatcha will detonate his bomb on the Liverpool bound train. He's supposed to arrive at Liverpool's Lime Street station where he'll plant his bombs, but if he hears that something's not gone according to plan, he'll detonate his bombs on the train. Check me out now before it's too late.'

Alex radioed through to the control room they had arrested Khan, '...and he claims to be an undercover MI5 man. Can you confirm please?'

'Confirmed,' George said, 'I repeat, it's confirmed, he is MI5, he's on our side.'

'Thanks control', she said turning to Khan. 'I'm sorry mate, but when you said that you're MI5, I thought you were just trying it on. Make that call, as we've two ISB officers on that train with Aatcha. It left Victoria ages ago and it's well on its way to Liverpool.'

Alex took the handcuffs off Khan, who then rang Aatcha. When he answered the phone Khan said, 'I'm on my way to Leeds now, the train's just about to leave Victoria. See you tomorrow. Allah be with you.'

'Thanks Moosa,' Aatcha whispered into his mobile phone, 'Allah be with you too my brother.'

Khan put his phone away and said to the two officers, 'The

priority now is in disarming the two bombs placed in the concourse.' He looked at his watch and said, 'They'll be going off in ten minutes.'

'Shall we order an evacuation of the station?' Chris asked anxiously.

'There's no need, it's simply a trip switch. I have to enter the code first before we can disarm it. Anyway, we wouldn't have to time to evacuate. Do your colleagues have the bombs?'

Alex organized for the two packages to be brought to them straight away. Within a minute, one of David's team handed Alex the two bombs. 'Tell your colleagues the package from outside the Arndale Center is a dummy bomb. It was planted to see if we were being followed. My two bombs are safe, I didn't arm them,' Khan said taking the bombs out of the bags. Each bomb was in a vacuum flask. In turn, he took each out of the flask, opened the side panel and entered the code on small digital pad to disarm the bombs.

Once he finished, Khan put them back into the bags and picked them up saying, 'They're safe now. The only ones we have to worry about now are the ones Aatcha's got with him. They've got a pathogen in each one. If they go off, a highly contagious disease will spread into the atmosphere throughout the immediate population. The problem we'll have with the pathogen is that for the first couple of days there'll be no obvious visible symptoms. Those contaminated will be carriers. It's after two days when the first symptoms can be detected and that's when the disease reveals itself. By then it's too late to save anyone. Let's go to your control and I can give you a full debrief there.'

Twenty-One

Friday 27th October
08.50 hours
Salford, Manchester

The train was about a mile out of Salford station as it headed towards Liverpool when David emerged from the train's toilet. Putting his phone back into his pocket, he walked over to Steve and said, 'We've got a problem Stevey. I can't speak now, but keep your eyes on Aatcha.' As the train picked up speed, other passengers found and sat in vacant seats allowing the two officers to talk without being overheard. 'Ahmed and Khan have been arrested but here's the best bit, Khan's an undercover MI5 officer. Apparently Sayfel's turned native on them. Their attack is today and they're using dirty bombs. The only bombs outstanding are the one's Aatcha's got with him. It's not a suicide attack, he's going to drop his bomb off at Lime Street station and go to St. Luke's church where he will be picked up. Merseyside's ISB are aware and waiting for our arrival.'

'How far is the church from the station?'

'About a five minute walk away. It's known locally as the 'bombed out church' as it got badly damaged by the Luftwaffe. It's been kept as a monument to those who died during the blitz. If Al Qaeda is waiting for him at the church, they'll most probably be waiting for him in one of the side roads that surrounds the church, most probably Bold Place.'

'How are we going to approach this?. Do we lift him now or do they want us to wait and follow him so we can get the Al Qaeda operatives waiting for him as well?'

'They've asked us to hold off and let him make his drop so we can follow him to St. Luke's. George told me Khan's got the codes for all of the bombs, so we should be able to disarm them after we've lifted Aatcha.' As some passengers edged their way down the carriage, David stopped talking. A man in his early thirties stopped, standing next to the two officers. He began to look at both of them. David stared back at the man and said, 'Have you had good look? Do you want a photograph you nosey bastard?'

'What did you say?' the man said out of embarrassment that he had been caught trying to overhear what the two officers were saying.

'I'm just telling you to keep your nose out our business unless you want it broken,' David said.

'One-all. I wonder if we'll piss anyone else off on this journey.' Steve whispered in David's ear.

*   *   *

Debbie turned to George and said, 'I can't raise them on the radio and David's mobile phone goes straight onto the answer phone again.'

'Keep trying him.'

'I will.' As Debbie spoke Craig came into the control room with Khan.

'Listen up everyone, here's the situation,' Craig said to all the staff in the control room. 'We've two MI5 officers in the Liverpool area watching St. Luke's church supported by Merseyside ISB officers. Merseyside's ISB have also got officers waiting at Lime Street station to pick up Aatcha. In addition to this we have West Yorkshire ISB officers in Leeds waiting for the car planned to pick up Khan. It's important we contact Hurst and Adams and tell them to still sit tight on Aatcha and wait until they arrive at Lime Street station before we lift him.'

'We're having trouble raising them at the moment. They're too far out to contact them by radio and I think they're struggling to get a signal on their phones,' George said.

Debbie shouted out, 'David's phone's ringing.' As David answered the phone Debbie instructed him not to speak, just simply to listen, 'We have the code to make Aatcha's bombs safe. Once he's deposited his bombs at Lime Street station, you're to arrest Aatcha. Merseyside's ISB will be there to back you up.'

'I've got that, thanks Debs. Speak to you soon.' He wanted to say more to her, but this was not the time or the place.

While she was speaking, Craig walked up to Debbie and said, 'Does Hurst know that he's not to do any heroics and to wait until they arrive at Lime Street before he makes a move on Aatcha?'

Wondering if he had been eavesdropping and she snapped back, 'Don't worry, he does.'

*   *   *

'We're to lift Aatcha when we arrive at Lime Street and Merseyside ISB officers will be there to assist us,' David said to Steve.

'So we just sit tight and enjoy the ride until we get to Lime Street.' He looked out of the window at the landscape that was unfamiliar to him and asked David, 'Where are we now?'

'We've just gone through Huyton. That's where we met our Chechen friend last Monday. Tell you what that seems like a lifetime ago.'

Not hearing what David said, Steve's attention was distracted by Aatcha who made an unexpected move. He nudged David and nodded towards Aatcha, 'Looks like he's making a telephone call. If it's to Ahmed or Khan he won't get a reply and that could be trouble for us. Once he gets no reply, we'd better get ready for him to do the unexpected, especially as we're pulling into the next station.'

As the train slowly pulled up at the platform of Roby Station, David glanced at his watch. It was twenty five past nine. No one got off the train, but another five passengers boarded the carriage where David and Steve were sitting. The new passengers had to stand as no seats were available. Neither David nor Steve had a clear view of Aatcha as the train pulled out of the station. David stood up and moved towards the door in his carriage. He saw Aatcha put his phone back into his jacket then lean forward in his seat placing his hand inside his bag. David nodded to Steve who remained seated and moved to the door in the second carriage. Because of the number of passengers packed into the carriage, David struggled to get a clear view of Aatcha. Aatcha stood up as the train was approaching Broadgreen station and, carrying his bag, walked over to the door in the first carriage.

As the train pulled into Broadgreen station, David wondered why he would want to get off here. 'As he's had no reply to his calls, he must have a change of plan if he fails to make contact,' he thought. As the doors opened, a passenger got out of David's carriage ahead of him and four people were waiting to get onto the carriage. Glancing over to Aatcha, he just glimpsed him getting out of the carriage and step onto the platform. David made his move. Stepping out of the carriage he followed his target. Aatcha walked along the platform to the exit. Located in the entrance hall to the station that comprised of the small ticket office and a small two person bench, the exit had two narrow doors that opened outwards. Acting like a funnel, it made the passengers form a slow moving queue as they left the station. As Aatcha could only make a limited progress in leaving the station, David used this opportunity to quickly glance behind him to see where Steve was.

Knowing the train was about to move off at any second, Steve aggressively barged his way through the passengers stood by the carriage doors. As he stepped onto the platform, the automatic train doors closed. Steve saw David disappear out of view towards the exit. He quickened his pace to catch up to him. Failing to see the bag placed on the platform by a passenger greeting someone who had been waiting for them, he tripped over, falling face first. As Steve cursed, a passenger he barged out of the way stepped over him. 'That's what you get for being so impatient,' the smart suited man said indignantly. Red faced through embarrassment, Steve picked himself up and hurriedly made his way to the exit. Looking ahead of him, both Aatcha and Hurst had left the station.

David walked out of the station, following Aatcha up Roby Road. Using two other passengers walking in front of him as cover, David glanced back again. There was no sign of Steve. Thinking he had been unable to get off the train in time, he accepted he was on his own. Walking thirty yards behind the two in front of him, he focused on Aatcha. He knew he needed back-up, but the question was how he could discreetly request it. Carrying out foot surveillance in such an open area, with little cover, his fair haired, six foot three frame was hard to conceal. Conscious of the fact he was constantly told he looked like a copper, he wanted to draw as little attention to himself as he could. The short debate in his mind concluded it was too risky to call George back in Manchester. If Aatcha looked behind and saw him making a call, David knew Aatcha would question such actions as having changed his plans, he would be more surveillance conscious than ever.

Walking towards the Rocket junction, all four were passing the small semi-detached houses when the two walking in front of Hurst turned right and walked down one of the residential side roads. 'Fuck,' Hurst thought, only having a clear forty yard gap between him and Aatcha. 'Just don't look back,' he said to himself as he followed Aatcha to the row of the small local shops positioned opposite the large junction. Hoping Aatcha had not noticed him on train, Hurst looked around the area making a quick assessment of the danger if he had to challenge Aatcha now. The traffic was heavy as it left the end of the motorway with drivers making their way into Liverpool. It was just as busy the opposite way, where vehicles were bumper-to-bumper making their way out of the city. At least there were no other pedestrians in the immediate area. That would minimize the danger and it reassured him a little if he had to arrest Aatcha right now.

Aatcha unexpectedly stopped by the newsagents shop next to a waste bin. Continuing to walk towards him, Hurst slowed his walking pace as he watched Aatcha looking into the bag he was carrying. Not knowing what he was up to and fearing that he could be about to leave the bomb in the bin opposite the newsagents shop, David placed his hand on his Berretta Cougar pistol and took the safety catch off. Quickly looking around the area again, he saw a young woman coming out of the newsagents pushing a pram with a child, who David thought could be no more than two years old. She stopped by the doorway of the shop and began to look into her handbag. The traffic in the area was still heavy. 'I'll have to take Aatcha out before he kills anyone,' he thought quickly, continually assessing the risk. As he walked steadily towards Aatcha, he saw him fumbling inside the bag. It had now come to the point where Hurst decided it was too risky to let him continue. He was twenty five feet from Aatcha when David drew his pistol and shouted, 'Ibrar Aatcha, stand still. Do not move. Armed police. Stand still.'

Startled at first, Aatcha made no move. Then lowering his arms, bringing the bag down by his side, Aatcha looked at the gun pointing right at him. Again the warning of 'armed police stand still' was shouted out. For a moment, Aatcha stood perfectly still. He did not even blink

'Put the bag down slowly onto the floor and stand away from it. Then slowly raise your hands so I can see them. Make any sudden movements and I'll fire.' As David shouted out his instructions, his heart was pounding. With his right index finger hovering over the trigger, he tightened his grip of the pistol. Every nerve in David's body tingled. Every one of his senses was on alert. He could taste the adrenaline on his lips as he concentrated on every move Aatcha made. Oblivious to any peripheral vision, he kept his eyes focused on Aatcha. The two men looked intently into each other's eyes. Neither showed fear. Aatcha could see the officer would kill him, while David could see the terrorist was waiting for that split second opportunity to make his move. During this momentary stand-off between the two, a woman behind Hurst gave an ear piercing scream. He did not take his eyes off Aatcha. He knew if he did, it would give Aatcha the chance to either set off the bomb or shoot him if he was armed. Time transformed into a surreal slow motion as he kept thinking, 'Do as I say, do as I say.' As the tension increased, perspiration began to meander down Hurst's forehead. His mouth was dry. His arms were stiffening.

Aatcha shouted back, 'Don't shoot, don't shoot.' He slowly bent down and placed the bag onto the pavement. Trying to stand up, Aatcha quickly brought his hand out of the bag and pointed something twoards David.

'Christ it's a gun,' David shouted out. Before he could react, Aatcha fired the weapon in his direction. As he had to fire from his hip, he could not get a clear shot. David felt the bullet from Aatcha's gun buzz past his left ear. Instinctively returning fire, David fired three shots. As the bullets ripped into his body, the impact hurled Aatcha backwards. There was a fourth shot. For a split second this puzzled David as he knew it did not come from his gun. He watched as the fourth shot hit Aatcha, causing part of his skull to splinter into the air, closely followed by blood and brains that scattered indiscriminately onto the pavement.

Steve ran up to Aatcha's lifeless body. 'Are you alright Davey?' Steve shouted over to him.

David did not reply. He just stood there staring at Aatcha's motionless body. A form of paralysis momentarily gripped him. Unaware of any sounds around him, his mind was only registering he had taken another person's life. 'Davey are you alright?' Steve asked again.

Quickly re-gathering his senses, David shouted back, 'I'm fine Steve. That was an arse twitching moment,' and he ran up to Steve and the dead Aatcha. For a moment the two men stood over the body. 'Fuck me that was close,' David said as he picked up Aatcha's bag. Looking inside, he saw was a vacuum drink flask. He carefully took it out and placed it upright on the floor.

'It's either the bomb or he came prepared because he didn't like what they sold from the drinks trolley on the train,' Steve quipped.

David stared at the flask, conscious of the danger it posed. 'This is the bomb, but I can't be sure whether or not he had the chance to arm it.' David put his pistol back into its holster and telephoned George. Waiting for George to answer, both officers heard sirens in the distance getting closer. 'Looks like the locals know we're here,' David said.

'I'll get Aatcha's gun while you brief George.' Picking up the weapon, Steve gave it a cursory examination and said, 'It's a Smith and Wesson thirty eight that looks more like a museum piece.'

David nodded back at Steve acknowledging what he said, but his hands were still shaking. 'Get a grip,' he said to himself as George answered the call. 'Hi boss, we've a problem, Aatcha's dead. Steve and I had to shoot him. We're by a row of shops at the Rocket junction in Merseyside. Inform Merseyside Police of our presence here. No one else is hurt, but we need to make the bomb safe.'

'Wait a minute,' George replied. David heard him ask for someone to tell Merseyside Police what had happened. 'Did he arm the bomb?' George asked David.

'I don't know. There is no ticking or anything.'

'I'll pass you onto Moosa Khan. He'll tell you how to disarm it.'

'OK, but it sounds like we're going to be joined by the local police shortly, so hurry up. I think someone's reported what's happened.'

'Stay calm and play ball with them until we confirm your presence.'

In a matter of seconds a marked police car screeched to a halt, just in front of the two officers as they stood on the pavement. The officer in the passenger seat threw open the car door and aimed a Heckler and Koch rifle at David, shortly followed by the driver who aimed his rifle at Steve. The officers' shouted, 'Armed police. Drop your guns slowly to the floor so we can see them and slowly lie face down onto the pavement with your hands behind your head.' David and Steve did exactly what they were told. As David began to lie down onto the pavement, a second Merseyside Police armed response car came to a halt. An officer walked over to David aiming his rifle at him, repeatedly telling him to lie still with his hands placed behind his head. The officer kicked David's legs apart. David tried to tell the officer he was an ISB DS from Greater Manchester, but every time he tried to speak, the officer just kept shouting at him to stay quiet. A second officer knelt down by David to search him. 'If you go into my inside pocket you'll find my Greater Manchester Police warrant card. We're GMP ISB officers and the dead man over was a suspected Al Qaeda terrorist. In that bag is a bomb that could go up at any minute,' David said.

The officer found the warrant card and told him to get up to his knees. As David got onto his knees he heard a shout from one of the cars, 'They're GMP ISB officers on a job and he's a DS.'

The officer that searched David helped him onto his feet. 'The bomb is in that flask by the dead man. We've got the code to disarm it,' David informed the armed Merseyside officers. 'Let me telephone my DI. It's not just any bomb, it's a dirty bomb. Tell your force control room to contact Merseyside's ISB as officers from your ISB were waiting for us at Lime Street. Tell them to get to St Luke's and check by Bold Place as soon as they can. They'll know what I mean.' He picked up his phone, 'It's me George. Everything's alright with the local police. Now how do we disarm this bomb?'

George handed the phone to Khan who started to speak to David. 'Open the flask and carefully remove the bomb. It will slide out, but do it slowly.'

'Give me a minute while I open up the flask.' David picked up the flask. Slowly, he opened the top and saw its lethal contents. A small red light was illuminated on the top. 'There's a red light on, is that supposed to be lit?'

'That means he's armed the bomb. It should have a forty-minute timer on it. Did he drop it when you shot him?'

'No, he placed it on the floor. Would that make a difference?'

'It could shorten or lengthen the time to detonation. Don't panic. Remove the bomb by slowly sliding it out of the flask.'

David slowly removed the bomb into the palm of his right hand. As he did this, Steve, with the assistance of the Merseyside officers stopped the traffic going past and tried to get people to leave the immediate area. Aware that he was stood alone, David fought to stay composed. He began thinking of his children, wondering if he would see them again. He also thought of Debbie and the irony that just as a relationship starts, it could all be over if he got this wrong. 'OK Moosa it's in my hand. Now what do I do?'

'At the bottom can you see a switch? It looks like the top of a ballpoint pen.'

'Yep, I see it.'

'Press that switch down and the side will come loose.'

David pressed the switch, half closing his eyes as he did so. Once again, he felt that dryness in his mouth and his heart pounding. Just as Khan told him it would, the side panel became loose.

'OK, now slide the panel down the bomb and you will see a small mobile phone keypad.'

'Done it, yes, I see it.'

'Type in the numbers five-eight-two-one.'

David slowly pressed the button on the keypad with his large fingers. 'Done, what now?'

'Has the red light gone off?'

David checked the device. 'Yes, it has.'

'Congratulations, you've disarmed the bomb. It will be exactly the same for the second bomb, but don't worry. I'll stay on the phone and talk you through it again.'

As there was only the one bomb in the bag, David felt sick to the bottom of his stomach. 'Are you taking the fucking piss or what, there's only one bomb.'

'He had two bombs when he got onto the train. Are you sure he didn't drop it?'

'Hang on.' David turned to Steve and shouted over to him, 'Can you see another flask where you are? Khan's telling me there's a second bomb.'

Steve and the officers standing by him had another look round the area, but they found nothing. Steve shouted back, 'There's fuck all here mate.'

Continuous waves of panic swept through his body at the thought of this bomb going off on the train, 'Moosa, he must have left the second bomb on the train. Put me on to George.'

'I've just heard there's a second bomb,' George said calmly.

'He must've left it on the train. Ring Lime Street. They've got to stop the train and get Merseyside's ISB to meet it. I'll go with Steve into Liverpool city centre.' As he spoke, Steve caught his eye. The both looked at each other knowing that time was of the essence if they were to stop the second bomb from going off.

Twenty-Two

Friday 27th October
09.55 hours
Broadgreen, Liverpool

'DS Hurst, I've got a message from our ISB, they'd like to RV with you at St. Luke's. I'll take you both down there now,' one of the firearms officers shouted over to David at the scene of the shooting.

'Thanks.' He shouted over to Steve, 'Jump in. We're going into the city centre. I'll just speak to the senior officer before we go.' As Steve got into the marked police car, David went over to the uniform inspector who arrived at the scene while he was disarming the bomb. 'Excuse me sir, but Merseyside ISB require that my DC and I to go to the city straight away. I'm aware that this may cause you problems seeing as how we've killed our suspect. Here's my card with my contact number on and here is my DI's number, he's the SIO on this job.' David wrote George's contact number on his card and handed it to the inspector.

'I know this is irregular, but this is not a regular shooting. Don't get involved in any further operational work. I assume it's your advice they want?'

'Yes sir and don't worry, I understand your situation. We won't do anything to embarrass you. I think I've done enough damage on your patch already.'

'That's an understatement DS Hurst,' the inspector shouted

back as David got in to the police car.

David was closing the front passenger door and the car set off with its blue lights flashing and sirens blaring. As the driver crossed over the Rocket junction and entered Edge Lane Drive, he said, 'I've never been involved in a Branch job before. It took some nerve to disarm that bomb.'

'Thanks. Are you going to cut through Wavertree Technology Park and go past Abercromby Square?' David asked.

'Yeah, but don't worry I'll have the sirens off before we approach St. Luke's. I can drop you off around the corner from the church if you want. You've got a good knowledge of Liverpool and your accent sounds like it's more from here than Manchester?'

'It is, I was born and raised here. I lived in the Dingle. Can I use the radio to get an update?

'Help yourself.'

'CH this is DS Hurst from GMP ISB can you put me through to my Merseyside ISB colleagues please?'

'Yes, go onto channel twenty-four, you can have talk-through.'

'Thanks CH.' David changed the radio channel and pressed the transmit button. 'DS Hurst to Merseyside ISB, come in.'

'DS Hurst, DS Curtis here.'

'Is that Andy Curtis?'

'It is Davey. To update you, we have two possible targets parked in Bold Place. We've met up with two Five officers and we've got transport on Leece Street and Berry Street. I'm holding back from the scene at the top of Bold Street. Two of my team and the two Five officers are on foot keeping an eye on them. We've contacted the BTP and the train's still on its way to Lime Street. Officers from Merseyside's ISB and the BTP are going to evacuate the station. We're in contact with a Moosa Khan who is going to help us disarm the bomb. What's your ETA to me?'

'We should be with you in less than five minutes. We're coming out of the Tech Park now onto Wavertree Road. We'll get out at Leece and Rodney Street and walk down to Bold Place. If they move off, lift them.'

*   *   *

'Someone's left this under this seat,' a young teenager said to his friend. Both of them were sitting in the seat Ibrar Aatcha vacated on the train. As the train approached Edge Hill station, one of the teenagers picked up the vacuum flask Aatcha left underneath the seat. He looked inside the vacuum flask as his friend went to grab the flask off him, 'Give it here Chris, it could be valuable.'

'I found it first.'

'Well open it and let's see what's inside.'

'It's only a flask.'

'It might have something valuable inside it. I saw it in this film once where a flask had diamonds in it. Go on open it. If it's just tea, we'll fling it.'

*   *   *

'I repeat will all persons clear the station concourse. Do not panic and walk to the nearest exit. Do not run,' said the reassuring voice over the public address system at Lime Street station. Throngs of people were making their way out of the station as uniform BTP officers guided people to the nearest exits, constantly telling people not to panic and not to run. Regardless of the warning over the public address system, there was still a mass panic as many tried to run out of the station. As people tripped over securely fixed seats on the concourse, it heightened the sense of panic. Some, realizing the police officers' attention had been diverted to deal with the emergency, took the opportunity to steal from the concourse shops. The surreal situation continued as the calm voice repeatedly continued with the message that boomed out over the utter chaos and panic on the station concourse.

*   *   *

As David and Steve passed Liverpool's Roman Catholic
Metropolitan Cathedral, referred locally as 'Paddy's Wigwam'
because of the distinctive design that did make it look like some
form of Native American tent, the driver turned at speed into
Hope Street. The officers lurched forward as the driver slammed
on the brakes to avoid hitting the large number of students from
the university opposite who were slowly crossing the road. David
instructed the driver to drop him and Steve off at the junction.
'We'll make the rest of the way on foot and thanks for the lift,'
David said slamming the passenger door shut. The two officers
ran passed the restored Georgian built buildings that now
comprised of shops and offices along Hope Street and turned
down the narrower Maryland Street into Rodney Street. David
turned to Steve, 'We'll be out of sight if we approach this way.'
Once in Rodney Street the officers stopped running.

Trying to catch his breath, Steve said, 'We're going to have to
pack the ciggies in. It's catching up with me now.' They crossed
Leece Street and walked down towards St. Luke's church still
breathing heavily.

Waiting for them in Bold Street, Andy Curtis saw the two
officers approaching. He walked towards them and said, 'I'm glad
you could make it. As there's no sign of your man, the two in the
car seem to be getting really anxious. Shall we lift them now?'

*   *   *

Chris looked to his young friend eager to find out what was
inside the vacuum flask. 'What's in it?' his friend asked.

'I don't know. There's some metal thing inside it with a light
on.' As the train was pulling up at Lime Street station, the two

lads saw a large number of uniform police officers standing on the platform, 'What's the police doing here?' Chris asked.

George passed onto Merseyside's ISB officers at the station the location of the seat Aatcha had sat in. As a result the station manager calculated the approximate position on the platform where Aatcha's seat would be when the train came to a stop. As the train stopped, the train guard spoke over the train's intercom requesting passengers to remain in their seats until they were told to leave by the police. As the police officers boarded the train, a mild panic ran through the passengers. Aiming for the seat Aatcha had sat in, Merseyside ISB and uniform officers pushed their way past the passengers standing in the aisle. As they got to the seat, they saw the two teenage boys who were open mouthed, thinking they must have done something wrong.

They dropped the flask and the device they found in it onto the seat and tried to run off. There were too many officers on the train for the youths to get away. One of the uniform BTP officers grabbed hold of Chris who shouted, 'We never stole it. It was just there, under the seat.'

DC Graham Stevens identified himself to Chris. 'It's alright lad, you're not in trouble. We know you found the flask. The man who left it reported to us. It's part of a valuable experiment that he's working on. That's why we need to get it and send it back to him.' The detective looked at the uniform officer and said, 'Take them away and one of us will come along later to get a statement off them.' He then turned to the two youths. 'You're not under arrest, but if you don't help us, we may find something to arrest you for. Do you understand?'

DC Stevens got onto his radio that had been patched into Greater Manchester's ISB and told Moosa Khan the situation.

'Is the bomb still in the flask?' Khan asked the detective.

'No, it's lying here on the seat.'

'Do you know how long it's been out of the flask?'

'No. Is that important?'

'Just stay calm as the boys may have interfered with the timing mechanism.'

'What you're saying is that this thing can go off any second?'

'Yes...' and Khan gave DC Stevens the same instructions that he gave David earlier to disarm the bomb. 'Has the light gone out?'

'Yes,' said the relieved officer.

'Congratulations, the bomb is now disarmed.'

The officer asked one of the other officers present to inform the station manger the device was safe and that passengers could return to the station.

*   *   *

'Aatcha was armed, so we must assume these two are as well. Are you and your team armed?' David asked Andy Curtis.

'Yes, and we've got firearms officers close by. They can make the arrest.'

'Good idea,' David said, thinking how he did not want to go through another shooting.

'Tango X-ray units, hard stop, Bold Place. The White Peugeot 405 parked half-way up Bold Place. Two males on board, one is in the driver's seat the other in the front passenger,' Andy Cutis instructed the other officers over the radio. He turned to David and Steve and said, 'They're literally around the corner. It'll be a silent approach. We'll wait here.'

'Where are they coming from?' David asked.

'Berry Street. Come on, we'll stroll up there. They'll be there by now.'

The three officers walked around the corner, past the church into Bold Place. They could see the two marked police cars had stopped the white Peugeot car. As the four armed uniform officers surrounded the car, one of the officers shouted instructions to the two occupants while other officers began to clear the immediate area and stop anyone approaching. The driver of the

Peugeot slowly got out of the car. He put his hands up in the air and, following the instructions he was given, went down onto his knees with his hands intertwined on the back of his head. A second firearms officer approached the driver and started to search him when a shout came up from one of the other officers, 'Stop or I will shoot.' The officer had his rifle aimed directly at the front seat passenger who was standing by the door refusing to go onto his knees. The firearms officer shouted, 'Grenade, he's got a grenade.'

Andy Curtis was the first to react, 'Oh shit!'

David looked at the man and turned to Steve and said, 'Isn't that Aatcha's cousin? What's his name?'

'Fuck me it is. It's Mohammed Aatcha. He's the one with the kebab shop in Ashton. So he's Al Qaeda as well!'

'You know him?' Andy asked the officers.

'He's the cousin of the lad that we've just shot. We had him down as an innocent associate. There was no intelligence to say that he was Al Qaeda. It just goes to show how fucking wrong you can be,' David said.

The three officers cautiously walked up to the car as David briefed Andy Curtis on how Mohammed Aatcha came into their investigation. As they approached, Mohammed looked directly at David Hurst and shouted, 'Have you arrested Ibrar?'

'Yes we have Mohammed,' David shouted back. He realized that Mohammed Aatcha had no idea his cousin had been shot. They slowly approached him and David raised his voice so it could be heard over the passing traffic, 'Why not put the grenade down Mohammed?'

'The pin's out, so one shot from any of you and your mates will die,' he said waving the grenade in his hand.

Steve whispered to both David and Andy, 'If he drops it, those firearms lads will cop it. They'll have no chance to get out of the way.'

David said, 'You're right about the firearms lads. We'll have to try and get them out of the vicinity.' As Andy Curtis reinforced the order to his officers to keep people away from the scene, David shouted to Mohammed, 'What are your demands?'

'Tell the armed coppers to move away and let us get back into the car. If we're not followed, no one will be harmed. Let us go or you'll have blood on your hands. The longer you delay, the more tired my hand becomes. I can't hold this grenade much longer,' Mohammed shouted back.

David turned to Andy and Steve and said, 'We've little choice but to do as he says.'

Mohammed watched the three officers talking to each other and shouted, 'You don't have much time. My hand's getting tired.'

Andy said, 'He won't be able to put the pin back, so it's going to go off anyway.'

'Oh fuck,' David said, 'he either drives off and then throws the thing, or drives off holding it and he'll blow themselves up. What's your shooting like Andy?'

'OK, but I don't know if I could hit him from here.'

'I could,' Steve said.

'I'll get the officers to move back and you'll have to shoot him as he gets back in the car. It's a big ask I know,' David said.

Steve's jocular persona accompanied by a cheeky grin was replaced with a look of steely determination. It was a look that David had seen many times in Steve before. Steve looked directly up Bold Place at Mohammed standing there, waving a grenade in the air and in a quiet but determined tone said, 'Trust me Davey, I'll get the bastard.'

David turned his back towards Mohammed and faced Steve and said, 'Get your pistol out now and stand behind me. We'll drop to the floor to give you a clear shot, but make sure your shot's true, you'll only have time to get one shot into him.' He then turned to face Mohammed and said to him, 'I'll tell the officers to back away from you. Can you hold the grenade long enough to let them drive away?'

He shouted back, 'Do it now!'

David did as Mohammed asked. The four firearms officers returned to their cars and drove off as the driver of the Peugeot got back in the car and switched the engine on. As the armed officers drove out of Bold Place David shouted to Mohammed, 'You've got what you want.'

Mohammed shouted back, 'Not quite you bastards.' He raised his hand holding the grenade, pulled his arm behind him indicating he was about to throw the grenade in their direction. As he did, David and Andy dived onto the pavement while Steve fired two rounds, hitting Mohammed in the chest throwing him backwards. As he fell he dropped the grenade. It trundled tantalizingly away from the barely conscious Mohammed as he lay motionless on the pavement. Four feet away from Mohammed, the grenade lodged in between two paving stones. On seeing this, the driver of the Peugeot drove off towards Leece Street. There was a loud bang as shards of hot metal flew off in different directions followed by a plume of smoke. If Steve did not kill Mohammed, the explosion of the grenade certainly did as the shrapnel ripped into his body. As David and Andy delicately stood up, Steve turned and said, 'Just a normal day at the office.'

'I think we're going to be writing this day up to when I retire,' David said.

With the other Merseyside ISB officers and the two MI5 officers, they ran over to Mohammed's limp and shattered body. A Merseyside ISB officer informed Andy that the Peugeot had been stopped and the driver was in the process of being arrested. Andy said to the other officers in his team, 'The circus will be down here shortly. Be professional. Remember this is a crime scene.' He pointed to two Merseyside ISB officers and instructed them to block off Bold Place and to preserve the scene. He told another two to check the buildings in Bold Place for witnesses. The three of them looked around and saw the explosion had caused the windows in the houses opposite to shatter, but no one else had been hurt. David was just relieved that no civilians had been killed or injured.

David turned to Steve and said, 'I'll phone George and brief him. Professional Standards and the IPCC are going to have their hands full investigating this lot. I just hope we don't get some prick of a detective super looking after the investigation. This job's far from over.'

Twenty-Three

'Don't fucking "but sir" me George. I've had a call from the head of Merseyside's ISB telling me how two of our officers have been running around wild on the streets of Liverpool killing people. Then to top it off, the two GMP officers that I'm told that are running wild are fucking Hurst and his sidekick Adams. And if things couldn't get any worse, the Chief Con's been on the phone and asked me to brief him on what happened. Fuck me George I'm livid. You promised me to keep me updated.' George kept trying to interrupt, but he could not get a word in. As soon as Paul Edge heard about the events in Liverpool, he contacted George to see what was happening and continued shouting at the DI, 'I told you to shut the fuck up when I'm talking George. You're finished in the Branch and with luck Hurst will be up on a fucking murder charge. You've all made me look like a right tit. I'm supposed be the head of the ISB not you George. And as head of this fucking department, I'm supposed to know everything that's going on, not what you fucking think I need to know. Have you any idea how embarrassing it is when the Chief's telling me what my officers are doing and I've no fucking answers because you tell me fuck all? I felt a right dickhead when Gamble's asking me for

275

answers. Do you understand? I'm the head of the ISB not you, not Hurst or any of his side-kicks, it's me! Have I got this through your fucking thick, obstinate head George?'

George finally managed to get a few words in and said, 'You've made that very clear sir that it's you that's in charge, but sir...'

'I told you before, don't fucking "but sir" me.' As Edge continued with his rant, George tightened his lips in anger. 'Now tell me this George, what are we going to do about the Al Qaeda attack on Manchester airport? Answer me that one? Then there's the murder investigation of Tony King. How am I going to fucking well man that one if you've got half of the department running around the Northwest on a fucking wild goose chase, shooting anyone that comes in their fucking way? If you've fucked up my promotion chances I'll have my pound of your fucking flesh.'

As Edge continued to rant over the phone, George held the receiver away from his ear where the tirade was clearly audible to those in the control room. As they heard Edge swearing and cursing, they had to suppress their laughter as they tried to concentrate on their own roles. Realizing he was getting nowhere with Edge, he cupped his hand over the handset, turned to Debbie and said, 'Do me a favor Debbie, could you find Craig for me. I think I'll need him to placate Paul Edge. He's that loud, I'm surprised I've not had a complaint from the hotel management to tone it down a bit.'

'Sure George,' she said and raising her eyes in disbelief at what she was hearing added, 'He's really gone off on one hasn't he?'

'I think that's what is known as an understatement. Be a dear and make it as quick as you can. I can only keep saying "yes sir" and "no sir" for so long before I explode myself with this foul mouthed ignorant prick.'

A couple of minutes later Debbie returned to the temporary control room with Craig. George was still on the phone to Paul Edge when he offered Craig the telephone handset. 'Do me a favor and deal with Mr. Edge. I can't get a word in edgeways with him,' George said.

'Certainly George, it will be a pleasure,' and Craig took hold of the handset and placed it to his ear. 'Mr. Edge, it's senior intelligence officer Craig MacDonald here from MI5.' Edge did not hear him as he continued his tirade of abuse. 'Mr. Edge please let me get a word in here. It's Craig MacDonald, the senior intelligence officer from MI5 here.'

Edge stopped speaking for a moment as it sank in that he was no longer talking to George and immediately changed his demeanor. 'I'm sorry Mr. MacDonald. It's just that my staff have let me down. What can I do for you?'

'Thank you Mr. Edge, call me Craig by the way, 'Craig said raising his thumb up signifying to George that he had finally calmed him down.

'Likewise, call me Paul,' Edge said sheepishly.

'Thank you Paul. I understand how upset you must be but please don't take too much of a dim view of George Byrne and his officers. They were acting under my orders. As my orders come straight from the PM and the Home Secretary, we were under strict instruction to keep the latest developments very firmly under our hats. As much as we wanted to, we simply could not let you in on the full picture. The airport attack was a diversion set up by Al Qaeda and we needed you to carry on believing that it was still Al Qaeda's primary target. Being the consummate professional that you are, I knew you would adopt the correct procedures at the airport and make Al Qaeda believe we'd fallen for their plan. George feels awful over not being able to let you know the truth. In fact both George and David Hurst pleaded with me to let you in on what was happening, but as my orders were from those on high, I couldn't. I have to admit, I do feel a bit of a shit not letting you know. Then to make matters worse, events occurred at such a pace this morning that our primary focus was in dealing with them as they unfolded. I simply couldn't allow anyone to take their eye of the ball and update you as to what was happening. I was just preparing a full statement for you that I was going to hand over to you personally this morning so you could answer any difficult questions from either the media or any police chiefs. Unfortunately Bernard Gamble beat me to it. So please Paul, I do understand your anger but I'm the one on whom you should be venting your spleen.'

Feeling like a fool having shouted and abused George in the manner he did, he said, 'I'm sorry Craig, but I'm still annoyed at George, a quick courtesy call would have helped. I understand the predicament you must have been in. It's just a shame that Gamble got to me first. I suppose it's just bad timing?'

'Yes, it was unfortunate. If only Bernard Gamble had contacted you in another ten minutes time you would have been fully in the picture. I would have already been in your office and briefed you on the events that occurred this morning and then you would have been able handle Bernard Gamble and the likes.' Feeling forced to lie in order to inflate Edge's misguided ego Craig said, 'Anyway reports from my intelligence officers at the airport state that you've done a splendid job. In fact you've done such an excellent job that George's teams and my officers could not have been able to catch the Al Qaeda operatives in the manner they did this morning. It's just been unfortunate that two of George's officers were placed into such a dangerous position in Liverpool. They had no choice but to kill the targets they came across. I can tell you this, their actions were highly commendable. Quite clearly the high standards you set has rubbed off on your officers. They're a real credit to you. I'll deal with the chief constable and have the PM contact him personally and apologize on my behalf. I could have him do the same to you if you want.'

Paul Edge calmed down as Craig explained the position to him. For a moment he thought how he would like a call from the PM, but then thought against it and said, 'Oh no Craig, there's no need for you to go that far. It's kind of you to offer but you will confirm to the chief constable that my actions were vital in the success of this operation?'

'Of course I will Paul. I'm sure you understand my position and the dilemma I was in.'

'Of course I do Craig and thank you for showing such confidence in me.'

'It's not a problem. I wouldn't be too surprised if there isn't a promotion in this for you.' After Edge hung up Craig looked to George and said, 'What an insufferable little prick he is. He's dangerous too. How the hell did he get to be a DCI?'

'I told you before, by greasing palms, having the black on people accompanied by bullying and intimidation. Thanks for that Craig. I see that you've not lost your touch with the soft soap.'

'Don't mention it. Anyway returning to the job in hand, I think I've sorted out Professional Standards and the IPCC regarding the investigation and the circumstances that led to the death of the two Aatcha's. Your two lads should be able to continue with their duties shortly. So Ibrar's cousin was Al Qaeda eh? That shows you how hard it is to identify these home-grown terrorists. What's the latest intelligence we've got in?"

Debbie said, 'I've been updating all of the latest intelligence to pinpoint where we are currently. Ahmed is in custody at Rochdale custody suite and DS Ray Baskin has organized interviewing teams. No interviews have taken place yet. The flats in Ashton and Granby Row are still being searched. Also Moosa Khan is still being debriefed by MI5. The Home Secretary's been in touch with IPCC and briefed them. The Home Sec's report has been forwarded onto us from MI5 via email. While David Hurst and Steve Adams can't go out on surveillance or fieldwork for the moment, they can interview the suspect who was driving the white Peugeot. Thames House hope to have both David and Steve fully operational by the end of the day. The interviews with the driver of the Peugeot will take place in Liverpool and they will be conducted by both David and Steve.

We've secured the services of Wavertree Road custody suite in Liverpool, where the suspect's being held. His name is Imran Younnis. He's a twenty-year-old, born in Oldham who was recently recruited to Al Qaeda. Apparently he was recruited by Al Qaeda twelve months ago at a mosque in Blackburn where the radical cleric Abu Al-Hajd was converting young Muslims to Al Qaeda.'

Craig interrupted Debbie and said, 'Isn't he the cleric that was recently sent to Belmarsh Prison pending extradition to Syria?'

Debbie replied, 'That's him. The Liverpool incident is the first time Younnis has come onto our radar. The intelligence we have on him shows he's currently unemployed and has been since he left school at sixteen. He lived with his parents until he was eighteen. For the past five months he's been living with two other males in a house in Oldham. That house is being searched by ISB officers and the two other occupants have been arrested and taken to the custody suite at Platt Lane police station. Moosa Khan has categorically confirmed that Sayfel has turned native and is acting as a double agent. Sayfel's last communication did not mention today's attacks, although it stated he brought timing devices and bomb triggers on Thursday morning. It made no mention of the pathogen inside the bombs. Khan says that Sayfel brought the pathogen up with him yesterday. Thames House see this as further evidence he's turned native especially as his last communication stated they would be carrying out their attack late Sunday or early Monday at Manchester airport. Clearly he was trying to throw us off the scent.'

Craig interrupted Debbie again and said, 'I'm sorry to keep butting in Debbie, but it's important we flag Sayfel up as the number one target. It's essential we find him before he does any more damage.'

'If anything of use is passed on by Khan during his debrief either Brian Maguire or Gordon Bascombe will pass it on straight away. At the moment they're still getting him out of role. Finally, regarding David Hurst and Steve Adams, Chief Superintendent Simon Knight from Merseyside Police Professional Standards Department is the officer in charge of the investigation into the shooting of Ibrar Aatcha and Mohammed Aatcha. They've given them clearance to interview Younnis.

'Regarding the IPCC's investigation there is corroborating evidence that both Hurst and Adams used reasonable force. A front seat passenger in a vehicle stationary at the traffic lights on the city bound carriageway of Edge Lane Drive, just a bit further up from Broadgreen Station recorded the event on his mobile phone. According to Merseyside Police, you both can clearly see and hear David Hurst give his warnings and that Aatcha fired first. Within the next hour they're sending this recording through to us, so we'll be able to see for ourselves what happened. The fact Ibrar Aatcha had a bomb is also good supporting evidence that the use of lethal force was necessary. As expected, the press is all over this one. As a result the press offices at both Merseyside Police and GMP are currently being bombarded with requests for information and interviews with police managers involved in the investigation.'

Craig responded first saying, 'We'll go to GMP headquarters and brief the ACC responsible for operations as I think she's best placed to handle this. It'll keep us out of the limelight.'

George nodded his head in agreement at this suggestion and said, 'That's a good idea. Sandra Parry is the ACC Ops. She's been in the post for the past twelve months. She's a bit of a flier as she's only thirty-eight years old, but she's alright. I'll get onto that now and then I'll speak to David Hurst and update him. I'll tell Paul Edge as well,' George said.

'Good idea George, it might be best to keep that jumped up little prick on board with us for now. Leave Edge to me. You arrange the briefing with ACC Parry.'

*   *   *

At four o'clock that afternoon in a side room at Wavertree Road custody suite David and Steve were waiting to interview Imran Younnis. Earlier that afternoon George had sent a GMP motorcyclist over to Liverpool to hand over the evidence found during the search of Younnis' house to put to him during their interview. They had already briefed Younnis' solicitor as to what they intended to cover during the interview and were waiting for him to finish his consultation with Younnis before they could start the interview. Steve was reflecting on how their briefing with Younnis' solicitor had gone. 'I've not come across him before', he said. He then mimicked the solicitor, a Mr. Clive Herring, saying, '"Is that all the evidence you have on my client? It's doesn't seem much to me. I hope you have respected his right to stay silent?" He's a typical provincial duty solicitor. Obviously Younnis hasn't been with Al Qaeda long enough to know the names of the solicitors they use. And regarding Herring, there's something fishy about him.'

David rolled his eyes at the poor quality of Steve's humor and said, 'All joking apart, he has the potential to be an awkward bastard who'll see this as his moment of glory. He'll know this job will attract a lot of media interest. He's probably pictured himself outside the steps of the police station giving a press briefing knowing that the world's media would be broadcasting it. He'll see this as is his five minutes of fame to enhance his own career. In my chat with him when he arrived at the station, he said that he normally dealt with property offences and serious assaults. This is his first terrorist case. Although he'd done a couple of murder jobs, this job was different to what he's dealt with in the past. It'll be just our luck to have a brief who wants to make a name for himself and start to act like an awkward prick.'

A few minutes later a custody assistant knocked on the door to the side room and informed David and Steve that Younnis and his solicitor were ready for the interview. David picked up the file he prepared with Steve and walked out into the main custody suite. There was an eerie silence around the custody suite. As the protocol of emptying out all of the cells prior to the arrival of a suspected terrorist had been carried out by the custody officer, only one of the twenty-three cells were in use and that was for David and Steve's prisoner, Younnis. With there being such little activity, the custody officer and the five custody assistants on duty that day that had little to do as they watched the two officers make their way to the one of the interview rooms. The custody assistant that accompanied the officers through the custody suite opened the door of the interview room and announced them to Younnis and his solicitor. It was a small cramped room that had a table against the far wall on which the tape recorder was placed. Alongside the recorder was a stack of blank cassette tapes piled up against a portable television with a combined DVD player. At the top of the wall opposite was a camera used for recording interviews. The claustrophobic atmosphere of the room was enhanced by the lack of windows, which restricted any natural light coming into room. The grim atmosphere was heightened by the smell of the body odors of the previous detained persons that had been interviewed over the years in that room. At one side of the table sat Mr. Herring and Younnis. As David and Steve entered the room Mr. Herring stood up while Younnis remained seated looking down to his hands that he placed on his lap. Watching Younnis constantly intertwine his fingers and tap his foot on the floor, David sensed Younnis' nervousness.

'Here we go,' Craig said to George at the incident room in Manchester as they looked at a screen relaying the pictures from the small camera placed inside the interview room, 'let's see if your two boys are as good as you claim. Let's hope it isn't too long before they get something out of the little bastard.'

As David offered his hand to Younnis, he introduced himself and Steve. Younnis stood up and shook hands with him. David was slightly taken aback by Younnis' behavior. He was used to trained terrorists never made eye contact or speaking to Branch officers let alone shaking hands with them. 'He's new to this game,' David thought. Then he thought that this could be a ploy by Younnis. 'Now he'll play dumb and plead his innocence.'

Neither officer knew Younnis, nor had they any idea how he would react to their questioning. What was evident was Younnis' fear that enhanced the charged the atmosphere in the room. Apart from constantly intertwining his fingers, both the officers noticed Younnis constantly biting his bottom lip. He was open eyed and kept alternating his gaze between David and Steve. Mr. Herring, sat on the edge of his chair was grasping his clipboard so tightly the whites of his knuckles were showing. 'He's keen not to cock-up then,' David thought as he looked at the solicitor out of the corner of his eye. After they introduced themselves to each other for the benefit of the tape, David explained how the interview would be conducted along with an explanation of the caution. Once he was satisfied that Younnis understood the legal points, David began his questioning of Younnis. 'What were you doing with Mohammed Aatcha in Bold Place, Liverpool this morning?'

Younnis stopped intertwining his fingers and grabbed the edge of the table with both hands. Pleading, he said, 'I'm not a terrorist boss. You must believe me. I share a house with Mohammed's cousin, Ibrahim Aatcha. I took Ibrahim to his family in Ashton early this morning and they asked me to take Mohammed to Liverpool as he had some family business there. All he told me was that he was meeting a business contact. I had no idea he was a terrorist.'

Looking Younnis right in the eye David, in a calm, passive tone asked, 'If you're not a terrorist, why did they ask you to take Mohammed to Liverpool?'

'Because I have a car.'

'So no other member of the Aatcha family has a car they could use to drive to Liverpool to meet this business contact?'

'I don't know, they just asked me.'

'Why should they ask you?'

Younnis paused for a moment. He was struggling to answer David's early questions. He was just saying the first thing that came into his head. 'I was there I suppose.'

'How do you know Mohammed Aatcha?'

'I've been to his family's kebab shop in Ashton before. I used to work there for a few months.'

'When did you work there?'

'About five months ago.' Younnis was desperate to change David's line of questioning. 'Please sir, don't tell the Benefits Agency, as I was claiming benefits at the time.'

His ploy did not work as David said, 'That issue's not important to me, I've no interest in what benefits you have or have not been claiming. So you've been living with Ibrahim Aatcha, who is the cousin of Mohammed Aatcha and you know the Aatcha family as you used to work at the family's kebab shop?'

'That's right boss.'

'While you were working in the shop were you living in Ashton?'

'No, but if I was working late I used to stay overnight at the flat they had above Ibrahim's uncle's shop. I still had the house I share with Ibrahim.'

'When did you work at the kebab shop in Ashton?'

'I worked there from March to August,' Younnis said feeling more comfortable as these last couple of facts were true.

'Did you know Ibrar Aatcha?'

'Yes, he is Ibrahim's older cousin. I met him in July. He'd just come back from Lahore University in Pakistan.'

'You knew Ibrar Aatcha because you worked at the kebab shop in Ashton for a few months, but you still lived in Oldham while you worked at the kebab shop and you only occasionally stayed in Ashton overnight when you worked late at the kebab shop. Is that right?'

'That's right boss.'

'Who else did you share the house with in Oldham?'

Again Younnis paused for a moment. He realized he had to tell the truth as he knew that they would have found out not only where he lived but who he lived with. 'Meshaq Yassin.'

'How did you know him?'

'He's a friend of Ibrahim's. He went to school with him as well as going to the same mosque.'

'Does he still live with you?'

'Yes.'

'How well do you get on with him?'

'OK I suppose. We sometimes go out together.'

'What do you know about Meshaq?'

'He helps his father with his market stall.'

'Where do they have the market stall?'

'They go to markets all over the North-west. They go to Liverpool, Oldham, Ashton...'

David broke the rule of not interrupting a reply by a suspect during an interview and cut Younnis short as he wanted to get to the real issue. 'So the three of you are all working on the side, all helping out with family businesses and then out of the blue you go to Ashton and you're asked to take Mohammed to Liverpool because you're the only one with a car. You then go to a side street, Bold Place in Liverpool by the bombed out church and you claim that you had no idea what Mohammed was up to. You're telling me that you had no curiosity as to why they should drag you out all the way to Liverpool, a city you don't really know. Didn't you think that this was strange?'

Younnis looked down at the table. He realized the officers were not going to easily accept what he was saying. He found David's constant eye contact unnerving. 'No boss.'

David created an uncomfortable pause as he scanned the papers before him. After reading the papers, he resumed his eye contact with Younnis. 'You're expecting me to believe that this was normal?'

'Yes boss, I had no reason to suspect anything.'

David let him continue with his implausibility. 'What did Mohammed have with him when you drove over to Liverpool?'

'He had a suitcase and a holdall.'

'Did you ask him what were in the bags?'

'Yes. He told me they were clothing samples.'

He was not normally an impatient interviewer, but with the events that had taken place that morning and knowing that Younnis was lying, David decided to start to reveal his hand. 'I think it's time to cut the bullshit. Let me tell you what I think happened. Al Qaeda recently recruited you, Ibrahim and Meshaq. I believe that Mohammed Aatcha also had a hand in recruiting you. You went to Liverpool to meet Mohammed's cousin Ibrar and you knew he was on an Al Qaeda mission. You knew that once you picked up Ibrar you were to take him to Essex so he could escape from the country. We have evidence confirming this. So Imran, you're in deep shit right up to your neck. I already know that you bought the rail tickets for Ibrar Aatcha and Moosa Khan at Victoria rail station on Thursday. You were not only seen buying the tickets, but you were recorded on the station's CCTV doing so. Once you purchased the tickets, you then left the station and met with Zulfqar Ahmed at The Triangle in Manchester. We have that meeting recorded too.'

Mr. Herring interrupted saying, 'Officers you told me that you had CCTV evidence that you wished to show my client, but you did not tell me exactly what it was. I need a break to brief my client further on this new evidence you wish to produce.'

David nodded in agreement with Herring as he said, 'I agree with you Mr. Herring. I suggest that just before we stop the interview we all watch the CCTV evidence together. Once you've seen it, my colleague and I will leave the room to allow you more time to consult with Mr. Younnis.' David then pressed the play button on the remote control, and instructed Younnis and Mr. Herring to watch the screen in the room. As the recording was playing David gave a commentary of the events as they unfolded, '... and clearly a male who looks exactly like you is seen here at the ticket counter. As you can see the camera zooms in here and you can clearly see this male. This male looks just like you. Do you have a twin brother or is that you Imran?'

Younnis made no reply. He just fixed his eyes on the recording. After it finished, David asked Imran. 'Is there anything you wish to tell me now before my colleague and I leave you to discuss this with your solicitor?'

Younnis said nothing as his eyes closed into a glare. No one in the interview room said anything as a David stared back waiting for an answer. Younnis broke off his stare, banged his fists on the table and shouted in such an aggressive manner that small amounts of spittle projected at speed from his mouth in David's direction. 'They told me you're all bastards. I'll tell you fuck all. You think you're so fucking smart? Trust me you won't win this. Trust me DS David Hurst, my brothers will hunt you down and kill you like the fucking snake in the grass that you are.'

David looked over to a horrified Mr. Herring whose eyes and mouth were wide open as he struggled to say anything in response to the aggression he saw from his client. 'I'll ignore your client's threats to kill me Mr. Herring. I think Mr. Younnis knows I wasn't lying when I said that he's in it up to his neck in this Al Qaeda operation. I'll leave you alone with your client now, so you can have a word with him as I think these events have just changed the direction these interviews are going to take. Imran, I must inform you that we have further evidence to put to you throughout the course of the day and if need be, the next few days. I know this is the first time you've been arrested and interviewed by the police. I suggest you speak to Mr. Herring at length while he advises you.' David looked at the clock on the interview wall, 'The time is sixteen twenty-one hours and the interview is now concluded to allow Mr. Herring further time to brief his client.' David and Steve gathered their paperwork and walked out of the interview room.

As they walked down the corridor towards the custody officer's desk, Steve lent over to David's ear and said, 'I take it you got bored there. What happened to letting them do all the talking and then steadily unpick their lies?'

'I got impatient. It's been a long day and I'm knackered. I just thought it was time to cut to the chase and stop him bullshitting us. This investigation is far from over and we don't have time to pussy foot about. I thought I'd show him some of our hand. Now he's reflecting with his brief over what happens next. Let's brief George and catch up on events.' As they approached the custody officer, David informed her the interview had been suspended to allow Younnis a further period of consultation with his solicitor and that he and Steve were waiting to receive the results of the search of Younnis' premises. They returned to the side room by the custody officer's desk.

Twenty-Four

Friday 27th October
15.30 hours
Hyde Park, London

Sayfel was sitting on a bench in Hyde Park, London. For a brief moment he was enjoying the solitude of his own company. In his mind he was evaluating the implications of what that morning's events in Manchester and Liverpool would have on his and Al Qaeda's plans. He heard about the arrest of Ahmed and Younnis and the deaths of Ibrar and Mohammed on the news bulletins. Although no names were given out, as he had planned the events, Sayfel knew who had been involved. He knew Ahmed was still alive as his solicitor contacted him, telling him that Ahmed was in custody at Rochdale police station. One advantage of Al Qaeda recruiting a number of solicitors around the country sympathetic to their cause was their ability to update Al Qaeda cells as to the progress of ISB investigations when they had suspects in custody. His main concern was for Younnis. Younnis had received very little training and he would not know any of the solicitors used by Al Qaeda. Sayfel's concern was that he may break down during his interrogation by Special Branch and reveal to them all he knows. On top of that, he knew Khan had been arrested but had heard nothing more about his whereabouts. The more he thought about it, the more Sayfel realized that Khan was not who he claimed to be. The prolonged silence on Khan's whereabouts became increasingly deafening. That silence confirmed to Sayfel Khan was a traitor. 'He must be an undercover MI5 officer.'

Trying to work out a plan of action to minimize the potential damage caused by Younnis or Khan's revelations to Special Branch and MI5, he was distracted by the normality of an autumn day in the park. He watched the ducks swimming past him on the lake. He envied animals and birds, their lives seemed so uncomplicated. He glanced at his watch. 'He's five minutes late,' he thought and began to look around, but he could not see any sign of his contact. It was getting cold and he was thinking how the autumn air was quickly being replaced by the chill of winter, but at least it was dry and sunny. He sat in solitude for a few more minutes, conscious of the sounds around him. He could hear small children playing, and saw two toddlers chasing what appeared to be their father. There was a dog barking waiting for its owner to throw a ball for it to fetch. He heard the roar of an aircraft's engines and he looked up to see yet another flight descending towards Heathrow Airport. As he looked up he was aware of someone standing behind him.

'I could have killed you then Sayfel. You're slipping. You've neglected your MI5 training.'

He quickly turned round to see Leonid. 'Where the hell have you been? You're late,' Sayfel snapped back at him.

'We've had some last minute things to sort out with your employer, MI5.'

Indignantly, Sayfel said, 'I've told you they're not my employer, no one is. No one owns me. I'm my own man.'

For once, Leonid noticed how Sayfel was not exuding his normal cavalier confidence. 'You look worried Sayfel. Something's bothering you.'

Avoiding eye contact, he looked down and shaking his head said, 'I'm finished with MI5. After yesterday's events they'll know I'm a double agent.'

'Why? What's happened?'

'The Al Qaeda boys you stayed with in Manchester were to have hit Manchester, Leeds and Liverpool this morning. I took the chemicals, explosive and the triggers they needed to do the job yesterday. The job was planned for this morning, but MI5 and Special Branch arrested everyone and killed Ibrar Aatcha and his cousin Mohammed.' Out of the frustration he was feeling, he began to pick up small stones and throw them into the lake.

Leonid sat down on the bench next to Sayfel. 'I saw that on the news earlier. No names were given out. The reporter only said that two unidentified males believed to be Al Qaeda terrorists were killed while three others were helping the police with their enquiries. As the shooting was in Liverpool, I didn't make any connection to the three men I stayed with in Manchester. I see a grenade went off in Liverpool. What happened there?'

'Ibrar was supposed to be picked up in Liverpool by his cousin Mohammed and a new recruit Imran Younnis. Once they picked him up they were to drive a pre-arranged location in Essex. It was a botched job as Special Branch shot and killed both the Aatcha's and arrested Younnis. I'm assuming it's Special Branch as I'm going by the intelligence I received from our own operatives in the area, but I wouldn't put it past MI5 to have carried out the killings and let Special Branch take the responsibility. They had inside information and it looks like Moosa Khan was also an MI5 officer working undercover. If that's not bad enough, we have a problem as Younnis is the one Special Branch arrested in Liverpool,' Sayfel said constantly picking up and throwing small stones into the lake.

'Why is Younnis a problem?'

Sayfel stopped throwing the stones and looked at Leonid. 'It's a problem as you put it because he's inexperienced. He's had no training in counter-interview techniques, so the chances are that it won't take the Branch long to break him down. When they do, he'll start telling them everything he knows. I've managed to hear from the solicitor looking after Zulfqar Ahmed in Rochdale police station. She found out from the Branch officers interviewing Ahmed that two experienced detectives from Manchester's Special Branch are interviewing Younnis in Liverpool. If those officers have been watching the Aatcha's and Ahmed, they'll be on top of the intelligence. That will make it harder for Younnis to lie his way out of being involved with us. Younnis has got some solicitor not on our payroll and more likely than not, the odds are the solicitor he's got will have no experience in dealing with terrorist cases. Like the proverbial lamb to the slaughter, he's really on his own.'

'What does he know?'

Becoming irate as Leonid's questions only served to reinforce his fears, he answered curtly, 'Trust me he knows enough to do harm to all of our cells in the Northwest. The Branch will be all over the flat he's sharing with two more of our boys in Oldham and they'll find enough to tie Younnis into our organisation. The worse case scenario is if they've found material in the flat that links them to the Rochdale, Bolton, Burnley and Blackburn cells. It's taken me years to start up and develop those cells. If the Branch find out what I think they will, then my former employer will also know what's being going on and cause even more disruption to Al Qaeda in the north and possibly in the whole of the UK.'

'It might not be that bad. Things might just look worse than what they actually are. Does Younnis know you personally?'

As he spoke, Sayfel again began to pick up and throw them into the lake. 'I met him a couple of times. One of those times wasn't long after he was recruited to Al Qaeda. Just like a lot of the younger mujhaids, he's quite impressionable. My main fear is if the Branch break him down then he'll start to make threats as he tries to be the big man and throws my name and the names of others into the ring.'

'Only time will tell on that one Sayfel. So what else happened this morning that gives you cause for concern? You mentioned that you think Khan's an MI5 agent.'

'This morning we first suspected the British security services had inside information when they managed to disarm all of the bombs so soon after finding them. We knew then they must have arrested someone who gave them the codes. It looks like it was Khan as he's not been detained at a police station and we've lost trace of him since he's been arrested. Added to that, we know it wasn't Ibrar as he was killed by Special Branch and Zulfqar is in custody at Rochdale police station. It doesn't take a fucking rocket scientist to work out who the traitor is does it? We had total trust in him. He's even been to a training camp in Pakistan! If that's the case, then MI5 must believe that I have what they term "turned native". The only reason they've put him undercover in Al Qaeda was to check on me. The bastards! They must've been suspecting me for a number of years now.' Sayfel paused for a moment as it dawned on him why Khan had gone undercover. 'I dread to think what information that bastard's passed over to MI5 on me in the last few years. They must have thought that what I passed over in the past few years was that poor and wanted to find out what I was up to. As a result of what's happened, I've told Al Qaeda that I'll go up to Manchester and kill Khan. That will prove to them that I'm still useful. Once that's done, I'll have to be smuggled out of the country and go to a safe house in Europe or if need be Al Qaeda could send me to Pakistan or Yemen. I don't want to go back to Pakistan. I've become used to too many creature comforts for that to happen. I need to know from you what the FSB can offer me seeing how I'm one of their agents.'

'Come on let's go for a walk so you can get off your chest what's in your mind.' As the two got up they started walking along the footpath closest to the lake. Leonid smiled and said, 'So you think that you're one of our agents now?'

Seeing Leonid smiling at the suggestion, Sayfel became further agitated and said, 'Don't you? What do you find so funny? Don't become a smart arse with me you Russian bastard. Remember, if it wasn't for me, you'd still be pissing in the wind over knowing what the Chechen fighters were planning, as well as the groups in Ingushetia and how they've organized themselves outside Chechnya. That's called working for the FSB in my book.'

'Don't misunderstand me, we're very grateful to you, but what you've done is nothing more than act as an informant and you've been well paid for the information you passed over. You're not an FSB agent and we don't owe you anything, just like you don't owe us anything. You're right, we would be "pissing in the wind" but trust me we would have found out what we needed to know in time without you.'

Sayfel grabbed Leonid's coat lapels and pulled him towards him and shouted, 'You fucking lying bastard. If it wasn't for me you wouldn't have got through the door with Al Qaeda in Turkey. You wouldn't have found out what you did without me. Not only did I get you into Turkey, I got you the false papers and the new identity as well as managing to get you in to the UK.'

Leonid placed his hands on Sayfel's and released Sayfel's grip on his coat. 'I'm the only friend you have at the moment as well as your only ticket out of this mess. All you did was speed things up. You're deluded in thinking how important you think you are to us. I don't want to rub salt into the wound, but remember the FSB is not some fledgling security service. Don't forget, the FSB's former name was the KGB. We have plenty of experience of looking after the Russia's security as well as protecting its interests in the world. On the other hand you and Al Qaeda are nothing more than a fly-by-night group. On top of that, you only had a few years MI5 experience before you joined Al Qaeda. We in the FSB, including our days as the KGB, have been a threat to the West for nearly a century. With that history comes experience in espionage, counter-espionage and counter-terrorism. We already had in place an intelligence network the likes of Al Qaeda can only dream of.

Russia can crush the Chechens and the Ingushetians any time it wants to. You know that and you also know we can crush you just as easily and hang you out to dry.'

Sayfel stopped walking and in a fit of rage said, 'I'm no insignificant fly that you can simply swat away. I suggest that you pay me some fucking respect.'

Unperturbed by this outburst, Leonid stayed firm saying, 'You need a reality check. Come on let's keep walking. I'll ask you again, what is it that you want from me?'

'I need you to get me out of the country. I need some money and a place to lay low for a while. I can arrange it with Al Qaeda to return to the UK in a year and when I do I can work for you again.'

Leonid could not help miss the opportunity for sarcasm and said, 'How about arranging for you to stay in a nice Dacha on the outskirts of St Petersburg along with a chauffeur driven limousine and a pension of fifty thousand in sterling a year?'

Sayfel could not believe his ears. If this was arranged, it would suit him perfectly. He pictured himself working for the FSB in Moscow being deployed in areas like Chechnya working undercover. 'Could you arrange that for me?'

Surprised Sayfel fell for his suggestion, Leonid said, 'Come on Sayfel, be realistic. If it got out that we sneaked you out of the UK and looked after you in Russia, it'll make relations between our two countries even worse than what it is now. The killing of the ISB police officer in Manchester is not helping our cause at the moment. Having Al Qaeda not us get you out of the country is your best bet.'

Sayfel tried to return to his normal arrogant self as he said, 'I told you. I don't want to go to some shit hole. I need you to look after me. It was me that helped you set up the Chechens. It was me that helped you go undercover as an infamous Chechen fighter. There must be some reward for that? It wasn't me that fucked up in Manchester. It was the FS fucking B. Why did your man have to kill that Branch officer? Don't forget, it was me who told you to go to Leicester to keep you on the trail of the Chechens. On top of that, did you know that Ahmed was going to kill you but I ordered him not too? It was me that saved your life.'

'That's why I took your advice and left Manchester with the FSB after meeting Petrov in the pub that night. I'm grateful to you Sayfel, I really am. I'll do all I can for you, but there's one obstacle and that obstacle is you. The question the FSB have to answer is what further use are you to them.'

Shaking his head in disbelief Sayfel said, 'Now you think that I'm an obstacle, for fuck's sake, I'm the one who handed the Chechen rebels to you on a plate. Don't forget that. I can offer you a lot more. You know that. There must be some currency in that for me with the FSB?'

'But I have to convince the senior managers in the FSB of that. As we see it, you can no longer access MI5 intelligence and Al Qaeda could have suspicions about who you really are and what your motives are. You'll have to show us that you're still useful to the FSB if we're to keep you on our books. You may have lost your usefulness in relation to what you can access from MI5, but you could still be of value with what you can give us in relation to Al Qaeda and their contact with the Chechen fighters and the Islamic groups in Ingushetia. In other words you need to be economically viable if you are to be of any further use to us. For us to take you out of the UK then house you and so on will cost money and we will want a return. We could assist you getting out of Europe once you've killed Khan and passed onto us the latest intelligence you find on the Chechen rebels and Ingushetian sympathizers currently in the UK, as well as in Russia. However it will have to look like you got out by your own means. In the meantime, and I stress after you have passed on more information to us, we can give out misinformation to Al Qaeda about you being a target for the FSB, MI5, MI6 and even the BKA in Germany. Before any of that happens, you'll have to finish off any loose ends here first.'

Sensing there was a grain of hope the FSB would help him, Sayfel said, 'The first loose end I'll sort out is Khan. I could also go after the Branch officer who killed Ibrar and Mohammed Aatcha.'

'How do you plan to do that?'

'I'll get in touch with the solicitor looking after Zulfqar. She'll get the officers' names to me.'

'That sounds a bit naïve Sayfel. You know it's not as easy as that.'

Angrily Sayfel said, 'I know that! I can get Khan in the next day or two, but it does not have to be me that personally that disposes of the Special Branch officers that killed Ibrar and Mohammed.'

'You realize that once you start targeting the military and the police, you will have stepped into a new area of operation and one where Al Qaeda will be under even closer scrutiny.'

'I know that, but this is a war Leonid and it's a war that I'm determined to win. I'm a patient man. I'll get them when they least suspect it.'

Leonid saw the hatred in Sayfel's eyes as he said, 'You're one ruthless man Sayfel. I'd hate to be your enemy. If you get it done this weekend will you have time to tie up these loose ends? What's your plan? Maybe I could help you?'

Sayfel gave an ironic laugh. 'You know better than to ask me that Leonid? I suggest that once you've stopped their attack, you let the Chechens get away from London. I know it may sound a ludicrous, but I'll make sure they're handed to you on a plate. I'll pass onto you the safe-house that Al Qaeda will let them lay low in. Once you have that, you can either kill them in the UK or smuggle them out and do what you want with them in Russia.'

'That sounds feasible, but I'll have to have this agreed with my controller first,' Leonid said handing Sayfel a mobile phone. 'I'll leave this with you and I'll contact you as soon as I can. Don't make any calls on it unless you really have to. Think of it as your lifeline. At the moment it might be the only one you have. When are you going back to Manchester?'

'As soon as I can.'

                    *   *   *

David was taking the lead in the fourth interview with Younnis. 'Imran I suggest that you stop wasting time. You're not helping yourself in refusing to answer my questions. You can see that we've enough evidence not only to charge you but to have you put away for a long time. Before your solicitor interrupts to tell me to stop the interview and suggest that we should charge you, we have a lot more evidence to put to you over other related offences. I strongly suggest that you start talking to us.'

Mr. Herring interrupted the interview, 'Officer you are starting to bully and intimidate my client. If you have enough evidence then as you say, charge my client. Your style of questioning is not considering the rights of my client.'

David stopped for a moment and slowly turned to look at the solicitor. 'Mr. Herring, never mind you're clients rights, your client's activities doesn't take into account other citizens' rights, especially their right to life. I'm balancing the rights of the many to the rights of your client. As far as I'm concerned, right now the right to protect UK citizens far outweighs the rights of your client. As I explained, I've other evidence to put to Mr. Younnis in relation to other offences. So come on Imran, let's stop pissing around and tell me the truth.'

'Officer,' Mr. Herring intervened raising his voice, 'You're becoming oppressive towards my client. If you continue in this style of interviewing, I will have no option but to have it stopped and report this to the custody officer.'

David glared at the solicitor and in a calm but forceful manner said, 'This morning I disarmed a bomb that, if detonated, would have released dangerous chemicals into the atmosphere killing hundreds if not thousands of innocent lives. Your client, Mr. Younnis has a hand in this morning's Al Qaeda operation. You've seen the evidence of that for yourself. Don't start to tell me when I'm being oppressive and intimidating. Trust me Mr. Herring you'll know when I am being oppressive and intimidating!' He turned to Younnis and said, 'Imran lad, basically you're fucked. Let me sum up for you what we know. You were recruited into Al Qaeda in Blackburn after Ibrahim Aatcha took you to a mosque there. We know that you received some basic terrorist training from Ibrahim and Ibrar Aatcha whilst working in Ashton. The job you had in the kebab shop was a front to your Al Qaeda activities. The evidence we got from your house shows that you were preparing for a trip to a training camp in Yemen early next year. Your computer's hard drive is full of extremist Muslim sites preaching hate and non-conformity to UK and Western legal system. You've been indoctrinated as a young mujahedeen. You're simply a foot soldier. You do know that as far as Al Qaeda's concerned you're expendable? We have evidence linking you to today's al Qaeda operation. You were controlled by Zulfqar Ahmed. You bought the tickets from Victoria rail station. Also you helped Ahmed organize the attack. Who controls Ahmed?'

Younnis went quiet for a moment. His demeanor changed from a cocky arrogance to being reflective and withdrawn. He looked down at the table and began to wring his hands. 'Can I have a drink of water please?'

Steve got up and opened the door of the interview room and shouted down to a custody assistant for a glass of water. He only had to wait a minute when the custody assistant handed Steve a glass of water. Steve made his way back to his seat and put the water on the table. He placed his hand on the top of Younnis' shoulder in a reassuring manner saying, 'Take your time Imran, we know it's a difficult decision for you to make whether or not to tell us the truth.'

Nervously and quietly he said, 'My mouth feels a little dry as if they find out what I tell you it could result in my death when they find me.'

David asked, 'Who is they?'

'Al Qaeda.'

'Go on, take your time.'

Mr. Herring placed his hand on Younnis' arm and said, 'I must remind you that you do not have to tell them anything, they have no evidence. They're on a fishing trip with this line of questioning.' Steve suppressed a muffled giggle as he related the solicitor's name to what he had just said.

David added, 'I have to remind you that you are still under caution. So take your time and have a think about what you want to say. I know it must be hard to weigh up the options of what may happen.'

After a few seconds pause, that seemed like a lifetime to Younnis, he took a sip of water and began to speak. 'I want to tell them Mr. Herring. There's a man in Al Qaeda in London called Sayfel. He's a senior man in Al Qaeda. He's powerful and he's also connected to MI5, or so Ahmed says. I've met him a couple of times. I remember him when I was first recruited. He told us why we had to fight. He really inspired me. He spies for us by giving MI5 information false information or half truths. He had an idea that Ibrar and the other two were being watched and that's why Zulfqar Ahmed instructed me to buy the tickets at Victoria station yesterday because they both knew that you weren't watching me. This morning me and Mohammed were to pick up Ibrar Aatcha and take him to a place in Essex. I don't know the exact location, as Ibrar was going to tell us when we met up with him. We were to meet Sayfel at this place in Essex and he would have papers for Ibrar and the others to leave the country. They'd arranged for a small boat to take them to Holland.

'I was then to take Sayfel to London where he had another job for me. Ahmed said that we should use my car as it was unlikely the intelligence services knew anything about me, and it was unlikely that any sort of tagging device would be fitted to my car. We had to meet Ibrar in that road by the bombed out church in Liverpool where you shot Mohammed. While we were waiting, Mohammed got a call from Ibrar to say that the others had been arrested in Manchester and that he thought Special Branch or MI5 would be at Lime Street station to meet him. He told us that he was getting off the train a few stops before the main station in Liverpool and that he was going to get a taxi into Liverpool city centre. He was going to deposit his bomb near to where we were waiting for him. Then he'd walk up and meet us and we'd drive off. He wasn't sure if he was being followed, but he thought it best to assume he was. He thought that getting a taxi would help throw you off his tail.'

'What do you know about this Sayfel character?' David asked.

'Only that he's a top man in London. He had inside information on what MI5 were up to and he said that kept Al Qaeda one-step ahead of them. Also he has connections with Chechens operating the UK as there's an operation they've planned for next week.'

'How do you know this?'

'Mohammed told me in the car this morning as I was driving to Liverpool.'

'Did Mohammed know Sayfel?'

'Oh yes, Mohammed had been to London to meet him many times. He received some training there and as well at some training camp Al Qaeda has in Scotland. I was supposed to go there last week but I had to stay in the Manchester to help with this operation.'

'What else do you know of Sayfel and this connection to the Chechens?'

'Mohammed said that Ahmed had told him that Sayfel also had inside information on the running of the Russian secret service, the FSB. This is why he's a top man.'

'Do you know what connections he has with the FSB?'

'No, only that he has someone on the inside of the FSB who gives him information which helps the Chechens. Ibrar and Moosa had a Chechen stay with them this week, but Moosa got suspicious of him and when Sayfel came up to Manchester. Sayfel gave Ahmed orders to kill him. Before he could do this the FSB man left the flat and never came back. Mohammed said that Sayfel was really angry with Zulfqar for failing to kill the FSB agent. They'll kill me now because of what I've told you. That's all I know.' Younnis then started to cry as he said, 'I'm a dead man now I've told you all I know.'

'You said that Sayfel told you that he had a job for you in London. Do you know what that job was?' Younnis was sobbing uncontrollably by now and David asked him, 'Do you want some tissues to dry your eyes?'

'Yes please sir.'

Once again Steve left the interview room, which David commented on for the purposes of the tape. David then leant across the interview table in a sympathetic manner and said, 'Imran, I know that what you're doing is a very brave thing. I know how brutal these people can be. Take your time and compose yourself.'

Steve returned to the interview room with a bundle of tissue paper and handed it to Younnis. Mr. Herring asked David, 'Do you think that this is an opportune time to stop the interview and let Mr. Younnis gain some composure and self-respect?'

'No not yet. I only want to ask Mr. Younnis about the "job" Sayfel wants him to do in London. If we find out now what it is they're up to it could save many lives. Don't worry. I can imagine that it's not an easy having to grass on those you know will kill you in revenge. I'd be reacting in the same way as him if I were in his position.' After Younnis had blown his nose and cleared the tears from his cheeks, he took another sip of water and David asked him again, 'What was the job Sayfel has planned for you in London?'

'I don't know the details, but he told me that it would help me rise up the ranks in Al Qaeda."

'He didn't mention a bombing operation and saying things

like you going to paradise?'

'Oh no, he didn't say it was going to be a suicide mission or anything like that. He just said that he had some work for me to do in London. He didn't tell me anything about it like when or where it would take place. I think he just wanted me to carry things round.'

David smiled at Younnis satisfied that he had got everything out of him that he knew about Sayfel as he said, 'Thank you for that Imran. I can't promise you immunity, but if you make a statement relating to what you've just told us and you're prepared to give evidence, we'll do all we can to ensure your safety. I suggest we stop the interview now and you have a chat with Mr. Herring. Then we'll put you back into your cell and I'll have my boss talk to Mr. Herring about what we can do for you so he can advise you accordingly.'

'I agree,' said Mr. Herring.

As David got up he looked at the young man sitting opposite him and thought, 'He's only a frightened shitty arsed kid. The bastards, what kind of animals recruit kids to do their dirty work.' George's voice echoed in his head that this is really a dirty game.

Twenty-Five

Friday 27th October
22.10 hours
Temporary Control Room, Marriott Hotel, Manchester

'Thanks for that David. Craig and I watched the interviews as they were relayed to from the camera in the interview room to the incident room here. Craig was impressed with your interviewing technique. He was surprised at how quickly you got the cough out of him. Now we know for certain Sayfel's the main man behind all of these activities. I suggest that you leave Younnis to the care of the Merseyside's ISB. Once we've got a statement, we'll start the relocation process for him. That's for MI5 to sort out. I'll get a Merseyside traffic car to pick you both up and bring you home. We've a lot to tell you including the lack of progress in the interviewing of Ahmed. I want you and Steve to have a go at Ahmed in the morning. He's not said a word so far, but with what you've got from Younnis you two can put that information to Ahmed. I'll speak to you later' George said to David and replaced the telephone receiver.

'Those two did well getting what they did out of young Younnis, in fact they've both done well all day,' Craig said. 'It confirmed for us that Sayfel's been one busy boy.'

'Not only is he one of the main men in Al Qaeda we've also learnt he's also got a connection with the FSB.'

'He's been running with more than the hare and the hounds,

305

he has been running with the bloody foxes too.'

George looked at his watch and said 'They'll be here within the hour, it's ten past ten now. They just have to finish off their initial statements for the Professional Standards in Merseyside and I've arranged for a traffic car to bring them here. At this time of night they could make Liverpool to Manchester in twenty five minutes if the roads are empty.'

'Fair enough George. Our night officer should be here shortly. We can debrief Hurst and Adams here before they go home and then brief them on what they have to do tomorrow. Hopefully they can do the same with Ahmed, what they did to Younnis.'

'Hopefully, but I don't think it's going to be as easy to prize him open like it was Younnis.'

*   *   *

A tired David Hurst parked his car at the old cotton mill that housed his flat. It was eerily quiet outside his flat and his tiredness made him feel the chill of the early winter night air. As he got out of his car, he looked over towards Manchester city centre and the lights giving an orange haze over the city skyline. He just wanted some quiet time to gather his thoughts and let the day's events to sink in. He walked by the Ashton Canal opposite to the entrance to the old mill and looked up at his flat and saw the lights on. He remembered that Debbie was waiting for him. When she spoke to him earlier in the day, she reassured him that he would not have to lift a finger when he came home. This was something he had not had for a long time. This time, when he walks through the door, there is someone ready to listen to him if he wanted to talk or just simply to be there. He had got used to coming home to a dark empty flat with no one waiting for him. Tonight it would be different.

He opened the front door of his flat and called out, 'Debbie, are you there?'

On hearing his voice she emerged from the bathroom wearing a toweling robe and her hair was all wet. 'You must think that this is all I wear when I'm not at work. I've just had a good long soak in the bath. I've not been back long myself. Sit down and I'll get you a drink. Do you want a coffee or something stronger?'

'A coffee please. If I drink any alcohol tonight I won't stop and I've got to be in handy tomorrow as no doubt you have to too. What a day.' As David eased himself onto the black leather couch in the living area he kicked off his shoes saying, 'I could sleep for a week.'

'I've just made this coffee,' she said pouring him a cup. She walked over to where David was lying on the couch and placed the coffee on a table by the couch. 'Have you had any second thoughts about our conversation this morning before you went off to Liverpool?'

He grabbed Debbie by the waist and pulled her on top of him. He gave her a hug and they kissed passionately. 'That definitely answers my question! How are you feeling after today's events?' she asked.

'Like shit.'

She stroked his hair and said, 'Do you want to talk about it or do you just want to lie quietly and have some time to yourself?'

'I just want you,' he said. Slipping the robe off Debbie's shoulders, he began to kiss her neck.

'I've wanted you all week.'

*   *   *

'Morning David and good morning to you too Debbie,' George said as he greeted them on their arrival at the control room early the next morning.

'Morning George and you can take that smirk off your face,' David said. 'What's on the agenda for today? Am I still going to be interviewing Ahmed?' he asked, hastily trying to change the subject.

'Yes and I think that's all you'll be doing today. Steve's already called in and he's on his way to Rochdale police station. He's got all the information you need. The officers who interviewed Ahmed yesterday are calling at Rochdale to brief him.'

'Do you want me to go up there now?' David asked.

'Get yourself a coffee first. I just want to have a quick chat over yesterday. Our firm's professional counselors have been on the phone offering their services to you after the traumatic events of yesterday.'

David rolled his eyes. On his list of people that he detested were psychiatric counselors that he saw simply as 'jobs-worth quacks'. 'I don't need a shrink!' he said.

'There's no need to be too hasty. In all seriousness are you alright after what happened yesterday? Have you slept on what happened?' George asked.

David smirked at George and said, 'Don't you start with that touchy, feely bullshit. George, trust me, I'm fine. I've no problem with the fact that the Aatcha's are dead. Killing them saved hundreds of lives. That's what's important. I'd kill those scumbags again if I had to.'

George smiled and said, 'Well you know I have to offer you their services. No doubt they will email you offering the same. Do me a favor and be polite in your reply, I have to admit I got a similar response from Steve this morning. In fact he said that he slept better knowing that those two "shit-heads" were dead.'

'The main thing is that you handled the Professional Standards and the IPCC so me and Steve can do what we're paid to do. That's what counts.'

'And don't forget the role Craig played in keeping you two operational. I don't know what you said to him yesterday, but you've got a new friend there,' George said turning his head towards Craig who was speaking to Debbie.

Craig looked up. 'What's that George?' he asked.

'I was telling David the vital role you played in keeping him operational after yesterday's shootings.'

He looked cagily at David and said, 'Think nothing of it David, it was a pleasure. For one from such humble beginnings, you now have friends in high places, even the PM spoke up for you. Not bad for a lad from the back streets of Liverpool, or is that the gutter?' Craig stood up and went to shake hands with him.

As he shook hands with Craig, David said, 'Better that a person rises up from the gutter than to have it all given to them on a silver plate like some in this room.'

'Tout che David. I take it there's no more hard feelings between us?'

David smiled back at Craig and said, 'Shall we call a ceasefire?'

Keeping hold of David's grip he said, 'Why not.' As Craig and David released their handshake he added, 'I'm not patronizing you. That really was a good show by you and Steve yesterday, especially when you disarmed the bomb. That truly was top drawer. Try and get as much as you can from Ahmed on Sayfel as you did with Younnis. That was good interviewing by you two yesterday. It's the Chechen FSB link I'm really interested in. Ahmed's an experienced operative and he's not said a dickey bird yet. Not that I'm denigrating your talents in interviewing David, God forbid. I think we might only get something out of him by asking our CIA colleagues to take him on a round the world flight, if you get my meaning. This having to abide by the law is a little hampering at times.'

'It's abiding by the law that distinguishes a totalitarian regime from a free and democratic state. The day we resort to underhand torture techniques to extract a confession is the day I resign. In fact I'd most probably join the other side.'

'I forgot about that left wing background of yours that comes out now and again. I'm surprised that you believe some of these naïve ideals.'

*   *   *

Taking the lead in Ahmed's second interview at Rochdale police station, Steve said, 'I appreciate you're exercising your right to remain silent but I want to show you this recording.' David pressed the play button on the remote of a portable television placed in the interview room. With Ahmed's solicitor, they all watched the recording of Ahmed and Sayfel taken from Piccadilly rail station on the previous Thursday. Part of the recording zoomed in clearly showing Ahmed and Sayfel talking to each other. The lack of a sound track added to the cold silence in the room.

Steve broke the silence, giving a commentary on the events they were watching. 'The man you can see on the left is clearly you Mr. Ahmed and the man on the right is known as Sayfel.' David pressed the stop button on the remote control while Steve asked, 'How do you know Sayfel?'

Ahmed stopped looking at the screen and returned to the posture he had adopted throughout their interviews of looking at his feet and making no reply. Steve said, 'This DVD recording is an object that shows evidence that you know or are acquainted with Sayfel. We have evidence that the bag he brought with him that morning contained explosives and bomb triggers, and possibly the chemicals necessary to make the bomb a dirty bomb. If detonated the bombs would've released a deadly virus into the atmosphere with the capability to kill thousands of innocent lives. They were placed in devices to be used in attacks in Manchester, Leeds and Liverpool yesterday morning. You've already seen the recordings of you placing devices in Victoria rail station yesterday morning. I'll ask you again, how to you know Sayfel?'

For the first time in the four hours of interviewing him, Ahmed raised his head and leaned across the interview table staring coldly into Steve's eyes. 'You've got me. There, that's what you bastards want to hear isn't it? It doesn't matter if I say fuck all or admit it. You'll portray me as a son of the Devil, an evil face of terror. I'm only sorry we failed. I wanted to kill thousands of you bastards.' Ahmed's solicitor put her hand on Ahmed's arm to try to stop him speaking. He grabbed her hand and violently took it off him. 'Get your hand off me. I'll only be happy when this country's system is overthrown. There, get that out in your press statements. Lie like you usually do. This is the shit that you want to hear me say. I'm laughing at you. You thought Sayfel was your man, your MI5 agent. He's not. You're asking me about him because you're not sure if he's still your man, but I can tell you that he doesn't work for you anymore. You'll never own him and you'll never catch him. Charge me and send me to your prisons. I've nothing else to say to you. I know who you are. You're the men who shot Ibrar and Mohammed. That's why you didn't interview me yesterday. You arrested Imran Younnis. You interviewed him and got your information by breaking down a boy. I'm telling you this, I'm no boy. I'm a man. Look into these man's eyes,' he said pointing to his own eyes. 'All you'll ever see is a hatred for you, and I'll not hesitate in killing you.' He spat in Steve's face. 'I've nothing more to say to you. Charge me with a million crimes. I have nothing else to say to you.'

Steve calmly wiped the spittle from his cheek, looked at Ahmed. He smiled at him saying, 'I've no further questions, David do you have any further questions?'

'No,' David said glaring at Ahmed. What he really wanted to do was to jump across the interview table and literally rip the man's throat out, but knew he had to remain calm.

'Ms. Nasser, is there anything you would like to say?' Steve asked with a half-smile on his face.

'No thank you, I will wait and see what decision you make regarding charging Mister Ahmed.'

Before Steve switched off the tape Ahmed looked at Ms Nasser and shouted, 'You're all the same, "no thank you" this "oh please" that. You're all weak. You're all fucking pricks.'

Steve calmly added, 'Mr. Ahmed, my profound apologies but I

thought you had nothing further to say. Is there is anything you would like to add to what you have told us already in this interview?'

He leaned across towards the microphone and said, 'Watch out for your families, they'll be dead soon. We'll find out where you live and kill you and your families. You won't be smiling then Detective Constable Stephen Adams. Sayfel will see to that. He is more than just Al Qaeda. He has connections with the Chechens. You think you're a smart arse, but you are nothing but a fucking prick.'

'Is that all Mister Ahmed or have you anything further to say?' Steve asked. Ahmed folded his arms and once again looked down at his feet. 'I'll take that as a "no" then,' Steve said as he reached over to the stop button on the tape machine saying, 'The time is now thirteen fifteen hours and the interview is concluded.'

David got out of his seat and opened the door to the interview room and called for the custody officer. The custody officer took Ahmed from the interview room and placed him in his cell. While David, Steve and Ms. Nasser walked towards the custody officer's desk, Nasser broke the silence. 'I must say I was very impressed at how you remained very calm and cool there DC Adams. I know many officers who would have reacted violently towards Mister Ahmed in that situation.'

'It goes with the job. He's just pissed off that we caught him that's all. What would have been gained if I hit him? Your man's going nowhere and he's looking at a long stretch in prison. In your heart of hearts you must know that Ms. Nasser.' Steve said.

'I will say that at this moment the amount of evidence you have against my client is substantial. However we'll have to wait and see if there's going to be a trial before I pass any comments at this stage. Nice try.' She turned to David and said, 'DS Hurst, I appreciate you have a lot of evidence to review, but could you indicate what your plans are regarding my client. Will there be further interviews with him today before you charge him?'

'Like you I can't make a comment on long term plans, but

for today there will be no further interviews with Mr. Ahmed. Trying to get us to say that we are going to charge him at this present time was also a nice try Ms. Nasser!'

Twenty-Six

Saturday 28th October
16.10 hours
Northbound Carriageway,
M6 close to Coventry

Sayfel was driving a rented car up the M6 motorway heading towards Manchester. An associate in the Brent based Al Qaeda cell rented a Vauxhall Astra under false details paying for the hire with a fraudulent credit card. During a counsel with other leading Al Qaeda members, Sayfel convinced them the primary threat was Khan. It had taken some powers of persuasion by Sayfel, but he convinced them that Khan's actions on Friday only confirmed he was a traitor to Al Qaeda and before he could reveal any further information to MI5, he had to be killed. Having inside information on MI5, Sayfel successfully argued he was the best placed member of Al Qaeda to carry this out. It was late afternoon and the fading late autumn daylight was hastened by the dark rain clouds. The continuous sound of rain falling on the windscreen accompanied by the sound of the car's windscreen wipers moving from side-to-side began to irritate Sayfel, causing him to turn up the volume of the car radio. He kept changing radio channels until he found something he could tolerate listening to. He hated hearing the mindless babble of radio presenters.

Prior to setting off for Manchester, he contacted Al Qaeda members in the Manchester area to try and find out where Khan was in order to keep observations on him. He knew he could find the ISB officers who killed Ibrar and Mohammed Aatcha as he knew the building where the Greater Manchester Police ISB department was located. He knew what the officers looked like, as Nasser, pretending to make a call, passed on the pictures she had taken of the officers on her phone at Rochdale custody suite. They were not his immediate concern, Khan was. There was always another day to take his revenge on the officers. He knew that once Khan was fully debriefed, MI5 would have more information on the running of Al Qaeda than they would ever have dreamt of. His concern was MI5 being in possession of Khan's knowledge on key personnel in the organisation, as well as their practices and procedures. The security services having this knowledge was potentially devastating to the UK based arm of Al Qaeda.

He knew the first thing the MI5 debriefing officers would have done was get Khan out of the terrorist role. Tomorrow would be different. Khan would start to tell them all he knew about Al Qaeda and importantly to Sayfel, what he knew about his involvement in the terrorist group. Knowing MI5 would cross check everything Khan told them on their intelligence systems, Sayfel knew it would take time, valuable time if Sayfel was to get to Khan before he revealed too much. This was now a damage limitation exercise.

*　　　*　　　*

Craig MacDonald and George Byrne accompanied by acting Detective Superintendent Paul Edge attended Greater Manchester Police Headquarters for a meeting to appraise the chief constable and the ACC on the progress of the investigation. On entering the chief constable's office, the chief constable, Bernard Gamble stood up and said, 'Come in gentlemen and take a seat.'

Paul Edge immediately sat down in a green leather studded

seat closest to Bernard Gamble's large oak desk and George realized it was up to him to make the introductions. 'Sir, Ma'am let me introduce you to Craig MacDonald, senior intelligence officer from MI5. I think you both know Mr. Edge?'

Bernard walked over to Craig and extended his hand saying, 'I believe we've not had the pleasure.'

'I can assure you Bernard the pleasure's all mine. Clearly Paul runs a tight ship,' Craig said as he shook hands.

Pleased to hear positive comments on his force, Bernard smiled at Craig and said, 'Thank you, I know Paul always prides himself on getting results, don't you Paul?'

'Oh yes sir, you know I do. Discipline and hard work is the recipe for success.'

'I agree to an extent. There are times we have to allow junior officers to use their initiative and experience. That's something we should never overlook, should we Paul?'

Shaking his head in an exaggerated fashion he said, 'Oh no sir, never sir.'

Bernard started discussing the main points he wanted to cover in the meeting. 'Paul, I've been worried about your team and the death of Tony King. How are they bearing up?'

'Fine sir, the trouble is we've not had time to dwell on it with so much going on yesterday.'

Nodding his head in agreement Bernard said, 'Of course, I can understand. How are David Hurst and Steve Adams after yesterday's events, in particular after the shootings?'

Seizing the opportunity to denigrate Hurst, Edge replied, 'The shootings are typical of Hurst's approach to policing sir. He has a gung ho attitude and a complete disregard for the law. To Hurst, the term "the use of discretion" means he can do whatever he wants to. He has total disregard to the consequences of his actions. I believe the shootings could have been avoided. He dealt with yesterday's events without any consultation with George or me. In summary sir, he's a loose cannon and I think we should seriously consider removing him from the ISB. My fear is that where Hurst leads, Adams and the rest of his team follows. He's clearly a bad influence and sets a bad example to the more impressionable members of his team that seem to hero worship him. In my opinion, Tony King's death only came about due to Hurst's negligence. Hurst's constant negligence during this investigation has led to three deaths, all of which were certainly avoidable.'

Bernard and Sandra began to look at each other in surprise when George, filled with rage, said, 'Sir, Ma'am I have to object...'

Craig seeing George's usual cool and calm demeanor disappearing rapidly, spoke over George and said, 'I can clarify the matter over David Hurst. I too would come to a similar conclusion if I only had the information Paul has.' Paul Edge looked over to George who was smiling and nodding his head in agreement. Craig continued, 'However I've only just received the interim report from Chief Superintendent Knight from Merseyside Police's Professional Standards department. Unfortunately, it only just arrived on my desk and I've not had the opportunity to forward it onto Paul. From the independent witness statements, both Hurst and Adams were left with no choice but to shoot Ibrar Aatcha in Liverpool. It was a similar dilemma faced by these two officers along with Merseyside's ISB in Bold Place. Adams had no option but to shoot Mohammed Aatcha. These are tragic events brought about through difficult circumstances. The officers had no time to consult the SIO for permission to shoot. The last thing I would want to do, especially as a guest of Greater Manchester Police is to embarrass Paul, but as I said this report only recently came into my possession.'

Paul Edge's cheeks flushed with embarrassment as he said, 'That doesn't account for Hurst's behavior when Tony King was killed. Once again Hurst was off glory hunting.'

Craig interrupted Paul, saying, 'I'm not trying to embarrass you here Paul, as I can understand fully how you arrived at your conclusions in relation to Hurst's actions. I ordered Hurst and members of his team to follow Ahmed. We needed to know as soon as we could what Ahmed was doing and who he was doing it with. From what I've seen of Hurst, he is not the type of DS to leave a scene endangering his team. If anyone is culpable, it is neither Hurst nor Paul, it's me.'

Bernard Gamble read the message between Craig's diplomatic words and said, 'That makes sense. I can see why you came to the conclusions you did Paul and we're not pointing any fingers of blame in your direction. This has been an operation that's had more than enough elements of danger to both the public and our officers. The main thing is, we've avoided those dirty bombs going off and a deadly virus spreading through the north of England. That's down to Hurst and his team. What I need to consider is where we go from here and what support I can give to the ISB.' Bernard then looked at Craig and added, 'And of course what support can I give MI5.'

Paul Edge said, 'Thank you sir, I appreciate that you don't blame me for what's happened.'

'Don't worry Paul, the fact that your promotion could become permanent is not affected by Hurst's or anyone else's actions in this investigation. When I have the PM and the Home Secretary complimenting me on the actions of my officers, I take that into account. Sandra, could you update us on what information you have on this operation?' Gamble asked.

'Yes sir, uniform support units have been assisting the ISB in the execution of search warrants, including firearms officers. Entry was gained to all of the premises and the searches were conducted. We're using the custody suites in Rochdale, Oldham, Ashton, Platt Lane and Bootle Street to detain the arrested suspects. There's been quite a lot of media interest in this and they're demanding all sorts of information. I'll be giving a press conference at nine o'clock tonight. George has kept me fully briefed on all of the developments and I have a draft here of the information we will release to the press. In addition to this we've had support from the local Muslim community leaders. I've passed on all the information we received from them and the local community to George and his team. I've also arranged for a meeting with you sir, me and a number of the community leaders for tomorrow morning at ten o'clock. Some of the information they passed over has, I believe led to a number of arrests of other persons suspected to be involved in acts of terrorism. Is that correct George?"

'Yes Ma'am, three persons have been arrested as a result of the information passed onto us from the community leaders and they're currently being held at Oldham police station.'

Bernard added, 'I've a lot of sympathy for the Muslim community when events like this happen. The vast majority of them are hard working, law abiding citizens who just want to get on with their lives. The problem is when reports of Islamist terrorist activity like this hits the headlines, it's just more ammunition for the racist groups to fuel further hatred towards minority groups. As usual the media tend to give a disproportionate portrayal of these communities by just focusing on the radical clerics and their supporters. If there's nothing further, I think we can reconvene on Monday morning at eleven, unless of course something else major happens between now and then. Thanks for taking time out from such an involved investigation to meet up. If there's anything further that you need or if you come across any obstinate senior officers in GMP let me know straight away, any time of day or night. There's nothing worse than an obstinate senior officer is there Paul?'

Edge completely missed the irony of the question as he said, 'No sir. There's nothing worse sir.'

As the three got up to leave the office, Gamble got up and ushered Craig, George and Paul out of his office when he said, 'Just before you go George, I want to speak to you about Chloe.' As Craig and Paul Edge left his office he closed the door behind them and said to George, 'Although I'm interested in your wife, that's just a ruse to have a quick word with you. Between us three, what's going on with Edge? Is he up to the job?'

George held nothing back as he reported on Edge's behavior during the investigation. Bernard shook his head and said, 'The problem I've got is that no matter how incompetent he is, I've had the likes of the PM telling me how pleased they are with him. What am I supposed to do, hang him out to dry when this investigation has gone so well? Just think how it would look George? I know who's doing the business in the ISB and I'll make sure it's recognized.'

*   *   *

Khan yawned and said, 'I'm feeling a little tired now. Can we break off and run through more stuff tomorrow. I need something to eat and put my head down. It'll make a change to have a proper sleep without wondering what my flat mates are up to.'

'Sure. We can discuss Sayfel and what he got up to in more depth tomorrow,' Gordon Bascombe said.

'As Chinatown's not far from here, I might go there and get a bite to eat.'

'I have to be with you at all times and that includes your recreation time. I'm afraid I'll have to join you.'

'I could do with the company and have a normal conversation without having double checking what I'm saying.' The two left the ISB offices and walked towards Chinatown.

As they walked through the busy Saturday night city center streets, Gordon asked Khan, 'What are you going to do when this is over?'

'I suppose Thames House will give me back my day job, hopefully an IT post. I could do with a break from field work and have some normality back in my life.'

'That wouldn't do for me. I like being out and about too much.'

'But you haven't been undercover for a number of years like I have.'

Just before they went under the ornate Chinese arch, two loud bangs shattered the hum-drum sound of a Saturday night. Khan fell to his knees clutching his chest. He looked down at his chest and saw blood pouring between the fingers of his hand. 'Gordon, I've been shot.'

Gordon laid Khan down onto the pavement. As the color drained from Khan's face, Gordon felt a sense of responsibility. Holding Khan close to his body he said, 'Hang on in there Moosa. I'll call for an ambulance, just hang on in there.'

As Gordon telephoned for an ambulance, he scanned immediate area for anyone that looked like they had fired the shots. Passers-by stopped to gawp at the dying Khan. A young man lurched forward to get a better view of Khan lying there as blood oozed out of his chest wound and shouted, 'He's been shot.'

Gordon got up and pushed the young man back saying, 'Give him some air, show him some respect.'

No one paid any attention to Gordon as others pushed past him to lean over Khan to see what was happening. In frustration Gordon took his pistol from the holster beneath his jacket and waved it in the air. 'If you don't move back I'll make you, now back off!'

The crowd were suddenly transfixed on Gordon's pistol and tentatively moved back. Seeing Gordon waving his pistol in the air a woman screamed, 'It's him. He shot him.'

As the crowd became hostile towards him, Gordon felt vulnerable. He took his MI5 identity card and shouted, 'I'm the police. This man was with me. Did anyone see what happened?'

The crowd went silent. They just stared at Gordon, who put his pistol back into its holster. In the silence he heard Khan moaning, 'God it hurts, I think I'm dying.' The blood from his wound was flowing onto the pavement, running towards the feet of the assembled crowd.

Gordon finally got a response from the emergency services operator. 'I need ambulance to the Chinese Arch in Manchester city centre. A man's been shot. I've no time to give you details, just get an ambulance here as quick as you can.' He put his phone back into his pocket and knelt down by Khan. 'Come on Moosa, hang on in there. The ambulance will be here soon.' Gordon picked up Moosa's head and rested it on his lap. The crowd thickened as more passers-by came to see what was going on. Their ghoulish nature exasperated Gordon and he shouted out, 'Get back! Give him room.'

As he held Khan's head in his lap, he could feel his body giving up the fight for life. 'Moosa speak to me.'

Faintly, Khan said, 'The pain's going. I feel sleepy.'

'Stay awake. Moosa don't close your eyes, come on I can hear the ambulance coming, just stay with me.' Khan closed his eyes and Gordon felt his body go limp in his arms. He looked up to the skies and shouted, 'Bastards, you fucking bastards.'

Twenty-Seven

Saturday 28th October
22.25 hours
Ancoats, Manchester

Late that Saturday evening David and Debbie were cuddling up to each other on the couch in the living room of his flat. Debbie had poured herself a glass of Merlot while David got himself a beer from the fridge. 'It's good of George to let us have tomorrow off. After a late breakfast I'll go over to Liverpool and call in to see Mum and Dad. I can then get to Goodison by three, meet up with me mates and make the four o'clock kick off. We're playing Chelsea tomorrow,' David said

'What shall I do?' Debbie asked.

'You can get my tea ready for when I come back. You're a woman aren't you, that's your job. Oh yes, and you can clean the flat as well, that'll keep you out of trouble.'

She picked up a cushion off the couch and started hitting David with it. 'I never took you for a misogynist.'

Shielding himself with his arms, he said laughing, 'I'm only joking. You can put your feet up with the Sunday papers or you could curl up with a good book. Just chill, do what you want.'

'That sounds good to me.' As Debbie spoke her mobile began to ring. 'Oh bugger, it'll be Craig. Can't he just leave us alone for five minutes?' As she picked up the phone from her handbag she saw it was Craig. 'It's him alright. This had better be important.'

She answered the phone, 'What do you want Craig?'

'I need you in straight away. Khan's been shot in Chinatown in Manchester and he's dead. Is Hurst with you by any chance? If he is then tell him to come with you.'

'My god. We'll be with you as soon as we can.' She put her phone back into her handbag saying, 'Come on, it's back to work, Khan's been killed.'

Stunned by what he heard, he got shot up off the couch. 'What happened?'

As Debbie reached for her coat she said, 'All Craig said was that he was shot in Chinatown.'

*   *   *

'George, I'm glad you could make it so quick,' Craig said with sense of relief. 'I'm afraid we've got another murder enquiry on our hands. Are there any ISB officers that Edge could spare to deal with it, as I don't want the local plod poking their noses in on this one?'

'Don't worry. I called Bernard Gamble as soon as you told me about the shooting. He's allocated Sharon Higham a detective superintendent from the Major Crime Unit. She's a good friend of mine from my NCS days. I contacted her as soon as I knew she was going to be the SIO. I've lent her a couple of ISB officers that we could spare. I also contacted Paul Edge and he agreed to DI Tim Johnson from our Airport Unit assisting Sharon, so you've got an ISB input in Khan's murder investigation.'

'Thanks.'

'By the way, I thought you were very complimentary about David Hurst with the Chief.'

'I might not like the man personally, but he's a damn good officer. I know a good thing when I see it George.' Craig laughed as he said, 'On the other hand that Paul Edge is such a self-centered creep. He just didn't recognize the put downs by Bernard. Bernard

Gamble's a former Branch man isn't he?'

'Yes, that was back in his days in the Met. From what I've heard from the SO13 officers that served with him, Bernard had the respect of most of the troops and I certainly remember him being a good, intuitive detective.'

As David and Debbie arrived at the temporary control room, Craig got up to meet them. 'Thanks so much for coming in at this late hour. There's a bit of a flap on that we need to bottom as soon as we can. Shall I order us a large pot of coffee?'

George said, 'I think we'll need it as it could be a long night. David I'm sorry but your day off tomorrow is cancelled.'

'Don't worry about it, I knew once we got the call it would be. How's Gordon Bascombe shaping up?'

'He's a bit shaken up but he's alright. It was only Moosa who got shot,' Craig answered.

Debbie said, 'We've been discussing it on the way here. We reckon Sayfel's back in Manchester. It has the hallmark of an MI5 hit written all over it.'

Craig sighed, 'I agree.'

David added to Debbie's observation and said, 'Linking it to Ahmed's outburst in his interview this afternoon, we learnt that Sayfel is involved with the Chechens. If you add that to what Younnis told us about Sayfel and his links to the FSB, I reckon Sayfel knows that Leonid's an FSB agent. If you ask me Sayfel's a triple agent! He'll work for anyone who offers him the right amount of money. I was thinking how you mentioned in an earlier briefing how SO13 and MI5 are going to be assisted by the FSB next week in foiling a Chechen attack in London. It wouldn't surprise me if Sayfel's got an involvement in that as well.'

Impressed with David's deduction of the situation, Craig said, 'I think it has more than just his fingerprints on it. Debbie, do you want to add something?'

'I've been going through the intelligence reports regarding the planned Chechen attack and the details that have come out of Petrov's debrief. Adding that to what Younnis told David and Steve about Sayfel having a job for him to do in London. With the connections that Sayfel has with the Chechens, it's my belief that this operation with SO13 and MI5 along with the FSB might not be as straightforward as we think. He simply can't be trusted. I think we must warn Thames House, SO13 as well as the FSB.'

Craig reflected for a moment and said, 'That's a good point. Sayfel's made sure that we keep our focus solely on activity here in the north.'

George added, 'It does seem more than a coincidence that Leonid ended up staying with our Al Qaeda targets. As Debbie says, the man can't be trusted. He may have set up SO13, MI5 and the FSB. I can see it now. We're at one location waiting for the Chechens only to find out Sayfel's assisted the Chechens in attacking a different venue.'

Debbie nodded in agreement and said, 'I agree. Sayfel's been very busy over the past few days, but as his plans are unraveling, he'll be feeling vulnerable right now. He'll be like a wounded animal and that makes him dangerous. When is the Chechen attack supposed to be taking place?'

'It's supposed to be late morning next Tuesday. Do you think it's a decoy?' asked Craig.

'Yes I do. If Sayfel's behind it, there's the possibility that he's set up the FSB as well as our own agencies,' Debbie said.

Craig stood up, stretched his arms above his head and rested them behind his head. This line of thought rejuvenated him. The possibility that finally they could be onto Sayfel's plans made him forget the tiredness he was feeling. 'George I'm going to make an executive decision. I suggest you contact Steve Adams. Get him out of bed, tell him to pack some clothes and that Debbie and David will pick him up shortly. The three of you are going to London. I'll inform Thames House that you will be there by...' Craig looked at his watch, 'David, George tells me that you can drive quite fast so shall I say you'll be there in three hours?'

David replied, 'Make it two and a half.'

Just as David and Debbie were about to leave the control room, one of the MI5 analysts working in the temporary control room interrupted their conversation. 'Excuse me, but I think there's something here that could be useful to you. A black Vauxhall Astra registration number Lima Echo Five Eight Oscar Tango Mike has been reported stolen by a hire company. Apparently it was hired out earlier today to male of Asian ethnic background by a company in Brent, London with a fraudulent credit card. Earlier this evening, a fixed penalty notice was issued to the car for illegal parking in Bale Street Manchester, just by St. Peter's Square. A uniform patrol was dispatched to check the car out fifteen minutes ago, but the Astra's gone. Looking at the time of hire, along with the time it was parked, it could be the car Khan's killer used. It might even be Sayfel.'

Craig said, 'You could be right, I'll pass this onto the uniform police, he might be using it to get back to London. Hopefully some uniform bobbies will spot the car. Put a flag notice on it that if seen, no one, including police officers are to approach the vehicle. If they do find it they are to secure the area until we arrive. The tide might just be turning in our direction in relation Sayfel.' He looked over to Debbie and David and nodded towards the door of the control room and said, 'I think it's time you two got going.'

Twenty-Eight

Sunday 29th October
01.30 hours
M1 Motorway,
Newport Pagnell Service Station

'Leonid, I need to see you now,' Sayfel said to Leonid on the FSB phone he gave him.

Stirring from a deep sleep, Leonid answered, 'Is that you Sayfel? Do you know what time it is?' Leonid focused his sleep filled eyes on his bedside clock that showed it was half past one in the morning.

'Yes I do. I don't care what time it is, I need to meet you right now. You told me this phone was my lifeline. I'm in danger and I need your help. Now! '

'Where are you?' he asked sitting up in bed.

'Somewhere on the M1, but I'm not telling you exactly, in case this call's being monitored. I've completed my business in Manchester and I'm heading home. Can you make it up to Luton?'

'You sound agitated, is everything alright?'

'Don't worry about me and don't keep me talking. MI5 might be trying to get a fix on the location of the phone's signal. I need you to meet me straight away as I've some material that might interest you.'

'What sort of material? Can't it wait until the morning?'

'It is the morning and you really need to see this now.'

'I know it's the morning but it's half one in the morning. Just

328

give me a flavor of what this material is.'

Sayfel was getting impatient with Leonid and said, 'For fuck's sake, I've told you to keep this brief. I'll tell you what it is when you pick me up.'

'OK, calm down. I'm not going to Luton. Meet me by the services in Newport Pagnell on the M1."

'Make sure you're on your own.'

'Don't worry I'll be on my own. I'll be there as soon as I can.'

*   *   *

A satisfied Craig replaced the landline phone receiver and said to George, 'Well that's Thames House briefed and up to speed. They're going to contact the FSB and get them to warn Leonid. He might be next on Sayfel's hit list. I've stressed to them that Sayfel appears to have lost it and that's made him dangerous. There's nothing else we can do right now.'

'I've heard from Sharon Higham. She told me the forensic team has sealed off most of Chinatown. They're also searching Bale Street where the Astra was parked just in case it was the car that Sayfel was using. In addition to that, I've told the Chief and Sandra Parry what's happened. They're happy to leave it to us to get the job done. We just have to leave it to our three along with the Met and your mob now to sort out Sayfel.'

*   *   *

'I'll have to sign you two in,' Debbie said as they walked through the main entrance to Thames House. Debbie showed the security officer her MI5 ID card while David and Steve produced their warrant cards. 'I'll sign for these two. They're Greater Manchester Special Branch officers. We're here to assist Jenny Richmond's team. Is she in?' Debbie asked the security officer.

'Yes she is. I'll buzz her now and tell her you're here.'

After signing in, they walked down the long corridor behind the security desk and went into a set of rooms through a doorway on the right. 'Stay with me and don't wander off, they get a bit funny about that sort of thing around here,' Debbie said to David and Steve.

'Don't worry we uncouth northerners won't show you up,' David said with a smirk on his face.

Steve added, 'It's a good job we tied the whippet up on the lamp-post outside. Have they got somewhere for us to hang up our flat caps?'

'Oh very funny! Jenny lacks a sense of humor, so for my sake, please just be on your best behavior.'

As they entered the suite of rooms, a smartly dressed woman with a bob cut wearing a dark trouser suit approached them. To David, she looked as if she was in her fifties. She stopped and looked both David and Steve up and down before turning to Debbie and said, 'Debbie, long time no see. How are you?'

'I'm fine thanks. Let me introduce you to Detective Sergeant David Hurst and Detective Constable Steve Adams.' Both the officers shook hands with her.

Jenny looked at the clock on the office wall and said, 'You three certainly made good time getting down here. It was just over two hours ago that Craig told me you were on your way down.'

A tired David said curtly, 'The roads were empty coming down here. Now do you want us to brief you with what we know?'

Jenny raised her hand and waved away David's impatience saying, 'All in good time, would you three like a cup of tea?'

Steve replied, 'I'd love one but my man here is a devout coffee drinker.'

Jenny said, 'We have that too and for you Debbie?'

'A tea would be lovely, thanks. We only had one stop on the way down and our driver,' Debbie pointed to David, 'let it be known that it was a toilet stop only.'

Before David could answer, Jenny said, 'You poor girl have you had to put up with a bit of machismo of a boy and his toy?'

'Well I think we broke some land speed records getting down here.'

Once again David let his displeasure show as he said, 'I got down here quickly because there's a dangerous target loose out there. The sooner we get him, the better it will be.'

Jenny stopped making the drinks and looked at David saying, 'Did I touch a raw nerve there?'

'Are all MI5 senior intelligence officers like you or do you go on a course on how to get under peoples' skin?' David asked.

Jenny smiled at David's abrupt nature as Debbie explained, 'David was the ISB officer who disarmed the bomb in Liverpool on Friday morning after he and Steve shot Ibrar Aatcha. It's been a stressful few days for all of us, especially with them losing one of their colleagues last Tuesday night. So we're all feeling a bit raw.'

Jenny softened her voice and said, 'So you're the officer who disarmed the bomb. From what I heard that was an excellent piece of work. In fact I heard that you two handled all of Friday's events very professionally. I'm sorry if I offended you.'

Surprised at receiving an apology, David replied, 'I'm sorry too, I don't want to get off on the wrong foot, but I'm tired, thirsty and hungry.'

Debbie added, 'At least that's only three of the four things that makes David bad tempered. You're lucky Jenny, when we first met I had to deal with all four and I took quite a broadside off him. But we've made friends since then.'

Jenny gave a wry smile and said, 'I can see that Debbie.'

As she was pouring the boiling water onto the drinks Jenny said, 'I can see where your reference to MI5 senior intelligence officers getting under your skin originated. You've had to put up with Craig MacDonald. I'd love to see how you dealt with him David.'

Steve said, 'Don't worry Jenny, they've clashed horns a few times, but there are longer gaps between the clashes as time's gone by.'

Jenny looked David up and down and said, 'You're obviously not a man to trifle with. Have you thought about a change and coming over to Five? We could do with someone like you in one of our teams.'

'I'm fine where I am thanks, I don't fancy going over to the dark side!' David said and Debbie elbowed him in the ribs.

They looked at each other and Debbie mouthed to David to be quiet, which Jenny observed. 'Oh no Debbie, never let someone hold back what they're thinking, it's always best to know where one stands.'

'I just speak to people as they speak to me,' David said.

Jenny handed the drinks out saying, 'That's enough jousting for now, here we are two teas and a coffee. Help yourself to milk and sugar. Let's go into my office and get to work.'

As they walked over to her office, David whispered to Debbie, 'I'm sorry but she wound me up.'

As Jenny was leading the way to her office she said, 'I forgot to tell you, I have excellent hearing.' They entered Jenny's office where she invited them to sit to begin their briefing.

*   *   *

As he hid by a set of trees at the far end of the car park of Newport Pagnell Services, Sayfel was feeling the cold. He put his discomfort aside as he kept watching for Leonid, as well as keeping an eye on the Astra he parked up by the entrance to the services. 'That bastard parking ticket,' he thought. He knew from the parking ticket the police would find out it was hired from Brent and link the car to the killing of Khan. As each minute passed waiting for Leonid, Sayfel's anxiety level increased.

Sayfel looked at his watch. It was a quarter to three in the morning. 'Where the fucking hell is he?' he mumbled to himself. He was getting colder by the minute. While his heart was telling him to go into the warmth of the service station, his head knew of the risk of being picked up by the CCTV cameras.

Sayfel watched a dark colored Mercedes entered the service station and park up away from the main service station building. He could not see if it was Leonid, as the driver remained in the car for a few minutes. When the driver's door opened and the interior light came on, he could just make out the driver was Leonid. Leonid stood by the car door and looked around the car park when he saw Sayfel emerge from the trees. Keeping his head down, Sayfel walked purposefully towards him. As he got to the car, a marked police Range Rover with two officers on board drove slowly past. Sayfel stopped dead in his tracks as the police car passed, but neither of the officers looked at him. Leonid got back into the driver's seat while Sayfel hurriedly got into the front passenger seat. As Leonid turned the ignition of the car Sayfel said, 'Drive slowly away, and don't bring any attention to yourself. Just get out of here now!'

'You didn't seem too happy at the presence of the police car.'

Sayfel was not listening to Leonid. He was concentrating on what the police officers were doing. 'Shit, it's stopped by the Astra. Now shut up and get the fuck out of here.'

'Calm down Sayfel, you're safe now.'

Leonid's reassurance had no effect. Sayfel looked at Leonid and snarled, 'Just do as I say. I'll know when I'm safe, and trust me we need to get out of here. I don't want to be here when they inspect that car.'

'What have you done?'

'If the officers inspect it, you'll find out soon enough.'

The police car stopped next to the Astra. The officer in the passenger seat got out walked over to the Vauxhall Astra while the driver radioed through to his control room, 'Just to confirm it's the Astra reported stolen from Brent yesterday evening. Cliff's checking it out now.'

Putting his hand on the driver's door handle, to his surprise it was unlocked. He turned to his colleague when a sudden burst of bright light momentarily lit up the whole of the car park followed by a large explosion. The blast hurled Cliff across the car park and rolled the police Range Rover onto its side. As the Astra exploded, fragments of hot metal were jettisoned at high speed in various directions of the immediate area. Some of the fragments ripped through the body of the officer that opened the door killing him instantly. Other hot fragments ripped into the chassis of the Range Rover rupturing the Range Rover's fuel pipes, igniting the leaking fuel. Causing the Range Rover to explode the police driver was killed instantly.

On hearing the explosion, Sayfel turned round in the front passenger seat to see the result of his handy work while Leonid watched the events unfold in the car's interior mirror. He turned to Sayfel and said, 'You mad bastard! You've just killed those two police officers and made it very difficult for the FSB to help you any further.'

'If you don't get me out of here, you'll be joining them. Don't bullshit me with this "I've made it hard for the FSB to help me" crap.'

Leonid looked down to Sayfel's hand and saw a pistol pointed at his chest.

Twenty-Nine

'Thanks for that,' Jenny said and replaced the telephone receiver. She turned to Debbie, David and Steve and in a solemn tone said, 'That was SO13. Two Thames Valley police officers have been killed at Newport Pagnell services. Thames Valley got a report of a black Vauxhall Astra parked some distance away from the main services building. The events in Manchester and Liverpool yesterday have obviously heightened public awareness as the service station staff was suspicious and called the police. When Thames Valley did a check on the registration number they confirmed it was the car hired from Brent and saw the flagging notice put on it by Greater Manchester's ISB. The flag message clearly said the vehicle should not to be approached. Those officers should have just followed the instructions of the flagging message and evacuated the immediate area and called for SO13 and the bomb disposal squad.'

David said, 'That's two colleagues you're talking about who have just lost their lives. This isn't the time for saying what they should and should not have done.'

'I'm sorry David. That was a bit insensitive of me. However that explosion tells me that our friend Sayfel will be back in the London area by now. I suggest you three go to your hotel and get

335

your heads down for a few hours. In the meantime I'll get my team in and we'll try to locate Sayfel. I suggest we reconvene at eleven in the morning, unless something else happens of course.'

*   *   *

As they checked in at the hotel in Kensington, David said to the night porter, 'Is there any chance of getting a drink before we got to bed? I know it's late but we've been working all-day and just travelled down here from Manchester. We just fancy a quick night-cap.'

'No problem sir. Would you like your drinks in the bar or in your rooms? And, do you want me to charge them to your rooms?'

David said, 'If it's not too much trouble, the bar would be fine thanks and please charge them to the room.' He turned to Steve and in a stage whisper added, 'Our hosts in MI5 can pay for that too.'

The three walked into the bar that had oak paneled walls with a number of paintings and old photographs of Queen Elizabeth, the late Queen Mother hanging from them. Walking across the thick pile royal tartan patterned carpet on which a number red and green leather Chesterfield sofas were located, David said, 'I tell you what, this is a much classier place than some of the flea pits the Branch put us up in.'

'I like the way you put the drinks on the bill that's being paid for by MI5,' Steve added laughing.

'Well we've worked hard for it and I'm sure their budget will extend to a few beers perhaps even to an Irish malt chaser,' David said.

'Let's not go over the top. Let's just have one, two at most as I think we're in for a busy day later. My firm doesn't mind a few extras on the bill, it's only expected, but let's not take the piss gentlemen,' Debbie said.

David pretended to tug his forelock. 'And if it is alright with you Ma'am can we have that Irish chaser with that? It will help get me to sleep.'

'Single malts of course,' added Steve.

'You two are incorrigible! So that's two pints of bitter, two single malt Irish whiskies and my own.' Debbie went over to the night porter and ordered the drinks. A couple of minutes later the night porter brought the drinks over on a tray to where they were sitting. After placing the drinks on their table, Debbie raised her glass and said, 'Here's to the three of us. We've got this far and here's to a successful and swift end to this operation with no more fatalities.' The three raised their glasses to that sentiment.

*　　*　　*

'So what do you propose to do now?' Leonid asked driving down the M1 towards London.

'It depends whether or not I can trust you,' Sayfel replied.

'What do you mean "if you can trust me"? What more do you want from me to show you that you can trust me?'

'I want you to arrange for the FSB to get me to Spain. To help you negotiate that with them, I've got more information about Tuesday's attack by the Chechens.'

'That seems reasonable. I'm sure I can persuade them and get you out.'

'That's funny, you didn't say that yesterday. According to you, the FSB don't owe me anything.'

'That was yesterday.'

'And yesterday I didn't have a gun pointed against your chest.'

'If I get you out of the country, you'll have to stay in the company of the FSB until we get the Chechens. After that you'll be free to go wherever you want. I can't work you out. You worked for MI5, you've been working for us and you've been busy with Al Qaeda. There's no rational pattern to what you do. Just whose side are you on?'

'My side, I told you yesterday, no one owns me, I'm my own man.'

'I don't get it. You must have a cause or a belief that you are fighting for? What are you really? Are you MI5, Al Qaeda, what?'

'Once I knew I was going nowhere in MI5, I realized I could make money by using the skills MI5 taught me. That's why I helped you. I've no regard for you or Russia, the UK, Islam, anything. They're beliefs are nothing more than something for desperate people to cling to.'

'It's a dangerous game you're playing Sayfel. If you keep thinking that way, before long you won't have any friends at all. All you will have are enemies. That's provided one of those enemies don't kill you.'

'There's always someone willing to pay for a killer to do their dirty work for them.' Sayfel said producing a large folded envelope from the inside pocket of his coat that he placed on the passenger side of the dashboard. 'That's the information you'll find useful. It covers the details of the Chechen operation, who the four Chechen's are and where they're staying over the next few days. In return for this information, I want you to get me out to Spain by tonight. You'll arrange for me to go to Vittoria. Pick me up by Admiralty Arch at four o'clock this afternoon. That will give you and the rest of the FSB the whole day to verify the information I've given you. If I suspect that you or the FSB are going to trick me, it'll prove to be fatal to you. You'll not see your family again.'

'That seems reasonable. Vitoria's in the Basque region. Don't tell me you've got involved with Eta?'

'That's none of your business. Your business is to get me out tonight. Understand?'

'Oh yes, having a gun pointed at you helps to understand exactly what you want.'

Thirty

David, Steve and Debbie arrived at Thames House for the eleven o'clock briefing on Sayfel and the planned Chechen attack. Jenny Richmond was chairing the briefing along with three other MI5 intelligence officers from Jenny's team. Once everyone sat down, she said, 'I would like to formally welcome David and Steve from the Greater Manchester Police's ISB to Thames House. I think you all know Debbie our northern area police liaison officer who travelled down with David and Steve early this morning. Their main interest in Sayfel is in relation to the Al Qaeda attack in the North-west on Friday and the murder of Moosa Khan.

'We had an interesting exchange with the FSB this morning. They're got serious concerns over Sayfel. I wouldn't say they're panicking, but they're worried about the reliability of the intelligence he gave them regarding Tuesday's proposed Chechen attack at the Langome Hotel. The FSB invited me for a breakfast meeting this morning. They showed me the details Sayfel handed over to them outlining the details of the attack, the Chechen fighters to carry it out and, to my surprise, the location in London they're staying at until Tuesday. Along with an FSB agent, one of our officers is checking out the address in Kensington as we speak, but initial reports indicate no sign of the four Chechens Sayfel refers to. They're going to give it another hour to see if there is any movement before deciding if we should enter the premises.

'The FSB also played a very interesting recording of a conversation between Sayfel and Leonid that took place in the early hours of this morning. The FSB gave me a copy and I'll play it for you later. Just to give you the background, Leonid received a phone call from Sayfel at half one this morning to pick him up at Newport Pagnell services. Leonid met him at the southbound side of the service station and took him to Dagenham. The meeting they had this morning followed one they had on Friday in Hyde Park. As a result of Leonid's report from both meetings, the FSB are treating Sayfel as an unreliable source. To show further good faith, the FSB have forwarded the details Leonid found out about Al Qaeda while he was undercover in the UK and throughout Europe. We've passed that onto Craig MacDonald in Manchester as well as MI6.

'The FSB confirm that Sayfel is responsible for the car bomb at Newport Pagnell this morning and the shooting of Moosa Khan last night. Leonid not only witnessed the explosion as he drove away from the services, but Sayfel admitted to him that he planted the bomb in the car as well as killing Moosa Khan. That's not the only thing of interest that came out of the conversation. It appears that Sayfel's totally disaffected with all the organizations he's currently associated with. According to the FSB, he's become a dangerous lone wolf. He doesn't appear to trust anyone. Sayfel wants the FSB to fly him to Vitoria in Spain later today as it looks like he's arranged business with Eta. God only knows what he's up to there. I'll play the recording for you.'

When the recording finished, Jenny asked if anyone had any observations. Debbie responded first and said, 'I think Sayfel being dropped off in Dagenham is a bluff to make the FSB and us think he's staying at another address. I don't think Sayfel's been as careless as you suggest. Prior to meeting the three Al

Qaeda targets in Manchester last Thursday, he orchestrated the misinformation that Manchester Airport was the target of the Al Qaeda attack. Knowing what we do now regarding the dirty bomb attack on Friday, clearly he was trying to throw us off the scent of what they were actually up to. Looking back, when Moosa Khan said there would be suicide bombers going on two aircraft, he was trying to make it sound unbelievable. If you replay the conversation from Tuesday night between the targets, there is a slight pause after Moosa mentioned that two Al Qaeda members were going to board planes. Analysis of the voice patterns that were carried out in Manchester last Wednesday afternoon shows that when Ahmed responded, he was thinking on his feet. I don't think the bombs' going off on the aircraft was in the original script that Sayfel sent them.'

'Sorry to interrupt here Debs,' David said, 'but when Steve and I were following Khan last Tuesday morning on foot around Manchester city centre, I thought he was behaving strangely. At the time I thought he looked more like a druggie desperate for a fix than a terrorist using counter-surveillance techniques.' Looking over at Steve he added, 'He's most probably clocked us two and wanted us to stop him so he could pass on information related to the dirty bomb attack.'

'I think that's quite possible as last week Moosa Khan was obviously restricted in his ability to pass on intelligence to his handler here at Thames House. When I spoke to his handler, there were concerns over Moosa's safety as he hadn't forwarded his weekly report the weekend before I joined David and his team in Manchester,' Debbie said, 'I think Sayfel knows what he said to Leonid was recorded and he's trying to send us on another false trail. Think about it, he wants the FSB to pick him up at Admiralty Arch at four o'clock on a Sunday afternoon. It would be too easy for us to lift him. He'll know we're desperate to get him and he'll also know the pressure we're under to have this operation concluded quickly. If he's been assisting Leonid, he'll know that we've been debriefing Petrov and he'll also know that MI5 will be in dialogue with the FSB. So, he'll have a good idea that the FSB will have informed us what was said. He may be hoping that in our eagerness to get him, we're more likely to fall for his ruse, gambling that we won't fully analyze the situation.

'From my analysis of the intelligence the FSB passed onto us, another reason why I think Sayfel's sending us on a bum steer is the suggestion that he wants to be flown to the Basque region of Spain. As far as we know, Al Qaeda has no association with Eta. Within seconds after the bombs went off on the trains in Madrid in 2004, Eta contacted the Spanish Government saying they were not responsible. Historically, national terror groups like Eta have nothing to do with groups like Al Qaeda. I think wanting to go to Spain is nothing more than bullshit. He knows our procedures and he's played us all very well.'

They all nodded in agreement and Jenny said, 'The ramifications of this don't bear thinking about.'

Debbie continued, saying, 'The analysis of his patterns of behavior indicate that Sayfel is not a "lone wolf" as the FSB suggest. In conclusion, my appraisal of the intelligence shows that Sayfel's still working for Al Qaeda and has connections with Chechens. He's given misinformation to the FSB regarding the Chechens. Look at how he's given the FSB the run-around sending Leonid all over the country. We shouldn't underestimate him. Sayfel's still politically motivated and he's using the misinformation skills we taught him at MI5.'

They all listened intently to Debbie's argument and her reasoning. Jenny said, 'Are you suggesting the Chechen attack planned for Tuesday is not going to happen?'

'I think there'll be an attack alright, targeting a meeting between the senior Russian politicians and wealthy Russian exiles makes sense,' Debbie said, 'but it will not happen the way we've been led to believe. I can't see them bursting in on the meeting all guns blazing as it says in this copy of the information Sayfel handed over to Leonid last night. It makes no sense for well-trained and experienced Chechen fighters who have overcome considerable difficulty in reaching the UK to be sacrificed in a death or glory attack. I think the Chechens are in the hotel now or soon will be, either later today or tomorrow. It's likely that one or more of them will be working at the hotel. It wouldn't surprise me if they've been working there for a few months now. Leonid didn't arrive in the UK until two months after he got out of Chechnya. That will have given Sayfel enough time to organize their employment at the hotel. I think it's going to be today when they plant the explosives, setting the timers on bombs to go off on Tuesday. By then the Chechens will be in another part of the country, that is if they haven't been smuggled out of the country by then. It reminds me of PIRA's attack on the Grand Hotel in 1984 when they targeted the British Cabinet. The explosives were timed to go off a few days after they planted them.'

'There's a degree of logic in what you say Debbie,' Jenny replied, 'This is something we have to take seriously. Has anyone got any other observations to make regarding Debbie's analysis?' David raised his hand. 'David you have something to add?'

'I think having an MI5 team tramping all over the hotel right now could scare off any of the Chechen targets that Debbie suggests could be working at the hotel. I suggest that one of SO13's senior bosses inform the hotel manager today saying they're going to start conducting sweeps in preparedness for Tuesday's meeting. This will include a security check of all of the hotel staff and guests booked into the hotel, including if any of them have booked in to stay over the next few days. As we're so close to the Russian dignitaries visit, it wouldn't be unusual for SO13's protection teams to be conducting the security checks from today. I'm sure the Chechens will have been briefed that this is a normal security provision taken by the police. In fact they'll most probably expect it, especially if Sayfel's been briefing them. It's just a thought.'

'That makes perfectly good sense to me. I think we should get the wheels in motion straight away. We could start a sweep at the hotel now for any devices already planted.' Jenny said. 'Debbie will stay at control here with me. David and Steve, I would like you to act as liaison with SO13. You can be the conduit between the Met and me. The sooner we get started the better.'

*   *   *

'Sayfel you mad bastard,' said Mo Shukar, a London based Al Qaeda operative and good friend of Sayfel as he greeted him in a cafe in Shepherd's Bush.

'Do you want a coffee?' Sayfel asked sitting at table at the back of the café by the counter.

'Too right, I'll join you for a coffee.'

Sayfel caught the eye of the girl behind the counter, 'Two Arabic coffees please.' The girl nodded indicating that she would bring them over.

'You just don't give a shit do you? Not only is Khan's murder in the news but you topped that off with killing two police officers with the car bomb at Newport Pagnell services. With the media going mental, you've got balls to sit here for all to see. Aren't you bothered the spooks will get you?'

'It's Aziz's uncle's café. If they or the Special Branch make a move on me here, they'll have a riot on their hands.'

'Total respect to you man, total respect.'

After the girl served the two men with their coffee Sayfel said, 'We need to stay calm and not get too carried away just yet. I've got an FSB officer dangling at the moment. I've passed false information to the FSB that our four Chechen brothers will enter the hotel fifteen minutes after the meeting's begun next Tuesday. I told the FSB agent they'll be armed and carrying bombs. They're expecting to pick me up later at Admiralty Arch at four this afternoon. I'm sure they're in some form of negotiation with the

MI5 so everything I've told the FSB will have been passed on by them to MI5. This afternoon, MI5 officers will be expecting me to turn up at Admiralty Arch when they think they can pick me up. When I don't turn up, MI5 will think the FSB lied to them to get me out of the country. That will really piss them off and instead of collaborating like I'm sure they're doing now, they'll be at each others' throats again. But first, I've a job I want you to do for me.'

'Just say what you want and it's done.'

'The Chechens are planting their bombs at the hotel today. I managed to get two of them working on the inside as hotel staff and another two Chechens have guest reservations for tonight. One of those on the inside has made sure that the rooms reserved for them are strategically placed close to where Tuesday morning's summit meeting takes place. I want you to act as a taxi driver and take them there. Pick up their equipment at this address in Lewisham.' Sayfel handed Mo a note with the address written on it. 'When you get there ask for Iram. She will hand over to you two suitcases with the explosives that they'll need. She'll then take you to the address where the two Chechens will be waiting for you.'

'What am I to do with Iram when I get to the address?'

'You'll pick up the two Chechens and Iram will make her own way back to Lewisham. You're to take the Chechens to the Langome Hotel. It's just off Oxford Street. Take their luggage in for them and keep your eyes open for anyone hanging around the hotel foyer that may be security officers. If you have the slightest suspicion they're there, don't enter the hotel and let me know straight away.'

'OK, but what about you?'

'Don't worry about me. When you make the drop, I'll be in the area of the hotel. Once I'm happy everything's fine, I have to get out of Britain for a while. I'm leaving this evening for Holland. From there I'm going to travel through Europe to Naples where

I'll be joining a ship for Algiers.'

'How long will you be there?'

'For as long as it takes,' Sayfel said as he put his arm on Mo's shoulder, 'Don't worry I'll be back within a few months.'

Thirty-One

'**D**o you need to see all of the personnel records or just those who began working with us in the recent past?' the manager of the Langome Hotel asked David and DS Ben Solaru from the Metropolitan Police's SO13 department. He was trying to be helpful but at the same time he was frustrated, as assisting the police was taking him away from what he considered other necessary duties.

'If you have them, we can begin with the records of those that started in the last twelve months, but if possible we would like to work our way backwards from the most recent,' David said.

'Yes you can do that, I'll bring up the staff file and you can go through it. I would like to be with you as you go through them.'

'That's understandable,' said Ben Solaru. Ben and his team were assigned by MI5 to work with David and Steve. While the two DS's were in the manager's untidy compact office, with paperwork strewn over the desk and a table by the door as well as the two chairs not used by the manager, the rest of Ben's team were working out the best surveillance locations to monitor all the comings and goings in and around the hotel. Ben turned to the hotel manager and asked, 'Is it possible to have a pot of tea sent up. I'm prepared to pay for it.'

'I can certainly go as far as providing tea and some biscuits for the local constabulary. Is that a pot of tea for two?'

'If possible could I have coffee please, strong and black?' David asked.

'Of course. I'll ring through the order for you.'

As the two officers went through the list of names, Ben said, 'Of course they're going to use aliases.'

'That's going to make it harder for us to spot them. I'm going for the fact that they're likely to use Eastern European sounding names. At least these files have the photographs of the staff members. That should help,' David said.

'True, but we can't rule anyone out. Chechens look European.'

'Here are five possible ones. What do you think?'

Ben looked at the five records and going through them, said, 'He's been here for three weeks, that one for five weeks, this one for seven weeks and these two for two months. But one of them is a very British looking woman and she's a trainee manager, educated here and a graduate from Exeter University. I think we can eliminate her. That narrows it down to four.' Ben asked the hotel manger, 'Are any of these staff on duty at the moment and can we access their duty roster for today and next week?'

The manager came over to his desk and said, 'Let me have a look. Ah yes, Joseph Grensky, he's a Ukrainian and he's on duty now. He's one of our porters and delivers room service requests on the second floor. Simon Duval's also on duty now. He's a trainee manager. Then there's Gregor Krenin. He's from Georgia. He's also on duty today. He's a porter and general assistant. You're in luck as I can arrange for you to see them. I'll just call up the duty rosters for you.' David got out of the seat behind the desk to allow the manager to bring up the rosters as the manager said, 'There you are gentlemen. Now do you want me to arrange for you to see those three?'

'Is there somewhere my colleague and I could go to discuss something privately?' Ben asked.

'If you promise not to access anything else, I'll leave you here while I chase up the tea and coffee.'

'Thanks,' replied Ben. After the manager left the room Ben looked at David and said, 'Grensky and Krenin are the two likely best bets. I suggest we contact MI5 and take instructions.'

'I agree. I'll call Jenny at Thames House.' David rang Debbie to get through to Jenny. 'Hi Debbie, listen we've two possibles here and Ben is sending the files through to you now. We've a Joseph Grensky and a Gregor Krenin. It might be worth checking with the Home Office to see if they got work permits and visas. If not they could be our men.'

'That makes sense. The files are coming through now.'

'See if Jenny will give us the green light to arrest them now. They're both on duty. If we're wrong, we're not losing out. But this looks too good to be true and it certainly fits in with your line of thinking. Once they're arrested, we can do a sweep of the second floor.'

'I'll tell Jenny. Wait a moment while I go and get her.' Debbie placed the phone handset on the desk as she went to find Jenny.

After a couple of minutes Jenny came onto the phone and said, 'Debbie's told me that you have a couple of possibles working at the hotel. Is Ben Solaru there?'

'I'll pass him over to you,' and David passed the phone to Ben, 'Five want to speak to you.'

'DS Ben Solaru here.'

'Hello Ben, Jenny Richmond here. You have the green light to arrest Grensky and Krenin. Before you arrest them, see if there's a back door you can use to leave discreetly. Let me know when you arrive at Paddington Green. A couple of our officers are in the area to see if there's going to be any further movement at the hotel. Pass me back to David please.'

'Sure.' Ben handed the phone back to David. 'It's Jenny she wants to brief you.'

'Hello Jenny.'

'David, you, Steve and a couple of Ben's team stay at the hotel until the sweep of the floor is completed. Once that's completed, I'd like you and Steve to return to Thames House where we can reassess our position.'

'Will do. Bye for now.' As David put his phone back into his jacket pocket he turned to Ben, 'Anything I need to know?'

'Not really. I'll make the arrests and leave a couple here to assist you with overseeing the sweep of the second floor. Are you going to stay in this office?'

'No, I'll go and join Steve. I'll have to keep a check on him as no doubt he'll have blagged lots of freebies from the hotel by now. Best of luck Ben and let me know when you're out of the building.'

'I will and thanks for your help David.'

As Ben walked out of the office, David picked up the printouts of the files of the men they suspected to be the Chechens and made his way to the ground floor to find Steve. Emerging from the stairway to the upper floors, he walked into the foyer and saw Steve sitting close to reception desk in the residents' lounge area reading one of the Sunday newspapers available for the hotel guests. David walked up to Steve to see a teapot and a cup along with a side plate that had the remnants of biscuits on the table next to him. Steve put down the newspaper, looked up at David and said, 'Afternoon leader.'

Looking at the empty plate and the teapot, David said, 'I can see you've been having a hard time of it.'

Steve grinned and said, 'I've got to blend in haven't I? I've only had a couple of pots of tea, a plate of sandwiches and they insisted that I try out the biscuits too. Do you want me to order you a pot of coffee? I'm on first names terms with the waiter now.'

'Which one's the waiter?' David asked.

As Steve looked around he could not see him. 'Typical, just when you want service, the bugger's not here.'

David took out the printouts from his jacket and showed them to Steve. 'For fuck's sake, please don't tell me the waiter's one of these two?'

Steve took the printouts out of David's hand and looked at the picture of both men. He pointed to one of the men and said, 'That's him, Gregor Krenin. I've been calling him Gregor as it was on his name badge.'

'You've only been waited on by one of the men we suspect is a Chechen.'

'How was I to know?' Steve asked, knowing this was not the time to pass it off with humor.

'When did you last see him?'

'A few minutes ago, just before you came down.' Steve pointed to a blonde haired receptionist behind the desk and said, 'She called him over to the desk and he walked off through that staff only door over there. He didn't appear to be in a hurry so I didn't think anything of it.' .

'Ben Solaru and his team are going to arrest him and that other one, Grensky. What did you tell Krenin you're doing here?'

'I just told him I was a guest and I had a few hours to kill before I met an old friend. Don't worry I used the name of a guest I overheard book in an hour ago and used his room number. So for the past hour I've been a Mr. Osman.'

'You're a fucking case. Go and settle the bill before the real Mr. Osman notices anything and the hotel staff get suspicious.'

As Steve went over to the reception desk David's phone rang and Ben Solaru told him the two Chechens had been arrested. 'Cheers, thanks for that and best of luck Ben,' David said.

'Who was that on the phone?' Steve asked putting the receipt in his pocket.

'Ben Solaru. You got away with it, our Chechen friends are on their way to Paddington Green. All we have to do now is sit tight until the techies have done the sweep of the second floor. Then we can go and find a pub and watch the match.'

Thirty-Two

Walking up the stairs of Oxford Circus underground station, Sayfel fixed the strap on the large holdall containing all he would need for his trip to Algiers and placed it over his shoulder. Stepping onto Oxford Street, he crossed the road and walked up Regent Street towards the Langome Hotel. He pulled up the collar of his coat and the peak of his baseball cap down. Sayfel decided to wait and watch events from the coffee shop opposite the hotel. Once the Chechens and Mo arrived at the hotel, he intended to make his way to Lewisham from where he would be picked up and taken to Ramsey Island in Essex, where a boat would take him to Holland.

After entering the coffee shop, he ordered a coffee and sat on a stool by the window overlooking the hotel. He glanced at the clock on the wall behind the staff preparing the drinks. It was twenty past two in the afternoon. 'They'll be here in ten minutes,' he thought. He reached over and picked up one of the free newspapers the coffee shop provided for customers and pretended to read it while glancing across at the hotel entrance, eagerly awaiting the arrival of Mo and his Chechen passengers.

*   *   *

352

As they were discussing their social plans for that evening, Steve began to stare out of the window in the hotel foyer at a figure sitting in the coffee shop across the road from the hotel. 'Are you listening to me? I said how about going for a good scoff tonight and a few drinks after... Steve...I'm talking to you,' David said.

'What? I'm sorry mate. Look at that bloke sitting by the window in the coffee shop over the road. I might be mistaken, but I'm sure that's Sayfel.'

As Steve spoke, David got out of his chair and looked over towards the coffee shop and said, 'You're right, it does look like him. Why would he make himself so obvious to us? Is that a holdall by his feet?'

Steve strained to look closely at the object at the base of the stool Sayfel was sitting on. 'It could be. It's hard to make out with the etching pattern on the bottom of the window. You don't think it's a bomb do you?'

'If it is, it's a bit too obvious. You keep an eye on him while I contact Jenny. There could be some MI5 officers who could get a better view and check him out.' David rang Jenny and told her what he and Steve could see. 'He has a blue baseball cap on with some sort of insignia on the front of the hat. He's wearing a green coat and he's just sitting there in full view reading a paper and drinking a coffee. It looks like he has a large holdall with him.'

'I'll send some MI5 officers over to deal with him. I'll be surprised if it is him and he's just sitting there in the open. He'll know we want him.'

'If it's him, that confirms Debbie's analysis and we should expect something to happen soon.'

'We'll check it out. You and Steve stay where you are and keep watching him. Do not, I repeat do not make a move towards him,' Jenny instructed David.

'OK Jenny.' He turned to Steve and said, 'Keep your eye on him. I'll get the hotel manager to show me a list of bookings of guests due today.'

*   *   *

Sayfel looked at his watch again and saw that Mo was late. He rang to check where he was. 'You're late. Why aren't you at the place yet?'

'The traffic's really bad. I'm about five to ten minutes away. Don't worry, everything's running according to plan.'

'Make sure it does,' and Sayfel rang off.

*   *   *

'He appears to be getting agitated,' David said to Steve walking back from the reception desk.

'He's just made a phone call, but he was only on the phone for a matter of seconds. Nothing's come over the radio, so I don't know if the MI5 officers are in position yet. Did you find anything out from the manager?'

'Two Russian guests are expected this afternoon, and strangely enough they've been booked into rooms on the second floor. It looks like Debbie was spot on with her analysis.'

David and Steve heard a shout over the radio from an SO13 officer, 'Mo Shukar's pulled up outside the hotel. Two men have got out and are waiting for Shukar to get something out of the boot. Shukar's a well known associate of Sayfel.'

David pressed the transmit button at the end of his sleeve and said, 'Jenny did you get that?'

'Understood. All officers hold their positions. Wait and see if the males and Shukar enter the hotel before you make a move. If they do, SO13 are to arrest them. I repeat if they enter the hotel, SO13 officers arrest Shukar and the two males. Zara and Charlie take Sayfel out now.'

By the time Jenny finished giving out the instructions, Shukar and the two other Chechens approached the reception desk. While the two Chechens were waiting to be dealt with by the reception desk staff, Mo Shukar placed two suitcases carefully by their side and said, 'Gentlemen I'll leave you now. I hope you have a pleasant stay.'

As he finished speaking five SO 13 officers surrounded the two Chechens. Realizing they had walked into a trap, Shukar began to run out of the hotel. David ran into him, bringing him down onto the floor, landing on top of Shukar. Screams broke out from hotel guests in the hotel foyer as a fight broke out between David and Shukar. Shukar repeatedly punched David in the side of the head, desperately trying to get the DS off him. The strength of Shukar's punches felt like a hammer blow. An intense pain reverberated in David's head with each blow Shukar landed on him. Ignoring the pain, David grabbed Shukar's throat as another of Shukar's hammer blow punches landed to the side of his mouth. The punch was so hard that for a brief moment it felt as though the whole of his jaw became detached from the rest of his face. He felt no immediate pain, just a numb sensation in his jaw. He retained his grip on Shukar's throat causing Shukar struggle for breath. Instinctively Shukar grabbed David's left hand and attempted to release the vice-like grip.

Feeling severe shooting pains in his jaw and a ringing in his ears, David's will-power gave him the strength to keep the grip on Shukar's throat. As he grabbed David's hand, David began to land a series of punches with his right hand into Shukar's ribcage, making it harder for Shukar to breathe. Even though he was struggling for breath, David would not loosen his grip on Shukar's windpipe as he knew he was gaining the upper hand in the struggle. A new source of strength surged through David's body as he continued to punch hard into Shukar's ribcage. Each punch caused an exhalation of breath from Shukar, but he did not have the ability to refill his lungs. As Shukar's strength began to wane, his body was becoming motionless, but David would not let go of him. He just stared at him and shouted, 'you spineless fucker. You're not so fucking hard when it's one on one,' and he tightened his grip even further on Shukar's neck.

Seeing this, an SO13 officer ran over to the enraged DS. 'Let him go Sarge, You're going to kill him,' he said. The officer knelt down by Shukar's head and loosened David's grip and looked up at Hurst who had streams of blood flowing down his chin and the side of his face from cuts above his left eye, which was beginning to swell. It took a few moments before David realized it was an SO13 colleague talking to him. The officer smiled at David and in a soft reassuring voice said, 'It's OK Sarge, we've got him now, you can let go.' As soon as David let go, the officer checked to see if Shukar was breathing. As Shukar gulped for air that quickly became evident to the officer.

David stood up slowly and felt dizzy. Wiping the blood from his eyes, he looked around to see where his best friend had gone, when he saw a scuffle taking place across the road outside the coffee shop. A woman was lying motionless on the pavement while Steve was fighting with Sayfel. Turning to the SO13 officers, he shouted, 'One of you to me now.' David ran out of the hotel into the road, dodging cars that sounded their horns at him as he scrambled across the road. In an instant all the pain he had been feeling ceased. His best friend was being battered and there was no way another officer was going to lose their life at the hands of Sayfel, certainly not Steve.

Focusing on Sayfel, David ran across the road and saw something shiny in Sayfel's hand as Steve was starting to lose the fight. Seeing it was a knife, David shouted, 'Sayfel, you're a fucking dead man. Stevey hang on.'

Sayfel's secondary hearing registered his name just enough to distract him in his attempts at killing Steve. He looked up to see David Hurst sprinting towards him. He recognized the bloodied officer running towards him from the pictures Nasser had sent him from Rochdale police station as one of the ISB officers that interviewed Ahmed. Added to that, just as Nasser had told him, he noticed the officer had a strong Liverpool accent and knew this was DS Hurst. Sayfel jumped to his feet as the big man, whose temper was clearly up ran towards him. Sayfel shouted back at the officer, 'You're too late Hurst.' and ran off along Regent Street towards Oxford Street. David pointed to Steve's motionless body and shouted to the officer following him, 'Look after him, I'm going after Sayfel.'

Thirty-Three

Sunday 29th October
14.33 hours
Regent Street, London

avid ran along Regent Street towards Oxford Street in his pursuit of Sayfel, dodging past people walking on the pavement or those who had simply stopped to stare at the chase. 'Come here you murdering bastard,' he shouted after Sayfel as he tried his best to catch him. Sayfel did not look back. As both pushed their way through the throngs of tourists and shoppers, Sayfel began to gain distance between him and the ISB officer. As Sayfel ran across Margaret Street, the driver of a car was forced to brake suddenly and sounded the car horn. David could see the front of the car was going to hit Sayfel but he placed the palm of his left hand on the bonnet and vaulted over it. Although Sayfel stumbled, he regained his balance and sprinted off down Regent Street, towards Oxford Street. 'You should have knocked the fucker down,' David shouted at the driver as he ran past the front of the car.

The pain from Shukar's punches returned and there was a constant buzzing in David's ears. In his determination to catch Sayfel, he tried to push the acute discomfort to the back of his mind. His peripheral vision continually narrowed as his eyes were fixed intently on Sayfel. Sayfel glanced behind him to see David was catching up to him. As he saw Sayfel glance behind him he

358

shouted after him, 'You fucking murdering bastard.' Running across Great Castle Street, David was unaware of the sound of screeching brakes. Glancing to his left, he saw the driver of a wagon struggling to stop and avoid him. His heart stopped for a split second when a further surge of adrenalin made him run that bit quicker. As he crossed the front of the wagon he felt the front of it brush his back.

David was running into more people as he crossed Great Castle Street towards Oxford Street. There was a burning feeling in his lungs as he was trying to run as fast as he could after Sayfel, who was again beginning to pull away from David. As Sayfel approached the junction of Regent Street and Oxford Street, David saw the pedestrian lights change onto the green man signal. 'Lucky bastard,' he thought cursing Sayfel's fortunate timing of the traffic lights that allowed him to cross safely into the now massed throngs of shoppers. By the time David reached the roadway, Sayfel had begun to run down the entrance to the Oxford Circus Underground station. As David was about to cross the road, the pedestrian lights changed to the red man signal. He was oblivious to this and did not check the road. He did not want to lose sight of Sayfel. He elbowed his way through the pedestrians who had stopped at the curbside shouting, 'Police, get out the way.' As he ran onto the roadway, David felt his legs go from under him and air gush out of his lungs. As he tried to fight for breath, he wondered why he was flying through the air.

*   *   *

That evening Bernard Gamble had called Paul Edge, George Byrne and Craig MacDonald to join him and Sandra Parry for a briefing on the developments in both the Manchester investigation and the events in London. The three men entered the Chief's office where he invited them to sit down. 'Gentlemen thank you for coming and taking time to join Sandra and I. Paul what's the latest on the condition of our two officers, DC Adams and DS Hurst?'

'Apparently the medical staff are keeping a close eye on Adams' condition to see if any of his vital organs were damaged as a result of the stabbing. Hurst was knocked unconscious after the car knocked him down in Oxford Street but the latest from the hospital is that he's drifting from consciousness to an unconscious state. He's not fractured his skull but is suffering from severe concussion as well as a fractured jaw. He also fractured his hip as a result of the accident and sustained severe bruising to his face from his fight with Shukar, but he's in no immediate danger.'

'That's good news.'

Paul Edge said, 'As a result of Hurst's actions we now have an officer fighting for his life. Also SO13 told me that Hurst was trying to kill Shukar. Members of the public present in the hotel foyer were apparently horrified and distressed at Hurst's violent behavior. This further demonstrates Hurst's of lack of thought for his position as a police officer. I mentioned my concerns about his behavior in our last meeting. It's totally unprofessional for a police officer to be seen trying to kill a person in front of the public. Fortunately, there was an SO13 officer on hand to prevent Hurst from killing Shukar. Due to these recent actions, I strongly recommend Hurst's removal from the ISB when he returns to duty. May I suggest he be removed to some uniform role that has minimal contact with the public?'

Bernard looked puzzled for a moment and said, 'I don't think that's a good idea Paul as I'm recommending David Hurst and Steve Adams for a commendation for professionalism and bravery. Also I was going to recommend that your position as temporary detective superintendent be made a permanent appointment. Now you and I shouldn't be getting off on the wrong foot in the first minute of your promotion by disagreeing over a decision that I've made. In addition to which, I'm looking to increase the personnel at the Branch. It might increase to such a number that you may be adding a pip to go with that crown on your shoulder that you've just earned. Of course, I can always reconsider that decision if you're determined to undermine me.'

Edge gave nervous cough and said, 'I would never dream of getting off on the wrong foot with you and in no way would I ever want to undermine you. Maybe I was a bit hasty in recommending Hurst's removal out of the department.'

'I'm glad to hear that,' Bernard replied, 'especially when the Home Secretary telephones me to congratulate me on the actions of these two officers. The Home Sec knows it's the same two officers that, in his view, performed professionally in Liverpool on Friday and in London today. He's impressed with both of them, in particular David Hurst. Perhaps one of the first things you should do as detective superintendent is to patch up your differences with him. When officers work hard and produce the goods, even if it sticks in your throat, you have to give credit where it's due.' As Bernard spoke, both George and Craig had to stifle their sniggers.

'Of course sir, you're right sir,' replied Paul Edge.

Craig interrupted the conversation and said, 'It's so remiss of me, and I'm surprised Paul's still talking to me. I really am showing my incompetence at not getting all of the relevant information to DCI, apologies I mean Detective Superintendent Edge on time. Once again, if Paul had been privy to the full facts perhaps he would not have such a jaundiced position in relation to DS Hurst.'

On hearing this, Edge turned and stared in surprise at Craig.

'I understand where you're coming from Craig and of course when we have the full picture we can always reappraise our first impression of what happened. That's right isn't it Paul?' Bernard said to Edge.

'Of course sir. If I had the full picture, then I would have come to a different conclusion in my judgment of Hurst's actions.'

'I knew you would see it that way Paul.'

'I do sir.'

Bernard Gamble addressed all of the officers. 'Overall, I have to say we've achieved a very positive result. The dirty bomb plot foiled as well as the Chechen bomb plot in London. The icing on the cake today, thanks to assistance from the Metropolitan Police was when Bill Andrews' team made an arrest in relation to Tony King's murder. A Russian businessman walked into Tottenham Court Road police station in London this morning and admitted the offence. Apparently he was on a drunken night out with two other men and his guilty conscience got the better of him. Paul, I must congratulate you and your department on a thoroughly professional job all round. Quite clearly you managed a very difficult and complex investigation extremely well and it's a credit to you.'

Edge began to bask in the glory of Hurst and Adam's work. He glanced over at George thinking that regardless of what happened, in his chief's eyes he was the top dog in the ISB, not George. Grinning, he said, 'Why thank you sir. I have to admit it was difficult at times and there were some difficult decisions to make, but I found Craig's presence and assistance invaluable when I had to make the decisions that counted.'

'I'm glad to hear that,' Bernard replied. 'Now that leads me to you George. With Paul being promoted that means there's a vacant position of DCI in the ISB. There is only one candidate that comes top of my list and that's you.'

Satisfied that his efforts had been recognized, George said, 'Thank you sir, but I like my current rank.'

'I can make it a temporary post and we'll see how it goes if you prefer. You never know you might get used to being a DCI.'

'Thanks all the same sir and I appreciate the confidence you've shown in me, but I really don't want it. However, Tim Johnson from the ISB's airport unit has passed his chief inspector's board. From what I've heard, he's been pretty impressive in managing the Khan murder investigation. I think he'd be an ideal candidate for the DCI's post.'

Looking surprised, Gamble asked, 'Are you sure George?'

'I'm absolutely positive sir. I couldn't think of anyone better for the DCI's post. He's got experience of working as a DI in the main ISB office as well as the airport sir.'

After pondering over George's suggestion for a moment, Bernard replied, 'Well I'll think about Tim Johnson for the post. I'm sure that you'll be pleased to have a DCI of Tim's caliber working at your right hand eh Paul?'

'If you say so sir,' he said, hoping Gamble would change his mind.

'I do say so Paul,' Bernard said looking squarely at Edge as he spoke. 'Well now that's all sorted I think that I've already taken up enough of your valuable time gentlemen.'

The three rose from their seats and walked out of the chief constable's office. They walked a few yards down the corridor when George grabbed Paul Edge by the arm and pushed him against the wall. George moved into Edge's face and said, 'You fucking tosser. You've got promoted on the backs of officers like Hurst and what do you do? You shit on them from a great height. I turned down the role of DCI so I don't have to work any closer with an arse-wipe like you than I have to. I'm watching you closely, one slip and I'll use my connections that you detest and have you out of the job before you can blink. Got it?'

Paul Edge cowered as the burly figure of George Byrne pressed his weight down on him. 'Get off me or I'll have you for assaulting a senior officer,' he spluttered.

'This isn't an assault, what David and Steve went through today, that's a fucking assault you brown nosing little shit,' George said, his face reddening with anger.

Craig got in between the two men and said, 'I suggest you go home George while I take Paul for a drink to toast his promotion. Paul, you have to see it through George's eyes. He's nurtured those two officers. They're more like family to him than work colleagues. Now come on Paul, I have a raging thirst that needs quenching and only the company of a detective superintendent will help to satisfy that thirst. What do you say?'

'Thanks Craig.' Edge walked away from George then turned to him and wagging the index finger of his right hand said, 'I'll overlook your outburst this once, but any repetition of that type of behavior and I'll finish you. I don't care how well connected you are.'

'Go fuck yourself Edge,' George replied and turned on his heels and walked away.

*   *   *

Debbie pulled back the curtain of the cubicle at Accident and Emergency where David was lying. 'So you're still with us then?' she said walking over to him. She kissed him and whispered in his ear, 'I thought I'd you lost you.'

The fractured jaw he sustained in his fight with Shukar made David struggle to speak but he managed to mumble, 'Sayfel? Did we get Sayfel? And Steve? Is he OK?' As he tried to sit up he clutched his head and moaned.

'Lie back and don't move. Just relax and I'll update you. First of all, Steve's fine. Sayfel stabbed him but it's only a flesh wound. Fortunately the blade didn't do any damage to any of his internal organs. He was unconscious because Sayfel had slammed his head on the pavement a couple of times, but like you Steve's also a tough nut. Fortunately all he has is concussion and bruising to his head. Both of you are very lucky, but you never know, both of your looks could have been improved when the swelling goes down. Sayfel's got away from us again and unfortunately he has another murder on his hands. He killed one of our officers, Zara Lloyd. She tried to stop Sayfel when he stabbed her. Steve saw this and ran over to assist. By the time Steve got across the road to Zara it was too late to save her. He ran after Sayfel and caught him. As Steve tried to restrain him, they ended up rolling round and fighting on the pavement.'

A feeling of guilt that he could not help his friend went through him as David said, 'I didn't see Steve leave the hotel.'

'That's because according to the SO13 officers in the hotel you were doing your level best to strangle Shukar. There were quite a few hotel guests in the area watching you two fighting. Of course they didn't know you were a police officer at first and one hotel guest was shocked when she heard you say "die you fucker". One of the SO13 officers explained the situation to her. This changed her view of what happened and wondered why you didn't kill him!'

'What about the Chechens?'

'We have four Chechens in custody as well as Shukar. The bottom line is that unfortunately we have no Sayfel in custody and to top it all off we've lost him altogether.'

'So they've no idea where he is?'

'No. Where he is, god only knows. Al Qaeda could be hiding him in the UK or he could be out of the country by now. The FSB want the four Chechens deported to Russia and Jenny's been dealing with them. We've no objections to them being dealt with in Moscow, but I'm sure the Chechens will. Craig sends his best wishes and congratulates you on your actions. He did say that you were a "good officer" but told me not to tell you. I think you've finally won him over. You and Steve are now both on sick leave and I've taken some leave so I can take you home and look after you while you recuperate. By the way I nearly forgot, Everton beat Chelsea three one. That should put a smile on your face, if you can call it a face at the moment.'

*   *   *

Usman Shah, a member of the Amsterdam Al Qaeda cell was driving across the border into Italy from Austria and said, 'Not far to go now Sayfel. We'll soon be in Naples. After what happened, I bet you're glad to get away from England for a while?'

'Not really I have some unfinished business there. The whole operation was a fucking failure. Eighteen months of planning, then total failure. We were so near but ended up so far from succeeding. I've a few names on my list that we need to dispose of and a certain detective sergeant from Manchester has gone straight to the top of that list.'

*   *   *   *   *